Revenge is Necessary

Stephanie –
Best wishes to
you + the family!!
Bill Mathis

Bill Mathis

Praise for Revenge is Necessary

"A snowy day in a Minnesota farm town. A chase ensues through the eyes of alternating characters. This sets the stage for secrets to be exposed."
—First place in the Chicago Writers Association's 2019 Annual First Chapter Contest

"'Betrayal is wicked. Revenge is necessary. Patience is a virtue.' A stunning collection of statements. The first is true; the second, repulsively human; the third taking on a frightening meaning when it follows the first two. Deception; intrigue; a loveable, hateable collection of characters; a quiet rural setting highlighting the challenges of farming; a blended family; an intriguing sidebar of love in all its forms; and last, but by no means least, an incredible tale of abuse, caring, loyalty, determination, courage, and revenge.

I'm amazed by the author's extraordinary gift and abilities in creating such thoroughly engaging and complex characters, not only in this book, but in his prior works as well. The depth of character development is incredible! Each character is "fully human" in appearance, in heart, in mind, and in soul."
—Ann Sitrick, Strategic Planning Consultant

"Revenge is Necessary is one of the most engaging books I have read in a long time. Before you've turned the first page it has pulled you in like a whirlpool. Enjoy the ride."
—Marty Densch, Retired Pharmacist, Freelance Writer, Film Critic and Prescreener for the Beloit International Film Festival

"Fabulous! Well done! Great story! The story was complex enough to hold interest, and the farther I got into it the harder it was to put it aside. The gay characters are integrated naturally and the mental health and societal issues handled beautifully. The characters are well rounded and believable. Love the Midwest farm setting and references."

—Steve Purdy,

Founder and Managing Director: The Automotive Heritage Foundation

Creator, Producer and Host: A Shunpiker's Journal Radio Program

Associate Producer: Sirens of Chrome—The Motion Picture

Chapter One

Junior: Shaw Philip Skogman, Jr., age 17

Saturday, March 26, 2011

Midville, Minnesota

Junior ran faster, his bare feet churning, sinking into the dirt drive, already muddy from three days of rain and now topped with three inches of heavy, wet, late-March snow. The grainy flakes whirled around him, pelting his skin, nearly blinding him. He didn't feel the cold yet. Where was he headed? Where could he go in his Fruit-of-the-Loom white t-shirt and tighty-whiteys at seven on a Saturday morning? His dad might come after him if he headed toward his boyfriend Beany's house.

The image of his father with the double-barrel shotgun bursting in on him and Beany in Junior's bed pulsed with every heartbeat. Beany's words as Junior raced toward the door still echoed. "Run, Forrest! Run!" The same words his mother screamed at his track meets. She loved the movie Forrest Gump. He knew Beany escaped down the back stairs as Junior flew down the front ones. Beany would be well on his way home. He was a fast runner, too. At least he had a place to run to for sanctuary.

Damn Beany. Sneaking into Junior's bedroom in the early morning, or middle of the night, still dressed, crawling into Junior's bed, ignoring the twin guest bed in the room. The bed his mother moved in over ten years ago when Beany started showing up in the middle of the night, coming in the unlocked back door, slipping up the narrow back stairway and into Junior's room without making a sound.

What caused his father to lose his marbles? Completely lose them. It's not like Beany never slept over before.

"Right, Junior. Duck right."

His mother's scream, sounding from the front porch, broke his thoughts. Made his heart thump harder. How could he be thinking about his bedroom and Beany when his father, at this very second, must have the shotgun aimed at him?

He dodged right, closer to the overgrown shrubs that lined the quarter-mile driveway. He heard the shotgun bellow and felt sharp stings on his left buttock, along the back of his upper leg. He ran faster, tried to crouch lower. Birdshot. At least it was birdshot. It smarted, but he was far enough away to realize it couldn't go deep. Must have caught the edge of the pattern. He dodged into the middle of the drive and quickly back to the right. Did that several times. Why? He wasn't sure. Maybe zig-zagging would make it harder for his dad to focus on a moving target. He knew what was in the other barrel of the gun. A slug. That would more than sting if it hit him. It would kill him. His dad was a good shot.

His mother's scream again tore through the wet, thick air. No words. It was followed by the shotgun blasting again and his dad bellowing. Was he in pain? Did he still have the gun? Did he have more shells? Junior threw himself into the ditch and lay in the cold sloppy mud and snow. Hearing nothing, no sound of a thud or a slug whistling by, he stood, turned and took several cautious steps toward the house. His mother's voice floated toward him through the heavy swirling snow. It was less shrill, but still urgent, her don't mess with me voice. "You're safe for now. Keep running. Don't come home."

What the hell did that mean? You're safe, keep running, but don't come home. He turned, lengthened his stride and settled into the eight-hundred-meter pace he ran for track. He sensed the front of his soaked t-shirt invading his nighttime warmth, but still, he didn't feel the cold. He stayed to the right of the drive, on the edge, the grass slippery beneath the snow. At 127th Street, he wanted to turn left, run one quarter mile to Milliken Road and go left a half mile to Beany's house. However, he figured if his dad was still capable, he might jump into his truck and head toward Beany's house down their Milliken Road driveway. If he shot at him once, wouldn't he shoot again? Junior remembered his father's words in the bedroom as he aimed the shotgun at him, "You're not my son." What did that mean?

Junior turned right, onto 127th Street. A half mile further was the small Lutheran church and cemetery where someone might be around and let him in. Why didn't he hear his dad's diesel pickup starting up? His dad must have ignored Beany who was probably home by now. Would he or his mom call nine-one-one? Would his dad show up at Beany's looking for him?

His feet began to sense the cold and the occasional small stone. He was glad the road was mostly dirt, not all gravel. How long did it take to get frostbite? He was approaching the fence of the cemetery when he heard a vehicle slowly splashing behind him. He glanced back. It wasn't his dad's pickup. Junior slowed to a walk as the old pickup eased to a stop beside him. He glanced in and saw Jens Hanson, motioning for him to climb in. There was a tarp covering something in the backend. It was shaped like a casket. Junior opened the door and slid into the warmth. He grabbed the blanket on the seat and pulled it around him like it was the last one on earth.

Chapter Two

Jens Hanson, age 51

Jens Hanson glanced at the clock. Six-forty-five a.m., Saturday, March 26. In the rear embalming room of the funeral home, he adjusted the frayed, plaid shirt on his father's body. He touched the ancient floral drapes torn from his parents' tottering farmhouse living room that lined the homemade wooden casket. Too many memories, good and bad. He shook his head, closed the casket and secured it. His father died, finally, yesterday afternoon. His mother thirty-five years ago.

Jens slightly opened the wide back door. He peeked to make sure no one was around, swung it out and blocked it. He pushed the cart holding the casket to the lowered tailgate of his truck. After sliding the casket onto the bed, he secured a tarp tightly around it before closing the tailgate. Returning the cart inside, he double-checked the room to make sure everything was in place, with nothing left for someone else to clean up. He pulled the note out of his flannel shirt pocket and propped it against the desk phone. *Sorry to leave so suddenly. Dad died. He's embalmed and buried. I appreciate you letting me work here over the past three years. I won't return. Jens Hanson*

No, I won't return here, he thought, as he laid the building keys next to the phone. *I did my duty. I don't want to deal with a funeral service and the hassles of buying a plot, trying to remember the names of the few people still alive and cognitive enough to remember Dad. Besides, I've embalmed and buried enough people in my lifetime. Now, it's time to take care of myself.* He climbed into the cab, started the

4

twenty-five-year-old, rusted, Ford F250 and placed his hand on the shift lever. His phone vibrated in his jeans pocket. A text from Connie Skogman. *Help. Junior running on 127. Shaw shot. Don't come to house.*

Windshield wipers on high and squeaking, Jens threw the lever into gear and headed south out of Midville. He turned right onto 127th Street, a straight, slender farm road that ran by fallow corn and soybean fields. He crossed Milliken Road; a quarter mile further, the Skogman driveway. Through the streaky wipers and wet heavy snow, he caught glimpses of white, then realized it was Junior running barefoot in his underwear. Easing to a stop, he noticed pelts and splotches of blood on the tall teen's left hip. Damn, what the heck happened? He motioned for the boy to jump in.

It seemed Junior couldn't climb in fast enough. He grabbed the car blanket, wrapped it about him as he shivered and his teeth chattered. His breath steamed up the windshield, he curled into a ball on the seat, his head nearly touching Jens' hip. Jens jammed the heat to high and flipped on the defrost. He drove five-hundred feet further and pulled into the cemetery, navigating barely visible lanes till he reached the back and parked behind a thick row of arborvitae and scrub brush. His old front-end loader and backhoe from the farm waited next to a soggy hole he dug late last night before he embalmed his father. He had no intention of towing it back to the family farm. He shut the lights off, left the pickup engine idling,

Junior seemed to be in shock. He didn't open his eyes or speak.

"Stay down, son. I'll be just a few minutes, then we're getting the hell away from here."

Junior gave a low moan.

Neither spoke when they heard the sounds of sirens coming down the road. In the dense and snowy air, Jens could see a county sheriff car and ambulance move slowly, ghost-like, through the slush and mud. Their sounds died shortly after passing the cemetery. Jens figured they ended up at the Skogman home, across the fields from the graveyard, easy to see on most days. Not today.

Jens stayed in the truck until, five minutes later, he heard the sirens start up again and leave, headed away, toward Summerville, the county seat. Probably take them forty minutes in this weather. The boy didn't say a word, just shivered and slowly seemed to bring his breathing to a normal rate.

Jens patted Junior lightly on his wet head, climbed out, gently closed the door, walked to the back and lowered the tailgate. He placed two pieces of two-by-six lumber against the gate and down into the grave to form a ramp. He guided the casket down the skids, between the dirt walls, leaving the tarp on. *Closest thing to a vault the old man will get*, he thought. He muscled the skids out from under the casket and threw them into the shrubs, jumped on the backhoe, fired it up and quickly loaded the dirt back into the hole, building it a little higher so it would settle level. He turned the backhoe off, climbed down and scattered some grass seed.

No one else was buried this far back in the cemetery. The row of brush and trees was a wind and snow break. He figured no one would notice the backhoe or the grave for some time. Very few people were buried here anymore. The old church was occasionally used for weddings, receptions, funerals or special community events, not regular services. Leaving the key in the tractor's ignition, Jens Hanson stepped toward the truck, wiping his face and hands with his handkerchief.

Now what? He planned to make this trip solo, leave town, keep in touch with Connie through texts and email, and never return. Now, there was a seventeen-year old, out, gay, boy in the truck who was clueless to what just happened at his home, or why. So was Jens, though he suspected something about the boy that the boy probably didn't have an inkling about. He wasn't sure Connie fully admitted the possibility to herself.

Chapter Three

Connie Marie Johnson Skogman, age 59

Connie loved her mornings, even the gray wet snowy ones. She secretly enjoyed the time between feeding her husband, Shaw, seeing him out the back door to attend to his equipment, his fields, planting, harvesting, and waking up Junior. Adding rich cream and sipping her coffee was a sacred act for her. After Junior left for the bus, she usually spent an uninterrupted hour reading and exploring the reference books she brought home from the local library where she volunteered twenty-five hours a week. Her alone time was an addiction, true, but not one that would ruin her health or injure those close to her. Ordinarily, today would be an even more special time. She didn't have to wake Junior for school or track and next week was spring break. She planned to increase her volunteer hours to assist with the avalanche of children rolling in. Junior would help his dad and might make a trip to The Cities—the Twin Cities, St. Paul and Minneapolis—to spend time with his sister, Emma.

However, today, Saturday, March 26, wasn't an ordinary day. Setting Shaw's breakfast in front of him shortly after five a.m., she told him she didn't feel well and left him to finish his breakfast alone. She went upstairs, crawled back into bed and cried. She wanted to talk with Jens, one of her two best friends, in person or at least on the phone. To share their sorrow on what would have been the sixty-first birthday of his older brother Hans who died suddenly, eighteen years ago on New Year's Eve. Over the years, the shock wore down, but the pain hadn't. Tears slipped down her cheeks. Tears of frustration as she realized she left her cell phone downstairs. Her cell was the only phone she used to communicate with Jens. While she was fixing breakfast, before Shaw came in, they texted about Hans. Texts of her love for Hans, how much she still missed him, plus her added sorrow for Jens over the death of his father. How it felt like his father purposefully planned to die on the birthday of his favorite son, and, as always, leave Jens to arrange the details.

Connie stretched and rolled onto her side, wanting to sleep. Going back to bed, telling her husband she felt ill, was unusual for her. Her children joked that Mom packed ten pounds into a five-pound bag, and on slow days, moved at the speed of light. Thankfully, no one in the family ever recognized she slowed down and took it easy on Hans' birthday or, on New Year's Eve, how she prearranged her family's activities and slipped away for some alone time.

She dozed a bit, then felt the need to use the bathroom. She was regular and consistent in her bowel habits. She always went between six-thirty and seven, usually in the bathroom off the back-porch mudroom after Shaw left the house and before she awoke Junior. She got up, in her panties and t-shirt, went into their master bath and sat down. She didn't like the feelings of sorrow this date always brought. You'd think, after all these years...

Connie sensed, rather than heard, the outside door of the mudroom close hard. Shaw rarely returned to the house this time of morning, but the heavy steps resolutely pounding up the back staircase could only be his. She heard him go past their bedroom, heard a door slam open and Shaw's voice roar through the large farmhouse, "Get out. You're not my son. Now go."

Connie heard Beany's voice shrill, "He's got a gun. Run, Forrest. Run."

She didn't know Beany snuck in last night, but that was not unusual for him. As she hurried to wipe herself, she heard stumbling and bumping from Junior's doorway, then steps running past her bedroom and lighter steps down the front stairs, followed by heavy ones. She rushed to pull on her blue jeans, struggling and tripping in her hurry. Why am I bothering to dress? What seemed to take forever was only a matter of seconds before she yanked her door open and sped down the hallway. At the head of the stairs, she caught a glimpse through the upper window of Junior racing across the yard in his underwear. She cleared the final stairs in one leap and was out the storm door in time to see Shaw move his finger from the guard to the right trigger of the double barrel, twelve-gauge shotgun. The gun he kept over the back door, the right barrel loaded with birdshot, the left a slug. He was aiming at their son. "Duck right," she screamed. "Duck right." Her bare feet felt the cold of the snow covering the porch.

She was still moving across the wide porch when Shaw squeezed. The gun roared. She saw Junior shudder, but keep running, then start zig-zagging. She gasped as Shaw turned to aim at her.

"You're next," he bellowed, struggling to keep his footing in the icy snow.

Connie saw red. Anger. *How dare he fire at their son and now aim a gun at her?* Self-preservation took over. She launched herself at him, grabbing onto the gun with both hands. She was tall, five-nine, and wiry strong. Shaw's feet went out from under him. The gun blasted. Connie lost her footing. Shaw screamed. Connie found herself half on, half off of her husband, him writhing in pain, she holding the gun.

She jumped up, laid the gun aside. She felt no pain. The blood on her jeans and bare feet was Shaw's. Not hers. His left lower leg looked destroyed. She could see ragged ends of both the bones sticking out of his blue bib-overalls. Fragments of bone mixed with muscle, flesh, tendons and skin were torn away, dangling or plastered into the floor of the porch. Blood spurted out. Everything rushed through her mind at once. She mentally calmed herself. Now was not the time to analyze the injury and recall everything she read and studied about human anatomy. The bleeding must be stopped. "Shaw, quit trying to move, lay still."

She glanced down the snowy, fog-like drive, glimpsed Junior cautiously starting back toward her. She used her tough mother voice to yell, "You're safe for now. Keep running. Don't come home." That much, she instinctively realized. Her son could not come home. Not right now. How long, she wasn't sure. Whether her husband lived or died, she knew her secrets could come out during this mess. That much she was sure of. She wanted to run down the driveway to hold Junior, hug him, try to explain, but now wasn't the time. Besides, she didn't want him to see the bloody porch, or Shaw, who was still conscious.

I have to stay in control, she kept telling herself as she raced back through the house, wondering what the quickest thing would be for a tourniquet. In the mudroom, she noticed a new bag of zip-ties, thirty-six-inch-long, wide ones, the kind always needed around a farm. She grabbed several and tore back to Shaw. Dropping to the floor beside him, she slipped one under his leg above the knee, slid the tip through and ratcheted it as tight as she could. The blood slowed. She placed a second one below the knee. Shaw screamed as she yanked it tight. The bleeding stopped. Shock was the next stage he would face. She ran back into the house, grabbed some large towels along with a throw blanket from the family room couch.

After covering him, she returned to the kitchen and used the land line to call nine-one-one. "This is Connie Skogman on the corner of 127th Street and Milliken Road. My husband just suffered a gunshot wound to the leg and needs immediate help." She hung up. EMS knew who they were and how their house was set back a quarter mile from both roads with a driveway from each. Grabbing her cell phone from the kitchen table, she texted Jens Hanson. He always told her he would take care of Junior or the girls if she needed him to. She hated to change Jens' plans to move away today, but had no choice. Neither did he. Neither did Junior, at least for now. As she placed her cell phone in her purse, she realized she found the phone on the table, not in her purse where she always kept it. Did she leave it on the table this morning, after she and Jens were texting? Before she told Shaw she was going back to bed?

She took a big breath, went to the mudroom, pulled socks on over her blood-covered feet and laced on her leather work boots. This was not how she thought her day would go. Her husband of thirty-five years, father to five of her children and two more from his first wife, went freaking nuts. She thought she might know one reason, but was that enough to set him off like this, to kill his son and wife? The guilt she always felt on this day sunk deeper, especially about the second secret, the one she hadn't admitted to herself since Hans died. She shook her head to clear it. No, she wouldn't give into the guilt. Whether it precipitated this or not, something must have snapped in Shaw, her silent, unemotional, dependable husband. The placement of her phone on the table and not in her purse felt odd again.

Confused, she hurried down the long hall, past the formal dining room, the library/guest room, and the living room, toward the open, two story front foyer with the main staircase to the second level. On the porch, she knelt beside Shaw. His eyes still looked angry, or was that the pain of a twelve-gauge slug shredding his leg? She didn't speak to him. Maybe there'd be time later. Maybe not. Either way, she knew their lives would never be the same.

A county sheriff car and an ambulance struggled up the drive, sirens blaring.

"Looks like the slug tore away the flesh, shattered both bones, plus the arteries, nerves, muscles…" The EMT shook his head.

He asked Shaw some questions and received short answers or hand squeezes. "This is a bad injury. We need to get you stabilized and to the ER. Now."

"Can he even keep the leg?" Connie watched Shaw's eyes flicker as she asked. She couldn't read them, but then, she usually couldn't.

"No idea. It looks bad. We're going to start some I.V.'s and get out of here fast. It's a good thing you got a tourniquet on him."

"I'll follow in my car." As the crew loaded her husband and the sheriff looked over the porch, Connie ran inside for her keys and purse. She heard a text sound. It was from Judy Sue Marsh, Beany's mother, her neighbor and other best friend. She pulled out her phone as she headed toward the mudroom door. *B says Shaw had gun. Heard shots. You okay? B says your car battery is missing.*

What the heck? This is getting crazier. Why was her battery missing? Connie tore back through the house and raced toward the ambulance. The sheriff was just getting into his car. She waved at him.

He blew his car horn and jumped back out. "Wanna ride with me?"

One of the EMT's noticed her, jumped out, opened the side door and told her to strap in next to her husband. Shaw's eyes were closed, but she sensed he knew she was with him. Tears came to her eyes. *My husband who shot at our son, tried to kill me, must have disconnected my car, and now I'm on my way to the hospital.* She swiped the tears away. *I have to stay strong for Junior, even if I can't be with him.*

Twenty minutes later, as they hit the paved streets of town, she saw Jens' text. *Found him. He's sleeping in truck. Call us. Love you.* She knew her son, he slept to drown out tension or conflict.

At the hospital, while Shaw was rushed into surgery, the sheriff asked if he could have a few words with Connie. "Can we do it over coffee? I need some. Bet you do too."

"Of course."

He led the way to the small cafeteria, got two coffees and motioned her to a table in a quiet section of the room. He took a sip and watched as she took several. "I'm Fred Cochran, County Sheriff. What the hell happened out there? Don't you got a son? Where is he?"

Connie looked at him, trying to think how she should handle this. What to say and what not to. "It's like my husband went nuts. Once in a rare while, he'll lose his temper, but he's never been violent or threatened anyone. He's usually very calm, almost remote." She sipped her coffee as the sheriff watched her carefully. "Our son is seventeen, almost eighteen. He's gay, but he's never told his father, nor have I. A friend of his, a neighbor kid who's his best friend, occasionally comes over and spends the night. He's almost seventeen. He must have popped over last night."

"What do you mean, he must have? Don't you know when he comes and goes? Doesn't his mother call or he ask you?" The sheriff looked perplexed.

Connie gave a brief smile. "That does sound confusing. This kid's been popping over unannounced since he was five. He lives a half mile away, no neighbors for several miles. We're isolated, you could tell that when you drove out there."

The sheriff nodded and sipped his coffee, still staring at her.

"Anyway, once his mother adjusted to the fact her only child was very independent and loved coming to my house, she relaxed. It's been sort of a joint effort on raising our only sons. You know, it takes a village type of thing. Only in this case, it takes two isolated farmwives to raise two gay sons." Connie tried not to show she noticed Cochran's surprised facial expression.

"Okay, whatever works. But how did your husband end up with a shotgun slug ripping his leg apart?"

Connie sipped her coffee. "Like I said, he lost it this morning. I think he saw the boys kissing. They must have been standing in the bedroom, it's got a bay window, and he noticed from his farm office. Anyway, he grabbed his shotgun, marched up there and ordered our son to leave. Yelled he was no son of his. He never said a word to the neighbor boy, Beany. Then, he followed our boy out on to the porch and shot at him as he ran down the drive. I think some birdshot hit him, not enough to do much damage. It was horrible. The kid was in his underwear, that's what he sleeps in." Connie wiped at her eyes. "He, my husband, started to aim the gun at me. I grabbed for it. It's a double barrel, Coach-type of gun. I know he keeps birdshot in one and a slug in the other. Anyway, the porch was slippery. We both fell and the gun went off. The slug must have gone through his leg."

The impact of everything that happened that morning hit her. She slumped back in her chair.

Cochran waited a minute. "Jesus, this story is crazy. Are you sure your son didn't try to shoot his dad?"

Connie started to rub her right shoulder. "I'm positive he didn't shoot his father. Give me a lie detector. All I was trying to do was get the gun away so my husband didn't shoot at me. I have no idea what came over him."

Cochran watched her pause, stop massaging her shoulder. "I can imagine. A twelve-gauge kicks like a mule. You said your husband didn't know the boy was gay? Think that might have set him off. It might have me."

Connie chose her words carefully. "Sheriff, I'd love to have a conversation with you about gay children. They don't choose it. To answer your question, I think he's suspected for several years. Seeing the two boys kissing confirmed what he's been afraid of. I've tried to tell him for years that being gay is normal and nothing to fear."

The sheriff seemed to think carefully. "Do you know where your son is? Where he would go? One of them big equipment sheds? Over to, what's his name's—Beany's? Should I send someone to go look for him? He can't be hard to find if he's only wearing his underwear. Kid's gotta be cold as hell, too."

"My son is a long-distance runner. He ran the Twin Cities marathon last fall and plans to run it again this October. My guess is he will run for a while and come back home through the field trails, a few of them are passable. Wearing his underwear isn't much different than his track outfit. He runs barefoot a lot around the farm."

She thought fast. Which building would he run back home to? "He must have heard the sirens. He'd come in the side basement door of the house and listen to see if anyone was home. Anyway, so few people drive down our road, I doubt anyone will see him. Running is one way he deals with stress and conflict. His father is fifty-seven years older than him, so there's never been a close, dad-son relationship. The older my husband gets, the more difficult he's become to get along with."

That wasn't true. Until today, she could barely discern any emotional change in Shaw from year to year, day to day or hour to hour. She knew the officer wouldn't be able to prove or disprove that. Even if Shaw fully recovered, what would his rationale be for shooting at his son? Senility? That's the only thing she could think of. Or was it? Her cell phone lying on the kitchen table this morning flashed through her mind again. "Sheriff, I need to use the bathroom."

In the bathroom, she was glad she had cell service. Quickly, she called Jens. "Don't talk if you're in front of Junior, just listen. I think Shaw may have found out about Hans. Don't tell Junior. I want to explain it. I still don't know why he shot at us."

"I can talk. Junior's in the gas station bathroom changing into

14

some clothes I bought him—"

"Good. Thank you. Try to keep him with you till I call again when I know more. Shaw's leg got shot when I tried to take the gun away from him."

"He tried to shoot—"

"Can't talk. I'll call soon." Connie hung up, washed her hands and returned to the sheriff.

Chapter Four

Junior

Junior heard the sirens, but it was like hearing them through mud. His left hip and upper leg still smarted. That was nothing compared to the pain of seeing his father waking him, brandishing a shotgun and shouting for him to leave. Dad never joked around with guns. Dad never joked about anything. Junior's birdshot wounds were nothing, he was far enough away to lessen the impact. No, the pain of realizing his own father shot him and the uncertainty of knowing what happened to his parents next was wrenching. He heard the backhoe fire up, roar for a few minutes, then shut off. A few seconds later, Jens got back in the pickup. Junior had no idea why they were at the cemetery.

He heard Jens shift the pickup into gear and they bounced out of the cemetery and onto the road. He knew they turned right, away from home. Away from whatever just happened. How long before he returned? Were he and Jens to just drive around a while? His mother's words to stay away slammed back into his mind. He winced and moaned and pulled the blanket tighter around him. Jens' hand softly stroked his head and face as he whispered, "Junior, you'll be okay. We're headed for Marshall to get you some clothes."

Junior heard Jens' phone vibrate, felt him lift his hand from Junior's head, twist in the seat to pull the phone out of his jeans and mutter, "That's good."

Jens turned to Junior and said softly, "Junior, your mom just texted that your dad is alive and should live and she's okay. She'll call us soon."

He felt Jens pat his shoulder. Still, he didn't speak. How could he respond when he had no idea why his father shot at him? How could his mom be okay when she told him to stay away? Who shot who? Anyway, what did Jens mean when he earlier said they were getting the hell out of the area? He shivered, curled his six-two body tighter on the bouncy pickup seat and managed to doze off.

He came to as he felt the truck slow and turn, then stop. Jens patted him again. He liked feeling Jens' pats. "We're at Walmart. What size clothes you wear? I'm going in to get you some."

Junior sat up and glanced out the window. The snow was now sleety rain. The clock on the dashboard said nine-zero-three. He was hungry. "Twenty-eight waist, thirty-two length pants. T-shirts, medium or large, but tall. Medium in underpants. Thirteen medium for shoes. Maybe a medium tall sweatshirt. I'm still chilled."

"About what I figured," Jens said. "Looks like they got a deli here. You particular on something to eat?"

"No. Anything should do. I'm famished."

Jens exited the truck, leaving it idling. He returned with several bags, tossing one with a long, day-old looking, pre-wrapped sub sandwich onto Junior's lap. Next, he handed over a large bag of chips and an oversized fountain drink.

"Hope you like cherry-coke. I forgot to ask. Got some fruit and cookies for later. Now eat, then change and we'll see how good of a queer eye I got for clothes."

He laughed as Junior jumped and stared at him. "Yup, I'm gay. Guess your mother never told you."

He pulled out his own sub and took a big bite.

"She never said anything like that. Only that she liked you a lot from taking care of you when you were little."

Trying to cover his shock, Junior broke open the chips, then dove into his sandwich. Jens was gay? Like him and Beany?

Both chewed and munched in silence. Junior inhaled a long slurp of his cherry-coke, his favorite soft drink. He stuffed his sandwich papers and napkin into their bag to throw away. Jens started the truck and drove across the parking lot to a Shell gas station. He stopped next to the men's room on the backside of the building. He hopped out and checked the bathroom door. "It's unlocked, make a run for it. Wave for me if you need any help with those wounds." Jens grabbed both used sandwich bags. "I'll walk these over to that trash can while you start changing. Here's a towel I bought in case you aren't totally dry yet. There's some stuff for your wounds, too. Best take care of them."

Junior gathered the clothes bags, looked around to see if anyone was nearby, and moved quickly into the bathroom. He pulled off his damp underwear, toweled himself off and squirmed around to look at his leg and hip. In one of the bags, he found first-aid cleaner and wipes, along with a tube of Neosporin, and another with drawing salve. He cleaned his wounds, noting they were mostly surface, applied the ointments and covered the deeper ones with Band-Aids to hold the drawing salve in.

Next, he sorted through the bags of clothes for his new underwear, glad he wasn't doing this in the seat of a pickup truck in a Walmart parking lot. He pulled on the other clothes, his socks, and picked up the bag with a shoe box in it. Great. They were Nike's. Good ones. The style he wore. He pulled them on and laced them up. The coke and shivering caught up with him. He needed to pee. Opening the door, he called to Jens, "I gotta use the john, too. Give me a few more minutes."

Jens smiled. "I'm not surprised. Any deep wounds that need to be checked out?"

"I don't think so, nothing looks very deep. Thanks for the drawing salve."

"I figured a farm boy would know what to do with it. Keep an eye on those wounds, don't want them getting infected. If it's lead, birdshot is not good stuff for your system if they're deep. 'Course, getting them surgically removed can be worse." Jens waved to close the door.

It felt good to use the john. Junior couldn't believe it had been since last night. He trotted back to the truck. His full stomach and the exercise brought him another kind of relief. Though it was momentary. As he climbed in the truck, his predicament and worries hit him. "Jens, what is going on? My dad told me I'm not his son and shot at me. Mom told me to keep running and not to come home. You said the two of us are getting the hell out of town." He slapped the dashboard. "Jens, what the hell is up? I want to go home."

Jens looked out his driver's side window for a long minute. Turning his head toward the windshield, he started the car and put his hand on the shifter.

Junior jumped across the seat, turned the key off and pulled it out. "No, Jens. Either you start talking or I'm jumping out. I'll run home, it's no more than a marathon. I'll find a way to call Judy Sue and Beany, they'll come get me. I'll do something."

He slumped over, tears of anger and frustration welling up.

Jens pulled him closer and into a strong hug, Junior felt himself start to relax as Jens said, "I know this is a shock. There are some things you don't know that your mom thinks you might learn in this mess. She wants to control the process. She and I go back a long way. She was like a mother and big sister to me growing up and was very close to Hans, my older brother by ten years…"

"Is he the one that died when I was a baby? I only heard his name a couple of times."

"Yes, actually, four months before you were born." Jens hugged Junior tighter. "Oh, man, your mom really needs to talk with you. She's planning to call soon. We'll just sit here till she does. I totally understand why you're confused and upset."

Junior yanked himself out of Jens' hug and leaned against his door. "Really? You totally understand all this shit? It seems pretty mucked up to me."

He grabbed the blanket and pulled it close, shut his eyes and zoned out. He felt powerless. He had no money, no phone, no coat and was twenty-five miles from home. His father was in the hospital in Summerville with a gunshot wound and there were things his mother might need to tell him. Just what was going on?

Jens took the key back and restarted the engine as Junior started to reach for the key again. "Take it easy, I'm just moving into a parking spot."

He did and, leaving the truck idling, he slid down in his seat and closed his eyes as if to wait.

Chapter Five

Sheriff Cochran, age 58

Deputy Sheriff Fred Cochran sat in the hospital cafeteria, trying to make sense of this situation. Connie sat quietly across the table as if waiting for him to resume the questions or conversation. He took a breath and slowly exhaled. "I hate to do this, but do you mind if I run out to the car and get my kit? I need to swipe you for gunshot residue."

"No problem, Fred, but I did wash my hands after using the restroom."

"Yup, I figured and I should have done it before. I just needed to hear what happened first. This is an unusual event for this area and I need to cover all my bases."

"And your ass," Connie said with a smile, seeming calm. "Go ahead. From what I've read, you'll probably find some on me. It doesn't matter. My son didn't try to kill him. My husband's the one who fired the gun at our son and his finger must have been on the trigger when it discharged as we were falling."

"Have you fired a shotgun before?"

"Of course. I'm a farm wife. Years ago, when my girls were younger, we raised chickens for the eggs. A fox got into the pen. Just once. The second time he got close, I nailed him."

Cochran watched her quickly look away from him. He went out to his car for the gunpowder and fingerprint kits. He thought there probably was gunshot residue on her and her husband. He didn't think she nor her son shot the older man. Or did she? There was something odd

21

about this situation. Why was she rubbing her shoulder? Did she fire a shotgun before taking a firm stance? Why did she look away when she said she nailed the fox? Would her son really just run the farm roads until he was ready to come home? Were some of the field paths remotely suitable to run in? In his underwear?

Back in the hospital, Cochran walked upstairs to the surgery area and asked the station nurse, "How's Mr. Skogman doing? I'd like to speak with him as soon as possible."

The nurse checked the computer. "He's in surgery for another hour and will probably be in recovery for at least two hours before he's conscious enough to answer questions. Even then, his ability to respond might be doubtful. Should we let his wife into the recovery room?" Her eyes glinted with gossip.

"Of course, she should be with him. I'll stop back in several hours to see if he can give me some more information."

Small towns and rural areas, he thought. By now, everyone in the county probably knew Shaw Philip Skogman took a shot at his son and ended up with a leg wound himself. Those phone lines running down the farm roads and all that cellular data in cyberspace must be red hot by now.

He took Connie to a side room, purposely near the nurses' station, leaving the door ajar like always, so as not to frighten the person, especially a female being alone with a male Sheriff. He wiped her hands, arms and upper chest. She willingly complied. "Your husband has about an hour more of surgery, then you'll be able to be with him in recovery. I need to talk with him a bit when he comes to." He looked at her closely for any reaction.

She was calm and gave a slight smile. "I understand. That seems logical in this situation. Maybe you can gain some insight. I sure have none."

He thanked her and checked her over. "Looks like there's some powder or residue on your shirt and jeans, too. Might be mixed in with the blood on your clothes. Mind if I swipe that as well? Next, I'll fingerprint you."

"Of course not. There's probably some in my hair, too."

She pointed out several areas on her clothes and body that might contain powder for him to swipe.

"Sheriff Cochran, if you need to go to the house, please feel free to do so. Anything you can find that will help us learn more about why my husband acted this way will be extremely helpful. I'm at a loss."

She didn't seem at a loss, that's what was confusing him. "Thank you. I was thinking I'd run out there now, then come back. Do you want me to bring your son if he's home or I run into him?"

He watched her sigh and turn slightly away from him. "Of course, tell him I'm still at the hospital and he's welcome to join me here. I'm not sure if he wants to be by his father or not. Sometimes he needs time to process things. Of course, you can't question him unless I'm present."

"I agree. Wouldn't think of it. Kind of hard to process things like this. Especially without some help." He thanked her again and left.

Sheriff Cochran's first stop was at the Marsh residence. The front door opened before he could ring the bell.

"Hi, I'm Beany. Mom thought the police might visit. Come in."

Beany stood about five-nine, slender shoulders, black hair and brown eyes with long lashes. He led the way toward their kitchen. "Please sit down. Would you like some coffee? Mom's feeding the calves. I'll ring the bell and she'll be right in."

He poured coffee and placed cream, sugar and a spoon on the table. From their enclosed back porch-utility room, Beany reached out the door and rang a yard bell. Returning to the kitchen, he poured hot water over a tea bag that smelled of mint, sat down and took a sip. "I can't stand coffee. It's tea for me." He took another sip, studying Cochran carefully. "I bet you want to know what I know, right?"

He seemed fairly mature for being almost seventeen. "Yes, but I'd like your mother to be present before I ask any questions of you. I'm sure your mother will have some insight too."

Beany half-smiled. He refilled Cochran's coffee cup. Tears came to his eyes. "I understand. I can't get over Dad Shaw and how he acted this morning. I was afraid for my life."

23

Judy entered the back-porch utility room that opened into the kitchen through an archway. Inside the back door, she slipped off her barn boots, washed her hands and came to the table, her hand out in greeting, the smell of calf manure wafting. She was short, sturdy and had thick, gray-streaked dark hair and the same large brown eyes with long lashes that Beany inherited. "Hi, I'm Judy Sue Marsh. We expected someone from your department to come by. If not, I was going to call."

"Thank you. I think the best thing is for me to listen to what you know about this morning and any background information that may shed light on the situation." Cochran pulled out his pad and pen.

"Well, we don't know exactly what happened," Judy Sue said. "Beany was over there early this morning, which is not uncommon. Since he was little, if he wakes up or can't sleep, he trots over to their house. They have an extra bed set up in Junior's room. Half the time, I don't know when I get up, if he's at my home or theirs. The same with them." She forced a smile at Cochran. "It sounds strange, but..."

"Connie explained that. It does sound strange, but actually sounds like the boys had two families in one." Cochran smiled to set them at ease.

He turned toward Beany. "So, if you were over there this morning, tell me about it." He took a sip of coffee and stretched back in his chair.

Beany leaned toward him, his face intent. "I woke up about four-fifteen, dressed, pulled a slicker on and slipped some farm boots over my shoes. I jogged over there. I do this a lot, as Mom said." He stirred his tea and glanced at Cochran as if to see the reaction on his face.

Cochran nodded.

"As I passed their garage, I was surprised to see the door open. It's never open that early and why would they leave it open during a snowstorm? So, I veered toward it and saw the hood was up on Mom Connie's car. She always backs it in. It's old and it's easier to drive straight out than back out, especially in bad weather." He carefully stirred his tea, sniffed it and took a long sip. "I noticed the battery was gone and several wires weren't connected. I thought that was odd. No one was around. I figured Shaw must have been working on it last night and forgot to close the door." Beany's face lit up. "Wait. I just realized there was hardly any snow in the garage around the door. If it was open all night, a lot would have blown in around the front of the car."

Beany shook his head and paused till Cochran finished making a note. "Anyway, I went in the mud room, slipped out of my boots, went upstairs and crawled on the bed with Junior. He was sleeping like a log. Usually, I'd get in the twin bed, my bed, but you know…" He blushed a little and looked away. "You know, sometimes it's nice to wake up in bed with someone and cuddle. Junior and I have been doing that since we were little, even before we knew we were gay and that we loved each other."

His mother smiled at him.

Cochran figured they did more than cuddle. He cleared his throat. "Did Junior wake up?"

"No, he didn't even know I was there. It was Saturday, so I knew we could sleep in."

"Did you undress? Take off your shoes?"

"Nope, just stretched out close to Junior and went to sleep."

"Then what happened?" Cochran drained his coffee and waved no to a refill.

"What happened?" Beany's voice was incredulous. "What happened is we were rudely awakened by Dad Shaw slamming the door open and yelling and shouting and waving a shotgun around. We both took off like bats out of hell. I mean, the man was crazy. His eyes bugged out, his face was all red. Next he yelled something about shooting Junior." Beany jumped to his feet, waving his arms like he was re-enacting the scene. "He cocked the gun and we both tore out of the room, almost knocking each other down. I went toward the back stairway. Junior went toward the front. I got a ways down the Milliken Road drive, past the garage, the door was closed now, and I could hear Mom Connie screaming and then a blast. I ran harder, then I heard another blast, Dad Shaw screamed. I heard Connie yell something about being okay, but to keep running. I knew she was yelling at Junior."

Beany sat down, panting, covering his face with his hands as if to blot out the sights.

His mother came over and put her arms around him. "He was worse than this when he got home. He told me what happened. I texted Connie if she was okay, and that her car was disabled. I was ready to call nine-eleven when we heard the sirens going up their drive. The 127th Street one." She looked at Cochran who had a questioning look on his face. "We didn't go over there. I was afraid of what I might find. We heard the sirens, so figured the police must have come, so there wasn't much I could do." She squeezed Beany. "Besides, he was so upset, I didn't want to leave him alone. His dad is on the road this weekend, selling our beef. It's all organic. He sells it personally to top restaurants and meat shops." She pulled out a chair and sat next to Beany.

Cochran flipped through his notes a few minutes. "Have either of you seen Shaw act this way before?"

"We knew he occasionally displayed a temper. When you've lived all your adult life next to someone, you know them pretty well," Judy replied. "I have never seen him out of control, threatening or waving a gun around. I'm still in shock. Usually, if he got mad, he just stared, maybe made a sharp comment, stalked off to be by himself or away from others. He's a silent type of man. You know how some Swedes are, not overly demonstrative, no matter how bad or good things are." She glanced at Cochran. "As for me, I'm half-Italian. Where do you think I got my dark hair and brown eyes from? Beany's dad has some Native American mixed in. The brown genes overrode anything else that may have been there."

Cochran stretched and shifted. "You got a bathroom I can use? I had coffee at the hospital with Connie and it's catching up with me."

Beany stood and pointed him to a bathroom off the porch utility room. *This is still odd,* Cochran thought as he stepped away. What triggers a stoic, usually calm, controlled man to shoot his son and threaten his wife, especially after many years of marriage? Plus, Connie said she thought Shaw noticed the boys kissing in front of the window, but Beany stated they were both sleeping together when Shaw burst in. Had Shaw snuck up there earlier? I think Connie would have heard him if he had. Guess this is another thing I gotta keep my ears open to.

Back in the kitchen, he sat down. "This is confusing. You seem to think so as well. Any ideas what's behind all this?"

Beany sat back down next to his mother. "I was so shocked. It's not like Dad Shaw was cuddly and close to me, but he's never been mean or nasty. When we were younger, he used to take Junior and me places. Sometimes we'd ride along in the big grain trucks to empty the load and get an ice cream cone on the way home. Never talked much, was just there. He was always busy working by himself or with his hired man."

"Who was that? He still around?" Cochran sat up straighter. He hadn't realized there was a hired man that might have been around.

Judy answered. "His name is Melvin Smith. He's worked for Shaw since I can remember. Melvin's an excellent mechanic and helps keep all that equipment up to snuff. He lives alone with his dog, Rusty, over in the old farmhouse, down Milliken another two and a quarter miles. Shaw rents that property and Melvin lives there to partly keep an eye on things on that end of Shaw's properties. Shaw owns two sections and rents more. A lot more, we think. He doesn't say. Melvin doesn't either."

"Yah, Melvin wouldn't hurt a flea," Beany said. "He's quiet, shy, hardworking, kind of a loner, a bit nervous-acting. Doesn't look straight at you when you're talking. He also delivers prescriptions to old folks from pharmacies in the area. Even has an old van he uses for that sometimes. Only times he ever yelled at Junior and me was when we were doing stupid kid things that could get us hurt. Even then, he didn't tell Dad Shaw on us." A flash of a smile crossed Beany's face as he continued, "Melvin even taught us how to play with Rusty when the dog was little and he was training him. Melvin loves that dog and Rusty's really smart. Anyway, today's Saturday and he should be off the farm. He'll start working weekends when planting comes and harvest. He may be out delivering prescriptions and putting in bluebird boxes, he's nuts about them. You want to go see if he's home?"

Cochran shook his head. "Not now. No other ideas of what could have gone wrong to trigger Shaw? He's not young. Have you noticed any signs of early dementia?"

"Shaw's a Swede. He's not out of middle age yet. How long you been around these parts?" Judy half-laughed.

Cochran chuckled. "A long time. I'm mostly Scottish, but I know what you mean with these Scandinavians living forever. One of my grandmothers was Norwegian and she lived to one-hundred and three. She was pretty sharp till she died." He shook his head. "Still, something had to have triggered him to act this bizarre. How long have he and Connie been married? I know she's a bit younger than him. Any other kids?"

"Well, yes. He had twin girls with his first wife, Alice. She..." Judy paused, looking at the floor. "Alice died October 10, 1975. Shaw found her dead in the bathtub. There was a prescription container for sleeping pills nearby. The twins were eleven and a half."

No one spoke.

Cochran cleared his throat. "I joined the department just before then. I remember hearing something, but didn't work on the case. It seemed pretty open and shut, as I recall. What a tragedy."

He watched Beany stare at his mother in shock as she quietly replied, "It just seemed such a surprise. I knew her fairly well, though she was also older than me, about Shaw's age. I'm sixty-two. She lived for those girls. Her older sister told me afterward she was planning a shopping trip with the twins to Sioux Falls that same weekend. It all seemed so strange. I guess you never know what someone's going through..."

"Mom, what did Dad Shaw do? I never heard this. I just knew Junior has a lot of older sisters and they all moved away from the area."

Judy patted his shoulder. "No, some things we don't talk about much and by the time you came along, that was pretty far in the past." She looked at Cochran who was leaning forward in his chair. "I'm feeling hungry. Would you like a fried egg sandwich? Beany makes a great one and we can talk a bit more while he makes it, then I have to get back to feeding calves."

Cochran made a note about daughters, and sat back in his chair. "Sounds great. Donuts don't last long." He glanced at Beany. "Do you help with chores, too?"

"Of course. I may be a bit femme, but I'm still a farm boy. I get the honor of feeding them this afternoon. I do the afternoon shift and Dad, Mom or I take turns doing the evening shift." He grabbed a skillet from the rack above the stove, spun around and said, "Get ready for the best gourmet fried egg sandwich you've ever had."

Cochran laughed. "He reminds me of my great-nephew in The Twin Cities. He's on the U.M. cheerleading team."

"Don't tell Beany or he'll leave tomorrow. He'd love that. He loves performing."

On his way to the fridge, Beany gave a cheerleading jump and softly called, "Go, team, go."

Cochran checked his notes. "Anything suspicious about the first wife's death being a suicide? An overdose?"

"Everyone has second thoughts after someone they know commits suicide. My discomfort may just be normal. There seemed to be no warning signs. It's hard to believe Alice could be on an anti-depressant and no one around her, including her family, knew. I have nothing concrete to base my worries on. That's why I never said anything. There was enough gossip floating around without adding to it. Besides, things seemed to work out with him and Connie." She paused and looked out the window. "Until today."

"How and when did Connie come into the picture?"

"We neighbors tried to help with the twins as much as possible. Alice's parents were dead and Shaw didn't seem comfortable sending the girls to their aunts. The twins were so lost. I took them to the library about a month after their mother died and Connie was volunteering. She knew who they were, their situation, and immediately took them under her arms. They fell in love with her and wanted to go to the library any time she was there."

Several minutes later, she and Cochran stopped talking as Beany slid plates in front of them with the most delicious-looking fried egg sandwiches he ever saw. Beany placed a cloth napkin, knife, fork and glass of orange juice for them. "It's a little messy, you might want to use the knife and fork. You'll definitely need the napkin."

Cochran cut into the homemade bread toasted to a golden brown, the egg yolk running, a hint of cheddar cheese wafting up. He lifted it to his mouth, chewed a moment. "The spicy mustard sets this off. You should patent this, Beany."

Beany beamed and sat down with his own plate. He delicately cut small bites with the knife in his right hand and ate with the fork in his left hand, like Europeans do, then wiped his lips.

Judy finished her sandwich much less daintily than Beany. "The end result is, the twins needed training bras and asked their dad to buy them some, plus suggested he get them some feminine pads. They knew they needed to be ready." She laughed. "I think he panicked. He contacted Connie and asked for her help. About that time, Mrs. Hanson died. She's the one Connie took care of for years. Started when she was only twelve and Jens was six or eight, I think. Anyway, Connie was twenty-four or so and it seemed like an opportunity for both him and her. He asked her to marry him. She said yes. They married six months after Alice's death. A year later, she had a girl, then three more, each two years apart. Her last one was born in 1983. Ten years later, at age forty-two, she had Junior. One year later, I was forty-six and had this guy. My first and only. My husband and I tried for years, gave up and were totally shocked and thrilled. That's why she and I are so close. Two old menopausal women raising young boys." She smiled at Beany. "Of course, that's why half the community thinks they're gay. Older moms who spoiled them."

Beany flitted his hand and scoffed. "Yes, all we did was sit around, put nail polish on, eat bonbons, and play with Barbie dolls. I mean, how much can farm moms and dads spoil their kids? Did you know Junior and I are in the same grade?" Cochran shook his head. "Yep, I skipped second grade because he kept teaching me everything he was learning and the teachers said I got bored and disruptive." He grinned as he whisked the dishes into the dishwasher, wiped the counters down and washed the skillet. "I gotta call Dad back with some figures he needs on our beef inventory. Do you have any more questions for me, Mr. Cochran?"

"No, thank you. Both of you have been very helpful. I'm still confused as to motive or reason. I'm heading over to the Shaw place, then back to the hospital. I'll tell Connie I saw you." He headed for the door, then turned back. "Say, any idea where Junior will run to? Or for how long?"

Judy looked startled and shook her head. "You mean he's not at the hospital with her?" At Cochran's shake of his head, she said, "I have no idea. I've been thinking of him all morning. He can run for hours, but why would he? Why wouldn't he be at the hospital?"

"Why wouldn't he come here? I half-figured he might be here when I came. Has he been?"

"No," Beany said. "If he ran just the outside of their two sections, he'd have been here by now. That's over six miles." He rubbed his eyes. "I figured he ran back home after the ambulance left and took Dad Shaw's truck into the hospital. That's why I didn't ask about him when you first came. Oh, please let us know if he's not at home. Oh, please God, I hope he's all right."

At the door, Cochran shook his head and turned back. "I don't want to pry or seem rude, but how do two gay kids get along in this conservative community?"

He looked at Beany. "Are you guys picked on much?"

Beany put his fingers to his temple and thought. "Kids are kids, but overall things are decent. The thing that helps is Junior and I started school with almost all the same kids we're in high school with. We all grew up together. It's not like we had to come out. Everyone knew us." He waited a moment. "Plus, I think it helps that Junior and I are into track. The high school is so small, everyone does a little of everything. Junior does cross country and track. I run the middle events, the four-hundred and eight-hundred and sometimes the two-hundred or mile. Junior's in the science club and on the yearbook crew. I'm in music, art and theater."

Judy smiled at Cochran. "I think Beany is right, though their freshman year, two big football jocks tried to give them a hard time. Connie and I asked the principal to have a meeting with the four boys. Not us. We didn't want to add to the over protective mama thing."

"What happened?" Cochran was intrigued with their story.

"The principal asked each of us what we had to say. The two jocks just mumbled something about not liking homos, it was in the Bible. So, I asked them how often they read the Bible and went to church. Of course, they didn't do either. Next, Junior gave them a copy of an article that said homophobic guys were usually hiding something about their own sexuality." Beany joined Cochran and his mother laughing. "That pretty much ended things."

~ * ~

Still laughing, Cochran stepped off the porch. He drove the short distance down Milliken Road and up the Skogman's driveway. He parked to the side of the house and walked around to the front. The gun lay on the porch floor slightly away from the blood. He guessed it to be about thirty-seven inches long, a standard size for coach shotguns. The melting snow and rain washed some of the blood, bone shreds and flesh toward and down the stairs.

Cochran pulled his gloves on, put covers on his shoes, stepped up the side of the steps, and walked around the blood as much as possible. He bagged the gun for further testing. Shaw was tall, at least six-three, he mused. If it was a longer gun, he doubted if the man would have hit his own leg. Maybe took his foot off. Of course, by the looks of it, he might lose his leg at or above the knee anyway. Still, the dynamics of how the gun went off during the struggle and where it hit Shaw were interesting. Something he'd have to think more about.

He pulled out his camera to snap pictures of everything he noticed. The front door was unlocked. After calling Junior's name several times and not getting a response, he wandered through the house, getting the lay of it, looking for anything out of place. He noticed small bloody footprints across the hardwood floor and down the hall that must have been Connie's. The gun rack on the back porch was over the door. A small cabinet on the wall was locked. It held a pistol and ammunition for it and the shotgun, both birdshot and slugs. He figured Shaw didn't take the time to unlock the cabinet for more ammo and relock it, which meant he only had the two loaded barrels. A pair of muddy boots sat near the door. They must be Beany's, they were turquoise. Upstairs, he could find nothing out of place in Junior's bedroom. Junior's cell phone, an older one, was hooked to the charger on the table next to his bed. Cochran left it there. The twin bed was made up, the double one not. The master bedroom, other than the rumpled bed, looked pristine.

Outside, about sixty-feet from the house, along the Milliken Road drive, the three-door garage was also unlocked. He noted foot tracks in the wet snow coming up the driveway, veering to the garage, then to the house. He noted the same prints, fresher, going back down the driveway. That fit with Beany's story. He could also see a set of truck prints with dual rear tires, entering and leaving the long driveway. A different set of foot prints led from the drive to and from the door where the Camry was parked. Could someone have driven in, opened the door, later driven out and shut the door? Beany stated Melvin didn't work weekends yet. Was Connie covering for someone else? Did Junior actually drive instead of run? His gut told him no. He just noticed Junior's bare footprints running away from the house down the front drive and the spatter and blood on Connie's body indicated she was accurate in detailing what happened. Did Shaw drive in and out? If he had, it must have been a quick trip. He shook his head and made several notes.

Inside the garage, a newer Dodge 2500 extended cab pickup with dealer stickers was parked heading out. It was locked. The hood of an old Camry was down. He opened it to find the plug wires unattached, no distributor, and no battery. He found the battery in the attached garden shed. It was past replacement age, but that didn't mean it was dead. Maybe Shaw removed it to take to the parts store for a new one? Made sense. Why would you leave the hood open for a while, then close it? Who did it?

Cochran went back to the Camry. It was unlocked. He checked inside. The car was farm clean. Dusty, worn carpets and seats, grease spots on the rear mats, the windshield slightly grimy with streaks of a handkerchief or Kleenex apparent. He popped the lever to open the trunk. There was a snow shovel, a bag of kitty litter, an emergency blanket kit, a partially filled, half-frozen jug of water, and some granola bars in a Ziploc bag. The spare looked serviceable. The jack and tools were there. Nothing else. He went back to the lean-to. There was a battery tester and charger, but not plugged in. Still wearing gloves, he attached the leads and plugged the machine in. The indicator floated to full. Good. Strong. What did he just prove, though? Had the battery been charged before and not re-installed? Was it good and not even checked yet? He still didn't know what this meant or how to interpret it. All he had was a fully charged out of date battery that may or may not have been recently charged, no distributor and spark plug wires unplugged.

He walked back to his sheriff's car and started it, turned it off again and got out. This was a crime scene. No one else should be around it until he gave the okay. He opened his trunk, pulled out the bright yellow crime scene tape, attached a sign to each door, and taped off the front porch, the back door and the side entry. Restarting his car, he drove toward the hospital.

What was there about this situation that didn't fit? An older man who uncharacteristically exploded, an attempted murder of his son, another attempt at his second wife, no evidence of the kid running down the road in his underwear, and his mother seemingly not all that concerned as to his whereabouts? Plus, add in a first wife's suicide. Why wasn't someone out looking for the kid? Why did Judy and Beany not seem concerned until he mentioned Junior wasn't at the hospital? Even then, they didn't offer to search for him. Connie rubbing her shoulder and her comment how she nailed a fox tickled his mind, too. She obviously knew how to handle a gun.

Chapter Six

Connie

Connie sat in the surgery waiting room, tiring of the wait. The surgeon and a nurse finally approached. The surgeon shook her hand. "I'm Dr. Patel, the surgeon. Your husband has extensive damage to his lower leg. Both the tibia and fibula are shattered. Just cleaning it out has taken us this long. It's clear to me the leg should be amputated below the knee."

"That's a big decision." Connie glanced at the nurse who didn't return her look.

"Besides the tibia and fibula, the bullet tore away muscle and nerves, destroyed arteries and veins. I consulted with a trauma surgeon at University Hospital in The Cities during the procedure, even sent him some pictures. He agreed with my assessment that we should clean everything up and amputate…"

"Would there be enough left to rebuild the leg?" Connie asked quietly.

The surgeon shook his head. "That's the issue. There isn't." He looked at her a moment to see if she was grasping the severity of Shaw's injuries. "Plus, shotgun blasts put a lot of residue in the air at the end of the barrels. Add in his overalls being ground in and bacteria from his skin means controlling infection is critical. The longer we wait to amputate, the greater the chance infection can take over. We have him on powerful antibiotics."

Connie felt him looking at her as he paused. She kept her face blank and motioned for him to continue.

"The good news is, your husband is in remarkable shape for his age. The bad news is infections of this type are difficult to prevent and can spread rapidly."

"So, are you asking for permission to amputate now?"

"Yes, we checked his medical records. Years ago, he designated you to have power of attorney in medical manners."

"That's only in case he is incompetent to make decisions. Is this something that can wait for him to decide? What happens if I won't make that decision? That I think he should make it. The man just tried to shoot me at close range with a twelve-gauge slug for reasons I don't know. If I tell you to amputate and he doesn't want it, what will he do to me if he recovers?" She stared into the surgeon's eyes, saw them flicker. "Can he be patched up enough till he regains consciousness? Is there a possibility he can survive with a chewed-up leg?"

Dr. Patel looked at the floor. "His leg needs to be amputated. I think it should be done in The Cities. We will discontinue the sedation so that he wakes up and can express his decision."

Connie sat next to Shaw in the recovery room. He just returned from surgery and appeared to be unconscious and probably would be for ninety minutes or more. A male nurse entered the room. "The charge nurse left a message that the police would like to talk with your husband as soon as he's capable. We'll check him when he starts coming to, you can spend a few minutes with him alone. Dr. Patel will return to seek his permission to transfer him to The Cities. Following that conversation, you will need to leave so the Sheriff can try to interview him in person. Of course, this depends upon how alert he is." The nurse studied her for a few seconds. "Was there foul play involved?"

Connie stomped her foot. "The question should be, why did my husband go instantly insane, try to shoot our son and me? My husband was injured when we struggled for the gun after he first shot at Junior and then turned it on me. I am totally confused and shocked. Tell Dr. Patel I hope he brings in a psychiatrist or mental health expert. I would love to see him transferred to The Cities. That will be his decision, not

36

mine."

The nurse's face registered his surprise. "You had no prior warning he was this upset?"

"None. I've been married to him for thirty-five years. He's been angry, occasionally, but never out of control. The police have never been called for a domestic incident. He's your typical old Swede, silent and stoic, even when upset. I'll stay by his side, but I need some help here." Connie turned toward Shaw's bed. "The police can talk with him as much as possible. Maybe they can find some answers. I sure don't have any." She plopped down in the recliner chair by the bed, reached over and hesitantly patted Shaw's hand.

As the nurse walked out the door, Connie's phone buzzed. It was a text from Judy. *How are you? WHERE IS JR??? Thought he was with you. Cochran says not. What's going on? Call if possible. Love you.*

Connie was the only conscious person in the room. She started to return Judy's call, but her phone buzzed. A call from Jens. She punched talk and lifted it to her ear.

"Mom, what is going on?" Junior shouted. "Is Jens kidnapping me? You said don't come home. Dad shot me. Jens says he knows stuff about you. What the hell is going on? I want to be with you. NOW."

"Oh, son. I love you."

"I don't care. I know that already. Just tell me what is going on. This is nuts."

Connie toughened her voice. "Junior, be quiet. Calm down. Don't talk, just listen. I don't want to hear your voice till I say so. Put this on speaker so Jens can hear, too." She waited till she could hear both men breathing, Junior sniffling. Her heart broke, but she had to control this situation. At least for now.

"First, I don't know what went wrong with your father. The front porch is a mess and I don't want you to see it. Second, the sheriff's department is investigating. They may want to interview you, too. Third," she paused, swallowed and took a deep breath. "Third, I have a secret that I'm not prepared to share yet." She lowered her voice, enunciating each word with force. "You have no choice in this. Right now, you must stay with Jens until I say you can come home. Don't argue. Don't question me. Don't beg. Don't cry." She heard Shaw moan and rustle. She knew the medical staff would be in momentarily. She brightened her tone of voice and added, "The gun went off and shot Dad through the leg. It's serious, but he survived surgery and is coming to now. The police are going to interview him. I'll call you when I know more, then we can talk about you coming to the hospital. I do want to see you, just not now." She punched end, slipped the phone into her pocket, reached over and patted Shaw's hand as the nurse and surgeon walked in and up to the bed. She hoped Sheriff Cochran was not outside the door, listening, but if he was, at least she could tell him Junior was safe with a family friend.

"My leg hurts. What happened?" Shaw moaned and tried to reach his leg, but the doctor held his hand in place.

"Easy there, Mr. Skogman. I'm Dr. Patel. I'm the surgeon who operated on you. A bullet went through your lower left leg. It did a lot of damage. We need to ask you about your wishes for further treatment."

"A bullet?" Shaw opened his eyes and looked around. "What happened? I got shot?"

Connie leaned over him. "Honey, something went wrong with you. All at once. You tried to shoot Junior. In fact, you winged him with birdshot. You started to aim it at me. I tried to take the gun from you and it went off. The slug tore through your leg."

"That sounds crazy. Why?"

"That's what we'd like to know."

Dr. Patel checked Shaw's vital signs and lifted the sheet concealing Shaw's leg which was in a metal frame and slightly elevated. He peeled back the edge of the coverings to check the area as he explained the wound. "Listen, we need to talk about your injuries. The slug tore through your lower leg, it shattered both bones and destroyed major arteries, veins and nerves."

Shaw looked up at him, his face grimacing.

"Your leg is so terribly damaged." He paused as Shaw groaned. "I need your permission to transfer you immediately to University

Hospital in The Cities where most likely they will seek your permission to amputate below the knee. They've already seen x-rays and photos and agree a below-the-knee should give you the best achievable result."

Shaw closed his eyes for several long moments. Opening them, he looked at Connie. "What's she say to do?"

Connie touched his hand, tried to hold it. He pulled his away. "I'm not making this decision, you are." She waited, but there was no reaction from him. Tapping his hand, she added, "More important than your leg is knowing why you fired at Junior and tried to shoot me." She got up and sat down across the small room.

Shaw glared at the surgeon. "I'm not going to The Cities. I'm not amputating. Not yet. Put me on antibiotics. I need more time to think."

The surgeon's shoulders slumped. "The longer we wait to amputate, the higher the risk of infection, the harder it will be to control and the greater the chances of blood clots. All of which you could die from." He paused as Shaw shook his head vehemently. The surgeon felt for Shaw's pulse. "Your wife is going to spend several minutes with you, then the sheriff wants to ask some questions. After that, you need to rest. The nurse will give you something more for pain and we've already started the antibiotics. We still may have to take you back in if there's additional bleeding."

Shaw's voice, though weak, was angry. "Another thing. I don't want any more drugs than necessary. You need to tell me what each thing is and what it's for."

The surgeon looked at Connie. She shrugged. She was confused. She'd never heard Shaw speak about drugs that way, other than he rarely took anything. He wasn't on blood pressure, heart, prostate or cholesterol drugs.

Shaw added, "Tell them only to increase the pain meds when I ask and to be ready to start reducing it soon. The antibiotics are what's important right now, not the pain. When's the sheriff coming in?"

The surgeon and nurse looked surprised. "You're in charge," Dr. Patel said. He left with the nurse.

Connie followed them out. It was obvious Shaw, though lucid, didn't want to talk to her.

~ * ~

Cochran lingered outside Shaw's room. He waited till Connie left before entering. He grasped the man's hand. "Hi, Mr. Skogman. I'm Sheriff Fred Cochran. We've met a few times over the years. How are you feeling? Can you focus enough to talk with me?"

"I'm in pain, but I can focus. Why do you need to speak to me?"

"Because, according to your wife and the evidence I've observed, you told your son he wasn't yours and ordered him to leave the house. You shot at him with birdshot, probably winged him." Cochran noticed Shaw's eyes flicker and glare at him. "Next, you turned the gun on your wife. She managed to deflect it and the bullet went through your lower leg."

"The hell you say. Really? She tried to deflect it?" His tone was sarcastic. He took a deep breath and seemed to calm himself. "Why would I do something like that?"

"That's what we're trying to find out. Do you remember seeing your son and the neighbor boy, Beany, kissing this morning? Maybe through the window from your farm office?"

Shaw closed his eyes. "What else?"

"Do you remember going back into the house about seven this morning, grabbing the shotgun, going upstairs, yelling at your son that he wasn't yours, ordering him to leave and pointing the gun at him?"

Shaw opened his eyes. "What else did she say I did?"

Cochran couldn't tell if Shaw was confused or obfuscating. "Well, your son ran down the front stairs, across the porch and took off down the driveway, the 127th Street one. You fired at him with birdshot. Connie thinks you hit him. Not much, though. Then, you turned on her, even told her, 'You're next'. She tried to take the gun away from you. The gun went off in the scuffle and the slug tore away your leg."

Shaw groaned and twisted. He muttered, "Really? She tried to take it away from me?"

Cochran thought it sounded like another sarcastic statement rather than a question. "One more thing, please. I need to take your fingerprints."

Shaw reluctantly allowed him to fingerprint him, then turned his head to the side. "It hurts when I talk." He closed his eyes and started to breathe regularly.

Was he sleeping? Why didn't he answer the questions directly? Cochran sat down in the recliner next to the bed. "Go ahead and nap. I'll wait to talk more when you wake up." He pushed the chair back. "I can use a nap, too."

He didn't sleep, but ran Shaw's answers and seemingly sarcastic statements through his mind. He waited about fifteen minutes, asked Shaw if he could talk more and left the room after receiving no response.

Chapter Seven

Shaw Philip Skogman, Senior, age 74

In the ambulance that morning, Shaw, in spite of the pain, remained conscious on the ride to the hospital. He knew Connie was next to him. He knew he didn't want to forget what he discovered on her cell phone that morning after she went back to bed. He focused on memorizing that text, forcing it into the reaches of his mind where he could recall it later, after the surgery he knew he needed. He knew his wound was bad. *Still, I'm lucky,* he thought. *If she hadn't slipped, I could be dead. Those texts I read on Connie's phone were the proof I wanted ever since Junior was conceived. Also, Junior left a note, a second one, on my desk in the farm office. This time, I needed to address his request. The note, combined with reading Connie's texts to and from Jens, set me off. I never lost it like this before. Is it my age? Will this open up my secrets I've concealed so well and for so long?*

In the ER, he felt the doctor and staff examine his leg, heard them ask questions, and explain to he and Connie what was going to happen. He'd been lucky. Had he been? Maybe if he died on the spot, no one would ever know…He felt the jab of a needle and drifted off.

~ * ~

As Shaw came to, he realized Connie sat next to him. Her voice sounded distant, unfocused. Must be on her phone. To who? Or was it whom? He didn't like being groggy. He heard the word secret. Secret?

42

She had one, a very big one. Had she figured out his? He had more than one. Why was she talking so strongly to Junior? Telling him to not come home? Shaw didn't look at her when she leaned over him. Why should he?

He knew the truth.

Now.

Finally.

Her truth.

Would she discover his? Should he tell her? Everything?

He listened to Cochran's questions. He asked his own back. He might be groggy, but he wasn't going to answer anyone until he had more time to think about things. He realized Cochran gave him something he could use as an excuse. Beany and Junior kissing. Except, hell, he knew they kissed, frequently. Even had sex. A lot of it. At least neither of them could get pregnant, like his six daughters could have. He was glad Connie put them on the pill and had long talks with them about conception and contraception. Still, the boys kissing was a good rationale. Neither Junior nor Connie ever told him the boys were gay. Beany? That took about three seconds to figure out, but again, no one ever told him that. Nope, he didn't care if the boys were gay, in love or in heat. Right now, though, he'd have to think about things. Right now, he needed sleep. Let Fred Cochran sit there as long as he wanted to. No, he wasn't going to The Cities or have his leg amputated. This just meant he'd die sooner than he planned. Which, given the information that could surface, might not be such a bad option. Easier than the legal mess that would ensue.

Chapter Eight

Junior

Junior roused and looked across the busy Walmart parking lot, at the gray skies still dripping a mixture of snow and rain. He poked Jens. "This is stupid. I want to go home. I want my phone. I want to go to the hospital and see Mom. I'm not sure about seeing Dad, if it's even possible. I want to talk to that cop, too. I got nothing to hide."

Jens squinted his eyes at him as if trying to decide what to do next. "Let me text your mom."

"Dammit. What are you? My daycare teacher? My new guardian? The keeper of the secrets? How long we gonna sit in this freaking truck, wasting gas in a Walmart parking lot? This is nuts."

Jens stared at him. "Look, kid. I like you, but I didn't ask for this detail…"

"Why are you doing this? Take me home."

"I can't. Not yet. I promised your mother…"

"Oh, God. What did you promise her? You'll babysit me till I'm ready for a nursing home? C'mon, just take me home." Junior slapped the dash, then waved the dust away. He slumped back in his seat.

Jens checked his watch. "Your mom doesn't want you to see the porch. Trust me. I've seen gunshot injuries. They leave a mess that will gag a maggot. Okay? Now, give me an hour or hour and a half, or till she calls us back. After that, I'll think about taking you to the hospital or to Beany's."

Junior startled. "You know about Beany? How?" He watched

44

Jens half-smile and situated himself to better see his face.

"I said your mother and I were close over the years. We've been close again the past three years since I returned to the area to care for my father. That's who I buried this morning. Your mom and I talk on the phone frequently and we text daily. We share a lot of life experiences. We have a deep bond. I'll tell you about it. Now, can you be patient?"

Junior reluctantly nodded. He rooted around in the bags and pulled out a package of cookies and an apple.

Chapter Nine

Jens

"Thank you. I'll try to be concise." Jens reached over and took several cookies. "My parents married right after World War II and tried for several years before my brother, Hans, was born in 1950. Mom was never a strong person health-wise. They doted on him and figured he would be an only child. Hans was precocious, bright, charming, one of those people who filled the room. He loved being an only child. Ten years later, I came along. Surprised the heck out of them. Mom was excited, never sure Dad was. Hans definitely wasn't. Suddenly, he wasn't the main focus. There was a baby who needed to be nursed and fed and changed and who cried. Hans hated the intrusion." Jens took a bite of cookie and chewed. "He soon figured out I wasn't going to leave either."

"How did your folks handle it?"

Jens smiled. "I think they were shocked their sweet perfect child didn't like having a little brother. Anyway, a year or two after I was born, Mom started feeling poorly. Vague symptoms the local doctors couldn't identify at first. Finally, when I was four, she was diagnosed at University Hospital in The Cities with MS, multiple sclerosis. You know what that is?"

"It's some disease that slowly makes it so they can't move, isn't it?"

"That's right." Jens took a big bite of cookie. "What do you know about your mom's background?"

"Not much. I know her mom died young, maybe when she was

ten or so and her dad seemed incompetent as a father. I think she went to live with you guys just before he died, too. That's about it."

"There's more, but that's a good summary. My dad could see that Connie's dad wasn't capable of parenting a child, especially a girl. He asked my mom if she thought taking another child in could be helpful or add to her stress." He smiled and looked out through the windshield for several moments. "My mom loved people. She met Connie who was desperate for some feminine touches and was excited to join the family. She came when she was around twelve. I was four, it must have been shortly after Mom's diagnosis. Hans was fourteen."

"How did he respond? If he didn't like you, why would he like a girl suddenly coming into his life?" Junior crunched a bite off his apple.

"By then, he'd grown up a bit and realized I wasn't going away. That didn't mean he liked me any better, just could ignore me easier. Plus, the local schools couldn't do much for his brightness so he moved to The Cities, lived with our uncle's family and went to the university high school. You know he went on to become an anthropologist of some note, don't you?"

"I think so. I don't know much else about him. Hey, when did you two develop such a close bond?"

"I think with Hans gone, only coming home periodically during high school and even less through college, it allowed Connie and my mom to develop a close relationship. At first, Connie became a loving big sister, then more of a mother to me as Mom slowly deteriorated. She was incredibly helpful to me. She seemed to understand my relationship with Hans right from the start. More importantly, she grasped that I felt different about myself and she made efforts to encourage me to be myself. Our bond developed even more as I realized I was gay and my mother grew sicker. At the end, we were both caring for her." Jens paused, stretched and looked out the window. "There's something about people caring for an ill person together that brings them even closer. I went through the same thing later, during the AIDS crisis…"

"You knew people who died of AIDS?"

"Yes, more than one. Many. I was an undertaker who served the gay community…My partner also died…" Jens reached over and patted Junior's arm. "I think that's a story that needs to wait. Just realize that one of the reasons your mom and I are close is that we shared in the care of and the love for my mother through some long, difficult times." Jens wiped his face as he noticed Junior wiping his eyes on the damp t-shirt he'd worn during his morning escape. He took a deep breath. "Anyway, Mom died when I was sixteen, Connie, your mom, was twenty-four, Hans was twenty-six."

"I thought Mom married my dad when she was twenty-four." Junior seemed ready to move back to the former conversation.

"She did, shortly after my mother died. My dad and I figured we could live on our own till I finished high school and went off to college. Dad always appreciated your mom, but was never that close to her. Connie was instrumental in helping me when I recognized I was gay. She read up on everything she could find. Even going to The Cities to read material from the university library and departments. Dad withdrew further from me. He wasn't interested in looking at what Connie was bringing home and trying to show him about homosexuality."

"Yeah, Mom's always been into library stuff and researching things."

"Umm, your mom managed to get an associate degree in Liberal Arts while caring for my mom and me. She thought of going on for degrees in Library Science and should have her Ph.D. and be running a university library someplace. She's that bright and capable."

"Okay, I kinda know how she met Dad when she was helping his daughters, the twins, and they got married and had four more girls, then I showed up late. I get why he wanted a wife, but never could figure out why she wanted him. I mean, he's nice…" Jens watched Junior take another bite of apple and stare out the window. "Well, Dad was, until this morning… Anyway, he's not…"

"Your dad's not a warm huggable person. He's a steady, usually even-steven type of man who says little, but always does what he says, and never in a flamboyant or spectacular manner. I always thought of him as kind of a cut rock, or a carved piece of granite. Like the cornerstone or foundation of a building. Not noticeable, but sure necessary."

Junior poked around for an empty bag to put his apple core in. "Didn't Dad used to be on the school board, the county board, and help some farm organizations?"

Jens nodded.

"I think that's a pretty good description of him. I never thought of him that way. Anyway, what's all this have to do with some secret about my mom? Why is she so uptight about wanting to control how it comes out? I still don't get it."

Jens was quiet. He looked out the window. Was he in his rights to share Connie's secret? How much longer could he keep stalling this kid until his mother was ready to see him? He and she had a strong trust relationship. He heard Junior sigh, waiting. *Given all the commotion and the predicament we're in, I'll tell him the secret I am positive about. The other one, the secret she's never confirmed to me, will have to come from her, if it's valid.* He turned toward Junior, sucked in a long breath and slowly let it out. "I think her secret was that she was in love with Hans."

"So, a teenage crush? He never lived around here, did he?"

"It was more than a teenage crush. It was an affair that lasted years. She, Hans and I were the only ones who knew of it. She was madly in love with him."

"For real? An affair? Why didn't she just marry him?"

"Because each of them married someone else. Hans married right after earning his bachelor's degree when he was twenty-two and your mother was twenty. At first, she was devastated, but they continued to see each other. Your mother married Shaw when she was twenty-four." Jens looked at Junior and the consternation on his face as he absorbed the information.

"You—you said years. The affair lasted years. When did it end?"

"Eighteen years ago, when Hans died. Four months before you were born."

"Dad never knew? Are you crapping me? This sounds crazy. An affair that lasted years between two married people who didn't even live near each other? My mother?"

Junior wiped his face with the towel he used to dry off. He stretched and kicked lightly against the floor, wriggled around in the seat. Sighing, he asked, "When did the affair start?"

"When your mother was sixteen, Hans eighteen, just out of high school. I didn't learn about them till I was maybe twelve. I mentioned how your mom loved to go to The Cities to do research and find books she couldn't get locally."

Junior blinked, his face blank of emotion.

"That's when they saw each other. Over the years, he would come to visit our dad, or stop by on his way to a state dig or conference. Several times, he flew her to a presentation he was making. Other times, once the twins were older, she'd leave the girls with Shaw for a weekend. She was always involved in library things. Even as a volunteer, she attended conferences all around the state. They'd meet up. At times, they might not see each other for a year, maybe more, but they always managed to keep in touch. Mail helped. The phone did, too."

"Yeah, Mom pays all the household bills, Dad wouldn't check." Junior scratched his head and looked out the window.

Jens was surprised, but kept his face neutral. This kid never let on that there could be more to the secret than an affair. He shook his head. Maybe Junior clearly didn't grasp the implications of his mother having an affair. He looked like he was losing interest. The kid needed to run.

"Okay, I get it, mom had an affair. But is it that big of a deal? I'm sure if Hans has been dead all these years, what difference does it make now? Hasn't she told Dad?"

Jens slowly shook his head. "No, she hasn't told him. I think that's why she wants to control how this information comes out. I think she's afraid…"

"Of what Dad might do? He already showed us that. If she's so afraid, why is she staying by him? Thanks for telling me this, but it still doesn't explain much." He dug through the bags, looking for more food.

Well, Jens thought, *it's not my job to explain there might be a consequence of his mother having an affair. Maybe there wasn't one, but why else would Shaw tell Junior he wasn't his kid?* Jens stretched. "Junior, do you know the park where the high school runs their cross country meets here in Marshall? If that birdshot in your ass isn't too deep, maybe you can take a good run while I stock up on some more food." He winked at the teen. "In fact, here's some money, run in and get yourself some running shorts and sweats." He pulled his wallet out and handed over four twenties. "Get a cheap pair of shoes if you want. No sense ruining the good ones I just got you, then I'll drive you over. While you're running, I'll try to reach your mom. I agree, hanging out in my truck isn't solving anything." He paused. "Just so you know, I was planning on leaving this area. Now that my father is gone, I have nothing to hang around here for. However, I'm not leaving until things are good for you. I promised your mother when you were born that I would back her up on anything she needed regarding any of her children. It's a bond I won't break."

"The birdshot in my butt isn't deep. Good idea. Weird. This is all so weird. I can't wait to run. I always think better when I do." Junior jumped out, slammed the door and jogged toward the store.

Fifteen minutes later, Jens pulled into a parking spot at the park. "I'll be back around this spot when you're done." He reached over and poked Junior. "You will come back, right? You're not going to try to run home on me, are you?"

Junior managed a smile. "Nah, but I am serious about stopping by the house and getting my phone, seeing Mom at the hospital and checking in with Beany. I can stay with them, too." He paused a minute. "Well, not sure I want to see a bloody mess on the porch just yet."

Chapter Ten

Junior

Junior did some stretches and exercises before jogging off. He'd run the park on several cross country meets before and remembered the course fairly well. It didn't matter. This was a chance to clear his head, not win a race. Clear his head, if he could. He never felt so confused in his life. He missed Beany, his color, his laughter, his love, or was it the sex? *It was both,* he thought. *Love and sex.*

Junior knew he was a bit like his dad, somewhat stoic and not given to exuberance. He knew he was also like his mother, somewhat reserved in public or with strangers, passionate, creative, curious, with a sharp wit and a zinger tongue at times. However, he never heard her speak to him in the tone she used today. Never. What was she so hung up about? An affair that ended eighteen years ago? Would Dad explode over that? Is that what set him off? Why did Jens look at him so oddly when he mentioned the affair? What else was there?

His mind drifted back to Beany. What would his life be like without him? Pretty damn dull, that's for sure. Beany was like day lilies and perennials that bloom forever. He was like jumping in the swimming pond Beany's dad built for the boys when they were little, off the 'crick' that ran through their properties. Mr. Marsh fenced it off so his cattle couldn't get to it and muck it up. Muck things up. God, things sure felt mucked-up today. Would this day ever end? How would it end? Would he be sleeping in his bed tonight? At Beany's? In the truck with Jens? That made no sense.

He felt his muscles relax and increased his stride and rhythm. The snow was mostly gone. The rain finally stopped and the sun was making half-hearted attempts to break through the clouds. He pulled the water bottle he bought in Walmart out from its shoulder strap, took a swig and glanced around at the sound of robins chirping. Must be the early ones. He wished he was running his farm trails. The ones he cut every year with the brush-hog through and around the fields. He loved running and watching the tiny shoots sprout out of the ground, the soy beans or the corn, whichever was planted in that particular field. He imagined the crops made different sounds as they grew. Squeaking as they peeked out of the ground; in the summer, the light rustle as the sprouts fluttered in the breeze. Later, in the early fall, their whispers, especially of the mature soy beans and the almost mature corn. Finally, the mature corn talked and gossiped and squawked, then grew raspy as it dried up.

Kind of like mankind aging. Where did that leave his dad? Seventy-four, yet Junior never thought of him as old. Hearing the man's age always shocked him. How could he have a seventy-four old dad? Beany's grandfather died at seventy-six and he was an old, old man.

Dad rotated the crops. He was a scientific farmer, recognized in the state, even over in South Dakota, as one of the top corn and soybean producers. He studied seed production, fertilizer chemicals, erosion, climate, and was a studious business man. He rarely bought brand new equipment, preferring to pick up a recent used piece. When a new combine could cost three-to-five-hundred grand, it made sense to his dad to buy used and maintain it well.

Junior trotted across a wooden bridge, noting the slippery spots on the worn decking. It was about the halfway point, a little over a mile and a half to go. He increased his pace. Three miles wasn't going to cut it. He'd do the route twice. Maybe thrice. He always liked that word. Much more concise than saying three times. Thrice. Concise. He glanced at the brightening sky. *Run, Forrest! Run.* Beany's words echoed through his mind. Those were the words his mom screamed at him from the sidelines, behind the fence at the track field or behind the rope at a cross country meet. Spectators usually chuckled when she shouted it, especially the ones who knew her, knew her quiet reserve mixed with her strong self-confidence.

Kids from other teams sometimes thought that was his name. "Hi, Forrest," they'd say.

"Nah, I'm Junior. My mom loved the Forrest Gump movie. She just likes to holler those words."

"Dang, I'd run fast too if my mom was yelling that at me. Does she give you chocolates at the end?"

Run, Forrest! Run. Except where was he running to? How many times could he go around the route and still get somewhere? Was running in circles any different than sitting in an idling truck, waiting for your mother to call to say you could come to her? Wasn't he safe? For God's sake, his dad was in the hospital. What could he do to anyone now? Had they discovered what made his father explode? Had they fixed him? How can I, Shaw Junior, go back to being normal when Shaw Senior fired a shotgun at me? When I still feel the sting of several pellets working their way out of my skin. Why did Jens look at me that way? Why did his mother keep her affair secret all these years?

He saw a port-a-potty ahead, off to the side of the trail. His bowels told him it was time to get rid of last night's dinner. He yanked open the door. Thank god there was toilet paper, damp, but useable. He pulled down his running shorts and sat. Was this running doing anything? Was his thinking becoming clearer? He wiped, pulled up his pants and stepped out onto the trail. He started walking. Running seemed to be a way to hide things, avoid them. He needed time to think about things, today, his life.

The first thing hit like a M-80 firecracker. His dad said he wasn't his dad. That meant he, Junior, wasn't Shaw's son. How weird was that? Wait. His mind struggled to sort out the look on Jens face, his mother having an affair and his father telling him Junior wasn't his son. Did that mean... Could it mean his father truly wasn't his biological dad? Was Hans his bio dad? He shook his head to clear it. That just seemed so preposterous, so unlikely. He even looked like Shaw. Maybe his dad was just mad about learning about the affair. None of this made sense. Or did it?

Another lightning bolt struck before the first one cleared. Who was in charge of his life? He was almost eighteen, had one more year of high school. He always depended upon his mother to help him sort things out. Now, she was acting weird as hell. His father said he wasn't his father. His mother had a long-term affair lasting from when she was in high school till he was born. A man he never met, Hans, might be his father. He needed to take charge of his life and find out some things.

A third thing exploded, almost like a meteorite. Could his note have triggered his dad? The note he left on his dad's farm office desk last night. Was that a part of this mess? Not that he caused it, but was his request somehow part of this puzzle? Why wouldn't it be?

Bam. Bam. Bam. It was time to get moving, not wait around. He saw the parked truck and quickened his pace to a fast walk.

Junior noticed Jens sauntering down a walking trail on the other side of the truck and paused as he came to the driver's door. He glanced in. The keys were in the ignition. Several bags of snacks and food rested in the middle of the seat. He slipped in, buckled up and cranked the key.

Jens startled at the sound, turned, threw his hands up in the air, like, what the heck.

Junior hit the button to lower the passenger window. "Get in, we're leaving. I'm driving."

Jens trotted back, climbed in the passenger side and buckled up. He started to talk, but Junior put his hand out.

"Don't talk, don't ask questions, don't touch your phone. I'm in charge of me now."

He drove to the hospital in Summerville. Jens followed him into the building. Junior asked for his dad's room number and was given directions. Walking down the hall, he noticed his mother, seventy-five feet in front of them, carrying a cup of coffee, enter the room. When they came to the room, the men could hear Junior's parents speaking. They paused and waited outside the door. Junior determined to not wait around, yet unsure how to proceed.

Chapter Eleven

Connie

After following the doctor out of Shaw's room, Connie wandered down to the main waiting room and sat, wondering when she should go back to Shaw's room. She noticed Cochran and realized he must have returned from visiting the farm and spoke with Shaw.

Cochran detoured to see her and started talking. "Shaw refused to answer any questions. Just kept asking his own. I think he was just pumping me for information." Cochran shook his head. "He's sharp, especially for all the pain he must be in. Listen, I'm headed back to my office to get some work done and check on other situations. I'll pop back later. Call me if you need." He touched Connie's shoulder and turned to leave.

Now, Connie sat next to Shaw as he breathed heavily beside her. He'd been sleeping for about an hour after the surgeon left. After he refused to be transferred and have an amputation. She stretched, needed coffee. "I'll be right back. I need some coffee."

He didn't rouse. She couldn't tell if he heard her, was sleeping, or just lying there with his eyes closed. The way it seemed he did with Cochran.

She returned with her coffee. Shaw's eyes were open, watching her. After she settled in and took several sips, he asked, "Why are you still here?"

She cringed. "Because I'm your wife. I want to see you recover. I really want to know what happened with you."

"Good question. I'm not saying. Figure it out."

"I don't want to play games. Tell me what it is that set you off so badly, you wanted to kill your wife and son."

"Figure it out. I'm going back to sleep. These drugs are wicked." He adjusted himself on the pillow and drifted off.

Connie stood, confused, angry, aching, physically and emotionally. Should she tell him what she figured he learned this morning? That she had an affair with Hans. There had to be more to it than that. No, she would wait. He had to tell her. There was no reason to untie the second secret, the one she kept tied tightly and hadn't considered in nearly eighteen years. She stepped into the hall and saw Junior and Jens near the door. Junior's face had a look of determination she never saw before. "You're here. What a surprise." She hugged both of them. "I'm so glad you are. I wasn't sure when to tell you to come or if you'd want to see Dad. In fact, I wasn't sure you'd want to see me. You must have so many questions."

Connie quit talking. She never rambled on like that. Of course, this wasn't about everyday chatter.

"Mom, can we go someplace and talk? Get out of the hallway? Half the staff is looking at us." Junior pulled his sweatshirt on; he was still wearing the Walmart running shorts and sleeveless t-shirt.

"There's a private waiting room near surgery. We can go up there." She led the way around the corner, up the stairs and into the room. She motioned to the chairs and sat down. "Why did you come here now?"

"Maybe because I'm tired of living in Jens' pickup. Maybe because I have no idea what's going on. Maybe because I decided to take more control of my life." Junior glared at her like he never had before. "Now, will you tell me what the heck is going on? What's your secret, though I think I know?" He glanced at Jens. "What in God's name is going on with Dad? Has he got a brain tumor? Sudden senility?" He settled back in his seat and motioned for Connie to talk.

Wow, she thought. *Junior has never been this assertive, nor so calm when he's upset.* "First, I'm sorry. I can't apologize for your dad, but I have kept a secret since I was sixteen. Even kept it from your father.

57

It sounds like Jens told you already, but I had a long-term affair with Hans, whom you never met. He died suddenly before you were born. We were single when it started, but we continued it after we each married. It wasn't frequent. It was intense. I always felt like we were true soul mates." She dabbed at her eyes. "I still miss him. Today is his birthday."

"So, what's that got to do with Dad going nuts? Did you tell him or something?" Junior's question seemed loaded.

"No, I have never said a word to him about it. I never felt the need to." Thoughts of her cell phone in a different position on the kitchen table this morning sparked again. "There's a possibility your father checked my cell phone this morning after I went back to bed. Jens and I exchanged several texts early this morning."

"Dad checks your phone?"

"He never has before." She thought a moment. "Right after we were married, he went into my purse for something, change, I think, for a parking meter. I read him the riot act about never going into my purse. It was a bug-a-boo that Jens' mom impressed on me. Ladies do not let men go into their purses. Crazy, isn't it? That always stuck, and I reacted when it happened. Usually, I try to respond. He never touched my purse again. This morning, I did leave my phone on the kitchen table. I don't think I've ever done that before. I always keep it in my purse or my pocket. I don't keep a screen lock on. Still, why he would decide to check my phone this morning is beyond me. If he did. If he didn't, then I have no idea what triggered him."

Junior looked at her for a long time. She could see the wheels turning. "Yes, but Mom, what does that have to do with him telling me I wasn't his son?" His words were heavy.

Connie swallowed. "I've always believed you were his son. His sperm hit my egg. A surprise? Yes, but a wonderful one." She stood, partly to quiet the butterflies in her stomach, stepped over and pulled her lanky boy into a big hug. "I'm glad you took charge. It was kind of stupid to keep you away from me. I'm sorry."

She wasn't ready to tell him her fears. The look on his face said she didn't answer his question and he possibly didn't believe her.

Junior held her tight for several moments before asking, "Tell me what Dad's injuries are. I heard him scream when the second shot went off. I was so glad when you hollered you were okay. I had no idea, and still don't, why you told me to keep running and not come home."

A nurse walked into the room. "Dr. Patel just checked your husband again. There's more bleeding and he needs to take him back into surgery to try and stop it. This is not unusual, plus they will check again for debris or anything that can lead to infection. Your husband agreed. We just wanted you to know. It should only take an hour or so and a short recovery time before you can see him again."

"Well, if he agreed, that's fine with me. As far as I'm concerned, he needs to make all those decisions."

Connie turned toward the guys. "I need to get out of here. Can we walk someplace close for coffee and a snack? I need to let Judy know that you are with me, too."

Over coffee and pie, she described Shaw's wound, that he needed an amputation, his decision to thus far refuse transfer and the surgery. She also mentioned how he wouldn't tell her why he behaved this way or what he meant when he said Junior wasn't his son. She didn't want to go any further. Yet. Junior stared at her and gave a slight shake of his head.

Walking back to the hospital, Connie called Judy and updated her. Junior pulled the phone away and talked with Beany. She couldn't help her smile at the change of demeanor in Junior when he talked with Beany. His excitement, his animation, his seriousness, his discomfort as he described getting shot. She never thought she'd approve of a love relationship between two teens. Of course, she never dreamed she and her best friend would be raising gay sons who grew up together and had been in love since they were old enough to jabber. She didn't hazard a guess, knew that Judy didn't either, whether these two would be together all their lives, or would eventually experience the heartbreak and pain of moving on to other relationships. Either way, she felt how they handled the two boys was beneficial for all involved.

The three went back to the surgery waiting room. No one spoke.

Each seemed deep in their own thoughts until an aide told them Shaw was out of recovery and back in his room. Connie sat next to him. Jens and Junior pulled chairs over near the sides of his bed. Junior kept looking at his dad's leg, and the I.V.'s attached to his arm. He scooted back when his father sighed and cleared his throat.

"Figure it out?" Shaw looked at Connie, his voice low.

"No. I told you I'm not playing games. You're responsible for being in here. You tell me what triggered you. Do you need to be examined by a psychiatrist?" Connie's voice was calm, but emphatic. "Junior and Jens are also here. It's your turn to talk."

He waited a moment, his eyes squinting, as if concentrating. Slowly, he said, "I'm perfectly sane. I looked at your texts after you went back to bed. You had an affair with Hans."

Connie leaned over and touched Shaw's hand. "I admit it. I'm sorry I never told you. After he died, what difference did it make? That was years ago. We've always been able to talk through issues before." He brushed her hand away. She straightened and pulled it back. "Shaw, I am sorry I didn't tell you about it, but I'm not sorry for having the affair. It had nothing to do with you. It was something special that started long before I knew you. It was infrequent. We were safe. More than that, we were soul mates. I loved you. I knew what you and I had was different, still good, but could never be anything similar. That doesn't mean I was constantly comparing the two of you. I wasn't. It was a small, but important slice of my life that was set apart from ours. I loved you, I still do, and I willingly bore your children. Now why did finding out I had an affair years ago set you off this morning?" She watched Shaw's neck and face muscles tighten as he glowered at her.

Junior scooted his chair closer toward the head of the bed. "Yeah, Dad. I can understand you being upset that Mom had an affair with Hans, but why shoot me?"

Shaw turned his face to see Junior, slightly lifted his right hand and pointed his finger at him. "Because you're not my son. It's impossible." Despite his facial look, his voice was emotionless, calm, matter of fact.

"How is it impossible?" Connie knew the fear in her voice was palpable. The knot on her second secret was coming untied. How could it be impossible Junior was Shaw's?

She knew how. She and Shaw had sex a week or so after her last encounter with Hans. She counted the days when the doctor told her she was pregnant. It was a surprise, getting pregnant ten years after Emma, but those things happened, especially with menopause. Her fear deepened. How could Shaw know Junior wasn't his child, as he was claiming? Why did he ignore Junior's request two weeks ago to take a DNA test for Junior's science project?

Shaw's slow words snapped her out of her reverie. "Junior can't be mine. I had a vasectomy three months after Emma was born." He was staring at her, his eyes cold, his lips curled in disgust.

Connie fell back in her chair, her mouth opening and closing. Nothing came out. Finally, she said, "You never told me. Why not?" The coffee in her stomach turned to acid. She wanted to retch, to run away from the impact of the double betrayal. She'd betrayed him with her affair with Hans. He'd betrayed her by never telling her he had a vasectomy. She betrayed herself by tightly wrapping and hiding the idea that Junior might be Hans'. After Hans' death, she convinced herself he was Shaw's. It was a triple betrayal, they both betrayed Junior.

His shoulders relaxed. He took a slow breath. "I didn't want more children. Six girls were enough. I'm fifteen years older than you. Having a son wasn't that important to me. I had to go to The Cities for a soy bean conference, scheduled it for the day after and came home."

"Aren't those decisions usually made as a couple?" Her voice was weak.

"Probably. I've always made the decisions important to me by myself." This time, his face turned red, like when he was angry. Almost sarcastically, he continued, "Besides, I figured you didn't want any more children. You told me you were going on the pill till you hit menopause."

"Why didn't you tell me when I got pregnant? Why did you seem to accept him as your son? You agreed to name him after you. Why is he in your will with the girls?"

She shook her head to clear away the emotions of how much she deceived herself. How deeply Shaw deceived her. How long he knew Junior wasn't his.

She watched Junior stand and begin pacing around the room. He turned back as his dad spoke. What was going through his mind? Would she lose him too?

Shaw glared at her, seeming to ignore Junior and Jens. His face curled into a snarl again. "I'm a patient man. I don't usually explode. I wait and see till I figure things out. I knew eventually, the truth would come out and I'd deal with things then. You might say I'm biblically slow to anger, but I do seek revenge. Usually, my revenge is better thought through than it was today."

"Revenge was shooting Junior? He didn't have the affair. He had nothing to do with this. He's innocent." Connie found her voice. It was incredulous.

She watched Shaw wait a moment, his face relaxing somewhat, the redness fading. "What set me off was the combination of finally knowing who you had an affair with, who the father was, along with Junior reminding me of the deadline for his DNA project. I felt boxed in." He shifted his good leg and groaned from the pain the movement caused his injured one. He closed his eyes a moment, straightened his shoulders and emphasized his words. "The slug was meant for you. I never intended to kill Junior. Just wing him to scare him away long enough to shoot you. Again, I should have thought it through better."

Connie gasped. His words were granite hard, no emotion, simply stated as fact. Cold hard facts. She shivered.

Junior shakily sat down. Connie still couldn't read his face.

Shaw continued, his words low, rumbling like thunder moving in. "I figured you'd either go chasing after him, which would give me a good shot or I'd be able to shove you down and fire. The porch was too slippery. I never got my footing. You couldn't keep yours either." He waited, apparently for Connie's breathing to slow. "I hate being betrayed. Always have."

They sat in silence. Finally, Connie said, "I don't know what to say."

"There's nothing to be said. I'd have killed you if I could. I didn't. You'd have killed me if you could have. You didn't, which means you'll live a long life as my widow. The children will all receive their inheritances. I'll be dead soon."

"You know that how?" Still stunned, Connie didn't feel bad about the sarcasm in her voice.

She knew her anger would come next. She sucked in a long breath. Stay calm. Stay calm.

Shaw looked past her and the men, as if checking the time on the wall clock. "I'm not having an amputation. Now, please leave. I need to sleep."

Junior stood, stepped next to the head of the bed and bent over Shaw's face. He stared directly into the man's eyes. "This didn't have to end this way." Junior emphasized each word. "You've ruined a lot of lives. I'll be glad when this is over."

Connie watched Shaw blink several times before muttering, "Boy, it's not over." He fell back on the pillow and shut his eyes.

Connie shook her head and pulled Junior gently away from the bed.

Jens pulled out his key and waved them toward the door. "Let's go home, your home."

In the hall, the two guys put their arms around Connie's shoulders. She put hers around their waists as they walked toward the exit.

Chapter Twelve

Shaw

Junior's words echoed through Shaw's mind. They hurt, worse than the pain of the gunshot. The boy he called son, named after him in spite of his knowledge that the kid wasn't his, just discussed his future, his possible death, like a mature man. Where was the boy's insecurity? Oh, well. What was done was done. He had things to do. Soon. Especially if he was going to die. And he was.

Shaw waited till the three left his room. He found the bed remote and adjusted the bed till he was sitting up more. He rang for the nurse who scurried in. "While I'm awake, I need to make some calls. Please get my cell out of my pants pocket."

She dug through his clothes and handed it to him. It held almost a full charge. "Do you know of a notary public close by?"

She gave him an odd look. "Yes, Miles Norton has a little office about two blocks away. I'll get you his number." She returned in several minutes with the number and stood waiting.

"Thanks, you can leave. Close the door."

He called the notary public, told him his needs, what to bring and to come over in forty-five minutes. Next, he called Melvin Smith and told him to be here at the same time. His phone call with Jack Walker, his family lawyer, lasted longer; longer and louder as Jack tried to talk him out of his plans. Shaw was sweating and shaking from pain when Melvin and the notary public entered his room. Telling them his wishes and signing the forms took several minutes.

He could tell Melvin wanted to stay and talk. Shaw told him to come back later, maybe in the middle of the night. Melvin was a night owl. As always, Melvin acquiesced. He hoped Melvin didn't want to try to talk him out of his intentions. Time ran out. Even if he had the amputation and lived, it would be impossible to keep his other life quiet. Especially with Cochran asking questions. Before falling asleep, he muttered to himself, "Betrayal is wicked. Revenge is necessary. Patience is a virtue."

Chapter Thirteen

Junior

Junior's mind felt like it was on a spinning-ride at the county fair. His father wasn't his father. Now he knew why it was nearly impossible. *Shaw stated it so coldly and matter of fact. I don't know how to take that in,* Junior thought, as his mother gave him a light squeeze. *Am I now supposed to instantly change who my father is? A man I never laid eyes on. In this very second?* He shook his head. *I need time to adjust to this, but I don't want to run from it either.*

As they exited the hospital lobby, Junior noticed the sheriff's car enter the lot and park not far from Jens' pickup. His mother must have noticed too. She dropped her arms from the guys' waists as Fred Cochran got out of his car and approached them.

"Guys, this is Sheriff Fred Cochran. He's been investigating the shooting incident," Connie said.

The men shook hands.

"How's your husband doing?" Cochran asked Connie.

"Not good. So far, he refused to consider an amputation, which is almost guaranteed to save his life. He refused to be transferred to The Cities. He—He said what triggered him…"

Cochran's mouth opened in surprise. "He did? My God." He shook his head. He looked at Junior, a questioning look on his face.

"I've been with Jens all day. He's a good friend of Mom's. I never touched the gun, but I can show you the pellets in my thigh and hip." He turned and pulled up the edge of his baggy running shorts, the ones he bought earlier at Walmart.

"I—I don't need to see. I believe you." Cochran stepped back as if surprised at Junior's bluntness. "Are you going out for a break, then coming back to be by him?"

Junior glanced at his mother who gave him a slight nod. "I doubt it. I don't know when I want to return. He's going to be here a while, so there's time. I don't think Mom does either. Right?"

Connie nodded.

Turning to look at Cochran, Junior stated, "Dad...Shaw just admitted to Mom that he fired at me with the intent of just winging me and was then going to use the slug to kill her. Jens heard him, too."

Cochran looked like his knees might buckle. He sucked in his breath and let it out in a slow whistle. "So, it was intentional? Something else wasn't wrong? Are you sure he doesn't have a brain tumor or something that caused him to go off halfcocked like this?"

Junior watched Connie step closer to Cochran. "I had an affair with a man that started before I was married and continued infrequently for years. It ended eighteen years ago. Shaw suspected and discovered proof early this morning..."

Junior interrupted before she could say more. Why, he wasn't sure. Maybe he didn't want to hear those words again. "Yeah, he also said he was biblically slow to anger, but always got his revenge. His intent was to scare me away long enough to shoot Mom."

Junior smacked his fist into his hand. Out of anger? Frustration? Pain? He wasn't sure. He needed time to absorb the fact Hans might be his father, maybe more proof, whatever that was. He knew he was upset. His mother patted his shoulder. He sucked in a breath and forced himself to calm down. "We need to go. My sisters have to be notified about Dad. Now, do you have any questions of me or my mother?"

Cochran's shoulders slumped. He looked down at the sidewalk. "No. Not now. You've been through enough. What a shock. I'll check with the D.A. She may want me to investigate further. I'll let you know. You need to think about pressing charges or not." He started to turn away, but stopped. "Listen, there is crime scene tape on your doors. I was going to run out and clean the blood off the porch. Don't think I need to investigate out there anymore."

Junior shrugged as if this was no big deal, but he was surprised. His house a crime scene?

Jens stepped forward. "I'm an undertaker. I can take care of cleaning up the blood and removing the tape."

"Oh, you're Jens Hanson. How's your father?" Cochran appeared to be relieved he didn't have to drive back out to the farm.

"He died last night. I buried him early this morning in the back part of the cemetery. The old Lutheran one by the Skogmans. Buried him behind the windrow. Used a backhoe to dig and fill. I planned to leave the area today, move south, but ran into this young man running down the road in his underwear with pellet wounds. I'll hang around till things settle down for Connie. Let me know if there's a fine for burying my father in the cemetery of a closed church with no custodian."

"I'm so sorry for your loss. I knew your dad a bit. It's been a long time coming. I can't imagine there's a problem with the burial. Not out there, doubt if anyone will even notice."

Chapter Fourteen

Cochran

Cochran took his hat off and scratched his head as the three walked away toward the truck. He knew shotgun wounds were messy, especially at close range. Why the hell wouldn't Shaw allow them to amputate? Transfer him to The Cities where several of the best hospitals in the Midwest were? It made no sense. He knew Connie couldn't override with medical power of attorney unless Shaw was incompetent. The man certainly seemed in control of his faculties. He'd seen a lot in his many years with the county, thirty-seven, however, this was perplexing.

Walking down the hallway close to Shaw's room, he noticed a nurse enter the room carrying a slip of paper. Almost immediately, she came out and closed the door.

Cochran stepped closer to her. "I assume that's Shaw Skogman's room, now."

"Yes, it is. He's a stubborn one. I don't know how he's standing the pain." She paused. "In some ways, he's right. He's got something to wrap up and he should while he still can. This is enough of a mess without leaving legal issues." The nurse motioned him over to a small vending area. "I only work the med/surge floor now, but for years, I did ER in The Cities. We saw a lot of gunshot wounds. Of course, the head ones are always the worse, but this one to his leg is terrible." She walked over to a coffee machine. "You got two dollars? My purse is in my locker and I need some caffeine. I bet you do too."

Cochran pulled out his wallet and handed her two dollars.

"Thanks." She pulled the first coffee out of the machine and took a sip of hers as the second one filled. Handing the second cup to Cochran, she said "See the bullet destroyed his lower leg, beyond repair." She sipped her coffee. "Yes, I wasn't in surgery, but I spoke to the nurse who was. She said it was messy. The doc told him he needed to have it amputated. Told him that would be the quickest way to get him back to farming. So far, he's refused. Sounds suicidal to me."

"Do you think he'd talk with me? There's some unanswered questions remaining..."

"You can try for a few minutes, but don't expect much. He's ornery. I feel sorry for him. On the other hand, rumor has it he intended to kill Connie. Who'd' a thought something like that?" She shook her head and walked away.

Cochran opened the door and quietly entered.

Shaw put his hand over the cell phone he was speaking on. "Go away. Don't have time. Yes, I intended to kill my wife. She had an affair. Junior's not mine. I had a vasectomy right after Emma. No, I hadn't thought of what might happen if I killed my wife." Shaw glared at him as he gripped the phone.

"Shaw," Cochran moved closer, bent over and whispered, "today, it was Connie. What about Alice?"

Cochran saw his eyes flicker. Was it fear? Surprise? Irritation at being interrupted? He couldn't tell.

Shaw waved for him to leave. He looked like he might explode any second.

Cochran surprised himself. Why did Alice pop into this? Had he thought about it? Was it the mention by Judy that she died? It did seem like a strange coincidence. Walking down the hall, something else struck his mind. It seemed odd that Connie and Junior didn't mention Shaw was not Junior's father, yet Shaw stated it right away. Why didn't they tell him? Were they still absorbing that fact? Wouldn't Connie have known or suspected? He climbed in his car and drove back to his office trying to decide where to start digging first.

Back in his office, he asked Irene, his clerk, to go to the archives and dig out all the records on Alice Skogman. Anything they had. He also asked Irene to hold all calls and interruptions unless they were a true emergency. He put his feet up on the edge of his side table piled with neat stacks of files and reports, removed his cap, and thought. Lowering his feet, he turned to his computer and Googled Shaw Phillip Skogman. It returned with information on Shaw, Philip with one L, Skogman. He perused the records. There were newspaper notices of Shaw being elected to the local school board and several terms on the county board, all years ago, plus several awards and appointments from various agricultural organizations. The newspaper stories mentioned he studied agricultural sciences, but never mentioned the school or the year. He found a 1962 marriage license to Alice, her 1975 obituary notice with him and the twins listed. Later, a 1976 marriage license with Connie, then birth notices for four more girls and Junior. He kept digging and found more, but not much. Shaw was the valedictorian of the Midville high school graduating class in 1954. No military records or newspaper clippings popped up of him entering or graduating from college.

He ran a search on just the last name of Skogman and the county. Most of the same things popped up, but several other Skogmans were mentioned. One was the November 1959 obituary of Fordham Skogman who died at age sixty-four. His wife, Helen Olson, preceded him in death by five months, also age sixty-four. Helen's obit mentioned a sudden illness as the cause. Fordham's a heart attack. Both obits mentioned the only surviving relative was their nephew, Shaw Philip Skogman. Next, he found Fordham's and Helen's only child, Lawrence, twenty-three, killed at Heartbreak Ridge in Korea in the fall of 1953.

Irene entered his office. He scribbled himself a note to check with just the name Skogman and to check out the land office upstairs in the county building. He thanked Irene for the files and arranged them on his desk. There wasn't room on his side table.

"Bossman, I did a little more digging." Irene turned toward him. "That situation with Alice always struck me as strange. I know, I know. We don't get many suicides. That's exactly why it struck me back then, even if I was a whole lot younger. I vaguely remembered a couple of strange calls coming in around that time. I dug around and pulled those files too. Ain't much to go on and it might confuse someone—not saying who—more than it helps. Take a look-see at them." She handed him two pieces of paper.

"Aren't you getting old enough to retire?"

"Yup, more than old enough, but I'm not leaving till after I get you trained. Now don't think too hard. I don't wanna smell rubber burning." Irene overemphasized closing the door quietly.

Irene was five years older than him and acted like she was his old spinster sister who was also married to the department.

Guess we both are, he thought. He glanced at the papers in his hand. Records of phone calls.

Date of Call: October 8, 1975

Caller Name: refused to say

Caller Number: refused to say

Address: refused to say

Reason for call: Female voice whispered her husband might kill her. She told him she wanted a divorce.

Name of other person: refused to say

Duration of call: 20 seconds. Caller stated, "He just came in and I have to get off phone."

Record of call two on October 10, 1975, indicated heavy breathing, a slurry woman's voice saying Hello, twice, then the phone cutting off.

Cochran recalled they couldn't easily trace calls in the seventies. The technology of electronic switching systems didn't arrive until the mid-1980's. If this was Alice calling for help, she could have been dead by the time the call slips were passed on to someone who noticed a connection between a suicide and two partial phone calls. What a shame. He put his feet back up on the side table, leaned back, scratched his ear and thought. Who else could he talk to?

Another thing struck him. The uncle and aunt dying suddenly so close to each other was interesting, especially at age sixty-four. Usually one spouse lasted a lot longer than the other. It was evident Shaw inherited the farm from his uncle and aunt, but where was he for several years after high school? He also realized there was no mention of Shaw's parents. He put his feet down and turned back to the computer. Only Shaw's Midville high school graduation was found. No articles of sports or achievements other than being valedictorian. He expanded his obituary search and found one for Philip Shaw Skogman, dated 1950. Shaw Philip was listed as the only child, and Dorothy, Dot, Gustafson, his wife.

Cochran pulled up the census records. The 1940 census sheet showed Fordham, Helen and Lawrence. The 1950 records were not available yet. By law, census records could not be released for seventy years.

How much land did Shaw own? Judy Sue mentioned more than the two sections they lived on. That he rented the property Melvin lived on. *I may be going down a rabbit hole,* he thought, as he pulled up plot maps for the county. He pinpointed where Melvin lived and clicked. The name Farm Holding popped up as the owner and tax payer. Who the heck was Farm Holding? He never heard of them before. The holding company's information was not accessible without a court order. He made a note to seek out more information on them later. Why would Melvin live on rented property owned by a holding company?

He shook his head to clear it and entered just the name Shaw. It wasn't a very common name, first or last. The list was longer than he anticipated. Still, he scrolled through them. Bingo. Up popped a record for a Shaw S Phillip at the University of Minnesota. Could this Shaw be the same Shaw lying in the hospital? Further results showed the same name at Worthington Community College. Both records explained his absence from Midville after his high school graduation, but why in heaven's name did he change his name? If he had. Cochran was intrigued. This man got weirder the more he learned about him.

He walked to Irene's area and poured himself a cup of coffee. It was cold. He didn't care. It was caffeine. She left for the day so he couldn't harass her. Restless, he glanced over her neat and orderly desk and smiled at the latest little desk plaque she ordered from some mail order house. *Dig Deeper.* He went back to his office and scrolled further for the combination of U.M. and Shaw S Phillip. Bingo again. In 1959, Shaw S Phillip graduated with a Bachelor's degree in pharmacy. His home address was listed as an apartment in Worthington. He checked that address and found it was above the Worthington Compounding Pharmacy.

Pharmacy? Not agricultural sciences?

Pharmacy.

How the hell was he going to confirm this?

Chapter Fifteen

Junior

After leaving Sheriff Cochran in front of the hospital, Junior, Connie and Jens walked to the parked truck. While Junior opened the passenger door, Jens grabbed the snacks and stuffed them behind the seat. Connie climbed into the middle. Junior slid in after her. Jens drove slowly toward the farm. No one spoke. Junior rode, spaced out, feeling as if he was having an out of body experience. His father's, well, Shaw's, words rattling around in his mind like the corn whirling out of the spout into one of their tall grain bins. He felt like he might suffocate from his thoughts rising higher and higher and swirling faster and faster, like being trapped in a bin as it filled around you.

His mother elbowed him, thankfully breaking his thought pattern. "I'm hungry. Are you?"

"Starved, Mom, but I don't think you should cook. Run through McDonalds or KFC."

"We're long out of town." Turning her head toward Jens, she said, "Drive through Midville and stop at Syds. It's Saturday. Hopefully, he's got something left. If not, I'll get some of his frozen sloppy joe or taco meat."

Junior grinned. He loved Syds food, whatever it was. Syds was a combination coffee shop, grocery store with the essentials, gas station, beer depot, and a restaurant that served one selection a day. There was no menu. You could have the selection for lunch, dinner or both. Whatever Syd or his wife fixed for that day was what was available. What didn't sell was packaged, frozen, and available to take home. Saturdays were usually roast turkey days. With all the fixins. Junior's mouth began to water. More when Jens brought the food into the truck.

There was mail inside the Milliken Road mailbox. Jens pulled out a package from an auto-parts wholesaler addressed to Junior, along with several flyers. It felt strange, riding up to the house with crime scene tape visible across the side door and both porches. Junior gathered some of the bags as Connie carried the food from Syds. He ran up, tore the tape away and held the door open for his mother and Jens. Entering the house felt uncanny. He glanced at the clock. Seven-ten. Twelve hours since he fled the house running for his life. It seemed a lifetime. How much could happen in twelve hours? More than he ever thought.

His mother stood in the middle of the kitchen, almost as if in shock. Junior pulled her into a hug. "Mom, all this happened in one day. It seems weeks, maybe months."

Both watched Jens scurry by, carrying a bucket smelling of bleach, some rags, and a sponge mop. He paused to wipe some bloody footprints off the kitchen floor and down the hallway.

"I know, son. I know." Connie reached over and touched the cup of coffee she left half-filled that morning. She seemed to notice Shaw's plate, cup and silverware placed neatly in the sink. The buttery frypan still on the stove, the crumbs around the toaster. She turned back toward Junior. Tears filled her eyes. "I am so sorry, Junior. So sorry this happened. This is all my fault."

"Is it, Mom? Really? All your fault? Dad—Shaw—got a vasectomy and never told you. Pretended I was his son all these years and discovers you had an affair and goes nuts, freaking crazy. I don't know what to think, but don't go taking all the blame."

"He said the DNA test also set him off. That, plus finding out who my affair was with, set him off as he said, 'like never before.'" She shuddered, then said as if she wanted to change the subject, "Listen, we can't function well without food. We need to eat. Go get Jens. He can finish the porch later."

Junior stepped warily onto the front porch. This too felt strange, like it was years since he flew across the slippery porch, jumped the steps and fled for his life. Jens was wringing out the rags in the bucket. He grabbed the mop and quickly worked it over the area. Junior could see no blood left on the gray floor. The bloody red water in the bucket caused him to shudder. That was his dad's blood, or who he always thought was his dad. It was human blood from a man who shot at him and intended to kill his mother.

Jens squeegeed the mop and handed it to him. "Carry this to the back room sink. I'll take the bucket and empty it over the fence. You don't need to watch. Go back inside and I'll be there shortly. I'm hungry, too."

No one spoke as they devoured the turkey, dressing, potatoes, gravy, home-canned green beans with bacon, rolls and pecan pie. Junior looked at his mom. "What are you going to tell the girls?"

Connie finished her last bite of pie, chewing carefully, thoughtfully. Jens and Junior waited. "The truth," she finally said. "The truth. I had an affair. Dad secretly had a vasectomy after Emma. He's wondered for years who really fathered Junior. Junior asked him to do a DNA test about the same time he discovered who my affair was with. He was convinced you weren't his son. He's carried this for eighteen years and today, he exploded. His goal was to murder me and wound Junior. The man's wanted revenge for all these years." Tears came to her eyes. She jumped up and started another pot of coffee. Putting her arms around Junior, she added, "This is all my fault. Can you ever forgive me?"

Junior jerked in his seat. Forgive her? He hadn't thought that far. Yes, it was her fault. Shouldn't she have known he was Hans' baby, not Shaw's? Had that possibility never crossed her mind? He glanced at the framed photo hanging on the wall of his mother and Shaw, taken on their wedding day at the courthouse. He studied it closely. It was frustrating. All his life, he'd been told he looked like his father. Looking at the photo, he could see a resemblance. The height, sandy hair, the hair line, the nose, the ears. His own lips and chin were a little different, maybe more like his mother's. What did Hans look like? He wasn't sure he wanted to know. This was all so new. What if Hans didn't look anything like him?

He shook his head to clear it, then stood and paced around the room, conscious of his mother's eyes following him.

He stopped and turned toward her. "Mom, can you tell me the idea Hans might be my father never crossed your mind? Honestly?"

His mother slowly rose. She turned away from him, looked into the family room, seemed to stare through the windows to the muddy fields. "No. I can't honestly tell you that the thought never crossed my mind. It did. Hans did visit me around that time at a conference I was attending near The Cities. We did make love. We hadn't seen each other in over a year. I made love with your father several days later. I remember when I finally realized I might be pregnant, Hans did flash through my mind, but I buried it." She sucked in a deep breath and stepped toward the family room. "You see, for well over a year before that, I skipped or had light periods. I missed some that spring and early summer. That's why I thought I was in menopause. I didn't think much of it till December when I visited the doctor for some vomiting and tummy issues that wouldn't go away. Doc asked if I could be pregnant. I laughed, said no. He tested anyway and, voila, I was four months along; another reason it was hard to pinpoint the time and man. Hans usually wore a condom. His wife never had children, he never said why. I even stopped taking the pill. The thought that I could get pregnant was as far away as the moon."

She turned toward him as Jens silently watched them from the table. Looking Junior in the eyes, she continued, "I think the question you want to know is, have I been hiding a secret all of your life as to who your father was?" She waited for a response from Junior.

He shrugged, muttered, "Yeah."

"I have always believed you were Shaw's son. I was thrilled when you were born a boy, Shaw Philip Skogman, Junior. I could not have carried the guilt of knowing you were another man's child with me this long. My guilt of a long, but sporadic affair with Hans was different. It's hard to call it guilt. It was another kind of love. I'm sorry it led to this, but I'm not sorry about the love he and I shared. It was special. I still miss him like hell."

Junior noticed a quick look between Connie and Jens. Jens

expression seemed to say he wasn't sure her words reflected her deepest thoughts. His mother's look said she wasn't sure either. What was that about? Coming to grips with the idea your father wasn't your biological father, your mother had an affair that resulted in you, and your supposed dad knew all along was confusing enough. Was his mom really that strong in her answer to his question? He sat back down. His mother's response wasn't as powerful as he would have liked. He believed her, but with some reservations that he couldn't deal with at the moment. Still, the idea of forgiveness was a hard concept to grasp in this situation.

His mother must have read his mind. "Son, you don't have to answer me right now about forgiveness. If I never had an affair or ended it sooner, this never would have happ—" She stopped like a lightning bolt struck her.

It did Junior too. He flashed her a surprised look. He hoped it was one of understanding. "I get it, Mom. I love you." He reached across the table, pulled Jens' plate of uneaten pie to himself and stabbed his fork into it.

His mom stepped over and hugged him. "You stink. Why don't you go shower and get some real clothes on? I'll text your sisters that Dad is seriously ill in the hospital and we want to have a conference call in two hours. Trying to communicate all this individually with six girls in four states and two countries is nearly impossible. I want them each to hear the same thing from me."

Junior went to his room, flopped down on his bed, picked up his phone and called Beany. He tried to briefly describe all that happened, but it took a while with Beany shrieking and repeating everything to his mom. When they hung up, there was no doubt in his mind that Beany would be over. When? That was always the unknown with that boy. His body tingled with the thought of Beany in bed with him. He tried to doze for a few minutes, yet his mind couldn't stop whirling. How should a person feel when, a month before turning eighteen, they discover their father isn't their father? How the man knew it all along and waited even longer to find out who the biological father was. Had Dad—Shaw— planned all along to kill his mother when he found out? Is that what he meant when he said he always got revenge? How did Hans die? Did he know he fathered a child? How does a woman not know who the father is? Hans' sperm must have nailed Mom's egg before she had sex with Dad. How long did that take? He sat up. To hell with this. I'm not googling eggs and sperm right now. I need a shower. Besides, I'm here. I'm alive. I can only deal with so much at a time.

In the shower, he checked his wounds, glad his tetanus shot was up to date. It felt like three pellets were still embedded but had moved closer to the surface. He was afraid to squeeze them, he might drive them deeper. After drying off, he applied the drawing salve, Neosporin, bandages, dressed in blue jeans and a t-shirt and went downstairs.

Jens was sorting through the cupboards and fridge, prepping a breakfast casserole that could be baked in the morning.

His mom said, "You look more refreshed. I've texted your sisters. Four have responded, two I'm waiting on. I'm going to go shower now. Could you check the upstairs guest room and make sure there are towels for Jens? He's still muddy." She smiled at both of them and headed for the stairs.

Junior poured himself a glass of milk and sat down at the table.

Jens poured himself some coffee and joined him. "Man, this sure is a lot to deal with. How are you holding up?"

Junior thought a moment. "How the heck should I know? I'm just trying to absorb everything. I mean, my dad said he's not my dad and shot at me. Which is probably why he didn't take the DNA test. He already knew the results. He intended to kill my mother because he finally confirmed she had an affair and with whom. Instead, he accidentally shot himself and who knows how long his recovery will take, or if he will recover. For years, Mom had an affair with your brother, who could be my father, but he's dead. Mom is sorry about all this, but not sorry about her affair and if she didn't have the affair, it's possible I wouldn't be here." He took a swig of his milk and set the glass down hard. "I don't think Shakespeare could have written something this freaking bizarre. To answer your question, I have no idea how I'm holding up."

Jens was sipping his coffee. He gasped, inhaled some and began coughing and sputtering. Tears came to his eyes. He slapped the table, hard enough to rattle Junior's glass of milk. Junior stared at him. He started to get up. "Are you choking? Should I do the Heimlich maneuver? Are you okay?"

Jens managed to shake his head. Slowly, he got his composure back. "I'm fine. It's just I was trying not to laugh and cry at the same time. You summed up your situation so well and it struck me as sounding hilarious. I mean, who could make something like this up? At the same time, I didn't want to offend you by laughing. It is sad." He took a big breath. "I'm sorry, it's just..."

Junior sat, rethinking his words. His face crinkled into a smile. He smacked his hand on the table, too, tipped his head back and started laughing. It felt good to laugh. In spite of the pain, it was good to bust a gut. Jens joined in. Something just happened. Junior knew, felt it down deep. There was a bond with this kind man who seemed so strange earlier in the day. The man who kept him away from his mother, at her request, he now realized, was dedicated to her as only a true brother could be. He smiled at him and enjoyed the warm smile that came back. "Maybe," Junior said, "maybe when this is over, we could write a soap opera."

"Maybe, but I think truth is always stranger than fiction." Jens paused, became serious. "Didn't your dad, I mean, Shaw, say this isn't over yet? Whatever he meant, it sounded scary."

Junior played with his empty milk glass. The laughter felt good, but there were more issues and he had no idea what they were. He thought of the DNA kit that must be still in his dad's office. If it still was. He didn't feel as if they should be worried about further physical attacks, but... His mother entered the room, interrupting his thoughts. "Mom, what did you say in your text to the girls?"

"I said Dad suffered a gun injury to his leg. It was serious, didn't look good because he's refusing the doctor's recommendations to amputate, and for them to make plans to return home ASAP. Be ready to join a conference call at nine-thirty." She checked her phone. "Good, all six can join." She looked at Jens. "When you raise them to be smart and independent, one shouldn't be surprised when they leave this no-man's land and live far away."

"I can't keep track. Where are they all?" Jens asked.

Connie answered, "Ellen is at The University of Alaska, Anchorage, teaching archeology." She smiled at Jens. "She was heavily impressed with Hans' work when she was growing up, when he visited and told her stories. Mary, the other twin, is in Prague, Czech Republic, working for a tech company. Gayle is a nurse in Seattle, Jane is a speech pathologist in Atlanta, Jackie is an English teacher in Mexico, and Emma is trying to break through as an actress in The Cities. That means she's also a waitress. She's going to coordinate all their transportation to the farm from The Cities. None of the girls are married. The twins each were, but it didn't last."

An hour later, Connie placed the phone on speaker as Junior slid a chair next to her kitchen desk. One by one, the girls announced themselves. There was silence until Junior nudged his mom and motioned for her to speak. Slowly, Connie spelled out the details, holding nothing back about her affair, nor the fact Hans was most likely Junior's father. It seemed odd to be part of a conversation about the fact that the man you called dad for nearly eighteen years, wasn't your father.

"He meant to shoot you?" Ellen sounded incredulous.

Her twin, Mary, whispered, "That would have been our second mother to die suddenly at the same home."

Emma sniffled, "Mom, it's hard to think of you having an affair all those years. Raising a family, doing everything you did. When did you have time and the privacy?"

Connie explained how infrequent their meet-ups were, that it was a unique situation and how she still loved their father.

"Mom, knowing you," Jackie said, "I can see how you had a second life and love totally separated from us and we never realized it. I mean that in a good way. You are still amazing to me."

Gayle, the nurse, had the most questions about Shaw's physical condition and what was being done medically. Each of the six sisters responded in various ways, but most expressed concern for their mother.

Emma was the one who asked everyone to wait a minute. "Junior," she said, "how are you doing? This is a lot to absorb. Has it soaked in that the man you knew as your father isn't your dad?"

Everyone on the call grew quiet.

"Well...I think I usually catch on to things fairly quickly...but this thing took me some time to grasp. I'm still wrapping my mind around it. I think I'm fine or will be okay... It's still a surprise. Out of the blue, you know? I don't know what else to say."

"That's good, Junior. We get it, we're shocked too," Emma said.

"Stay strong, little brother," Ellen called.

It ran through his mind that Ellen and Mary were not his blood sisters. He shook his head to clear those thoughts. It was too much to deal with at the moment. Besides, would it matter?

Junior noticed his mother seemed to vacillate between strength, fear, sadness, and appreciation for her children as she answered their questions and listened to their comments of support. No one judged her or criticized her, for which Junior was thankful. Each seemed shocked at the actions of their father. His sisters discussed their travel plans already in progress. It appeared four of them would arrive Sunday night in the Twin Cities and drive out late in a rental minivan, one was flying in Monday morning and would ride out with Emma.

During the call, Junior again realized how he barely knew his older sisters as he was only eight when Emma left home for college. Yet, somehow, this call strengthened his sense of family and connectedness to each of them. They were all in this together.

After the long conference call, and a light snack, Junior kissed his mother, hugged Jens and went to his room. He was delighted to find Beany. Not surprised, but delighted. Beany told him he didn't want to interrupt anything, that's why he snuck in. He and Beany ran downstairs so Beany could hug Connie and meet Jens.

"Houdini strikes again," his mother said.

Jens said that after everything he heard from Connie about Beany, he was glad to meet him.

Back in his room, Beany pumped Junior with questions. Junior did everything he could to answer. It was such a confusing day.

"How do you feel, knowing that Hans might be your father, not Dad-Shaw?" Beany asked. "I'm still calling him Dad-Shaw, not to tease you, but that's who he has been all my life."

"I understand. I'm still thinking of him as Dad, I guess there's part of me still not as certain as he sounds. He said he had a vasectomy after Emma. I don't know whether to call him Dad, the mean bastard who shot at me, or…"

The thought flicked through his mind about being called Junior. He didn't want to deal with that right now. Adjusting to the idea his dad wasn't his dad felt so odd, heavy, scary. Something he needed to take his time to accept. But only after he obtained as much information and facts as possible.

Beany hugged him. "You don't have to figure anything out right now. I'm sad he could die over this. I don't understand why he won't go for an amputation. I'm mad he shot at you. I'm disgusted he never told Mom-Connie about the vasectomy. They could have had this all straightened out back then." He paused and gently rubbed Junior's cheek. "Don't take offense, but is there any chance Dad-Shaw was wrong? That he might be your father? I mean, how do you truly know he isn't?"

Junior stared at him, could almost see the wheels turning in his best friend and lover's mind. "I'm fairly certain he isn't. There's one way to find out…"

"Actually, there's two." Beany pointed toward the hall as they heard Jens close the guest room door.

Junior pulled Beany into a strong hug that quickly led to sex. Teen age boy sex, hot and fast. They fell asleep in each other's arms.

Around one-thirty in the morning, they woke, dressed and slipped down the back stairs. Junior took the keys off their hooks in the mud room and they walked to the farm office and turned on the lights. His note and DNA kit were right where he left them. Apparently, Shaw threw the first kit away. Junior's other note, about ordering the distributor for the Camry, was also there. He thought a moment. That meant his father checked his mom's phone, was upset, grabbed the note about the distributor from the back door Junior taped it to, came out to his office, laid the distributor note down, saw the note requesting him again to swab his mouth for DNA, and lost his freaking mind. Junior told Beany, "He could have ignored the DNA kit, I told him the deadline and he could have stalled past it by just being too busy. It's the science class project you and I signed up to for extra credit. It's not part of the Ancestry program. If Dad only found out who Mom's lover was, well, maybe he would have confronted her. But…"

Beany hugged him. "Didn't you tell me he said something about always seeking revenge? He'd have done something, maybe not yesterday, but eventually. I think your dad was patiently devious. Now, do you still want to do this?"

"Yes, it will help. I hope."

They walked to the small equipment shed for Shaw's work pickup. Junior drove to Beany's house and waited, lights off, while Beany slipped in and got an extra DNA kit he didn't need. Each student participating in the extra-credit assignment were supplied four swab kits. Beany only needed two because his parents were the only ones he tested. Junior drove to the hospital and they entered through the emergency entrance. The main entrance was closed overnight. "I need to visit my dad," Junior told the sleepy clerk. She pointed them toward the med-surg hallway and mumbled the room number.

There was a low light over Shaw. He was breathing heavily. A monitor softly beeped, several bags hung from a pole dripping into his arm and leg. Junior poked him gently, he didn't respond. He felt warm. Junior squeezed his hand, hard. Still no response. Beany opened the kit, pulled out the swab, and as Junior held his dad's mouth open, swirled it around in his cheek and put it back into the tube. Shaw gasped, startled and jumped. Pain must have ricocheted through his body. He screamed.

The boys were gone from the room in seconds. They rushed down the hall and stopped at the nursing station. "Mr. Skogman just woke up in pain. Maybe he was dreaming, because he jerked and I think that's what hurt him. We were just going to sit with him a while in case he woke up and wanted to talk, but he's in too much pain. We'll come back."

Beany's flair for acting could have earned him an Oscar, Junior thought. The nurse looked at them with an odd expression, shrugged her shoulders and marched off to check on Shaw.

On the drive home, part of Junior felt guilty, a bit sad, yet still angry. His bird shot wounds still stung. Emotionally, part of him was numb. Beany was the only thing that felt like life right now. He wanted to laugh over Beany's acting job, but knew they caused his dad pain. Was it fair to hurt him?

Was it fair to get shot by him?

To be coldly told by your dad that he wasn't your dad?

They drove home in silence and went back to bed.

In the morning, sitting down for Jens' breakfast, Junior slid the DNA test kit across the table. "Jens, I want you to take this. It's easy. I just need to know scientifically who my father is. Hans is dead, but your results should tell us if you're my uncle."

His mom said, "That's an excellent idea."

"There's more," Beany said. "We got Dad-Shaw's sample in the middle of the night. This is what science is for. He was sleeping hard, but then he woke up and kinda jerked which hurt him. He didn't know we were there."

Connie gasped. "You did what? Honestly? Oh, my goodness."

She slumped back in her chair, quiet, looking out the window. Turning her head toward Junior, she reached over and patted his hand. "I hope you didn't cause him too much pain, but I do think that was a wonderful idea. I'd love to have more confirmation one way or the other, and I can see how you need to know even more than me." She stood and picked up her coffee. "Please, though, don't make any more visits in the middle of the night without my knowledge."

She stepped into the family room to sit in her favorite rocking chair, turning it toward the window overlooking the fields.

Beany and Junior looked at each other and shrugged. "We won't, Mom. I'm not sure how often I want to visit anyway."

Chapter Sixteen

Connie

March 28, 2011, Monday Evening

Connie turned her rocking chair to face her children. Everyone was quiet. All six girls made it home by noon that day. Four managed to arrive Sunday night in Minneapolis around the same time and rented a minivan, getting home in the middle of the night. Emma waited for Ellen to land Monday morning and the two arrived around noon.

The family spent that afternoon at the hospital with Shaw. To Connie, he appeared weak, gray and in a lot of discomfort. A nurse explained the medical team worked on him for several hours earlier to stop another blood leak. Dr. Patel, along with another man, came in while the family waited for Shaw to come out of his grogginess. "The longer this goes on, the less likely of a favorable outcome," the doctor said. "We have additional concerns, the need to clarify communications."

He wiped his face, shook his head, and shuffled around on his feet. "This is Abe Jordan, our social worker."

"What concerns now?" Connie and the kids looked at each other with expressions of surprise.

"We have new information about whom we can communicate with." Abe Jordan seemed calm, yet stern. "First, let me emphasize that your husband and father seems to be of sound mind."

He turned toward Connie. "That's what I came to speak about. First, power of attorney only applies when a person is not able to make decisions for themselves. Mr. Skogman still is. In addition, yesterday, he had a notary public visit and he signed a new medical power of attorney and living will which overrides you and your children's legal power. Only Melvin Smith is allowed to make health-related decisions now. Mr. Smith has indicated he will only do what Mr. Skogman desires, should he become incapacitated."

The gasps echoed around the room. Several of the girls began crying. Connie stood up, stomped her foot and faced Shaw. "Melvin Smith? You son of a bitch. You did what? Is that legal?"

Shaw didn't look at her.

"I'm afraid it is." Jordan waited till she looked at him. "According to our legal team, you could probably appeal it, but that will take time and money. The form is usual and valid."

Gayle moved closer to the bed. "Dad, that means none of the family can receive information about your medical condition?"

Shaw closed his eyes a moment. "Yes, except I added you to the HIPPA or whatever they call it permission. Only you."

Gayle turned toward Abe Jordan. "I take that to mean he doesn't need a psychiatric evaluation to determine his competency? I have my Masters in Nursing and am working on my Nurse Practitioner certification."

"God dammit." Shaw stirred and groaned. "I'm sane. It's my life, not yours."

Abe Jordan shuffled on his feet before looking at Gayle. "There is no indication Mr. Skogman is not of sound mind."

There was silence as the impact of his actions settled in.

Connie stomped her foot again. Turning to the children, who still looked in shock, she gathered herself. "I think it would be best for me to go home now. I do think it's wise for you girls to spend as much time with your father as you're comfortable with. Maybe your presence will bring him to his senses."

Junior got to his feet. "I'm with you, Mom. We can take the truck home. The girls have the minivan they rented."

The girls nodded.

Mary hugged her mother and said, "I don't blame you."

"You better drive," Connie said to Junior in the parking lot. "I'm too upset to be safe behind a wheel. How dare he? Melvin? Melvin?" Her voice almost shrieked as she climbed in the truck.

"I know, Mom, why Melvin? What would he know about Dad's wishes? What do you know about him? He's always been a nervous little mystery to me. I don't get it." Junior put the truck in gear and drove carefully out of the lot.

"Obviously, I don't know him well. This stuns me, too." Connie looked out at the late afternoon sun trying to dry up the fields and roads. "He and your dad go back to before I came into the picture. After all these years with Shaw, I can't remember when he hasn't been around in some capacity. Once in a while, he says he has to deliver a prescription to someone. I have seen him in a van that says Prescription Delivery on it. Shaw says it's something he likes to do to help people, mostly older ones."

"Even before you married Dad…Or…Shaw…"

Connie reached over and patted Junior's leg. "I know, son. It's got to be difficult for you to know what to call him. I'll understand either way. Please forgive me if I keep referring to him as your father. Hopefully, we'll know definitively someday. Maybe it will be easy to figure out how to address him, then."

She paused, looked out the window again. Why did she say know definitively someday? Why was it so hard to finally admit to herself that she covered up that Hans was Junior's father? She glanced at Junior. "Yes, to answer your question, Melvin was around before we married. I thought it was mostly out of the goodness of Dad's heart, but over the years, I've realized the man is truly a skilled mechanic and has a strong grasp of agricultural business. A few times, I've made some suggestion to Dad about something regarding the farms and he said he had to discuss it with Melvin. I quit making suggestions. Obviously, Melvin had more knowledge than me, no matter how much I read and studied." She waited a moment. "All these years and I can't say I know the man. Isn't that odd? He rarely looks me, or anyone else, in the eyes when you do talk with him. He always seems in a hurry to do something or go somewhere. Other times, on rare occasions, he's been friendly and almost outgoing."

Neither spoke the rest of the way home.

Several hours later, the girls arrived home, looking drained. Beany and Jens fixed omelets, American fries, bacon, toast, jelly and juices. No one asked questions or spoke about their father. Connie felt it was as if everyone was too worn out emotionally to talk about him. *After we eat,* she thought, *then we'll be ready. We have to be.*

Mentally, she replayed the conversation with Abe Jordan regarding the power of attorney. The only other time she ever felt so much anger and hatred toward someone was when Shaw turned on her with the gun. She was his wife. The wife he intended to kill. For a few seconds that afternoon in the hospital, she wished she had the gun. She mentally shook her head, determined to keep such ideas away. This was the here and now. Her job was to guide this clan through the next few days. After that, she could think about her life, the farm, and most importantly, Junior. When everyone finished eating, she motioned everyone into the family room.

Jens and Beany finished loading the dishwasher. They pulled kitchen chairs to sit in the archway between the kitchen and family room. Everyone was looking at her. Waiting for her, and, though each of them was very independent, she knew, in this situation, they were depending upon her to shepherd them through a phase of their lives she was partly responsible for. She remained quiet, looking at the twins, thinking about all they went through with the suicide of their mother, their father's quick remarriage, and all the adjustments they made from a shy, insecure, self-conscious mother, to a strong, confident stepmother. The fact they started calling her mom when they were fifteen was proof, in her mind, they made a successful transition. That, plus the fact they left home and successfully established themselves as independent, self-reliant women, said a lot for their transition. Each of the six girls told her at various times throughout their adult lives how thankful they were for her pushing them to leave the inbred, farm-driven, dull life of their community.

She cleared her throat. Tears started to form in her eyes. She wiped them away. "We have a lot to talk about, but first, I want to again apologize for my role in this mess…"

"Mom, don't apologize again." It was Gayle, her ER nurse daughter. "What's done is done. Right now, our main focus should be about Dad and the next few days. Obviously, we won't have much say in his treatment, but we can think about the next few days. Shall I be the spokesperson and update Mom, Junior and Jens about after they left?"

"Heck, yes," Emma said. "You're the nurse and best one to understand his condition and the legal ramifications."

The girls grew silent, watching their mother, Junior and Jens as Gayle began pacing. "The bottom line is, Dad will die soon. He wants to die. He won't say why." She pulled a napkin off the table and wiped her eyes. "He has ordered the medical staff to discontinue his antibiotics starting tomorrow night. He will continue his pain meds at a reduced level for as long as he can stand it. For some reason he wants to be able to think clearly a while longer. Though the pain meds won't be necessary when he goes into a coma, hospice might keep him on them as well as heavy sedation to ease his transition."

"It's like suicide," Connie whispered. "Why? Why all of a sudden? He found out who my affair was and who Junior's father is. He failed to kill me, but why does he want to die? We could divorce, split things up. I just need enough to live comfortably on, and I'm sure there's enough assets for that. Why? Why? I just don't get it."

"We don't either." Mary stood. "All of us hugged and spoke with Dad. I asked him, again, if he understood the consequences of his decision. He looked us in the eye and said, 'If that's what it is, then that's what it is. I'll see you tomorrow.' Can you imagine that? Then he turned his head away and closed his eyes."

No one spoke. Beany and Jens got up and brought in homemade cookies and offered tea and decaf coffee. Mary rummaged in the pantry and brought back bottles of red and white wine, which Jens opened and found glasses for.

Connie took several sips of her Riesling and looked around the room. She sighed. "He clearly wants to be in control, even of his death.

So, how do we plan for this?"

Gayle looked at her mug of tea. "I think we should visit tomorrow, two or three of us at a time. Not say much, not beg him, not offer our opinions. Tell him we love him, try to talk about fun times growing up, or our lives, what we're doing now. If he brings anything up about his condition, then respond, but try not to argue or beg."

Junior cleared his throat. "This may sound sarcastic, but can any of you remember fun times with Dad? I mean, laugh out loud, giggle, practical jokes, him laughing at our silliness or us at his mishaps. For me, he was just there. He answered my questions as quickly and efficiently as possible. Maybe there's a reason for the way he responded to me, but how was he with you girls?"

No one spoke for several minutes. Eventually, Ellen spoke. "Junior, that's a tough question. I've been searching my memories to see if I had any of those experiences before our mother, Alice, died." She looked at Mary who shook her head. "The only emotion I remember was him yelling at Mother a couple of times, something about her being sneaky. I had no idea what he was referring to. I just remember being so surprised that he yelled or showed any emotion, especially anger."

Mary smiled at Ellen. "I remember that as well. It seemed shortly before Mother died." She paused and looked around the room. "I'm guessing our recollections of him showing emotion only involved a brief smile or nod. If he was mad, he got red in the face, may have snapped a reply, but usually marched off in silence. That was rare. Am I right?"

There were nods, but no one spoke. The only sounds were of drinks being sipped and cookies bitten into and chewed.

Connie cleared her throat. Nodding at Ellen and Mary, she said, "You two certainly went through a lot. I'm so proud of what you have done with your lives." She looked at her other five children. "I'm proud of each of you too, but you've had the same mother, good or bad, your entire lives. These two went from a quiet mother who suddenly died, to a stepmom who didn't let any grass grow between her toes. I'm still amazed you two made the transition as well as you have."

"Mom, so are we." Ellen stood and laughed. Her infectious

sounds broke the solemn tension. The whole room erupted into laughter.

Several others stood and stretched. Gayle called out, "I think we have enough of a plan for tomorrow. We're going to have to take this a few hours at a time." She went into the kitchen, and poured herself a glass of red.

Jens found the big popcorn popper and started filling a roaster pan. Beany sliced some apples. Everyone settled back in the family room, somehow in a lighter mood.

Gayle looked at Junior. "I understand you're sending in DNA on Dad and Jens. That was smart. Sometime, part of our conversation should be around what those results might show and how well prepared you are emotionally either way."

Junior's cheeks reddened, like he was embarrassed. "I just hope I didn't make things more painful for Dad. Getting the sample wasn't very fair. We didn't ask him, just did it and left."

Connie said, "Oh, son, I'd have been tempted to do the same thing…" She wanted to say, 'but I would have taken it from his leg'. She didn't. "No one here is going to come down on you."

"I understand. I don't think the results will change much, but at least it can lead to more proof. I think I will be okay." Junior half-smiled.

"Yeah, either way, y'all are still stuck with little Junior." Beany giggled, then sobered. "I'm sorry. I shouldn't joke around."

Connie smiled. "I agree, Beany. We are stuck with Junior. Thank goodness."

The twins, Ellen and Mary, glanced at each other, stuck their arms out and raised their thumbs. "We were twenty-eight when he showed up, but we're still glad we're stuck with him." Ellen winked at Junior.

Connie watched her family chat and catch up. She loved being a mother, having her entire brood home, along with Jens who seemed to fit right in. How long would he stay? She hoped for a while. The conversation with Abe Jordan slammed into her again. She raised her hand, waved it around.

Emma giggled. "Umm, Mom. You don't have to raise your hand to speak. Remember, you're the mom, you're in charge."

When the giggles died down, Connie began. "I'm sorry to get serious again, but can any of you think of any reason Dad would choose Melvin to be his medical power of attorney?"

Everyone shook their heads.

Ellen said, "Mom, I have no idea, but I can tell you he's been involved with Dad since I can remember, so that's over forty years. How old is he?"

Connie thought. "I'll have to double-check our employment papers. I'm guessing in his sixties, maybe even early seventies. I write him a paycheck once a month. It's usually cashed in a day or so. It's a decent salary, plus he gets his housing and utilities free. I don't get it. Why him?"

"Because he's always done what Shaw said." Jens edged his chair forward and set his wine glass on the floor beside him. "I spoke with Melvin several times yesterday. He seemed a little jittery. I got the impression he thinks he's kind of a partner with Shaw, plus he's a great mechanic. Several times, he mentioned the word we, meaning Shaw and him. I don't know anything else, that's just the impression I got. I know he's desperately concerned about Shaw."

"Then why will he let him die? Sorry for the sarcasm." Connie stretched and yawned. "It's time for me to go to bed. I assume you all found someplace to sleep."

"I have." Beany grinned.

"Hush, boy." Jackie looked at her mom. "You sure have slipped in your old age. If we wanted to have our boyfriend sleep over with us, in our room, with the door closed, you'd have had a fit. Tagalongs get all the breaks."

Jane, the quietest one of the clan, stood up. "Umm, Jackie, do you really want to go there? Remember the basement? Remember me unlocking the side door, not once, but several times when you were in heat with...what was his name? Some farm boy that pushed his motorcycle up the drive so no one could hear him? Besides, who went with you to Worthington? Worthington, for god's sake, so no one you knew could see you buying condoms? You hadn't talked with Mom yet about going on the pill."

"Enough," yelled Jackie. "The difference is Mom condones Junior's relationship. She didn't know about mine."

"Are you positive about that? How do you think that tire went flat one night? The one on the motorcycle hidden in the brush at the end of the garage. The time you had to wake us up for someone to drive him home at two in the morning." Connie smiled triumphantly and waved goodnight.

Beany stage-whispered to Junior. "Think Jackie's condoms are the same ones we found in that old dresser in the basement?"

Chapter Seventeen

Shaw

Tuesday

Monday afternoon, after the girls left, Shaw had another angry call with Jack, their lawyer. While they spoke, the nurse kept checking his vitals. He ignored her, figured she was eavesdropping anyway. It didn't matter. He knew his temperature would start to rise after his final dose of antibiotics later tonight.

Tuesday morning, Gayle, Mary and Emma arrived around ten-thirty. He tried to smile. Emma scooted up on the bed beside him and hugged him. She was the most huggy one of the bunch. "Dad, how you feeling?"

"A little worse, still conscious and my brain's good. That's all that counts right now. It's my time. Don't start begging and pleading. Now, why don't each of you take several minutes and update me on your lives."

"Dad," Emma cried out, tears running down her face. "How can you act this way? You've never been the Mr. Rogers type, but this is nuts. Why do you want to die? Did we do something so wrong that you want to up and die rather than fight? We'd still love you with a false leg. We wouldn't care. It's not like you have a bad heart or cancer." She put her head to his shoulder and tried to put her arms around him.

"Dammit, Emma," Gayle said, "remember we were going to stay calm and just talk about our current lives."

Shaw felt Emma cry harder into his shoulder.

He hated mushiness. Had never cuddled his kids. The only cuddling he liked was shortly before and after sex. He pushed Emma off him. "Get back. I just told you not to beg and plead, now, leave me alone." He grimaced from the pain his movements caused.

Gayle pulled Emma away from the bed and hissed, "Stop it. Get hold of yourself. Good grief, this isn't about you or us. It's about Dad and the family."

Mary glared at her father. "Dad, do you want us to hate you? Is that your game? You screwed up, lost your cool and instead of trying to make life better for yourself and your family, you want us to hate you. Why? What are you hiding? Do you think if you're dead, we won't find something out? Is that it?"

Before he could reply, Gayle said, "Girls, just sit here and be quiet. He obviously doesn't want to communicate. We obviously love him and want to be with him. Let's just sit awhile and not talk." She turned her face toward him. "Dad, we'll be here for a few more minutes. We'll tell the other girls when they visit this afternoon to not say a word."

The three sat down, Emma still crying.

He didn't look at them. He felt so weak. He wanted to drift off, but knew he had more to do. Emma's sniffling became louder. It bugged the hell out of him. Gayle and Mary now were trying to comfort her, whispering to her, patting her. Mary began sniffling, too, poking around for tissue.

Without opening his eyes, he growled, "Just leave now. Tell your sisters not to come today. You can all come when I'm worse, if that will make you feel better." He watched over the top of his glasses as they gathered their coats and purses and left. Each with a look of shock. Did he feel bad for them? For his behavior? At this point, what difference did it make? Yes, he screwed up. He reacted rather than responding. He should have planned better, but he didn't. He made a mistake, a rare one, and at seventy-four, he would die. He wasn't afraid of death. There was no afterlife. *Sometimes,* he thought, *our society puts too much emphasis on keeping old people alive.* For what? A few months more of contact with family? Frequently for a family who didn't have the time or resources to care for their aged relative when they most needed the help. No, he didn't have any fear of dying. Nor did he feel guilt over some of his actions over the years. They were necessary.

He thought more about his life. Did he want to die so he could keep some of his life hidden? Could he have the amputation and return to a normal life? No, at this stage of the game, the family was going to find out anyway. The door to my secrets has been cracked open. The rest will spill out and my life can never be normal again. The best decision for me and the family is to die. However, look at all I accomplished. The family will better understand me when they read the story of my life.

I hope.

He twisted and tried to get comfortable.

Chapter Eighteen

Connie

Tuesday

Connie woke at her regular time of four-fifty. Couldn't help it. Her routine was to have everything prepped for Shaw's breakfast before she went to bed. It was always something simple, but filling. A slice of breakfast casserole she could reheat in the microwave. French toast ready to dip and fry or eggs to whip and scramble with bacon, plus toast. Whatever it was had to be ready to slide on the table between five-oh-five and five-ten. The coffee was on a timer. She usually joined him for breakfast. There wasn't a lot of deep conversation, but some. Usually about what he might need from her that day, driving a load of grain out of the field to the bins, run to the implement dealer for parts, extra sandwiches for hired hands working at peak harvesting time or a late-night dinner for them. She would always update him on her plans with the kids. He'd finish eating, nod, get up, and if no one else was present, stand behind her, clasp her shoulders, bend over and kiss her on the top of her head. "Thank you," he always said. Then he was gone. Her silent, unemotional, rock steady husband who only showed emotional excitement between the sheets. He was an occasional, but good lover. Not great and definitely never inventive like Hans, but Shaw did surprise her the first time they made love. She got used to the short time of cuddling before and after intercourse, even the lack of variety in their positions.

She liked the consistency of being with him. With six, then seven, kids, school, their homework, a large farm, cooking, laundry, housework, Shaw was the constant, the one thing in her life she never worried about being inconsistent or springing some huge surprise on her at the last minute. Even when he grew angry, which was rare, he was consistent. His face would get red. He might snap something sarcastic or ask several short questions, but then he walked away, usually out to his farm office. He never mentioned it again, unless there were decisions to be made, facts to be shared. Several times, Connie exploded at him. He sat, listened, seemed to mentally sort through her issues, somehow would arrive at the kernel, the heart of the matter, and say, "I can do this and this or, I can't do this, but I can do such and such. That should clear up your problems." He'd get up and walk away.

This morning, she didn't worry about breakfast. No one would be up, expecting it at five-ten in the morning. She went downstairs and checked that the coffee was set, slipped on her farm boots and a jacket and went to the office. Melvin usually arrived and checked in at five-thirty. Occasionally, he showed up in his delivery van; otherwise, his farm truck. She wanted to be waiting for this quiet, sometimes jittery, yet also unemotional little man. *Almost a smaller version of her husband, but with less self-confidence and, somehow, he seemed less trustworthy,* she thought.

Melvin didn't seem surprised when he entered to find her at the desk and the coffee ready. He tipped his hat toward her and poured himself a large mug. She motioned for him to sit next to the desk, the place she knew he regularly sat when talking to Shaw.

"How's Shaw doing?" he asked, looking at the desk.

"I'm not optimistic. Besides, you should be telling me. Will you?" She sipped her coffee and looked over the mug at him.

Melvin shook his head and took another sip. "I suppose you were surprised Shaw changed things around." Surprisingly, he didn't look uncomfortable or nervous.

"Shocked is a better word. What was the reasoning? Were you surprised?"

"Yup, I was a bit surprised. The only reasoning, I can tell ya is what he told me. He didn't want an amputation. He didn't want to be transferred. He didn't want someone overruling his wants. He asked me. I said yes. I most always say yes to him. His reasonings are most times right." Melvin sipped his coffee, his pale blue eyes never leaving the desk or his mug. "I talked with the nurse last night, heard they're switching his care to hospice. Still hope he pulls through."

"How the hell can he? He went off antibiotics, didn't he? Does he want to die? Is that some of his right reasonings?" Connie slammed her cup onto the desk. "Melvin, this makes no damn sense. You do realize that, don't you?"

Melvin glanced at her for a second, then focused on his mug. "I get that it don't seem right to you, but to me, well, Shaw always has a plan B. This ain't my plan B and wouldn't be yours, but it's his. I figure we'll find out in time. How? I just ain't sure yet, but we will." He drained his coffee and stood up. "I'm sorry I can't give you answers you'd like better, but I gotta run all the way to Worthington to pick up parts for the picker. The jerks wanna charge us two-hunnerd to deliver them. Ain't right, not at this time of year. In the fall, maybe. Not the spring when we can't get in the fields yet and we got time to repair stuff." He turned toward the door.

Connie stood. He turned back, still not looking at her. "Melvin, I think you and me should meet sometime when you don't have to run off. I'd like to get a better picture of this operation. I pay the bills, but that's about it. You and me need to work together. I may be counting on you a lot. I also hope you keep me in the loop with Shaw's medical situation."

"Why, thank you, Connie. Can't say I'm not glad to hear that. I'm guessin' Gayle will keep close tabs on things and can tell you." He touched his cap again and left.

Connie thought the tone of his voice was sarcastic, but decided it was just his way of showing grief. She waited till his work truck drove by. She started poking around, her mind going in all directions. Focus, she kept reminding herself. Focus. Where was she to start? Her main role in the operation was to write the checks for the bills that came in, keep them organized and transferred to the accountants. She spent two to four hours a week in the office. At harvest season, she sometimes spent several hours a day, driving a truck or helping out wherever needed. Those times, she reduced her volunteer hours at the library. The name of the business the checks were written on said, 'Skogman Farms.' She didn't handle the income. Didn't even balance the checkbook.

Regarding the farm business, Shaw told her years ago, "Just write the checks and mail them. I'll approve the bills before I give them to you. I won't give you the bills if I don't think we have the money." He snickered, a rare thing for him. "Of course, that won't ever happen."

How many pieces of property did they own? She knew it was at least two sections, twelve hundred and eighty acres, making them the largest landowner in the county. How much additional land did they lease? How did that work? She thought their accountant handled leases and the income. She never saw the checks written to the farm, their income, only the bills she paid. How much debt did they hold? Most farms, even big ones, carried tremendous amounts of debt. Did they? She knew Shaw was shrewd and a careful businessman. He loved farming, but it was definitely a business.

At home, she kept a household checkbook balanced monthly. Come tax time, she signed the returns for their joint home account that the accountants prepared. She knew Shaw paid himself a salary from Skogman Farms, thought it was around forty-thousand. The farm paid her ten-thousand a year for her doing the bills and helping elsewhere when needed. They had a joint savings account with a current balance of twenty-thousand dollars, most of it set aside for Junior's future college expenses. When the girls were in college, each was expected to pay half their housing expenses, all of their spending money, and help out their parents with the tuition by finding scholarships. Several times, she told Shaw their savings account was getting low and he told her he'd sell some stock or investments. She never inquired about their investment portfolio, the farm finances or even how Shaw determined his salary. The thought that might have been a mistake niggled at the back of her mind

She opened the door to the back office. A place she rarely entered.

There was a huge old safe with a combination dial and heavy-looking handle. Shaw said it was his uncle's. She never saw it used or opened, and figured the days of dealing in cash were long over. File cabinets lined one wall, some with stickers signifying the years of the records contained. She glanced through several to find old bills and invoices going back to the sixties. Several cabinets were locked. They had no designation. She went back to the office and checked through the top desk drawer for keys. None fit the locked cabinets. There weren't keys for the two locked ones in the main office either. *Made sense,* she thought. You wouldn't just leave keys laying around. Shaw never carried a big wad of keys on him. She thought the sheds were keyed alike. She tried the lower desk drawers. The bottom left one was locked. She didn't want to wait till Melvin returned. For some reason, she wanted to be able to get into anything she wanted. Dammit, if her husband was going to die, she needed to know everything.

She pulled an old pearl-handled letter opener out of the top drawer. This was an old desk and couldn't be too complicated. She slid the blade along the lip of the drawer till she encountered the bolt. It didn't budge. She tried it from the other direction and pulled and jiggled the drawer with her other hand until the lock retracted. *Guess I have a new career*, she thought, as she saw a ring with cabinet keys on it. She heard voices, quickly pulled up the ring of keys and slipped them into the top drawer as Junior and Beany burst in.

"Mom-Connie, we're fixing the Camry today and then you may never see us again." Beany enveloped her in a warm hug and kissed her cheek.

Junior slipped in a more reserved hug. *Better than Shaw's, definitely not like Hans,* she thought.

Chapter Nineteen

Junior

Junior stepped back from his mom's hug. He was in a hurry to work on the old Camry. "Hey, Mom. I need that—"

"What do you need from me? This is your project. You're the one who wanted to tune it up by yourself. I've been patiently waiting. I can't start driving my new truck till I start the insurance on it. I wasn't going to start the insurance on it until the Camry is listed with you as primary driver." She paused and poked his arm. "In fact, I wasn't aware you started work on the Camry. You never told me, nor did your fath...Shaw. I was shocked to find the car not drivable when Shaw was injured and I needed the car to get to the hospital."

"Sorry, Mom, it's only been laid up a few days. This Dad thing put me behind. Now, he said he'd leave some tool to measure the spark distance on his desk. Is it here?" Junior edged around her. "Yup, here it is. Okay, Beany, we just got to gap the new plugs, install them, attach the new wires and adjust the distributor. Or do we gap the distributor and adjust the plugs?"

Beany shook his head. "I might know, but I'm not telling you."

Connie shook her head. "You could wait till Melvin gets back. I'm sure he'd help or at least tell you how."

"Mom. Melvin? Somehow that feels weird now."

"I know, son. He and I talked this morning. He didn't have any more answers. I think he was surprised Dad asked him to be power of attorney, but he's so used to doing what Dad asks that he didn't dispute it." She waited a second. "Son, somehow we have to establish more of a relationship with him. He knows more about running this place than anyone else."

"I know, Mom. Listen, Dad *told* him to be his power of attorney. He never *asked* him to do anything. If he did, it was always a question Melvin couldn't say no to." He gave her a squeeze and the two boys ran out the door.

Junior opened the garage door and patted the old Camry. "I've watched and helped, but never done this by myself. My first car. I can't wait to start driving it to school and not take the bus."

"I can't wait for you to take me places. Like Chicago, New York City, Los Angeles."

Junior opened the hood and started checking the wires. "The plugs are already in and these are new wires. We need to connect them to the distributor. I'm surprised. Dad must have stuck them in while I was waiting for the distributor to come. Whew. That makes things easier. Doesn't it?"

"It doesn't matter, dear. Beany is here. Now go get the battery. You do know how to hook it up, right? You're not color blind, are you? Know what a plus and minus look like?"

Junior gave him the finger and went to retrieve the battery from the lean-to as Beany pulled the distributor out of its box.

Forty-five minutes later, Junior slid behind the wheel, held his breath, and cranked the key. The car started, but the engine ran rough. Very rough.

"Something's wrong," Beany hollered. "Shut'er down. Let me check the distributor again."

The guys tinkered and rechecked the wires. Still the engine ran as if not all cylinders were firing. It was lunch time, so they ran in to eat lunch.

The girls were talking about their dad when the phone rang. Connie answered, listened and hung up the phone. "That was Gayle at the hospital. It's not looking good. She said hospice is in charge now and Dad wants us to visit about five this afternoon."

"All of us? Or just the girls?" Junior asked.

He noticed his mom's jaw tighten. Her age lines around her mouth and eyes stood out more. "Gayle first said the girls. She must have been calling from his bedside. I heard him mumble something, then she said the whole family."

Junior sighed. "That just makes me feel so welcome." He took a final bite of the grilled cheese with bacon and downed his milk. "Let's go, Beany. I'd rather be frustrated with the car than sitting around in here."

As they opened the garage door, Melvin drove up the Milliken drive. He stopped in front of the garage, got out, and walked over to them. Rusty trotted after him, and sat waiting for Junior's and Beany's pats. He lay down after they did. Junior wasn't sure how he felt about Melvin. It's not like they had a close relationship. On the other hand, he'd been around him his entire life.

Melvin said. "Just stopped to see your dad. He ain't doing too good."

"Yeah, Mom just told us he wants the family to come at five. Are you going to be there?" Junior stared at him, not smiling.

"Yup. He wants me there, too. I ain't plannin' to stay long. This is a bit awkward, but it wasn't my idea. I got nothin' against you all. He's a stubborn man. Always has been."

Junior shuffled his feet, bent over and patted Rusty again. He wasn't sure how to respond.

Melvin stepped closer to the car. "See you two put in the distributor. How's it runnin'?"

"Rough," said Beany. "It's not firing on all four. Want to hear it?"

Melvin listened as Junior started the car, then waved at him to shut it off. "Don't think one of them plugs is gapped right, maybe another one is off, too." He looked at Junior. "Hey, this going to be your car now?"

Junior couldn't help his smile. "It's mine if I can put in new plugs, wires and distributor. Beany's helping."

"Well, then, I'm sorry I interfered. I saw those plugs on Shaw's desk last Friday and figured he ran out of time to install them. I was in early that Saturday morning and thought I'd save him a bit of time. Because they were out of their boxes, I guessed he'd already gapped them, so I just brought 'em over and popped them in." He leaned in and touched one of the wires. "I started to attach the wires and realized the distributor was missing, so I trotted back to the office to look for one, but got an emergency call from one of our tenant farmers that a pipe broke in their kitchen and he needed help. As I jumped in my truck, I noticed old Beany here goin in the back door. I put the garage door back down on my way out."

"So that's how the door went down. That means you weren't around when Dad Shaw went crazy?"

"Nope. I was way over on M road, trying to get a rusted shut-off valve to turn. I didn't know nothing till Shaw called me later that day from the hospital, man could barely talk." Melvin shrugged like he didn't want to talk any more about it and stepped closer to the car. "Want me to gap these things?"

Junior asked, "Could you show us? I'm trying to learn this stuff myself. Here's the gap thingy."

"It's a feeler gauge, not a thingy." Beany looked at Melvin.

Melvin tried to hide a smile, but failed. "Yup. That's the name. Now, pull those plugs and I'll show you. Can't take long, I gotta get some paperwork done in the office that we're behind on."

"Doesn't Mom pay the bills?" Junior pulled the wires and began wrenching out the plugs.

"Yup, your mom pays the bills. But there's a lot more paperwork that your dad and me do." Melvin demonstrated how to use the gauge.

"What kind? Don't you have accountants?" Beany looked over Junior's shoulder as if to confirm he was doing things correctly.

"Of course, but someone's gotta get stuff ready for the accountants. Besides, there's lots of records that gotta be kept for other reasons, like the government, taxes, county, rental income, income checks, holding payments…" He startled and shook his head. "Hey, looks like you got the hang of things. If it don't run smooth, find me and I'll take another whack at it. Rusty, heel."

Melvin scurried to his truck and drove to the farm office.

"He's odd," Beany said. "Just odd. Nice, but why'd he jump when he said holding payments and then rush off? Are they like investments? Wouldn't Dad Shaw handle any investments? Or your mom?" Beany put the last plug in and connected the wire. "Try it now, my almost-skilled mechanic."

Junior twisted the key. The engine purred. Beany slammed the hood down and jumped in the passenger seat. "New York, here we come."

Junior put the car in drive and drove Beany the half mile to his home. He came back and asked his mother to call the insurance company.

Chapter Twenty

Jens

Tuesday, 5:30 p.m.

Jens ordered four pizzas to go, grabbed a craft beer from the cooler and slid into the wooden booth closest to the front door of Katie's Beer and Pizza. Three of the six booths were already filled. He used the wine/beer opener attached to the wall on a string to pop his beer cap and took several long slugs. He'd have a wait. Katie's could only bake four pizzas at a time and sixteen inches was the only size they offered. If some were already in the oven and you ordered more than they could bake at the moment, you had a choice. Take them one at a time as they came out of the oven, which, if you were dining in, meant they came at staggered times, or, if you ordered them to go, wait till they could all go in at once and come out at the same time. Either way, they came boxed. No pizza pans, plates or silverware if you were dining in.

Dining was not a word used frequently for Katie's. If eating in, you used your fingers to eat and the paper towels on the roll in each booth as napkins. Carry out, you paid up and left. Eat in or carry out, the waiter charged you seventeen dollars for each pizza, three dollars for each individual beer bottle or can sitting on your table, ten dollars for each six-pack, and twelve per bottle of wine. The staff gave you the stink eye if you asked for a glass for your beer. Katie's didn't offer draft beer. A grubby handwritten poster listed the eight mixed drinks they served. If you asked for a drink not on the list, the bartender ignored you or, at best, grumpily pointed to the sign. For wine, which customers opened themselves, the staff condescendingly gave you small disposable glasses. A sign over the bar read, *Don't like Our prices? Go to Walfart or dumb Domminoes. Don't like Our service? Go to Hell.*

It was the best pizza in the state. They didn't take phone orders, so people waited for hours on weekends, which meant they could drink more beer and wine. Besides the typical mundane American beers, they kept a surprisingly good rotation of craft beers and decent wines, plus they held a package license to carry out beer and wine. Jens wasn't sure if the current owner was the third or fourth generation of Katie's. He wished he still carried a pen knife to add his initials to the carved-up table top.

It felt good to get out of the hospital room. It was clear Shaw was giving the family time to say goodbye. In the room, he squeezed Shaw's hand, told him he enjoyed knowing him, and wished him the best. What the hell else can you say to a man who has chosen to die rather than to have his leg amputated? A man who intended to kill his wife and shot at his son, who changed his power of attorney to his farm assistant rather than let his wife have any control.

Earlier that day, after lunch, Gayle told the girls one of the nurses told her Shaw was busy reading pages and pages. The nurse said the lawyer brought them over.

When everyone entered the room at five, Shaw seemed alert in spite of the painkillers. He looked like hell. Like a man dying. He half-smiled at them and weakly thanked them for coming. Gayle asked him if he had anything to say. He said no and thanked them again for coming. Next, Gayle asked him about the papers he'd been reading before the family's visit. "Are you going to share them with us? Will they explain some things?"

He managed to whisper, "No. Not today. My lawyer has them back with him. I just wanted to review them. You'll see them in due time."

That was when Jens left. He drove into town separately with the intent to get the pizzas and meet everyone back home whenever they arrived. Before leaving, he set the timers to turn the twin ovens on warm in case he got home before the others. No one expected the visit to be a long ordeal.

Jens took a sip of his beer. He had to admit living in this family setting was nice, in spite of it being due to a tragedy. He was lonely. The past three years had been hell. His father never adjusted to Hans' death. Jens knew his dad always liked Hans better. Oh, he knew growing up, he was loved, but his dad had a lot on his plate. What with an ill wife, a live-in helper, Connie, and trying to keep a farm going when it seemed the only way to keep up was to get bigger, plus, life in general.

Jens' reverie was broken by Fred Cochran coming through the front door. Cochran grabbed a beer, placed an order at the bar, and looked around for a place to sit. Jens waved him over.

Cochran sat down and popped the cap off. "Don't worry, I'll keep the bottle in front of me so you won't get charged for it." He took a long drink. "That tastes mighty good." He squinted his eyes at Jens in concern. "How's the family holding up? Any updates on Shaw?"

Jens smiled his thanks. "Update on Shaw is he called the family to meet him at five this afternoon. He cancelled his antibiotics and hospice is taking over."

"Other words, he's dying. I assume the girls were there. Was Connie and the boy there? Anyone else?"

The way he said anyone else struck Jens as odd. "Connie and Junior are there. I'm not sure how they can hold up, but they do. Watching the man die that wanted to kill you is pretty gut-wrenching." He took another sip of beer and checked how much was left. "Melvin Smith was there. Didn't say anything. Apparently, Shaw wanted him there, too."

"Isn't that just the oddest thing?" Cochran took a long pull on his beer and looked at Jens' bottle. "You need another one. They were just prepping your four pizzas when I ordered mine. They put mine in ahead of yours with two others. It's going to be a while before they start yours." He clambered out of the booth and returned with a six pack of the type Jens was drinking. "Figured we can each have a couple and you can take the rest home. I'm sure they won't go to waste."

"Thanks. You on or off duty?"

Cochran's smile almost split his face. "Glad you asked. Technically, I'm off duty, but as sheriff, I'm never off. That's about to end. I had me a little talk with the county administrator and the elected board supervisor today. My deputy sheriff's been making talk of applying for a sheriff opening up north. He's getting tired of waiting for me to die or move on. I told them it was time for a younger guy. The detective position is open and why don't I take the detective position for several more years and Kevin can run for sheriff? He's got about fifteen years in under me, got a good name, no one's gonna run against him, especially with my blessing. The county board meets Monday and can appoint him as acting sheriff till an election." He lightly slapped his hand on the table and looked around. "Hope I wasn't talking too loud. Don't want word to get out yet."

Jens laughed. "Well, congratulations, I guess. I don't blame you for wanting to get out of the head spot. Why don't you just retire?"

Cochran studied his beer bottle. "The main reason is, I ain't ready to be retired. I enjoy working and fifty-eight isn't that old. A second reason is, I love detective work. The third reason is…" He started peeling the label off his bottle. "I just plain don't know what I'd do with myself."

"Don't you have a family?"

"Nope. I'm a lifelong bachelor. Folks are dead, sister's in Tucson, the brother's in Bradenton, Florida, and I hate the heat."

The way he talked made Jens look at him, think about him, in a different light. He's lonely. Never married. Small towns. Rural area. Dedicated his entire life to keeping it safe and no one to share it with. Plus, he's good-looking. He looked up to see Cochran looking at him. He seemed to blush and Jens felt his own cheeks growing warm.

"What about you? That Connie's quite a woman, ain't she? They're quite a family, in spite of Shaw. How long you planning to stay around? Thought you said you were heading away from here after things settle down with Connie. Where to?"

"I thought someplace warm, but after these days with Connie and the family…" He drained his bottle and popped open another one. "See, I've been alone with my dad for three years. They were rough. I can go anywhere and work as a mortician. In fact, I have enough reserves to buy or start a funeral home if I wanted. I don't want those headaches…"

"I think after burying people forever, then three years tied down so tight with your dad, you're lonely."

His words struck Jens. How could this man be so intuitive? Yes, I am lonely, just like I think he is.

Both men were quiet until the waitress appeared with a single pizza. "Here, Sheriff, yours is ready." She glanced at Jens. "You understand how our high-tech system here works, right? We could get his in before we could start baking your four."

Jens laughed. "Yup. Hasn't changed much since I was a kid."

He looked at Cochran who looked like he had more to say. Jens sure had more he wanted to ask him about, if he dared. He handed the roll of paper towels to him. "Get started. No sense you taking this home to eat alone. I might try a piece for an appetizer."

Cochran tipped his bottle at him and opened the cheese, sausage, pepper and onion beauty. He stuffed a piece in his mouth, quickly guzzled some beer as if to stop the burning cheese and managed to mumble, "Have a piece."

Jens took a piece, then set it back down in order to tear off a paper towel. No sense in dripping grease down his wrist. He picked it back up, chewed and swallowed. Sucking in a breath, he said, "You're right, I'm lonely and staying with Connie's family made me realize that."

Cochran chewed and motioned with his hand to go on.

Jens decided what the heck, this guy felt like someone he could talk to. Something that hadn't happened in years. It felt risky, but sometimes you had to take risks. He took a sip of beer and began. "I lived in The Cities ever since I started college. I'm gay. I got my bachelor degree in mortuary science from U.M. I worked for several funeral homes during college and right after. The AIDS crisis hit, so I bought out an older couple's family business and began offering services for AIDS deaths. It wasn't very lucrative, but it served a need not many other funeral homes wanted to serve. I met a man, Thomas, who joined me in the business. We became romantic partners as well. Unfortunately, he had AIDS and died in 1993, shortly before the crisis began to wane." He glanced at Cochran, gathering himself to answer the question he figured the man would have. "I was always careful, insisted on precaution. I never got infected."

Cochran gave a slight nod, blinked, and looked away.

Jens continued, "My building was in an ideal location. I sold it for a ton of money. I freelanced till Dad got sick." Jens didn't look up while he was talking. He stumbled on. "Dad never fully accepted me as gay. He was glad I loved the Twin Cities and could live my own life there."

He stared at his bottle. Did he say too much? He heard Cochran clear his throat and looked up to see the man pulling out a handkerchief and wiping his eyes. What was that about?

Cochran blew his nose. "You been through a lot. All that death, all that loss, all those lives lost because of government inaction and social prejudice. Thomas. Your dad. Now Shaw. Damn, Jens, that just hit me hard. Stuff usually doesn't. Not anymore. Not after everything I see."

He attacked another piece of pizza.

Neither man spoke for several minutes.

"Aren't you lonely?" Jens barely glanced at him when he asked.

Cochran handed him another piece of pizza. "Shut up and eat. I'm the one that's supposed to ask the questions." His smile was warm. "Yeah, now that you ask. I am. I love this county and area, always have, always will. I never dated. Didn't want to. Too afraid. First of women, then of what people might say…"

The waitress arrived, carrying an insulated carrier. She pointed at Jens. "We trust ya to bring this carrier back, seein as you're with the sheriff."

She laughed as Jens pulled four bottles in front of him and pushed three in front of Cochran. "Gotta keep things straight, huh?"

She looked confused when Cochran and Jens burst into laughter.

"Maybe I'm not too sure about doing that anymore," Cochran

muttered as Jens handed his credit card over and told her to add in two more six-packs. Cochran reached into his pocket, pulled out his cell and handed it to Jens. "That's my private cell. Call your number, then we'll both have each other's."

Jens punched in his number, then pulled his phone out of his pocket when it rang. "Got it. We need to talk."

Cochran stuffed his phone back in his pocket. His face grew serious. "I agree. Just realize, there's some things we can talk about, some things we can't."

Jens shook his head, feeling confused.

Cochran wiped his hands off on the paper towel. "Jens, let's just say there's more questions about Shaw. That's all I can say. Give my regards to the family."

Jens couldn't help smiling on the drive home. Fred Cochran was gay and lonely. He wasn't happy about those facts, just smiling at the coincidence. What did that mean? Would his life change? Would he see Cochran again? Somehow, he couldn't call him Fred. Everyone called him Cochran or Sheriff. The man was still solid, only a hint of flab. Looked like he worked out frequently. And those eyes. They looked like they could stare into your soul, in a good way. Unless you were guilty of something.

A horn tooted. Jens laughed as Junior crept pass him in the old Camry. Connie waved, but wasn't smiling. *She doesn't have much to smile about*, he thought. Cochran flashed through his mind and he found himself smiling again. The words to John Prine's song, *Illegal Smile*, floated between his ears. Guess he could do both, be sad, and smile at other times. Still, just what did Cochran mean, regarding more questions about Shaw? What else could there be besides the vasectomy and waiting eighteen years to learn the person who might have fathered Junior? Slow to anger? What did Shaw mean by that? Sharing his papers in due time? Was he changing his will? He wished Hans was alive, he was always good in rough times. Even if he always put him down, Jens trusted his brother's wisdom. It was just his big-brother's self-confidence bordering on narcissism that was sometimes hard to take.

Chapter Twenty-One

Cochran

Cochran watched Jens struggle out the door with the pizza container and two six-packs. *I should go help him,* he thought. If he did, he was afraid he might give into the emotions he kept stuffed and locked up for so many years and follow the man home. Right now, he wanted to jump up and yell, "I'm gay." What would people think if County Sheriff Fred Cochran jumped up in the middle of Katie's and shouted out that news? Another thought flashed through him. Jens was AIDS free. What would he have thought if he wasn't? Didn't matter, just more crazy thoughts. He stuffed another bite of pizza into his mouth. A bite he hadn't intended to start. He watched his calories carefully and exercised hard so he could keep up with his younger deputies.

Being a full-time detective was another reason he wanted to shout. He spent ten years as a detective and loved every minute of it, just like putting large jigsaw puzzles together, finding the colors, the borders, those pieces that seem to have no meaning, but eventually become important. What would people think if he stood and hollered, "I'm going to be your gay county detective,"?

Man, someone's going to put me in a white jacket if I'm not careful. He finished the unwanted piece of pizza and reached for his beer. Out of the corner of his eye, he noticed Melvin Smith reaching for a beer in the cooler. Melvin looked around and must have realized there was no place to sit because he turned and started to put the beer back.

"Melvin, I got a seat," Cochran called through the noise

enveloping the tiny place.

Cochran couldn't read Melvin's expression. Was he pleased? Scared? Shy? Whatever it was, he blinked and sat down. "Thanks," he said as he popped the cap off his beer.

"You just come from the hospital?"

This time, Melvin's face showed surprise. "Yup. Shaw ain't got much more time. Stubborn old fool." He took a sip of his beer. "How'd you know I was there?"

"Jens just left. He was waiting on some pizzas to take back." Cochran pushed the paper towel roll and the pizza a few inches across the table. "Have some. It's more than I need to take home for leftovers. I can't afford to lose my girlish figure, you know."

"Don't mind if I do." Melvin pulled off a piece and bit into it.

"How long you been with Shaw?"

Melvin's eyes narrowed slightly, as if he wanted to be cautious in his answer. "Long time. Real long. Guess I just happened along at the right time." He gave a half-smile and took another bite.

Cochran learned years ago to not show emotion or surprise when talking to folks. Just the facts, please, just the facts. That wasn't quite how Jack Webb said it in Dragnet, but it was close enough. He didn't have the facts, yet, but somehow Melvin's words sounded hollow. He smiled warmly. "Have another piece, you gotta be going through a lot, along with the family. How you holding up?"

Melvin chewed and swallowed. "Me? I'm okay. Shaw's been good to me, but Connie told me the other morning she wanted to keep me on cuz I know more about the business than she does." He sipped his beer and reached for another piece of pizza.

Cochran waited till the small man took a bite. "I thought Connie already knew a lot about the place. You mean you fixing things and keeping the farming going? I'd guess she knows a lot about the business end with commodities, cash flow and keeping those leases straight."

Melvin mumbled, "Nah, she don't..." A flash of smugness crossed his face, then his eyes startled. He chewed faster, took a swig of beer. Glancing at Cochran, he added, "She'll be okay, 'specially if I keep all that equipment runnin' and them renters happy."

Cochran smiled nonchalantly and watched him eat another piece and finish his beer. "You want to take the rest home? I gotta go check my messages and make a few rounds. Hopefully, it's a slow night and I can get home to some sleep. Hey, you got emergency prescription deliveries to make?"

"Thanks, Sheriff. I'm hungrier than I figured I'd be. Thanks muchly." Melvin's eyes blinked. "Nah, I only deliver regular scheduled ones with forty-eight hours' notice. The old folk seem to appreciate it." He closed the lid on the pizza and laid three dollars and two quarters on the table. "This'll take care of my beer and tip." He left as quietly as he entered.

What is that man hiding? Cochran waved over the waiter and settled up. Why was he not more specific about how long he knew Shaw? Why did his eyes blink when Cochran mentioned pharmacy deliveries? Also, why did he start to correct Cochran on how much Connie knew about the place, then change it? Did Connie know much about the operation or not? He was beginning to wonder how she could, what with two secretive men around while she was raising seven kids. He headed back to his office. He had more digging to do, plus he wanted to print off some notes and have a chat with the D.A. tomorrow.

He smiled all the way to the courthouse. That Jens was quite a guy. He wanted to skip down the hall. Instead, he put his serious face on as he waved at the evening desk staff. He couldn't wait to be full-time detective again, or see Jens.

He sat at his desk for ten minutes, thinking about Jens. Was this puppy-love? At his age? What was that connection they both seemed to share while eating pizza? Was he imagining that Jens felt the same way? He didn't think so, not by several looks Jens gave him. What would it be like to be in love? Finally. After all these years of tamping his feelings and desires down so tight he could barely feel them. Tonight, in just a few minutes, it felt like they finally exploded from the pressure. He groaned at the thought of being alone with Jens. He stood and paced around his office. Stop this, right now. He sat back down and turned his computer back on, occasionally pinching himself to stay focused.

Chapter Twenty-Two

Connie

After the family time with Shaw, Connie rode quietly in the passenger seat of the old Camry. She didn't even smile when Junior carefully passed slow-moving Jens. That man never drove fast. She simply nodded when Junior said, "Guess he wants the pizza to get home safe. I'm only doing forty-five."

There was so much she wanted to ask Shaw. In any other situation, a wife would spend his last days and hours by his side. She wanted to pick his brain. Besides the why of wanting to kill her, she wanted to learn everything she could about their operation. She had no idea of their overall size, financially or land-wise. Were they millionaires or barely getting by? She was pretty certain they weren't broke. Only once, shortly after they married, did he say things were tight and to watch household expenditures for a while. Several months later, he told her things were fine again, some payment came through that had been held up. Ever since she moved in, all the mail went into the box at the Milliken Road driveway. Both the personal and the Skogman Farms mail. A few times, working in the office, paying bills, she noticed Melvin bring in some mail, but it never occurred to her to ask where he got it.

She didn't like this feeling of being out of control, of not knowing things she should. Except, how could she? Why would she? When she moved in and married, she was dealing with two distraught pre-teen girls who needed help making it through the day without a meltdown. She was trying to adjust to a husband who had been living his life this way for over fourteen years or since his uncle died and he'd taken over the farm. It wasn't her role to come in and demand answers about a growing farm business. She knew books, fiction, nonfiction, literature, poetry, authors, how to research, where to find reference materials, how to learn things that interested her. Mostly, though, she knew kids and people who needed her help. She knew Shaw didn't need her in his business, but he did need her to mother his daughters, to keep the home fires burning, so to speak, to love him, to accept his silent ways. She needed his stability, plus the freedom to have and raise kids, to nurture them, teach them to be independent and self-sufficient, to love others, to be good citizens, to respect others. She always figured they made a good team. Other people sure thought so.

She looked out the window at the fields that went on and on. A road every mile delineating a section, six-hundred-forty acres, all the way west into South Dakota, south into Iowa, north to the forests, and east to The Cities. How could they have been a good team? Was she kidding herself all these years? Covering up her guilt over Hans? Kidding herself by ignoring and stuffing the fact that Junior might be Hans' son? She glanced at Junior, concentrating on his driving. No, she wasn't trying to cover her guilt about Hans. What she had with him was so unique, it was hard to describe. If there had been no Hans, she wouldn't have Junior. She sighed as they turned into the drive. Now was not the time to think about guilt. Whether she and Shaw were a good team. Whether she should have asked more questions or been a bitch about understanding the business. Now was the time to prepare to bury her husband, to make sure her girls were stable, her son was secure, and, to learn more about the business.

As Junior pulled to a stop in the garage, she unhooked her seatbelt and picked up her purse. She heard the cabinet keys from the office softly clink. All the keys from the entire desk were in her purse now. She also carried the bag of Shaw's clothes from the hospital she requested, along with his dead cell phone. She knew his master keys to the buildings were in one of his pants' pockets. She also knew Melvin opened the bottom desk drawer, the one she picked open. She knew, because she placed several of her head hairs over the edge of the drawer and somehow, they ended up in the drawer. Guess more than one person knew how to pick that lock. When would he ask her about the keys? Why did something seem so curious about him? More than curious, threatening? Why was his name on some papers she glanced at?

After they finished eating the pizza, Gayle spoke about Shaw's condition. "Dad fell asleep before we left. He could slip into a coma anytime now. It's unlikely he will be conscious again." She stood from the loveseat as if she was going to give a lecture to a group of students. "We think he will die in in the next five days. Hospice nurses are in charge now." She looked at each person as if to see how they were handling that information. No one burst out crying. "There are five stages of grief; denial, anger, bargaining, depression and acceptance. What step do you think we are in now?" She sat down and waited. "Each of us doesn't have to be at the same stage," she added.

"Can it be a combination?" Mary asked. "Right now, I feel anger, plus depression at not being able to do something, to fix it. Is that okay?"

"It's absolutely all right. Grief is not linear. It can go in circles, out of order and interweave. The important thing is to learn to recognize it and acknowledge it, guilt-free. It's human." Gayle reached over and patted her mom who was sitting next to her.

Connie scooted forward. "Thank you, Gayle. I'm so glad we have your expertise with us." She took a big breath. "I really feel a mix. Definitely some denial, how could he do this, act this way, be so cold? That, mixed with anger. Part of me wants to bargain, to have a chance to work all this out earlier, go back in time, and part of me wants to move on. To accept it and get going with what's next. I'm learning there's a lot about this place and operation I know nothing of…"

"Mom, kids," Gayle glanced around the room, then took her mother's hand. "Don't rush the steps. Don't try to speed the process up or think a person can skip some of the steps. Know that you will go through each one at some time or another. My point is, in your hurry to move on, don't bury them. It's trite, but we will need to take our lives one day at a time for a long time."

Ellen got several bottles of beer and walked around the family room, refilling glasses. "As for me…" She sat down. "Well, Mary and I, being older than the rest of you, Dad doesn't seem that old. Many friends our age have even older parents while some have parents in their seventies who are dying. So, the fact that our father is dying at this age may not feel the same as for you younger kids." She sipped her glass, twisted a finger in her blonde-gray hair. "I guess I'm trying to say, it's not Dad's age that's shocking, it's how he chose to act." She slammed her glass on the end table and jerked herself to a stand. "It's how the damn fool chose to end his life. It just makes me so angry…" She threw her hands up in the air. "Guess that means I'm in the anger stage." She smacked one hand into another and shook her fist at the window. "Damn him. Just god damn him. I so want to hit something."

"Me, too. Me, too." More me toos filled the air.

Junior pulled Jens to his feet. "Come on, Jens." They ran out the back door and returned, carrying a fifty-pound bag of seed corn they double-bagged into a burlap sack. Junior set it on the kitchen table, pulled the chairs back and began punching it, hard. Jens went to the other side of the table to brace the bag upright. Junior grunted as he hit. He danced around like a boxer, swinging and swinging, till he broke away and sagged into an easy chair, crying.

Ellen stepped up next, only she screamed and yelled, "Damn. You. Dad. Damn you. Why? Why? Why?"

Barely a word was spoken by the others as each adult child punched the bag. Some hard, some soft. Some speaking. All with emotion. Connie was the last family member to step up. The others wiped their eyes and gathered behind her.

"Go, Mom," Gayle whispered. "Let it out."

Connie screeched, "A—i— i—i." It was almost blood-curdling. She karate-chopped the bag, shouting out each hit. "One…Two…Three…Four…Five…" At ten, she stopped and fell back into the waiting arms of her seven children. Somehow, they managed to fold to the floor in a heap of hugs and sniffles.

No one noticed Beany slip in. He didn't make a sound, just sat on the kitchen floor and watched, his eyes even larger, tears slipping down his cheeks.

For nearly ten minutes, there was silence, only broken by the antique clock ticking from the family room. Emma set life in motion again. "That was therapeutic. Great idea, Junior. Listen, do we want a service for Dad? He didn't like churches." She wriggled her way out of the pile and found a pad and pen.

The others slowly made their way to the chairs and couches. Beany and Junior sat on the floor, leaning back against a bookcase. Emma dropped to sit on the floor in the middle of the room. "This is somewhat of an awkward situation." They all broke into laughter. "What? Did I say something funny?" Emma looked confused. "Oh, I get it. Yep, this is an awkward situation. We should have filmed this for Dr. Phil. Maybe that could be my breakthrough in acting."

"Okay, kids, settle down now." Connie overemphasized her motherly words. "It feels strange to start planning your father's service when he's still alive. Who knows how much longer he might live? I've heard of people in comas and in hospice lasting for days and weeks longer than expected."

"Mom," Gayle said, "You're right. However, most of them did not have an infection. He could hang on for a while." She thought a moment. "He's also at higher risk for a blood clot. However, I think it's important to at least sketch out some plans. We can fill them in after he dies."

Emma continued. "There are no secrets in this community, yet I feel Dad knew a lot of people who respected him and would want to express their condolences."

The family discussed various options for a service and location. It was already accepted Shaw would be cremated, so they weren't discussing a funeral and burial. Jens stood up. "I feel a little out of place. On the one hand, I feel like I've known each of you all your lives through my relationship with your mother. On the other, I haven't been around enough that you'd know me."

"That's okay," said Ellen. "I think we've known you're a close friend of Mom's. So, speak up."

"The other day, when I met Melvin, he showed me around the shop in Shed One. He acted upset over Shaw's condition and said he wondered how he will fit in for the long term. Except, it didn't seem genuine. Almost like he knows something no one else does. He's a hard guy to read. Anyway, the idea just struck me. What about using the large equipment shed, Shed One, for a gathering place? It has a cement floor, the equipment could easily be moved outside, it's heated because the shop is in there, has a bathroom, and it would be easy to clean out. I think that would take the stiffness and awkwardness out of something, as opposed to the church or school. People could come dressed as they are." Jens sat down, a look of embarrassed concern on his face, as if he spoke out of turn or said too much.

Jane jumped out of her chair. "I love it. That's Dad. We could get chairs and tables rented in from Marshall, maybe even find a caterer."

The family discussed several other ideas as Emma made notes. Ten minutes later, she said, "I think that's a good outline. We can fill in the tasks and details later…" Her voice trailed off.

"This is strange, isn't it?" Connie stood. "I think it's time to read, watch TV or go to bed. We need a break."

As good nights and hugs were shared before bed, no one spoke about all their emotion punching the bag of corn. Instead, Connie thought, there was a calmness that their anger had been addressed, at least for now. She knew hers was. At least for now.

Chapter Twenty-Three

Cochran

Technically, he was off the clock. Technically. The desk staff knew not to bother him when he came in at odd hours unless something was important. Sometimes, one would joke about building a master bedroom onto his office because of all the hours he spent on the job.

He glanced at his citations and certificates hanging on his wall. He was proud of each one, but wondered where he would hang them next week. As detective, he would have a low walled cubicle. He glanced at his diploma. His assistant, Irene, was the only one around long enough to remember it took him seven years to get his Associate Degree in Law Enforcement in 1982 from Worthington Community College. She also knew some of the extra time was because he took every psychology and sociology class he could, plus working full time as a rookie patrolman for the sheriff department didn't leave much extra time. He was hired by the sheriff's department at age twenty-one right after his discharge from the Army where he served as a Military Police Officer.

A photo of Cochran's parents, taken with him at his graduation from community college, hung next to his diploma. The photo showed their pride in him. The first college degree in their extended family. They couldn't have been more excited if it was a Ph.D. It was a college degree. His older sister had a diploma and license from a ten-month beauty school program. They were proud of her, too. In their minds, though, it didn't compare to a real college degree. His younger brother dropped out of high school, had problems holding jobs until he ended up repairing and replacing ties and rails for the railroad. It was structured, hard, demanding work that somehow, he could focus on. It also kept him on the move where he wasn't expected to build responsibilities of a home, marriage or family.

Cochran sometimes wondered if his brother didn't have fetal alcohol syndrome. Not severe, just enough to affect his judgement abilities. Growing up and as a young adult, the guy made some crazy decisions. Not that his parents were drunks. They were never out of control, falling over drunk. They just drank beer or wine from the time they got home till they went to bed and all day on the weekends. That included during his mother's three pregnancies. Hey, in the fifties, cigarettes and beer were considered normal nutrition in their neighborhood. Both parents died in their late sixties of lung cancer. Cochran never smoked, not even as a teen or in the Army. He still feared lung cancer.

Jens flashed through his mind. Cochran pinched himself, hit the keys and dug deeper. He was grateful for the computer and information technology seminars he took over the years, including forensic data research. After an hour, he tired of saying, 'WOW.' He stretched and settled back and made a list. When he finished, he printed off a copy and slid it into his portfolio case. He sent a quick email to Jennifer Logan, County D.A., requesting to meet with her as soon as her schedule allowed. He expected a reply by seven-thirty in the morning. Like him, she started early.

Notes:
Saturday, March 26, 2011
Shaw Philip Skogman, age 74
Facts:
Ordered his son to leave home at 7:00 a.m.
Shouted son wasn't his son
Threatened him with shotgun
Fired birdshot at him, winging him in left buttock and upper leg
Told his wife, Connie, he would kill her

Turned toward her at close range to fire, she managed to grab onto the gun, both slipped and fell, gun discharged, destroying his lower left leg

In hospital after initial surgery, informed wife he intended to kill her and wing son

Reason: he discovered she had an affair that ended eighteen years ago

Reason: he had a vasectomy twenty-eight years before so son couldn't be his

Never informed wife of vasectomy

Wife never informed him of affair, the lover, Hans Hanson, died unexpectedly, sudden heart attack?? Eighteen years ago

Refused transfer to University Hospital

Refused amputation

Discontinued antibiotics

Had medical power of attorney and living will changed to Melvin Smith, his longtime farm assistant and mechanic, removing his wife

Other:

Shaw's first wife, Alice, died of suicide in 1984 from overdose of anti-depressants, drowned in bathtub while twin daughters were at relatives. Apparently, no neighbors or relatives knew of sleeping pills

Shaw's uncle and aunt, Fordham and Helen Skogman, died five months apart from sudden illnesses in 1959 at age sixty-four. He inherited farm

Shaw changed his name to Shaw S Phillip, using AKA to register at Worthington Community College, after H.S. graduation.

Pharmacy licensing records indicate that in 1954, a Shaw S Phillip earned Bachelor degree in Pharmacy at U.M. under that name

<u>Pharmacy License still current under Shaw S Phillip WITH AN AKA (Also Known As) Shaw Philip Skogman</u>

1960 census showed him at farm as owner under Skogman name

Melvin Smith

Melvin Smith is an enigma. He appears on county voting records since 1964.

Smith is very vague about how long he's known or worked for Shaw. Voting records would indicate otherwise.

I called family-owned pharmacy in Summerville and asked if Melvin delivered prescriptions for them. Was told Melvin did almost all non-emergency deliveries in rural areas, not towns, between here, to South Dakota Line and to Iowa line, no towns, just rural areas. He delivers for pharmacies in Worthington, Marshall and Summerville. Pharmacist thought he'd been making deliveries since he could remember as a child in mid-60's. He thought Melvin was a Licensed Practical Nurse, too.

State license records show Melvin Smith as a registered L.P.N through the year 2001 at several addresses owned by Skogman or Farm Holding.

Other

Discovered holding company called: Farm Holding Company

Checked state registration records. Principals are not listed, would require probable cause and warrant from court.

Address in Worthington, Minnesota shows office on 2nd floor of small compounding pharmacy, Worthington Compounding Pharmacy, (started in 1932), still operating

Worthington Pharmacy building and business owned by Farm Holding. Does FH own other types of businesses? Why a pharmacy?

Farm Holding is privately held, little information is available. Application for State Registration said its purpose was to "buy, sell and lease farms in southwestern Minnesota, northern Iowa and eastern South Dakota; invest in commodities; provide management services to farms in arrears; to own other businesses as seen fit."

A plat survey shows a number of properties in this county and adjoining as belonging to Farm Holding.

Educated guess is that Shaw Skogman AKA Shaw S Phillip is a principal and possibly/probably Melvin Smith.

At eight-thirty Wednesday morning, tired from a night of restless thoughts about Jens, Cochran sat across from Jennifer Logan, County

D.A. for seven years. Late-thirties, five-one, plump, thick glasses, closely cut dishwater blonde hair that went in all directions, usually dressed in black polyester pants that scuffed the floor, a light blue dress shirt that never stayed tucked in, and a navy blue jacket whose pockets bulged with notes. Cochran knew Jennifer didn't look like the person who could get a paper bag convicted. She earned an excellent reputation working in the state D.A. office, grew tired of the big city life, the state politics, and moved back to her childhood home in Marshall when the chance opened for her in Summerville County. Cochran knew she and her husband, a home-based writer, were raising three young boys while Jennifer's sister was in the armed services.

"First, I need to update you before the rumors start..."

"Rumors about you or me, Fred?" Jennifer pointed to a second cup of carryout coffee waiting for him.

"Me, of course. There's no rumors about you. I'm hoping that on Tuesday morning, I will be the county detective and Kevin will be the acting Sheriff till he can get elected next year."

Jennifer pulled her perpetually smudged glasses off and wiped them with the tail of her shirt. "Really? You stepping back? You got a cardiologist following you around to treat people when they find out?"

Cochran laughed. "Nope. It will shock some, but it's time. Before you get all nosy and ask why, I'll tell you this much, the official reason. I love detective work, always have, but I've done enough as the Sheriff. I ain't got that many tricks left in my bag, so it's time someone else stepped in. Besides, Kevin is younger, has a bachelor degree and we need to keep all the experience he's gained here in this county, not export it somewhere else."

"Wonderful." Jennifer eyed him carefully, the look he'd seen testifying in court, either at him as a witness or at the perpetrator. "Now, what did you mean by official reason? What's the unofficial? C'mon, spit it out."

He wiggled around on the chair like he was guilty of something and she was grilling him. "I—I decided it's time I had some personal life." He didn't know what else to say. He wasn't even sure himself what that meant.

"About time," she replied, smiling warmly. "I hope that includes meeting someone special, you deserve it."

Cochran felt his cheeks grow warm and his head get dizzy. This was all so new to him. How could he control it? He shook his head to clear it. He couldn't look at Jennifer.

Jennifer broke into laughter. "You have, haven't you?"

His mouth opened and closed like a fish flopping on the wooden pier at his pond. He shook his head, tried to speak, but nothing came out. He lifted his cup to his mouth, glad the coffee was lukewarm, ready to take a sip.

"Oh, my God, Cochran, you're guilty as hell. I got you nailed to the wall." She laughed harder. "I won't press my case. You can spill the beans when you're ready. I just hope he's cute."

At that, Cochran inhaled, choked, turned his head and spewed coffee across the chair next to him as Jennifer roared.

When he quit choking and sputtering, she tossed a box of tissues across the desk. "Wipe that up, get your eyes, too. I'm not saying another word till you're ready. I'm glad you might have figured yourself out. Now, do you have a business reason to be here?"

Cochran gathered his wits and slid his notes across the desk to her. "These are just my rough notes. I want them back. I'm just picking your brain, seeing what you think about me pursuing this further. I plan to talk with Kevin next week, once he's officially the acting sheriff."

Jennifer skimmed the page. "What's your gut telling you?"

"There's not much we can do about Shaw, the man's going to die within the week. He's admitted to winging his son and threatening to kill Connie. Even stated his reasoning. Connie doesn't deny the affair, but claims she always thought the boy was Shaw's. She was shocked to find he had a vasectomy."

Jennifer looked at him and sipped her coffee.

"Plus, add in it appears likely that Shaw was operating under two names, these other deaths, the holding company, and things seem awfully odd, maybe more than a coincidence. Taken individually, they're not too alarming. Taken as a whole, they raise a lot of questions. At least in my mind. What about yours?"

Jennifer handed the sheet back to him. "Off the record, I agree. I don't see enough probable cause to seek a warrant yet, but you might be close. I recommend you keep digging. Nose around, show Kevin soon, today, if possible. Make sure you're documenting everything, then you both come back to me. We can then decide about calling a grand jury together. I won't say a word about this to anyone, you shouldn't either. Other than to your side-kick, Irene. That woman can keep more secrets than a dirty big-city cop." She stood up, came around her desk and chucked him on the shoulder. "Another thing, Detective. I think I'd hit the property and tax office upstairs, check things out, ask a few questions, especially about that holding company."

Cochran saluted her and left, a smile on his face.

Chapter Twenty-Four

Connie

Wednesday morning

At five a.m., Connie poured herself a cup of coffee. She was still full from last night's pizza, didn't want breakfast, but needed caffeine. Gayle wandered in from the family room, poured herself a cup and sat down. "Mom, I couldn't sleep and came down here about three-thirty so I wouldn't wake Emma with my tossing and turning. About four, I saw lights and a pickup pull by the office and park in shed three. I'm pretty sure it was Melvin. Who else could it be?"

Connie felt a shiver run through her. "I know he comes in early sometimes. He mentioned the other day he's got a lot of paperwork to keep up on now that Dad's..."

"Dad's incapacitated? I know, Mom. What words do we use till we get comfortable saying Dad died or when Dad was alive? He's dying, maybe today. How do we adjust? This living in limbo sucks." She looked up at her mother. "Just why the hell does he want to die? Us kids would still love each of you if you weren't together. This has to be about more than Junior not being his son. I don't get it."

Connie set her cup back down and pulled Gayle into a hug. "You have been so helpful, I'm not sure what we would do without you here, explaining and guiding..."

"But he's still my father. He's your husband. Then he went crazy." Gayle swiped at her eyes. "Guess I'm still dealing with denial.

Think the corn bag will help with that?"

Both chuckled through their moist eyes.

It was five-ten. Connie glanced through the window at the lights in the farm office. Pulling back from Gayle, she said, "Will you think I'm rude if I go out to the office now? Something keeps telling me to make my presence known earlier today."

"Mom, you're juggling so much. Can't the farm stuff wait till Dad is settled?"

"Logically, yes, but I need to learn more about this place. Much more." Connie pulled her briefcase from the mudroom closet.

"Wow. A briefcase to go across the driveway to a farm office? Aren't you overdoing it a bit?" Gayle laughed.

Connie shook the case so Gayle could hear the keys rattling. "I need something to carry all these keys. I'll be back shortly."

At the farm office door, she paused before quietly opening it. She poked her head in, expecting to see Melvin sitting in his usual chair, drinking coffee. He wasn't there. The door to the back office was closed. She could hear sounds and light grunts from someone. Next, a sound like someone slapped the wall or a door. She tiptoed across the room. Butterflies, more like bats, beat in her stomach. She decided to listen for several minutes. She hoped it was Melvin in there, but why the weird noises? More grunts, heavy sighs, an occasional slap. Why did he close the door? It was frequently left open.

She softly grasped the knob. It was locked. She set the briefcase down and reached into her pocket for Shaw's master ring that she pulled from his jeans the hospital had sent home. It held five keys. One for each of the four out-buildings, plus what? Thankfully, each had a number stamped into it. Number one had to be for this building. Two, the big shed and shop, three and four were for the smaller sheds, and One-A? Maybe this was for the back office.

The key slipped in quietly and she turned the handle. Taking a big breath, she swung the door wide. Melvin was kneeling before the old safe, spinning the dial, his face close to it. Sweat seeped down his face, his glasses were smudgy, his nose runny. As she stepped into the room, he startled, struggled to get to his feet, but fell against the safe and the file cabinet next to it. His legs sprawled awkwardly in front of him, his eyes darted with fury. Connie almost stepped back and closed the door to run. Instead, she decided to go on the offensive and stepped closer. She used her super angry mom voice. "What the hell are you doing? Why is this door locked with you inside the room? How long have you been trying to open that safe and what in tarnation do you expect to find in it? Gold?"

He scrambled to a stand. "I—I was just tryin' to open this old safe." He wiped the sweat off his forehead, looked at the floor as if he needed to think how to reply. "It's always somethin' Shaw and I messed with when we had the time. Just kind of a pastime. A challenge, ya know."

Connie looked around the room, noticed a tiny screwdriver stuck in one of the cabinet locks she knew she had the key to. She pointed toward the cabinet. "What's going on there?"

"God dammit," he yelled. "How the hell can I get my work done when you stole the friggin' keys? I was trying to get some papers I needed out of there."

"What's the reason you couldn't ask me for them?"

She thought quickly. She hadn't time to go through the cabinets yet, but yesterday, she opened this one and glanced in it. The top drawer contained files with Farm Holding Company records. She never heard of Farm Holding Company until that moment. She hadn't the time to explore further, so she closed the drawer and relocked the cabinet.

She held her hand up to him. "Don't move." Connie stepped into the doorway and picked up her briefcase. Opening it, she pulled out the keys and walked over to the cabinet. She glanced at Melvin. If his looks could kill, she'd be dead meat.

Her second try unlocked the cabinet. "Now if you tell me which file you want, I'll be glad to find it for you and you can show me what information you need and tell me the reason why." She glared at him. "I'm waiting. I'll be glad to help you."

He lowered his eyes, took a big sigh and forced his face into a pathetic smile. "Sorry. I can't quite adjust to losin' Shaw and getting' used to you bein' around. I'll come back, work on stuff later. Just leave it unlocked."

He turned for the doorway, but Connie stepped in front of him. "Melvin, I'm not leaving it unlocked, nor are you going into those files without me present. Now, can we sit down and you tell me why they are so important? Why they always remained locked? And why you've been in here since four this morning, trying to get into that cabinet and the safe?"

His face grew red, his eyes big and dark behind his thick glasses. She thought he might have a stroke. He stomped his foot and clenched his fists. "I don't report to you. I'm a partner and you don't know shit about these operations. Now step back and let me get to work." He stormed around her and out the door.

A minute later, as she tried to settle her nerves, she heard his truck tear by the office and watched it go down the Milliken drive.

She sat down at her desk, breathing heavily. Who was this man? What did he mean by partner? Who was Farm Holding Company? Why had Shaw never mentioned it? What in god's name was in the safe and files worth spending over an hour trying to open? She turned on her computer and looked up locksmiths. She emailed several about her needs, not expecting a reply until eight or after. One out of Worthington called her back in twenty minutes. Ben was very understanding, gave her some good suggestions, said he was an early riser and promised they would be out between nine and ten. Next, she texted her kids and Jens. *I'm not leaving office. Bring me coffee, food and moral support.*

Jens and five of her kids flew into the office. None of them carried anything to consume, except Ellen who struggled behind with the coffee pot and pizza box. "Junior's still sleeping. Cold pizza will have to do. Can you explain why you've moved to the office and need moral support to write checks at six in the morning?" She tried to laugh as she shakily poured her mother a cup of coffee.

Connie sipped the coffee. "Thank you. I didn't think my text would wake all of you up. Guess you're early risers, too. A locksmith is coming between nine and ten. Hopefully, I can move back to the house after they leave." She tried to smile. "I'm having electronic locks, the ones you punch in a code, put on the house, the four outbuildings and the back office. I'll choose several codes for others to use on the four buildings, but not the office, back room or the house. I'll have the master." She took in a big breath.

"Mom," Mary exclaimed. "What the hell are you talking about? Start from the beginning."

Connie took a sip of coffee and looked around the room. She pointed to the sleeve of coffee cups next to the office pot. "Why doesn't one of you start that pot? The rest of you find a chair or get comfortable on that old couch or the table." She told them about her first meeting with Melvin, went on about the keys and noticing the Farm Holding Company records she knew nothing of. She expressed her shock at finding Melvin at the safe this morning, his attempts at getting into the file cabinet, his surprise and his words that he was a partner. She stopped talking and waited for comments from her stunned kids.

"Partner? What's he mean by that?" Gayle shook her head. "Are he and Dad partners in another business?"

"Maybe they used it when they lease farms?" Emma looked around the room.

Mary climbed down from the table she was sitting on. "There's only one way to find out. Let's check out the files."

Everyone, except Ellen and Connie, jumped to their feet in excitement and curiosity. Ellen spoke above the commotion. "Wait a minute. I got a gut feeling about this. Something's not right. Do we really want our fingerprints all over those files? Are we sure it's a legit business? Doesn't it seem odd that Dad had another business that none of us, including Mom, knew about? What if we mess up stuff that might be needed later?"

Connie stood. "I agree, Ellen." She glanced at the clock. "Why don't Ellen and Jens stay with me to do some exploring? There's a box of first aid gloves with the big kit in that closet we can wear. The rest of you go back to bed, or clean the house." She looked at Gayle for confirmation.

"I'll call the hospital in an hour for an update. No one thinks Dad will make it through Sunday. So, I suggest we tentatively plan for a Monday service. We can always move it back. Some of us need to get back to our homes next week, so we could begin making tentative travel plans for the middle of the week." Gayle pulled her siblings into a hug with their mother. "This is so crazy. Mom, if there's any way to put some of this farm stuff off till after Dad is gone, I would."

"I know, but I have this deep sense we're going to learn more about your dad and somehow Melvin's in the middle of it. I don't trust him. I can't."

Gayle led her troops to the house as Connie, Ellen and Jens donned gloves. "I think we should first start with the cabinet Melvin was trying to get into," Connie said, retrieving the keys from her briefcase.

She again unlocked the cabinet and slowly pulled the top drawer open. It took them several minutes to figure out the system.

"Each file is for a different property," Jens said. "Look, here's the property Melvin lives on. Here's one near Marshall..." He kept pulling up the successive files so they could read the addresses. He returned to the front of the drawer and opened the first file. It contained all the records regarding obtaining the property, price paid based upon payments, title and who the property was leased out to for farming.

"My god. What does this mean? There has to be sixty or seventy files with properties in Minnesota, South Dakota and Iowa." Connie stepped back and thought a moment. "Let's see what's in each of these lower drawers, then check the other cabinets."

The second drawer held another file folder for each property that included 2011 bills, expenses and receipts for income, land rental, and crop sales or percentages going to FHC. The third and fourth drawers held 2010 and 2009 records. The next three cabinets went back another twelve years to 1997.

Connie opened the last cabinet with trepidation. Talking with Jens and Ellen, she realized there had to be incorporation records for FHC someplace. At least a file with information on where to find the lawyer or bank vault where they were stored. Just as she pulled the top drawer open, the office phone rang. She hustled to answer it.

"Is this Connie?" The voice sounded cautious, but familiar, not someone she readily recognized.

"Yes, this is Connie Skogman. Who's calling?"

"This is Ben, from Worthington Security. I just need to check something out." His voice sounded hesitant.

"Yes, go on."

"You're the person in charge there, right?"

"Yes, as I told you, my husband Shaw is dying, he's in a coma. I'm in charge now." She felt a lead sinker slowly slip down her throat.

"This is weird. I'm sorry to bother you, but Melvin Smith just called and ordered me to come change locks on everything but your house."

The lead sinker hit her gut. She cleared her throat fighting to stay calm. "That is odd. What did you tell him?"

There was a long pause. "Well, I thought about it and how strange he sounded. I told him I wasn't free till tomorrow afternoon. He said he wasn't sure if he could wait that long, but to plan on it and if he found someone else, he'd let me know." She could hear him take a deep breath. "That guy is so weird. Anyway, I doubt he can find someone else who do what we do. Listen, we got an early start and will be there in twenty minutes. Take care."

Connie sank into her office chair. Jens and Ellen came into the room. "We heard your end, but what was that all about?" Ellen refilled Connie's coffee.

"Melvin Smith ordered the same security company to change the office and shop locks. The guy, Ben, told him he was booked and couldn't do it till tomorrow. Melvin said he might try to find someone else." She put her hands over her face and fought for composure.

"He did what?" Ellen. "Who does he think he is?"

Jens said, "A partner..."

Connie broke in. "You know, it's bad enough Shaw is dying in this manner, but why is there so much strange stuff going on that I knew nothing about?" She sat in silence as Jens and Ellen patted her shoulders. Straightening herself, she sipped her coffee, wiped her eyes and stood. "No time for self-pity. I just have to learn what I don't know. Did you find out anything else?"

Jens held up a file. "This is a copy of a Farm Holding brochure. It says to call Phillip Smith. It's a pretty old file of miscellaneous things." He shuffled through the papers. "Hey, you need to see this. This looks like an old copy of a Doing Business As Form registered with the state. Melvin Smith is listed as a partner with Shaw Philip Skogman who is Doing Business As Shaw S Phillip in the Farm Holding Company."

"Oh my god. Does that mean my husband had a second name? It sounds like he rearranged his name. So, that's why Melvin thinks he's in charge." She glanced at the page Jens showed her. "He added an L to Philip. That has to be him. Who else would go into business with Melvin with a name like that? It has to be Shaw trying to hide his real name. Doing Business As...Why is he trying to hide his true identity? Who the heck is Phillip Smith?" She let go of the paper. "I'll bet it's a combination so no one knows who it is. Now, go back and check the first cabinet, top drawer, and see if our farm is one of those files."

Jens returned with a file. "I need to do more digging, but it appears on the map that's included in each file, that this half-section we're sitting on is not part of Farm Holding, but the other half and the full section to the west might be. I—I found a file for my dad's property, too." He stopped talking as they heard the sound of a vehicle driving in.

"Quick," Connie said, "lock up everything and put the keys back in my briefcase, then run the briefcase to the house. Hurry."

Jens was back in time to meet Connie and Ellen outside as a service truck with a small cherry-picker lift, ladders on the top and metal panel doors on the sides pulled by the office, turned and parked behind Shed One. The sign said Worthington Security.

Connie breathed a sigh of relief. She wasn't sure why. She knew more surprises were coming. Maybe changing the locks gave her a small sense of strength, of control. She put aside the idea of trying to figure out the holding company for the moment. She and Jens walked around the building to meet them.

"Hi, I'm Ben, this is Lou and Lyle, my sons. My wife stuttered when the doc told her she delivered twins."

Connie immediately felt at ease with him. He appeared to be in his late fifties, her age, with a shaved bald head, tightly trimmed graying mustache, goatee, and twinkling blue eyes.

Connie thought the twins were about thirty and resembled their dad, except with hair and much leaner, as they quickly began unlocking panel doors, pulling out tool kits and boxes of new locks. Ben explained how the locks worked and told her to think up a six-digit master code that only she would know. "Don't make it easy. Make it something only you would know. If it's someone's birthday or anniversary, change or reverse at least one of the numbers. Anyone who knows you can usually figure out who your childhood friends were or ex-boyfriends." Ben started to laugh, then his face changed to horror. "Oh, I'm so sorry. I need to drive out and come in again. Please forgive me, that was so thoughtless."

"It's okay. You took me back a second, but right now, a bit of levity helps." She hoped her cheeks didn't look as hot as they felt. Hans' birthdate was on her mind. "Let me show you where we will need the new locks, and then I have several other questions about security." Connie turned, but noticed Ben's twins were already crossing the drive toward shed three.

Ben held two locks in his hands. "These are for your office and one-A. Two is the big shed and shop, Shed One, which the office is attached to and three and four are across the drive by the bins. We also brought new vehicle openers and will reprogram the big shed doors. After that, we'll install the locks on your house." He looked at the confusion she felt on her face. "You realize we have been here before, don't you?"

She shook her head.

"You and me need to sit down and talk a bit. Hopefully, you have some coffee." Ben started for the office door.

Connie paused. "Ellen, please go tell Junior to come out here. He needs to be in on this and understand the system."

"Good move, Mom. It won't do any of us any good when we're

all so far away." Ellen looked at Jens. "You stay too, Jens. Won't hurt."

Junior trotted out of the house, looking all excited. "Wow. New locks with codes. Cool." His face sobered as he looked at his mother.

She knew she looked like she was in shock. She was.

The four sat down in the office. Ben opened the conversation. "You look surprised, like you didn't know we have been providing you electronic surveillance, computer support and security services for nearly thirty years."

Connie swallowed. "I didn't. When did you start?"

Ben scratched his head. "Sometime about 1983. Shaw said you were pregnant and he wanted better security, plus he wanted to get in on the whole computer and technology movement that was taking off." He waited till she looked at him again. "I think the reason we never met was because he always said you were doing something with the kids. Sounds like you had a bunch of girls. Who's this guy?" He pointed at Junior.

"I'm Shaw Philips Skogman, Junior. They call me Junior. I was born in May, 1993."

"He never mentioned you."

Connie thought Ben must have noticed the surprised looks on her, Junior's and Jens' faces, because he quickly added, "Not that he would have. Shaw didn't talk much about personal stuff and it's not like we were out here more than once a year. Most things, we handled through the computers. In fact, Shaw always asked us to park behind Shed One, so you probably wouldn't have known we were here anyway."

Junior shook his head, a look of confusion on his face. "Mom, didn't you pay their bills? Why didn't you recognize the name?"

"All our bills have been paid by Farm Holding Company. Their office is in Worthington, but sometimes the payment envelopes were stamped from the Summerville post office." Ben looked at Connie. "That's why it took me a minute to realize we were talking about the same place. We never truly worked for Skogman Farms, just knew it was run by the same men." He stood up. "I sure am sorry about Shaw. Hard guy to know, but a fair businessman, always paid within ten days. He or Melvin called us right away if there were problems. They didn't try to fix things themselves like most places. Speaking of Melvin, that little man is strange. I liked doing business with Shaw best."

Jens looked at Connie. "Ben, can you start at the top here? Assume we know nothing about what Shaw installed and explain it to us."

"Sounds like a plan. First, though, Connie, I need you to take a few minutes to punch in your master code. Don't write it down for me. You're going to walk around with me and punch it in each lock. Next, you decide several additional five-digit codes for family, Melvin and so forth. Shouldn't take more than ten minutes. Just be consistent."

Connie turned to the two locks sitting next to Ben. He showed her how. She already decided the code. Seven-zero-three-one-five-seven. It was a date she mulled over in the back of her mind since Ben told her to come up with something. It was a variation of the date Alice died. *It popped into my mind and somehow seems significant,* she thought.

When she and Ben came back from coding the ten locks, including the house, Ben walked over to the bulletin board mounted on the adjoining wall the office shared with Shed One. He ran his right hand down the right side of the frame, pausing two-thirds of the way while his left felt along the bottom frame toward the right corner. "Come over here. Junior first. Put your fingers below mine, now slide them down. At the same time, slide your left fingers toward the corner. Feel anything?"

Junior's eyes got large. "Yes." He backed away so his mother could feel the hidden switches.

"Okay, Connie. Now squeeze those switches hard at the same time."

She did and shrieked as the three by five-foot combination cork and white erase board swung open to the left. A monitor stared at her with a plethora of wires that ran to several electronic boxes with blinking lights.

"That looks like a jacked computer and separate hard drives," gasped Junior

Ben smiled and picked up a remote. He clicked it and four live scenes filled the monitor. One was a video feed of the back and side of their home; one of the bins and sheds three and four, one of the garage and one of the entry to the office and big door of Shed One.

Connie sat down and put her head in her hands. Through her fingers, she whispered, "And this has been going on since…?"

"The one aimed at the house?" Ben rubbed his bare head. "Since about December 1992. It was after Thanksgiving and before Christmas. I remember it because Shaw was in a panic to get it in."

"That bastard. That dirty bastard." Connie raised her head to look at Jens who nodded as if he too understood the significance.

Junior took a bit longer. "That must have been right after you told Dad you were pregnant with me…" He stopped talking at the warning look on his mother's face. "I don't believe it. Almost eighteen years, he's been waiting?"

Connie glanced at Ben. He looked confused. Should she fill him in? She realized Ben provided services for other things to the farm, but did he know it included spying on the client's wife? Did he realize that? Weakly, she said, "I guess he wanted to make sure we were safe."

Ben stepped over to the coffee pot and refilled his cup. "Yup. That's what I thought it was all about. He never said there was any other reason. He paused as he studied his coffee. "He probably wouldn't have. He always seemed to know exactly what he wanted." He took a sip of his coffee, grimaced, and added creamer and sugar. "I forgot how strong you guys make this stuff. You wanna know where the cameras are hidden?"

Reluctantly, Connie stood and followed Ben outside, along with Jens and Junior.

Ben pointed to the large roof of Shed One. The office was attached to Shed One like a lean-too. "See that cupola up there? One camera covers your house and the 127th Street drive, the second one, the garage and the McMillan driveway, the third one is for sheds two and three and the bins across the drive, and the fourth camera is located in that bin and covers shed four, the fuel station and those older bins."

Connie scratched her head. "I had no idea there were video cameras up there. The next question I have, is there a hard drive? How long does it save things? How far back does it go?"

"Good questions." Ben led them back into the office and explained the hard drives, the size of the computer to manage the entire system and the fact that it was one of the most powerful in the area. He rubbed the top of his head again. "Guess as long as I've explained this much, I might as well tell you the rest of what this system does."

Connie groaned, refreshed her coffee and sat down. "There's more?"

Lou and Lyle stepped inside to speak to their father. One of them, Connie wasn't sure which one, looked at Junior. "Hey, aren't you the kid that did so well in the Twin Cities Marathon last fall?" Junior smiled. "Yah, I thought so. We were in it too, but we were in the middle of the pack, not almost leading it, like you were. Congratulations."

Connie watched Junior blush as he said, "I wasn't almost leading it. I was still over three minutes behind the winner, almost four."

Lou and Lyle laughed. "Yup, three to four minutes. That's pretty bad. Now, let me see, I think that was still eight to ten minutes before us." They shook their heads as they turned back to Ben and asked their questions.

Ben watched them leave, then turned and looked at Connie. She could sense his pride in his boys and thought he recognized hers in Junior. Without thinking, she softly said, "Run, Forrest, run." Ben gave her the thumbs up.

Ben pointed toward the door. "The boys are going to start on the house locks now. Do you mind if they double check your computer system over there? We never did anything with it. Shaw said he'd plug it into the T- one line we ran to the house that's tied into the office computer."

"Go ahead. Who knows what they'll find?" Connie waved her hand. She was tired and needed to be thinking about her husband's memorial service, not this stuff, but she felt glad over the connection with Ben with their sons being distance runners.

"It's slow," Junior said. "I can tell you that much. If I need to do something for school, I'll come out here because the office computer is so much faster." He peered again at the hidden set-up. "Can you change the view of the cameras from here or do you have to climb up to the cupola?" He picked up another remote. "I bet this does it, right?" He touched a button and a video of another farm flickered on. "What the heck? Where's this at?"

Ben checked the letters on the frame of the video. "That's another farm, I think. If you give me a minute at the computer, I can show you all the other places under surveillance."

"My God. When will this end? Why would he need to watch other farms?" Connie started to stand, but sat down as the intercom buzzed. She noticed their private home line button was lit up. "Yes." She listened and turned to Jens and Junior. "That was Gayle. There's some confusion at the hospital."

Ben gave a slight bow and stepped outside.

Connie punched the speaker button. "This is Connie. How can I help you?"

"Connie, this is Abe Jordan. I'm so sorry to bother you, but Melvin Smith is here, insisting that because he has power of attorney, he can make funeral arrangements for after your husband dies. He's trying to line up a funeral home to embalm him and hold services. Is that accurate? He claims the recent change in power of attorney provided by your husband gave him full authority to make final plans. I read the document and don't agree, but he's insistent."

"God damn that man." Connie slumped back in the chair, fighting tears as she twisted her hair between her fingers. "Abe, I have no idea what was changed. Give me your number and I'll call you back as soon as I talk with Jack Walker, the attorney. He should know." She hung up. Junior tried to hug her. "Don't touch me. Just stay by me till this is over, then you can hug me." She pulled out her cell phone and pushed call on one of her contacts. "Jack, this is Connie. Melvin Smith is at the hospital, trying to make funeral arrangements. Shaw's not even dead yet and the family is already making other plans. What gives?" She laid her phone on the desk and pushed speaker so Jens and Junior could hear.

"I warned Shaw Melvin shouldn't be given medical power of attorney. No. Absolutely not. That power of attorney is only if Shaw is incapacitated and unable to make decisions for his care. It ends when Shaw dies. I'll call the hospital and tell them Melvin has no say. I'm so sorry for this confusion."

"Jack, we're all confused. Thank you." She reached for the phone to punch it off, but didn't. "Jack, is there anything you can do to keep Melvin away from here, off the property, till I have time to figure this place out?"

They could hear Jack clear his throat. "You're talking about the farm right there. Your house, the office, the sheds and bins. Right?"

"That would be a start. Jack, you and I are going to have to have a long talk soon. Now can you keep him away from here till after we get Shaw in the ground or whatever we do with him?"

"I can try. I'll tell the Sheriff to warn him. If that doesn't work, we'll get an order of protection issued. Has he harassed you?"

"Damn near. Thank you."

"Connie, I know you're going through a lot. I'll be in touch." The phone connection clicked off.

Connie stood and let Junior and Jens envelop her as she sobbed. "What is Melvin trying to do?" She shook the men off of her. "Can you two stay and deal with Ben? I've learned enough to keep my head spinning. I need to go clear it, do laundry or something. The man's not even dead yet and Melvin wants a bloody funeral for him." She straightened her shoulders and marched for the door. "Damn that man." Outdoors, as she walked by Ben, she ordered, "Ben, I appreciate your help today, Jens and Junior will carry on with you. Listen, I want the camera on the house stopped immediately. Show the guys how to do that, please." She didn't wait for Ben's response.

She slammed the back door and stormed into the kitchen.

"Mom," Emma said, "We have a question about—"

Connie slapped her hand on the counter. "Deal with it. Ask your sisters. If it's about the memorial service, I don't give a damn. Call Melvin, let him plan the whole freaking ceremony…"

"Mom, what's wrong?" Jane moved toward her as if to give her a hug.

"Don't, 'but Mom' me. Don't ask me, 'what's wrong?'. What's right is the question. Nothing is. This is like those Russian dolls. There's always one more. Two men around me for thirty-five years... Living double lives...Shaw, damn him...Shaw... Just let the dead bury the dead. Okay?"

The girls stared at her as she poured herself a glass of water. She drained it and wiped her lips with the back of her hand. "I'm going to take a nap. If anyone dares to disturb me, they better be prepared to roast alongside their father."

She gently set the glass on the counter, turned, gave a brilliant smile, waved like a queen and walked toward the stairs.

Forty-five minutes later, she was back in the kitchen. "All right, girls, you can start 'but momming' me again."

"But Mom, can we still play with these?" Emma handed her a Russian doll.

Chapter Twenty-Five

Jens

Ben reentered the office and showed Jens and Junior how to easily turn off and on each of the cameras and how to play the video back from the hard drive or watch it live in the office. He spent the next two hours, explaining the complexities of the system. He checked further into the system for several minutes as they watched him.

"Guys, I knew nothing about the purpose of these live feeds surveilling other farms. I told them they have that capability and showed them how they might set cameras up to do so, but they never told me their reasons. I assumed it was for security purposes. I know they store seed and fertilizer in several remote places, at least that's what they told me."

Junior put his hand up to stop Ben. "Okay, but did they handle all that stuff from this computer? The one here in the office? Mom and I don't spend a lot of time over here, but there's never a problem when we just pop in. Plus, I used the computer quite a bit to research school projects and print stuff off. I never saw these feeds on the computer."

Ben smiled. "Two things. One, you and your mother could only log in through one entry point. Your father and Melvin had another password and site to log in through. Second, didn't your dad usually have a laptop in his truck? Melvin has one also."

"Dad did," Junior exclaimed. "He never let me use it and he locked it in the office every night. So, that means he could check on anything from wherever he was. I bet he had a cellular connection for it

149

too." He began pacing around the office. "I was rarely in Melvin's truck, so I have no idea if he had a laptop or not. Listen, is there a way to figure out the address or location of those farms being watched?"

Ben said yes and pulled up the feeds on the desk monitor. "Yes, see, here's the GPS location." His fingers flew over the keyboard. "Here's an address. Want more?"

"Yes," Jens said. "Junior, run back to the house and get that briefcase with the keys."

Ben wrote out several of the addresses.

When Junior returned, Jens opened the file cabinet, the first one they looked at earlier. He pulled open the top drawer and began flicking through the files. Shaking his head, he said, "None of these file addresses match the farms being videoed. What gives?" He checked back through them.

Ben shuffled around. "I know nothing about these files, or why places were being watched. I thought everything was for security." His phone rang some jazz tune. Ben pulled it out of its holster. "Hello? Yes, Melvin. Okay, I'll see you tomorrow. What?" He walked into the main office. "Melvin, I'm on a call right now. I'll hurry back to my office and check that out and get it corrected as soon as possible. Yes, I'll see you tomorrow." He turned to Jens and Junior. "What the hell do I have myself in the middle of? Connie knows nothing about the holding company or the security system. Melvin said he just received a text that the camera on the house is not working and he wants it fixed ASAP."

Junior's eyes got big. "That means he hasn't checked the hard drive on his laptop. Quick, can you do something so he can't log into them? He doesn't know you're here. Mom told the lawyer to keep him away from here. The man is dangerous."

Ben rubbed his head. "Technically, as far as I understand, Melvin is a partner in the holding company and has say over those operations…"

"Technically," Junior yelled. "Technically, my dad shot me. Technically, it was birdshot in my ass. Technically, he tried to shoot my mother with a slug and admitted he wanted to kill her. Technically, Melvin's hiding all kinds of things from us, like the holding company."

He stomped over to Ben, leaned over and stared him in the eyes. "Now, technically, are you going to help us or not? If not, get your ass out of here and Jens and I will tear this system apart with our bare hands and run it through the corn auger."

Ben stepped back. "Junior, I'm in the middle here, but there are two parts of this system. One is for the Skogman Farm whose owner hired me today. The other relates to the holding company. So, here's what I think is the best solution." He paused and looked at Jens and Junior with a look that acknowledged they were watching him like a lion inspecting its prey. "I'm going to make sure the high-speed internet to the house is connected and set your home computers up to it. I'll send the video security feeds monitoring your house and the buildings only to your house, so you can see what's going on. We'll set up a small hard drive in the house." He walked around the room, ticking things off on his fingers. "I'll text Melvin that I can't fix the feeds to him today and will deal with it tomorrow. Even then, I won't send them to his laptop. I'll also install WIFI in the house so you can use your phones and laptop, that way you'll have more flexibility." He reached for Junior's hand to shake. "Technically, I can do all that." He winked as Junior slowly gave him his hand.

Jens half-smiled. "What's that leave Melvin? We have no idea if Shaw's death leaves him the entire holding company or not."

Ben smiled. "This way, Melvin can still survey those other properties. The issue is, the holding company records are here." He scratched his head and thought a moment. "You know, if I was you, I'd make damn sure he wasn't allowed on this property until this is straightened out."

"I agree," Jens replied. "Listen, before you leave, review with Junior and me how to readjust those cameras. I want more coverage of both driveways, if possible."

"We'll add a wireless camera to the front of the house. Junior will have the remotes to re-aim all the cameras. Now, we got a lot to do. After things settle down with Melvin, I'll come back. Judas Priest, what a mess."

Jens and Junior played with the equipment, practicing how to maneuver the cameras, re-watch past recordings, the hard drive data went back for three months. For a few minutes, they tried to look at the other properties, but realized Ben adjusted the settings so they couldn't. He told them they could only watch the Skogman Farm images, not the holding company ones until it was clear the family also had ownership in that business. Junior and Jens went into the house so Ben and the twins could orient everyone on how to log into the WIFI and hook up their laptops and phones to the now fast feed.

After Ben and the twins left, Jens wondered what to do with himself. He told Connie he was going back to the office to make sure everything was locked and closed up. She hugged him. "I'm so glad you stayed. You've been so helpful. I still need you, just to know you're here."

"I'm not moving on for a while. Not till I know everything is over with Shaw and stable with you. Right now, I may run back to Dad's farm to get some more clothes. By this time of the week, I planned to be far enough south to where I didn't need long pants and sleeves and heavy socks. I didn't pack much of those, just summer clothes I hoped to wear almost permanently. Besides, I need a suit or something dressier than muddy jeans and a flannel shirt for the memorial service, whenever it is."

"Don't bother with a suit. Wear what you want. You're not conducting the service." She wiped her eyes. "We're fine in here. The girls are doing a great job, getting everything planned. We found an undertaker who will pick up Shaw and cremate him when the time comes. The hospital staff are surprised he's still hanging on."

"What about Melvin?"

"Jack, our lawyer, just called. He said Melvin has been warned to stay away from the farm and he agreed not to deal with funeral arrangements." She wiped her hand across her forehead. "I don't have time to think about him or anything else, other than my husband's dying and planning to get him off to wherever he's going. Now, go, get out of here for several hours, if you need. Thanks for checking on the office. Beany just arrived, so I figure Junior will keep him involved for a while.

If not, the girls will. They've already asked him to make fried egg sandwiches for dinner." She smiled and gave him a gentle shove toward the door.

~ * ~

Jens double-checked the office, made sure the back office was locked, even played with the lock-code a few times. It only worked for the code Connie gave the family members. The window alarm system was armed. He shook his head as he glanced at the bulletin board, amazed at the system and the secrecy Shaw developed. He didn't blame Connie for not knowing about it. It was obvious Shaw and Melvin had a second life. He wished he knew more about it. He turned off the coffee maker, decided to finish the last half cup while it was still warm, and sat down at the desk.

Seeing his family farm in the Farm Holding Company files surprised him, but after a moment, it didn't shock him. He never expected to inherit it. Days before his father went into a coma, the old man told him a holding company owned it and made payments to him for years. That was how the old man managed to stay in the home. "They kept the taxes and insurance up, gave me enough each month to live on and pay my medical bills. They own the farm outright when I die. Kinda like them reverse mortgage things."

Jens sighed aloud, Shaw and Melvin now owned his family farm. He shook his head, unsure whether to be angry, thankful or just perplexed. He settled on being perplexed. Something about this whole thing seemed wrong, but he couldn't put his finger on it. If Shaw and Melvin owned it or held the deed on it, why didn't his dad say something, tell him it was them? Did his dad know who the holding company was? He decided to dig around and see if he could find any other paperwork at their old farmhouse when he picked up some clothes. He turned out the lights, double-checked the new lock and left for the twenty-minute drive to his childhood home. The one he never wanted to return to.

At the driveway, he was surprised to see security posts installed on each side of the driveway. A heavy chain lay across the ground. In the ragged circle drive sat a large dump truck, towing a heavy-duty front-end loader with a back hoe. He parked behind the trailer, close enough so the driver would have to move the truck in order to unload.

"Can I help you? Sorry, just had to take a leak." A short stocky man in bib coveralls stepped from in front of the truck, buttoning his fly

"This was my dad's place. I stopped by to pick up a few clothes and look for some papers." He stuck his hand out. "I'm Jens Hanson. This is the old family farm. My dad died last weekend. I'm hanging around with some friends till I leave town. What are you doing here?"

The man shot a wad of tobacco juice toward the ground. "We got a contract to demolish the old place. Tear it down, haul it away, dig out the foundations, level the basement, clear the trees and brush. Guess it's gonna be more corn and soybeans."

"Who ordered the demolition? Seems awful quick."

The man laughed. "It's always fast with this outfit. Someone dies, if it wasn't theirs, it becomes theirs." He spat again. "Farm Holding Company. I do most of their demo work. Go all over the area. Couldn't tell you how many I done, but it's a lot."

"Who do you work with? Who's your contact?"

"Some guy, a Phillip Smith. Says he's a partner. Can't say as I ever met him face to face. Things are over the computer and phone and ten days later, bingo, a check is in my mail." He shifted uncomfortably around on his feet. "Listen, how much time you need in there? You know if the bathroom is operational? Course, don't matter if it ain't, does it. Go on in while I take a dump, then I'll shut the water off at the well. The well stays. Just be gone before I need to get my rig off the trailer. Course, there's more than one way I can do that too." He laughed.

This is weird, thought Jens, as he opened the sagging screen door. Nothing changed since he left. The fact the house was going to be torn down didn't bother him. He even considered torching the place when he left last Saturday, but figured someone would figure out who and he didn't want the hassle. He found an old suitcase in the hall closet and pulled some work clothes—jeans and flannel shirts—from his room. Not that he had many. He did have several pair of dark dress slacks, white shirts, ties, black leather shoes, always black leather shoes if you're in the funeral business, but didn't take any. Instead, he grabbed a long wool dress coat. Enough was enough. A few more pairs of underwear and socks and he was set for clothes.

He could hear the equipment operator grunting away in the bathroom as Jens went into his dad's room. He poked through all the paperwork again. Same stuff he looked through many times. The dresser caught his attention. Barely visible, a thin gold chain hung over the corner of the mirror frame, the rest of it hidden behind the mirror. How had he missed seeing it there in the three years he was home? Gently, he lifted it. The rest of the chain with a dusty cameo on it swung from behind the dresser. *My word,* he thought. I bought this at a farm and home auction when I was ten or eleven. Connie was with me. Mom was less mobile. I didn't have the ten dollars, so Connie loaned it to me and I paid her back at two dollars a month. She wouldn't let me give it to Mom till it was fully paid for. Said unless I had equity in something else, I shouldn't give gifts that weren't paid for. Mom was thrilled when I hung it around her neck. I learned so much from Connie about handling money. Jens took a deep breath and slipped the cameo into his pocket.

He rummaged through the top drawer which held decrepit, raggedy socks. The second drawer held farm t-shirts and long underwear. Something caught his eye. It was an envelope. An old one, somewhat yellowed with age, the seal no longer holding. The writing on the cover was in pencil, and said, *December, 31, 1992 -- Dad, Give this to Jens to give to Connie the next time he sees her. Thank you. Hans.* He caught himself getting dizzy and sat down on the ancient spongy bed, still smelling of old age and death. December, 31, 1992 was the night Hans died of a sudden heart attack.

Jens heard the toilet flush and the bathroom door open. He knew he didn't want to read this letter with anyone else around. Slipping it into his shirt pocket, he picked up his suitcase and waved goodbye to the man still struggling with his bib overall hooks.

The man smiled. "Surprised you're not all emotional about this place coming down."

"Actually, with my memories of this place, I should be thanking you." Jens climbed in his truck and carefully turned it around. He stopped at the end of the driveway and threw the car into park. Hans letter was burning a hole in him. He pulled the envelope out of his pocket and started to open the letter. His brother's last known written words. What would he say to Connie? Jens thought a moment. Connie would have known she was pregnant by then. Would she have told Hans her thoughts on the baby possibly being his? His phone vibrated. He put the letter back into the envelope, opened his suitcase and placed it on top of his clothes. *Connie's got enough on her mind,* he thought. The last thing I want to do is add to her guilt, I'll give this to her later. Besides, it seems intrusive if I read it.

Chapter Twenty-Six

Jens

Jens' phone buzzed as he started the truck. It was a text from Cochran. His heart thumped loud enough, he thought the man back in the house might hear it. *Need to talk. Got time?*

Yes. He barely hit send when the phone rang.

"I need to see you. Got any time?"

"What about? Yes, I have time. Where?" Jens wondered what this was about. Cochran sounded so urgent. "What's wrong?"

"Don't want to say over the phone. Some things are good, some bad and some I can't figure out yet. Do you mind coming over to my house? Coffee shop is too public right now."

Jens couldn't figure out Cochran's emotions. He sounded upset, anxious, confused and secretive. "No problem, give me your address. I'm just leaving my dad's old place."

"Oh, good, you're close. About five minutes." Cochran gave him the address and hung up.

Jens started to feel nervous. What was this all about? Was it about Shaw? Melvin? He and Cochran? His body tingled at the thought of hugging the man and looking into those wonderful eyes. A few minutes later, he recognized the driveway from Cochran's description. He drove by this place many times in the past and always wondered who owned it. Split rail fence along the road front, pine trees lined the winding driveway that seemed to go on forever. Rusted, antique farm implements sat every few hundred feet adding a country feel. An old plow, a wooden horse-drawn wagon, an early John Deere tractor with steel wheels, everything neatly placed. The drive finally circled in front of a small story and a half farmhouse, painted white with green trim. A porch wrapped the front and side of the house. A newer white Jeep Wrangler sat in the circle. The garage fronted toward the small barn, both in good repair. A garden sat waiting for spring and, through a light grove of woods, was a pond, probably encompassing two acres, with a wooden pier. A stream seemed to enter and leave the pond.

He was greeted by loud barking. A gigantic dog ambled up to the car, wagging his tail. He quit barking and sat, as if waiting politely for Jens to get out. Jens stepped out of his pickup and held out his knuckles for the dog to sniff. After one sniff, the dog rose to all fours, stretched his head up and gave Jens a sloppy lick on the cheek.

"Rufus, no kissing." Cochran waved and laughed from the porch. "I got him trained to sit till people get out of their car, but I can't get him trained to not kiss everyone he meets. Hell of a guard dog, ain't he?"

"What kind is he?" Jens stood at the bottom of the three porch stairs, looking up at Cochran. Loving those eyes.

"An English Mastiff. He was the runt of the litter, weighs about one-fifty. His parents went around one-seventy to one-eighty." Cochran waved Jens up the steps and pointed into the house. "Kick your shoes off in the little room there. I can get you some slippers if you want. Somehow, my Scottish mother thought she was Japanese or Chinese and never allowed shoes in the house." Cochran led him into a homey, bright kitchen and pointed to a chair. "Want coffee, tea? A beer?"

"Tea sounds good, today's been a lot of coffee." Jens sat down. "What's this all about, anyway?" He hoped he didn't sound rude, but he was anxious about many things involving Cochran.

Cochran slapped several boxes of tea on the table, set two big mugs down and pulled the teapot off the stove to a hot pad waiting on the table. "I'm a tea drinker at home. These are my favorites. Help yourself." He waited till each had their tea. "I hope I didn't confuse you, but I wanted to update you on some things I'm discovering about Shaw that I think you might have some insight to." He squirmed on his seat. "Plus, I guess at a personal level, I wanted to see you again. I—I thought about you all night. A lot. That scare you? You can leave anytime, I'll understand."

"Haven't heard anything scary yet. Let's start with Shaw."

Jens tried to look calm as he lifted the mug and blew on it. Focus, concentrate, business first, then pleasure, or whatever would happen or not happen. What did he mean by personal level? Should he tell him he thought about Cochran a lot last night, too? He glanced across the table to find Cochran smiling at him. *God,* Jens thought, *I haven't felt like this in years and we just met last night.*

"Okay, everything looks like a go for me to be the official county sheriff detective, come Tuesday. The county board should approve it Monday night. The supervisor's been nosing the word around and no objections. So, for the next few days, Ken, the deputy sheriff, is pretty much taking over and I'm devoting most of my time to this stuff with Shaw and Melvin. It's kinda weird. Say, what do you know about this Farm Holding Company?"

"We just discovered it today." Jens told him about Ben showing them the security system, the hidden cameras, the computer.

He paused. How much should he share? Would Connie care? He doubted it, but wanted to be sure. "Hold on, Sheriff. I want to double-check with Connie that it's kosher to say a few more things involving the family."

"It's detective. Better yet, Cochran."

Jens called Connie and briefly told her where he was and with whom. "Is there anything you don't want me to share or explain?"

"Heck no, Jens. I'm glad you're talking with him. Bring him back for fried egg sandwiches if you want. We're actually doing quite well around here. Kind of going into the waiting stage." Jens heard Connie's forced smile through the phone followed by a deep sigh.

Jens shook his head. "Are you sure you're all right? Should I come back?"

"No, I'm fine, but I'm glad I quit digging in those damn files. Beany made me hot chocolate with marshmallows, which is helping.

Don't forget to ask Cochran for dinner." She hung up before he could reply.

Jens laid his phone on the table and took another sip of tea, conscious of Cochran watching him. He turned toward him and said, "Okay, Detective, Connie found Melvin locked in the inner office at five ten this morning, trying to get into the safe and file cabinets, but she already had snuck the keys out of the office. He'd been there since four and he left angry, she said. We went through the cabinets. Connie had never been in them before. She barely knew what was in the inner office."

"What did you find?"

"A whole other business..."

"Farm Holding Company, right?"

Jens nodded.

"Did you find anything listing the principal owners as Shaw S Phillip and Melvin Smith?" Cochran spelled out the last name of Phillip. "I suspected this earlier in the week. Got any idea how much land Farm Holding might own, lease or control?"

"We did see those names together. On a Doing Business As form. Guess he really has two names."

Cochran said. "Beginning to look like it."

"As to the property, I'm guessing there were sixty to seventy addresses in the file in three different states."

"Holy crap, I only found the ones in this county and a few surrounding. This is big, huge." Cochran sipped his tea and studied Jens for a moment. "What else you know? Connie okay?"

"I think she's okay. Beany made her hot chocolate." He watched Cochran smile. God, that's a beautiful smile. "Anyway, that's mostly it so far, except Melvin tried to make funeral arrangements for Shaw before he's dead. Jack Walker, the lawyer, was going to deal with it and try to keep him off Connie's property. He told Connie Melvin has no say now or after Shaw is dead."

"Ya, Jack called me and I walked over with him to talk with Melvin. He pulled his confused act and started to leave. Then I told him I thought it might be wise if he stayed away from the farm. He cussed me out, said he and Shaw were partners. He had a business to run and that office was his now." He took another sip of tea. "Well, by then, I knew by checking the plat maps the farm buildings weren't part of Farm Holding, so I told him unless he could prove he leased or owned that specific property, he better stay away till he, Connie and some lawyers can sit down."

"I think you're finding out stuff before us. What did Melvin do then?"

"Well, he sputtered and fumed a bit. Next, I asked if he could tell me about this Farm Holding Company. Said I really had to dig to find out about the organization. It seemed pretty secretive. Only thing is, I told him, if you're a partner, it ain't with Shaw Skogman. I'm betting it's with a Shaw S Phillip, spelled with two L's. If so, how do you explain them apples? He said, 'Ain't none of your damn business.' Then stomped off like a banty rooster."

"So, he didn't deny it. What did the lawyer say?"

"Jack? He looked at me kind of funny and said, 'I think old Shaw had some secrets wrapped around that holding company. Nothing illegal, that I could figure, just secretive and kinda sly. I didn't set it up, but did handle several property transfers for Farm Holding over the years. Plus, I never could figure out Shaw's relationship with Melvin.' He thanked me for joining him and said he'd call me if anything else came up." Cochran looked out the window a moment. "Course, I didn't tell him I'm spending almost all my time on old Shaw and Melvin."

Jens stood up, he needed to pee out some of the strong coffee he'd been imbibing all day.

Cochran pointed to the hallway. "Second door on the left. Leave a quarter. Water ain't cheap."

Jens peed and washed his hands. The bathroom was spotless. He didn't have any change, so he slipped a dollar bill under the tissue dispenser. When he returned, a package of mint Oreo cookies sat on the table, along with some napkins. Jens set back at the table. "Hey, these are my favorite store-bought cookies." He pulled several out. After several bites, he asked, "What else are you checking out Shaw and Melvin on? I thought the lawyer said their holding company was legal, just sly."

Cochran chewed a few times before swallowing. "I did some checking. Many of the properties Farm Holding owns, they acquired when the owner died."

"So? Why wouldn't that be the case? An old farmer dies, someone's going to buy the farm. You gotta be big to buy them nowadays." Jens felt a pang at realizing that was exactly why their farm was gone.

"Yeah, that's pretty common thinking." Cochran paused and bit into his cookie.

Jens thought it was more to give him time to think than because he was hungry after eating six or so cookies. "There just seems to be a lot of coincidences between the deaths and the time the holding company takes ownership. Like days."

Jens stood up. "Holy crap. That's what they did with Dad's farm. They been paying him enough to live on, plus the taxes, almost like a reverse mortgage. The place was theirs. Farm Holding now owns our family farm." He walked over to the sink and poured himself a glass of water. "Good well water." He set the glass down. "Cochran, when we were going through those files today, I saw our farm in there. Now, I've been around here for three years, I never saw anything from them. My dad never mentioned them by name, just said some holding company was taking it and not to worry. Things were so bad between me and Dad and he was so sick, I didn't bother to ask. Doesn't that sound weird? Today, the contractor was there to demolish the place and turn the house and barn area into a field."

"What?" Cochran jumped out of his chair. "Already? Today? That quickly?"

Jens shrugged and motioned for him to calm down. "Think about it, if the deal was done years ago, they were just waiting for him to die. Why wouldn't they move fast?"

"How much did they pay your dad each year? For how many years? What's the place worth and how much did they give for it?"

Jens sat back down. He pulled a pen out of his shirt pocket, along with a scrap of paper. "Just a minute, I handled his banking this last two years. I seem to remember about a thousand dollars being direct deposited every month, I have no idea from where, no name, just letters and numbers. Plus, his social security, that was about nine hundred, and he had a few old C.D.s that brought in about two hundred a month till they ran out last year."

"Jens, how many years was he getting a grand a month? Estimate."

Jens thought. "The only thing that comes to mind is Hans was trying to work with Dad on his finances when he was home. That's the same time Hans died. All I remember is just before I left, after Hans' memorial service, to go back to The Cities, Dad said he'd be all right financially. He was able to figure out something that would bring in monthly payments, he used that term, payments. Enough to keep him alive and pay his utilities, food and medicine, and his beloved truck payments."

"When was that?" Cochran was pacing around the kitchen.

"About eighteen years ago."

Cochran pulled a small calculator from a drawer. "A thousand a month times twelve months a year, times eighteen years. Let's see, that equals about two hundred and sixteen thousand dollars. Seems like a fair amount, but today, in 2011, farm prices in this county, not just tillable acreage, is going for over five grand. Now how many acres you got total?"

"Three hundred acres. Holy shit, that's one-point-five-million." His mouth dropped open.

Cochran sat back down. "Let's say, eighteen years ago, those prices were fifteen hundred dollars an acre, not five G's, that would be four hundred fifty thousand bucks. That doesn't sound fair to me, even with adding in property taxes they been paying. Didn't you ever think about an inheritance or being able to sell the farm when your old man died?"

Jens slowly shook his head. "I wanted as little to do with my dad as possible, especially after he knew I was gay. After my mother died and Connie moved on, he acted like Mom's illness and death was my fault. I couldn't wait to leave home and never wanted to return. My visits were few and far between. Even after Hans died, I tried to stay away. Finally, he got so sick, I knew I had to come back to care for him. I swear the old goat lasted three years just to spite me." He grabbed a cookie and stuffed it into his mouth. After he swallowed it, he said, "No, I never worried about an inheritance. Never wanted one." He grabbed another cookie, looked at it and slid it back in the package. "Get these damn things away. I'm turning into an emotional eater."

Both men laughed as Cochran put the cookies back in a cupboard.

Jens turned over the slip of paper he jotted his figures on. "This is interesting. Something I missed telling you earlier." He explained the farms that were being watched by the system, how Melvin apparently could set cameras up and watch the results later from his laptop.

When he said they could find none of these four addresses in the files of land controlled by Farm Holding, Cochran jumped to his feet and grabbed the slip from Jens. "Do you know these people?"

Jens shook his head. Cochran sat down at his small desk and fired a laptop up. He poked and scrolled several minutes. "Come over here and look. All four of these people are elderly. Why are they watching them?"

"Waiting for them to die?" Jens looked at Cochran. He wished this business stuff would end so they could get to the personal.

"Why haven't they already signed them up?" Cochran scratched his head.

"Because they don't need the income and they want their property to go to their heirs. Maybe. That's a thought." Jens thought it sounded like a lame reason.

"I think that could be it." Cochran checked his watch. "It's still light out and two of them live close. Let's go pay them a visit. You wanna drive? Everyone knows my Jeep. Your truck looks pretty common around here."

"You mean old and rusty? I was going to get me something sleek and sexy when I got south." Jens slipped his shoes on and the two headed for his truck.

Cochran climbed in, slammed his door and buckled in. "You still planning to go somewhere?" His voice sounded wistful.

"Not sure."

Jens controlled his urge to slide across the seat and pull Cochran's head into a kiss. He looked out the side window, anyplace but at Cochran. They just met and shared each was gay last night. Did Cochran even say he was gay? Not directly. What happened if he tried to kiss him and got smacked? Too soon. Patience. He shook his head to clear it. "Give me directions to where we're going." He drove slowly down the drive. "Oh, yeah, Connie invited you for fried egg sandwiches."

"Beany making them? Is that still considered business hours or personal?"

"Well," Jens said, lightly poking Cochran. "There's personal and there's personal with a capital P." He felt his face flush. Did he say too much too soon?

Cochran was quiet. Jens didn't dare look at him. What seemed forever was only a short ride down the driveway before Cochran cleared his throat and said, "Shut up and turn." Looking straight ahead, Cochran pointed right. The roads became even more narrow till Cochran said, "That must be it. Pretty decrepit-looking old house. The barn has caved in, but the fields look great."

Chapter Twenty-Seven

Jens

Jens parked in front of the rundown house. It reminded him of his old house, the one that was torn down today. He wasn't sure if he wanted to drive by again to see what his old place looked like as a heap of rubble.

Cochran knocked on the front door. An aged voice called, "Come in. It's unlocked."

He pushed the door open. Jens recognized the smell of old age, medicine, saturated adult diapers and canned vegetable soup. A shrunken elderly man tottered toward them, using a cane. "I'm Loren. What can I help you with?"

Cochran shook the old man's hand. "I'm Sheriff Cochran. This here is Jens Hanson, almost a neighbor. We got some questions to ask. Is that okay?"

"Sure. Let me turn the soup off. The wife is dozing anyway. That medicine they delivered today bothered her tummy again. I rubbed her good with skin cream, just to make her feel better. She seemed to fall to sleep." He returned and pointed to the couch. "I wondered if you was Phillip Smith and was here about them damn papers that keep coming and his phone calls. I keep tellin' this guy ta show up so I can yell at him in person, but guess not." He eased down into a cracked vinyl recliner. Papers piled high on the lamp table next to him.

"What are the papers about?" Cochran glanced at Jens.

"Farm Holding Company wants my land. I've already told 'em I ain't interested, haven't been for years. It's all in my will to go to my

166

grandsons. They's the ones that can sell it and use the money for their graduate schools. They're smarter than hell, both of 'em, and going on to be doctors in something or other. This way, they won't have to take out any big loans."

Jens leaned forward. "How much is Farm Holding offering? Wouldn't it be simpler to take their offer and turn the money over to your grandsons?"

"Hell, they don't want to pay market value. They want to put me on some kind of land purchase agreement. They'll pay the taxes and insurance, farm the fields, give me a cut and pay me a monthly stipend. All in exchange for title to the land. That's it. Good deal for them, not for me and my grands." The old man's eyes flashed with anger. "Six years, they been bugging me. Now that my wife took sick, they began bugging me even more."

"What's wrong with your wife?" Jens leaned across the coffee table and patted the old guy's knee.

"Nothing 'til about six months ago. The doc put her on blood pressure pills a year ago. 'Bout six months ago, someone changed them. She was taking those hard things. I think they're called tablets. Now she's taking those softer things that look like you can pull them apart. She ain't been good since they switched. Doctor says they're the same thing." Loren wiped his tears away. "We're old as hell, but been healthy up till all this started. I got the A-Fib, but wasn't a big deal till the doc added another medicine too, at least that's what the pharmacy says. Then they switched mine from the tablets, to them other kind, too." He picked up a medicine container and tossed it over. He rummaged in the drawer of the end table and tossed another prescription over. "These here are the tablets afore they switched them. The delivery guy also started bringing us skin cream. Said our skin looked dry and to use this stuff." He picked up the bottle of over-the-counter skin cream.

Cochran's eyes widened. "The delivery guy said you needed this? What about your wife?"

"He gave her another kind of lotion. I mean, the guy says he's a nurse." Loren struggled out of his chair and shuffled toward the bedroom.

"You gotta realize something, seven months ago, we was both taking two mile walks every day, mowing the lawn, shoveling the walk and driveway, driving to The Cities to see our son and grandkids. We ain't doin nothing now. Can't. Don't have the energy." He called back. "I'm just gonna check on the little lady."

Cochran turned to Jens. "You got cell service out here? Look this up and see what the pills look like and their side effects. See if there's any numbers on them."

The cell strength was barely strong enough to use. They compared the picture to the tablets and the letters stamped in. They matched. Cochran handed the capsule to Jens to search for. It looked similar.

"Wait," Jens said. Not wanting to say it out loud, he handed his phone and the capsule to Cochran. Cochran looked the capsule over carefully. "No numbers on this capsule," he whispered.

Loren returned to the room. "What drug store do you use?" Jens asked as he checked the other prescriptions against the internet.

"The one in Marshall, near the doctor. Melvin, that's the name of the guy, the nurse that delivers. Bout every four weeks, he shows up, brings our prescriptions, asks us how we're doing, takes our pressure, checks our pulse and says he'll update the doctor. He's friendly enough, a little nervous sometimes. He usually brings us fruit or a donut."

"He ever ask about the farm? What your plans are with it?" Cochran asked.

"At first, he did. Now he don't."

"What about papers? Do you have to sign something for delivering the prescriptions?" Jens tried to keep his voice level.

"Oh, hell yes. Sign here, then there. Every time. Guy says it's for Medicare records." Loren looked at them carefully. "You being the sheriff, why you stopped by asking all these questions? Something wrong?"

"Well," Cochran chose his words carefully. "We've had some concerns about holding companies preying on the elderly. We've also had some reports of drug companies bilking Medicare. We're just going around, asking some of you older folk if you're having any problems." He showed him the capsules in his hand. "Mind if we take these as samples? Just a precaution. I'll take a tablet as well." He pulled out his camera and shot pictures of the containers.

Jens noticed the labels looked different. Same pharmacy, different font styles. The labels on the newer bottles with the capsules looked older, less modern.

Loren looked at Cochran, confused. "Course not. Don't understand why, but go ahead. Should I talk to the drugstore or the guy who brings the stuff?"

Cochran pulled a small plastic bag out of the hip bag he always wore, put the pills in it and wrote on the bag. He stood and casually stretched. "Nah, we'd prefer you don't mention our visit to anyone. We got a couple other places to check. This is all precautionary. You understand how that is." He handed another baggy to Jens. "Put a little hand cream in here. Who knows, might as well check everything."

There was a sound from the bedroom. The old man said, "I'll keep my mouth shut as long as you get back to me one way or the other. Hang on, the missus musta woke up." Moments later, he stuck his head out of the bedroom door. "Wanna meet the bride? She's feeling perky right now."

Jens could tell Loren's wife had been a beautiful person. Her eyes sparkled in spite of her greasy hair, well-worn flannel nightgown and smell. She grasped his hand. "It's nice to see someone besides that old man who lives here." She looked at them closely. "Is one of you a doctor? Something just ain't right with these pills, but when I call, the nurse says they are the ones the doc prescribed. Tell ya what, I feel a lot better when I don't take them. It seems like they got stronger. So strong, I sometimes throw them up. Then I feel better."

"I'm not a doctor," Jens said, "but have you thought about getting a second opinion?"

"We have, the trouble is when we tried, the new doctor wasn't taking any Medicare patients at that time. Guess he was waiting for some old person like us to die off so he could take another one."

"Well then, I would demand an appointment soon, plus you should take these bottles along and show him the pills." Jens patted her hand.

She smiled at him. "I think we'll do that tomorrow. Loren can call the neighbors to take us, they're young and keep wanting to help us. I keep mentioning to the man who delivers the pills how these things make me worse, but he says it's just side effects and to keep taking them, how in the long run, they're better for me than not taking them." She looked up at her husband. "Did you tell them we might have bluebirds coming in?"

"Nope, didn't see how that pertained." He looked at Jens and Cochran. "This same delivery guy, Melvin, is all excited about bluebirds. He goes around, setting up bluebird boxes on those little posts. He put three or four around the yard and one right in front of the house."

"I love bluebirds. Hope some nest, it's almost time for them to arrive." Jens thought they could be arriving any day.

Cochran handed the man his card. "Do me a favor, call me on my cell number with whatever the doc says about your pills or if this guy drops by before your next delivery is due. And I wouldn't mention I was here. Okay?"

The old man watched as Cochran tapped the man's name and number into his cell phone. Loren followed them to the door and closed it behind them.

"I bet there's a camera in that bluebird box," Jens said getting into the truck.

"No bets. Drive around the circle, go past the box about twenty feet and let's walk in from behind it."

Jens parked and they walked up to the box, staying directly in back of it. Cochran lightly ran his hands around the roof and back. "Here's hinges with a screw to hold the back in." He pulled a jackknife-tool out of his pocket and gently undid the screw. "Yup, there it is. No bluebirds going into this box, there's no room."

"Any way we can turn it off?" Jens peered over Cochran's shoulder.

"Yup, there's a switch." Cochran looked around. "You click it off. How long before you think Melvin checks his box?"

Jens reached in, found the switch and pushed it. The signal light went out. "Not sure how often he checks. This electronic stuff is new to me. Now, where next, Sheriff? I mean, Detective."

Cochran pulled out the scrap of paper and gave Jens directions to the next farm. Two miles down the road, Jens slowed down and pulled closer to the edge of the road as a long white Ford pickup approached and moved over so they could pass each other on the narrow road.

"That was Melvin," Jens said.

"Must be out making his rounds to check his boxes. Wonder what he thinks or does when he finds the switch off?"

"Don't know. It might be hard for him to accuse someone. I bet he stays quiet and stews about it. Hey, do you think Shaw was part of this? That's another sixty-four-thousand-dollar question." Jens pulled into the driveway Cochran pointed to. "Surprise, surprise. A bluebird lover lives here, too. We going inside?"

"Yeah, just a quick check. Park so the bluebirds can't see you. It's dark. We'll stay to the left and try the back porch. That's where the lights are on."

This time, it was an elderly lady caring for her husband. Same story. Though old, both had been in good health till the medication switched from tablets to capsules. The medications were from the same pharmacy. Cochran bagged samples of their pills and took pictures of their containers. He also bagged some skin cream, the same brand as at the old man's house. Their delivery man sounded like the same bluebird-loving guy, also named Melvin. This couple wanted to leave the farm to their nephew who farmed ten miles away, but wanted to expand. Their two hundred acres would be a big help to him. Farm Holding Company had been after them for several years. Never in person, just letters and phone calls from a Phillip Smith. Cochran got the Farm Holding number they were to call. He got their contact info and left his card.

Leaving the home, Cochran walked ahead of Jens and got in the driver's seat. "You drive too slow. I'm starved, but I want to get these pills back to the office and have a staff member get them over to the state lab for a rush job. Something's not right with those capsules not having any numbers. I'll send the pics too."

When they were almost to the end of the drive, Jens told Cochran to stop and wait. He jumped out and approached the bird house from behind. Bending over, he swiped his finger in the mud. Carefully he reached around, felt for the opening and smeared mud on the lens of the camera. He trotted back to the truck. "I didn't turn this one off. It will be blurry, that's all."

Cochran laughed. Twenty-five minutes later, Cochran left the Sheriff's office and waved Jens back to the passenger seat. "Get back over there. I ain't relinquishing the wheel. We're less than twenty minutes away with me driving, thirty or more with you. A fella could starve to death by then." He slid behind the wheel. "My guys are on it. I'm starved. Think Beany's kitchen is still open?"

"Okay, Dale Earnhardt. I'm not afraid to admit I drive slow. I bet Beany's just getting started. I'll text Connie we're on the way." He waited a moment. "She says a big thumbs up. Say, how long will the lab take? The pills being changed, I can kinda see, but skin cream?" Jens jumped as Cochran turned into Connie's driveway and caught sight of a bluebird box near several small pine trees that lined the 127th Streetway. "Dammit, I'm seeing bluebird boxes all over. That one faces the house."

"I'm not stopping. Melvin will notice when he checks the camera." Cochran's stomach growled. "Let's ask Connie about any more bluebird boxes. The pills will take a couple of days, unless I get a court order. I put a rush on it. The skin cream was just a precaution. I doubt anything will come of it either, but this old detective was taught not to ignore anything."

Beany was starting his prep work, ordering people to set the table. Junior was his able-bodied prep chef, putting a salad together. Jens was glad to see the family was not in a gloom and doom mood.

"Hi, Sheriff," Beany squealed. "I knew you'd be back for more of my cooking."

Connie hurried over. "Sheriff, I'm so glad you could join us. As you can see, at the moment, we're doing quite well. Nothing is settled, and we can't move on with our lives, but we're all right for now. We think the memorial will be next Monday. I hope you can attend." She offered him a beer or glass of wine. He took the beer.

He briefly explained the changes in his status. The room grew quiet as he said he would be spending a lot of time digging into the holding company business as well as the relationship and actions of Shaw and Melvin.

"You mean there's really more? It sounds like Dad did have a second life and business we knew nothing of." Ellen sipped her wine and looked sad.

"It sure looks that way. I'm sorry," Cochran replied. "There's some interesting aspects we're finding that I'm not allowed to discuss yet." He paused to sip his beer. "I may be needing more information from you guys."

"I'm sure that's fine with all of us." Connie pointed to the sink on the back porch. "You two go wash your hands and grab a seat. I'm so glad I bought this big old table at a farm sale years ago. Eleven fit perfectly around it."

After the first round of sandwiches and salad, Cochran accepted a second beer. Leaning back, he asked Connie, "I haven't been out here much. Are you into blue-birding? I noticed a house on the way in."

"Oh, heavens. I used to be. That was something the twins were into when I first became their stepmother. We really got into it when the other girls came along." She sipped her wine. "I think Melvin's the one that keeps it going. He got real interested in it years ago. Once in a while, I notice he's got some boxes and posts in the back of his truck, so he must still be interested."

Jens was glad Cochran didn't look at him. Even more happy when Junior exclaimed, "We saw you drive up the driveway." He pointed toward a small monitor mounted above the kitchen desk. It showed feeds from all the cameras. Junior looked at Cochran. "They only come into the house now, not the office. Melvin can't see who's coming and going anymore."

"That's good. That man is strange." Cochran glanced at the time. "That was great food, but I need to get back. That is, if my driver can spare the time."

Jens blushed as he stood. "Got nothing but time. Let's go."

Connie followed the two to the back door. She pulled Jens into a hug. "I am so glad you and Cochran are friends."

Jens didn't dare look at Cochran.

In the truck, Jens kept glancing at Cochran who fidgeted all the way home. Butterflies, or live chickens from Beany's eggs, bounced around Jens' stomach. Neither spoke. Jens was afraid to. He felt like a teenager again with his first kiss and make-out session with a boy. He slowed to turn into the driveway. Slamming on the brakes that sent both men toward the windshield until their seatbelts jerked them back, Jens yelled, "Bluebird box. Over there."

"You dummy. I got boxes all over my property."

"Is that your property? That box looks straight down your driveway."

"Keep driving. Hell no, that property's not mine. My neighbor has boxes, too."

Jens put his foot back on the accelerator and drove slowly up the drive. "I'm getting paranoid about bluebird boxes. That much, I can tell you."

Jens and Cochran noticed Cochran's Jeep Wrangler at the same time. "What the hell? My tires are flat."

Jens pulled behind the Jeep so his lights were on the fancy Wrangler. It had the hard top on and what looked like winter tires. Big ones. All four flat.

"Someone pulled the stems. I can't see any punctures." Cochran was on his knees, feeling the tires. "Oh, crap. This one's been punctured from the back side." He crawled to check the others. "This one too. One front and one back are slashed. All four with no stems." He stood and looked at Jens in the harsh lights. "You thinkin' what I'm thinkin'?"

"I'm thinking Melvin got suspicious about the two of us driving by. Especially when or if he stopped and found the camera turned off and mud on the other one. Either way, he had plenty of time to get over here and leave again."

Cochran slapped his hand against the truck. "You any good at changing tires? I got my summer ones in the garage, they're already mounted, which helps. I don't want to drag a tow truck out tonight."

Jens opened his door. "Get back in. We'll drive down to the garage and load your tires. You got a service jack?"

"Yup to both. Sorry about all this. I think we stirred something up visiting Loren and his wife and turning off that camera." Cochran punched the code for his garage. "I'll check the summer tires first."

"I think not being able to watch Connie's house may have set him off, too. Then when he realized we were at Loren's, he figured things out, drove over here and did your tires in."

Jens followed him into the garage and helped him pull the tires from a rack, check their pressure and load them in his pickup. "However, is there another way to prove Melvin was here? I'm thinking you might have other enemies."

"I've got an old camera system. We can check it later. Don't know how good it will be. May be time to put a good one in." Cochran started toward the pickup. He paused, looked longingly at Jens. "Sorry, I gotta get this taken care of. Who knows what else could happen?"

"I understand," Jens reluctantly replied and chucked Cochran's shoulder. He wanted to pull him into a hug. He heard several barks from the house. "I think Rufus misses you. Too bad he wasn't outside when someone was messing with your tires."

"Hell, the only harm he might have done was to kiss Melvin to death. Besides, Melvin's got a dog and would have liked the affection. Rufus is not a watch dog. Damnit."

They loaded the jack, a board to rest it on and rode back to the Jeep to begin the arduous task of switching the heavy eighteen-inch wheels. They put the four damaged ones in the back of Jens' truck so he could drop them off at the tire store. When they finished, Cochran parked the Jeep inside the garage. He locked the garage and walked slowly over to Jens. Both were sweaty, grimy, with scrubbed knuckles and grease on their hands and breathing heavy. "If it was warmer, we could take a dip in the pond."

Jens didn't know how to answer. The tension was so thick, he felt like he needed a sword to slice through it. Neither looked at each other. Jens felt like if he even glanced at Cochran, he would try to pull him into an embrace and kiss. He wasn't ready to trust his gut yet. This guy was still the Sheriff, just figuring out himself. Jens didn't dare push things. He turned toward his truck. "I'll run these in first thing in the morning. Bye."

He walked away, fighting not to turn back. He heard Cochran's throaty goodbye. As he pulled away, he saw Cochran standing, watching him, his hand partially raised. Rufus was barking in the house.

~ * ~

That night in his bedroom, Jens removed his shoes and three quarters rolled out. He sensed something in his shoes all evening, but not enough to investigate. Sort of like his socks bulged. Given the age of his socks, that wasn't uncommon. He laughed. He grabbed his cell and called Cochran. "Umm, three quarters just rolled out of my shoes."

"Took you long enough. I always make change. I wondered how long you would walk around on them without noticing." Cochran paused a moment, his voice sounded hoarse. "Listen, thank you for all your help tonight…I—I hope we can see each other again…This is all so new to me…Not the detective stuff, I mean…the gay stuff, being gay, saying it out loud, finally feeling like a whole person."

Jens heard him clear his throat, blow his nose. He wasn't sure how to respond. He'd been there before, but at a much younger age and with Connie's help. "Is this the first time you've said that out loud? You're gay?"

"Yes. It really hit me the other night at Katies. I felt like jumping on the table and shouting it out. Am I crazy for feeling like this? Do other guys feel this way when they fully realize who they are? Did you?"

"Yes, I think that's true for every gay or queer person. I was much younger, but had similar feelings." Jens went on to tell him about his self-realization as a teen. How Connie helped him, how gay friends had similar feelings. He couldn't help but ask, "Cochran, have you ever been in a relationship before? Straight or gay? Did you ever mess around as a teen or in the army?"

Cochran was quiet. "No, never. Mom was raised Catholic. Even though we rarely went to church, she nagged us something terrible about the evils of sex before we were married. Dad mentioned a few times not to play with ourselves too much and never, ever with another guy. I just accepted it. I was always so busy with sports and jobs. I didn't make time to date. In the army, well, the guys going nuts trying to get laid turned me off. I thought I was better than them, had more self-control." He chuckled. "I tried dating a few women after I went on the police force."

"How'd that go?"

Cochran's laugh rang through the phone. "It was a woman who told me I was special. Took me years to figure out what she meant."

"Did she mean special because you were so good in bed or special for other reasons?"

Cochran snorted. "It wasn't for my performance in bed. I got snowed in at her place and we ended up sleeping together. She was a young widow, no kids, one bed. I could tell she wanted to have sex, but wasn't going to make the first move. I had no desire for her, strange because she was very attractive. I was so dense. Part of me felt guilty about sleeping with a girl before marriage, part of me felt confused. Shouldn't I feel something sexual toward her? Part of me thought it was too soon in the relationship for sex. In the morning, over breakfast, waiting for the snowplows to come, she said, 'I think you are a very special man. I like you and would like to remain good friends, even go out together. However, I think we each need to keep looking for the person right for us. I don't think we're right for each other, except as good friends.'"

Jens nearly choked laughing. "She knew, Cochran. She knew. How did you answer her?"

"Talk about being stupid. No, not stupid, just totally unaware of myself. Even worse, afraid to find out who I was or might be. I kept telling myself she wasn't the right woman and when I met the right one, I would know it. Feel something huge, like a miracle would hit me and I would sweep her off to bed. She and I remained good friends, lots of people thought we were dating, then she met someone, married, and moved away."

"Cochran, didn't you think about being gay? Weren't you attracted to men? Didn't you ever wonder about men? You've worked out with other guys, showered with them. Their bodies looking good never crossed your mind?"

Cochran waited before replying, "I was too afraid to even let those thoughts even flit through my mind. I purposely kept myself busy. I married the county sheriff department. I volunteered for community groups, Rotary Club, the Lions, made sure I was at every high school event."

"What woke you up? You seemed ready to admit it the other night. That didn't happen the moment you sat down with me at Katie's Pizza."

"That's right. Ten years ago, my sister realized her grandson was gay. My niece, the kid's mom, put the word out that she and his father didn't care and if any of the family had a problem with him being gay to consider ourselves uninvited from family events. It was an eye-opener for all of us. I watched the kid grow into a fantastic young man. He's now a senior at U M and on the cheerleading squad, getting a degree in marketing."

"Is that the only reason?"

"No. Shortly after that, Jennifer Logan came in as the County District Attorney. She hired an assistant district attorney who is gay. I realized my nephew and the assistant D.A. being gay was as normal as the color of your eyes and going bald. That still didn't alleviate my fears of coming out. How would I do that? What would it look like? I looked at some of the dating sites online. Some were about nothing but sex and the ones like Match.com, well, I was scared to death to sign up. When you showed up, I figured you were gay and thought I'd give things a few weeks. You know, see if I was interested in you and vice versa. If you moved on like I thought you intended to, I'd take the leap and join Match."

Both men were silent, listening to each other's breathing, as if neither knew what to say next. Jens decided to break the tension. "So, by waiting to figure me out, you were just trying save money on a membership?"

Through their combined laugher, Jens heard Cochran gasp, "Damn you, Jens. You saw right through me. Now get some sleep. Some of us have to work for our pay and I need my beauty sleep."

At seven the next morning, Jens ran the tires into the tire store. He was back by seven forty-five. Around eight thirty, Cochran called. He sounded like he was trying to cover his nervousness with humor. "I'm counting out some money to save for a date. Would you go out with me? Or do I need to sign up and go through Match?" He took a quick breath and rushed on, "Actually, I'm at the tire company. They just finished switching my tires back. They'll keep my summer ones till I can haul them back home."

"So, for our first date, you want to take your tires home in my truck? Is that what you're asking? No steak and wine? Just hauling your sorry-ass tires back?"

"Well, I could bring a bottle of Boones Farm in a bag and we could run through McDonalds."

"It's a date. What else you got going on today?"

Cochran sounded more relaxed. "Can't tell you everything. Don't want to lose my job if I told everybody what I did or how little I do." He laughed. "I can tell you this. Loren called me at six-thirty this morning. Said that delivery guy was just there and he was checking his bluebird boxes. Said Melvin seemed a bit upset. He even asked if anyone else had been here."

"Hope he said no."

"He did. Told him no one was by and he didn't appreciate being called so damn early. Guess Melvin said he was sorry. Loren thought Melvin worked on the bluebird box out front."

~ * ~

In the kitchen, Jens showed the family his skinned knuckles and explained about Cochran's tires. He didn't tell them about the bluebird boxes. He sat down and poured himself a bowl of Cheerios while Emma buttered some toast for him.

"That's all that happened?" She gave him a saucy look as she placed some toast in front of him.

"That's it. Just a fun evening, changing the Sheriff's tires. Nothing else."

He didn't look at her. He was sure his face was red.

"Sure is a shame." Emma winked at him.

The family grew quiet as the phone rang. Gayle picked it up. "Skogman home, this is Gayle." She listened, then spoke, "Just a moment. I'm going to put you on speaker." She punched the button and laid the receiver down.

"This is Jadine from Hospice—"

"He's gone, isn't he." Connie's voice was soft.

"Yes, I'm so sorry. He passed on about five minutes ago. We didn't expect it this soon, but we weren't shocked. Apparently, he had a blood clot. He went quickly. I've notified Melvin who said to call Gayle. Does anyone want to come see him before the funeral home picks him up?"

Jens watched Connie look around. Everyone shook their heads.

Gayle replied, "No. Thank you for asking, but we will not be coming in. Please express our appreciation to your team and the hospital for all they did for him and us. Goodbye."

Connie sat, staring at the floor, the dial-tone sounding across the room as Jens watched the girls wipe their eyes.

Ellen came over and gently hung the phone up. She muttered, "He didn't pass on. He died. He's gone. His spirit lives on through our memories, the good and the bad..." She stopped as she realized everyone was looking at her. "I'm sorry. I guess I was saying out loud what I was thinking. I hope I haven't offended anyone." She pulled her mother to a stand and the family crowded around.

"That's my archeologist," Connie said, wiping her eyes. "I agree, one hundred per cent."

Jens wondered how would they handle the next steps? He'd been through this process frequently from the other side, and three times as a family member. Would Connie and the girls break down? Fall apart? They showed such strength thus far, but was there a tipping point?

He watched Connie. "Well, I'm now a widow and you are now fatherless. At this time of our lives, I wasn't prepared for this, nor were you. But here we are, let's finalize plans for the service." She paused and looked at Gayle. "Let's not get too task-oriented, though. Why don't we go into the family room, sit and take several minutes to remember your father?"

Jens watched her hug each of the girls individually as they went by her. He got a box of tissues from the bathroom, passed them around, and sat with them in a silent tribute to a complicated man. He sensed each person still felt a cloud hanging over them about what else they might discover about Shaw.

Chapter Twenty-Eight

Junior

About nine that Thursday morning, Junior and Beany meandered into the kitchen in their running clothes, sweaty and smelly. "Just did twelve miles," Beany said as he guzzled some water.

Connie pulled them into the hallway. "Boys, Shaw died while you were out running, just before eight. There was a blood clot." She looked up into Junior's eyes.

He pulled her into a hug. "How are you doing? This is all so weird."

"It is strange, but I'm all right for now. At least we've had several days to grasp the idea he was dying. It's not like he keeled over driving tractor."

"Still, there's more stuff to figure out." Junior let go of her and stretched.

Beany squeezed Connie's arm. "Now, we know one thing for sure and can begin making plans."

"You sound like the girls." Connie patted their backs and pushed them toward the kitchen where Junior poured two bowls of cereal as Beany popped bagels into the toaster and dug out the milk, cream cheese and jelly.

The girls were looking over the outline Emma printed off for the memorial service. They were calm. Junior wasn't sure if they were calm because they were tired of being sad or if it was that Shaw died and they could now make plans.

"What about catering?" Jane asked

Gayle said, "I love the idea. But why cater? Make it a pot luck. That way, everyone is helping with the experience. Besides, some of my favorite memories of school and church events were the pot lucks..."

"You liked all those hot dishes?" Mary exaggerated her amazement.

"You betcha." Gayle laughed. "Actually, the only traditional hot dishes I remember were the ones with the cream of mushroom soup, canned vegetables, some mystery meat and covered with crushed potato chips or crackers, brought by the same little old ladies. They must be dead by now. I do recall others brought more progressive things."

"Like the Jell-O salad mold with canned pineapple, grapes, maraschino cherries, and cottage cheese? I thought the stuff was growing penicillin till Mom made me try it. It wasn't that bad. I kind of miss it." Jackie giggled as Beany mimed gagging himself.

Jane looked at her mother. "Mom, what about seeing if Syd could fix up a batch of sloppy joes and we invite everyone to bring a salad or dessert. That way, we won't have two dozen hot dishes that all taste the same. He could provide beer and wine, too. I can make up a cooler of pink lemonade in Dad's John Deere water cooler. We can serve on decent disposables..."

"I can ask my friends in Marshall to play," Beany yelled. At everyone's frowns, he added, "We're a string quartet. We play light classical." He beamed broadly as the family laughed.

"I think we have a plan," Connie said. "Now, when should we have it? The local paper comes out Friday, tomorrow. The deadline is noon, today."

"Let's keep it on Monday," Junior suggested. "It's a teacher's institute day tacked on to spring break, so everyone is off school. That still gives everybody enough time to prepare. Say, start at three o'clock?"

Connie looked at the girls. "Why not eleven-thirty? That way, it's a luncheon. I think by then, we'll want this to be over with. We'll need to get on with our lives." The girls nodded.

Lists were made, tasks assigned and the girls got busy while

Junior did the few dishes. Beany started calling his musician friends.

The land line rang. Connie picked it up. Junior watched as she quickly sat down, her face drawing tight. Beany and his sisters noticed too as everyone stopped talking and watched their mom.

"Yes, Melvin, we know Shaw died. Thank you," she said quietly.

She listened for several more minutes. Though Junior couldn't make out the words, he could hear the emotion from the man's voice.

"Melvin, I don't want you on the property, even if it is to pick up more bluebird boxes. By rights, I should hang up on you." She listened some more. Raising her voice, she snapped, "I just said no. Shaw just died. We are planning his memorial right now and have enough to deal with. You are not to step foot on this property till we meet with a lawyer. The only thing I will consider is asking Junior and Jens to load some up and bring them to your house." She listened several more minutes. "Melvin, as they say, that's my final offer. Call me back to arrange a time." She hung up.

"I'm not sure why I'm accommodating him about stupid bluebird boxes. Why the heck is he worried about them now? Maybe he doesn't know what to do with his time because he can't come here." She groaned. "Guess I want to keep some communication open so when we sit down with a lawyer, I can learn more about this place."

"What the heck, Mom. Dad, Shaw, just died and Melvin wants his bluebird boxes? Isn't that weird?" Junior watched Jens' face. Something was up, but he couldn't read what the man was thinking.

Jens finished his coffee. "Connie, I'm more than willing to deliver bluebird boxes, but first, I want to make a call..." His voice trailed off as everyone looked at him. "I can't explain it right now, but it might be an opportunity to learn more about what Melvin does."

"God, this situation gets stranger and stranger. Who'd a thought Melvin was into bluebirds?" Gayle muttered. "I'm with Junior. Why the hell are they so important now? Isn't there something else that needs to be attended to on some of the other farms? Why wouldn't he be sitting at home grieving? He and Dad have been together since Noah's flood. Bluebirds?"

Junior followed Jens outside. "Can I listen in?"

"Yes, it might tie in with what you already know." Jens touched several keys and put it on speaker. "Cochran, we're on speaker. Junior is here with me. First, are you aware Shaw died around eight this morning?"

"Yes, just heard that. Please give my condolences to Connie and all of you. I was going to stop by a little later. Figured you all are busy making plans and didn't need interruption at this time. Now, what's second? I'm listening, go on."

"Melvin just called Connie and wants to come pick up bluebird boxes and posts. She told him he can't be on the property, but would consider Junior and me dropping some off at his home. She doesn't yet know what we do."

Junior's eyes got big. He mouthed, "What the hell?"

Cochran's voice was strong. "Bet you're thinking what I'm thinking. What can we do to track him?"

Junior looked at Jens in amazement. "Like those transponders they put under cars in the movies?"

"Like that, son. Exactly like that. Now, don't you think he'll see them when he installs the posts and builds the boxes?"

Junior stepped closer toward the phone. "They're already built. He builds the boxes a dozen at a time, wraps them up like they're glass dolls and then loads them all fragile-like. The man is crazy about his bluebirds."

Cochran snorted. "Hey, Junior, Melvin ever said he saw a bluebird in one of his boxes?"

Junior thought a moment. "Nope, now that you ask. It's just those boxes and posts he gets excited over."

"Okay, men," Cochran said. "Let me make some calls. Tell Connie to stall Melvin till around noon so I can find some transponders. Glad I'm still Sheriff so I don't have to get permission." He paused. "Hey, Jens, maybe McDonalds and Boone Farm tonight?"

"Sounds good." Jens hung up the phone.

Junior saw Jens' face flush. "What was that all about?" He paused. "What's going on?"

Jens laughed. "Let's just say that Cochran and I might be developing something similar to what's going on with you and Beany."

"For real?" Junior didn't know whether to hug Jens, jump in the air or act adult-like. "You and the Sheriff got something going?" His voice came out shrill, like a girl's. Definitely not adult-like.

"Might have. I think we're both very surprised. Time will tell." Jens waved his hand as if to stop Junior from asking more questions. "Can you show me where these crazy bird boxes are?"

Junior went inside to get the keys. Beany said he was headed home to help his folks and came outside with him, then headed down the drive. Junior led Jens to the back side of the shop where a garden shed sat, about ten by twelve foot in size. Inside were two dozen cedar poles, a post hole digger, a small toolbox and a dozen nesting boxes, each wrapped in bubble wrap. "For Pete's sake, since when did nesting boxes need to be bubble-wrapped?" Junior grabbed one off the shelf.

"How tightly are they wrapped? Any tape?" Jens eyed the one Junior held.

Junior turned it over in his hands several times. "Just a small piece to hold it in place. Want me to unwrap it?"

"NO." Jens turned and slowly looked around the small shed. "Sorry I yelled, kid. I just wanted to make sure there's not a camera in here. Keep holding that, now set it back and pretend to be counting the posts." Junior pretended to count posts as Jens carefully looked around. "In case he has a camera in here, I just didn't want him to later see us unwrapping the boxes. Okay, I don't see anything."

"This is crazy. Why is he so careful with wrapping wooden nesting boxes?"

"Try this. Pick one up in each hand. See if one is heavier than the other. I'll do the same."

This is weird, really weird, Junior thought as he hefted two. "Wow. This one is heavier. Not a lot, but definitely heavier. I'm setting it against this wall."

By the time they were done, five of the nesting boxes seemed heavier. All five had a small blue mark on the tape. "Okay, buddy," Jens said. "Try your skills at unwrapping one and wrapping it back up the same way. Take your time. I'll dig a screwdriver out of the toolbox."

Junior stuck his tongue out as he concentrated on delicately undoing the tape and unwrapping the box. Jens handed him a screwdriver and pointed at the screw to remove. When it was loose enough, Junior pulled the door open like it might have explosives in side. "Holy crap. That's a battery-operated video camera with an SD card. Man, Melvin must really be into birding."

Jens looked carefully in it. He needed to see a transponder to see how much room he needed. "Wrap it back up as carefully as you unwrapped it. We may be unwrapping more if we get some transponders." Jens punched Junior's shoulder.

Junior groaned as if he was injured. "Can you tell me why we need transponders to follow Melvin around so he can study stupid bluebirds? I don't get all this cloak and dagger stuff for freaking birds."

"Can you wait for an answer? We have one more thing to do and then it will be more than clear to you."

Jens kept the screwdriver in his hand as Junior locked the door. Walking toward the house, Jens said, "We're going for a little hike, about a mile long. Let's head out the Milliken Road driveway."

"Can't we jog it?" Junior was bored and frustrated.

"Sure, I need a bit of a workout."

The two started a slow jog, out to Milliken Road, right to 127th Street, another quarter mile and a right into their other driveway. Partway up the drive, Jens slowed to a walk. "See that bluebird house? We want to approach it directly from behind."

"You gotta be kidding me. It's the same as those boxes with the cameras." Junior halted and bent over to look at the back of the box. Jens handed him the screwdriver and watched as he carefully undid the screw and pulled the door open. "Freakin' A, why doesn't this one show up in the house?"

"Because it's too far away to be wired into the computer. Melvin stops by, or your dad used to, downloads the media card or switches it, and watches it on their laptop or the big computer. He's got bluebird boxes all over, recording people."

His anger hit like tornado. Junior stepped back and raised his leg to kick at the nesting box. He felt Jens grab him and pull him back.

"No, don't. If you want to take this out, make it look more like an accident."

Junior slowed his breathing. "What difference does it make? I just want the damn thing gone."

"We believe Melvin is suspicious we're on to him and the bluebird cameras. If we just tear this out right now, I think it will fully confirm his suspicions and we don't know what he will do next." He took the driver from Junior and screwed the door shut. "Now, let's reverse our steps. I'll try to go at a faster pace."

They didn't talk on their fast jog back. As they neared the house, Junior poked Jens' shoulder. "Hey, isn't your front-end loader still at the back of the cemetery? Isn't it time it's moved? I've always wanted to drive one. Can I go get it for you? I'm sure there's room to store it in one of our sheds." He tried his best to look innocent.

He must not have succeeded because Jens burst out laughing. "Great idea, the key is in it. Good luck not hitting anything, the steering's a little loose."

I love that man, Junior thought as he jogged down the driveway. He wanted to wave at the bluebird box, but contained himself. I'm so excited for Jens and Sheriff. He seems like such a good guy and now he's going to be a detective, that's even cooler.

On the backhoe, he flipped the seat over and sat down. The starter ground ominously, but then caught. Thank goodness. He didn't want to drive something else over here to charge the battery. He checked to make sure the stabilizer feet were up and the back bucket secured so it wouldn't sway. The front loader controls worked well as he practiced moving the bucket up and down to dump the water out of it. *Jens should have left the bucket angled down,* he thought, *but then, the man did have a birdshot victim in his truck, waiting for him. God, was that only five days ago?*

He put the tractor in gear, eased up the clutch, and drove slowly around the perimeter of the cemetery. On the road, he shifted into third gear and pulled the accelerator down till he was cruising at a whole seven miles an hour. Shortly, he realized the speedometer was stuck at seven. He eased into their driveway and drifted further and further to the right, the tires meandering onto the long grass. He lowered the front-end loader to about twelve inches off the ground and leveled the bucket. He glanced behind him. Yup, he was leaving some good tracks in the soft spring dirt and grass. Oops. The birdhouse post snapped about a foot off the ground and went flying. Junior shifted the tractor into neutral, coasted to a stop, jumped off, turned and looked ahead toward the house and hopefully the new camera. He threw his hands in the air like, oh my, what just happened? He picked up the nesting box, the post, and threw them in the bucket.

After parking the rig, he walked in the back door to find the family clapping. "You deserve an Oscar," cried Emma. "Even I can't act that well."

The laughter quickly subsided. "To think, we've been under surveillance. In our own home," Connie clenched her fists as if fighting to maintain control. "Who knows for how long?" She turned to Jens. "Are these nesting boxes somehow part of this scheme of whatever Farm Holding is doing?"

"It appears that way. Cochran is spending almost all his time on it. The fact we're on to Melvin's tricks can't leave this room." Jens looked at each person till they nodded.

"This is serious," Junior said. "How involved was Dad in all this? Do we even know?"

The emotional high from wiping out the bird nesting box was over. That felt good, for about four minutes. Now reality was back. They still had no clue as to who their father was or what he did. If Shaw was his father... He wasn't, but sometimes Junior allowed himself to still waffle. The DNA tests would take at least six more weeks. They weren't high priority for the testing company. This father thing is an adjustment, he kept telling himself.

His mother wiped her eyes. "No, we don't know what Shaw was involved in. That's what is scary. We could lose this whole farm if there's malfeasance and someone sues us." She blew her nose and took in a big breath. "I need to talk with Jack, our lawyer. I know he knows more than me. I'm going to call him and ask him to come out here. I want him on my turf, not me on his. A grieving widow in her own home is harder to snow than one in his office."

"Wow, Mom. That's strong," Gayle stepped over to hug her. "Mom, just who does the lawyer represent? Us or Melvin?"

Connie slowly responded. "That's a good question. He's our family and the farm lawyer. I'll ask him what he knows about Farm Holding." She shook her head. "I'm positive he doesn't represent Melvin. Jack's always been very helpful to others in the community. He said he had no problem coming out here on the weekend."

Junior glanced at the monitor and pointed. A sheriff's car sped up the 127th Street drive and swung to a stop at the front porch. Jens hurried to open the door. Junior followed. A short wide deputy handed Jens a small box. "Here's three transponders, all we could spare. Cochran said to rush them out. Don't know what the hell's going on, but sounds interesting. They're activated, our guys will pick up the signal. Guess we'll be driving more of these farm roads for a week or so."

"We're just tracking bluebirds," Junior said before he could stop himself.

"Right. And brown cows give chocolate milk." The deputy winked at Junior and left.

Jens opened the box. "These are the perfect size. About two inches by an inch and a half wide and inch deep." He carried them back into the kitchen and showed them to the girls who were waiting in anticipation. "Junior, where is the birdhouse you accidentally knocked over?"

"On the back porch. Want me to get it and we'll check out where we can hide these?"

While everyone watched, they quickly opened it. Several girls gasped when they saw the camera. Jens said, "There's plenty of room up against the roof at the front. I bet you have some double sticky tape around here which will work fine."

As Junior returned with the tape, the phone rang. Gayle handed it to Connie as everyone quieted down.

"This is Connie, who am I speaking with?"

Junior thought, *You'd never know Mom was in tears ten minutes ago. She is so strong.* He watched her eyes grow serious.

"Yes, Melvin. You do want Jens and Junior to bring the bird boxes and posts to your place." She made a face at the family. "In one hour. Exactly one hour. Two o'clock. I get that. One hour, not before or not after." She drew circles with her finger around her temple. "They're supposed to handle the posts and boxes gently." She drew circles again. "Melvin, for God's sake, they're wooden boxes and posts. The eggs aren't in them yet."

She shook her head and held the phone out so the family could hear Melvin hollering about how he loved bluebirds and caring for them was a privilege and he made sure their homes were just right and in the right locations and on and on he went. Connie slapped the mouthpiece against her stomach as Junior and Jens broke into guffaws. She waved for them to quiet down. "Okay, Melvin. I get it. The guys will be there at two o'clock sharp. You don't have to repeat yourself. Goodbye." She started to hang the phone up. Junior noticed a glint in her eyes. "Melvin," she yelled. "Hang on, I forgot to tell you something. It's about bluebird boxes. You there? Good. Listen, Junior was driving Jens' frontend loader to our house and the steering is loose and he clipped that nesting box out near 127th Street. He said he's sorry." She covered the mouthpiece again as laughter erupted. "Quiet, guys." She uncovered the mouthpiece. "You what? You want the pieces?" She looked at Junior and shrugged her shoulders.

"They're in the dumpster," yelled Junior.

"No, Melvin, he's not going to dig them out and bring them to you. Goodbye." She slammed the phone down.

"Damn, this is worse than menopause. One moment, I'm in tears and fearing for our future, the next minute, I'm arguing over bird boxes with a crazy man spying on us and want to laugh at the insanity of it all…" Her voice faded off as several kids hugged her.

Junior patted his mother on the back, then looked at Jens. "Mom, we're going to go load the precious cargo. Maybe we can rename the farm Bluebird Acres. Sounds appropriate, doesn't it?" He laughed as his mother shook her fist at him.

Jens and Junior loaded the posts and digger into the back of Jens' truck. They opened the three boxes with cameras and easily stuck the transponders against the front wall and roof, not noticeable until removing the camera. They rewrapped the boxes and placed all of them on the floor of the cab. "He's got to have a supply of cameras someplace. Where do you think he keeps them?" Jens asked as he swung Melvin's toolbox into the truck bed.

"Probably someplace in his shop. We got time to look, I'll run get the keys from Mom."

"Umm, you don't need them, remember?"

Junior laughed. "Oops, I forgot."

They entered the shop through the side door and began looking around the parts area. Stairs led to more storage for smaller parts. They poked around on the wobbly plywood floor. "Look, here's a metal cabinet. Hope it's not locked." Junior turned the handle and pulled it open. "Looks like we hit the mother lode." He pulled out a box and began reading the specs. "Works in heat or cold, battery-operated, up to a thirty-two gigabyte SD card, motion detector adjustable to avoid plant and tree movements, ninety-day guarantee." He handed the box to Jens. "This means Melvin has to drive around and download the data or swap out the card. Bet it doesn't take long." He poked around the cabinet some more. "This is cool. I'd like to play with these."

"I doubt if he'll miss them," Jens said. "If he does, it will be kind of awkward to accuse us of stealing the equipment he was using to spy on us. Don't forget, you have the one you so carelessly drove through. You can experiment with that one."

They arrived at Melvin's house thirty minutes early. Jens backed his truck around so it lined up with the back end of Melvin's four-door diesel Ford pickup. Jens lowered his tailgate as Junior lowered the one on Melvin's truck. "Keep your eyes open for anything odd. Try not to talk much," muttered Jens as he slid a post from one truck to the other.

"Hey. I said two o'clock, not one-thirty." Melvin stormed out of the house. Rusty following him. The dog sat next to Melvin.

Junior thought Rusty must be about ten years old now. He hoped Melvin would signal the dog to 'release' and let him run to greet Junior. The dog loved him and Beany. Melvin taught them how to play with the dog and maintain the dog's consistent training when they were little and Rusty was a puppy.

Jens glanced at Junior. Neither spoke. They just kept sliding posts from one truck to the other.

"I don't want them in the truck yet. It's too soon to load them." Melvin's face was red.

Jens tossed the post hole digger on the ground in front of Melvin. "This where you want them? We're trying to help you out and you're standing around, bitching like a goose on her nest."

Melvin sputtered; he was so angry he couldn't get his words out. He bent over, picked up the digger and held onto it like it was his child. Rusty whined as if he wanted to be released. Melvin angrily signaled him to stay.

Jens smiled at Junior as if they were simply helping out a good neighbor. "Junior, start putting the nesting boxes inside Melvin's truck. Put them on the back-seat floor. They should ride safe there."

Melvin stared as Junior piled four boxes into his arms and placed them on the floor behind the driver's seat. Junior moved carefully, trying to look around without being too obvious. He brought four more as Melvin remained on the other side of the truck, still frozen. Junior noticed there were three shoe-box sized packages wrapped in brown paper lying across the passenger side floor, behind the front seat. They had Priority Mail stickers attached, but no address labels.

Jens handed Junior the last four wrapped nesting boxes, then faced Melvin across the truck bed. "Was that gentle enough, Melvin? You want to open them to make sure there's no damage?" Jens spat on the ground. "Jesus H Christ, Melvin. Nesting boxes wrapped in bubble wrap? I heard you birders were crazy, but this takes the damn cake.

Melvin, how many bluebirds you sighted? How many are nesting? You reporting weekly to the bluebird society in St. Paul?" He and Junior walked to their truck.

"Where's the one Junior broke?" Melvin finally moved, stepping toward Jens who was sliding into his truck.

"In the dumpster. Don't worry, we held a funeral service for it. Empty nesting boxes are precious to God." Jens spat out the window again and slowly drove off as Junior rolled in laughter. "What a dumb shit."

Back home, as Jens went to his room, Junior updated the family on sticking the transponders into the boxes and their time with Melvin. Jens walked back into the room as Mary said, "I don't understand this nesting box set up. There's cameras. For what? How do they work? Now, you've added transponders to three of them. Can someone explain this? All I know is we've been spied on and now someone is trying to spy on the guy spying on us who's also spying on old folks. And we're not even old." Several other voices chimed in, asking for more explanations, too.

"It's like this," Junior said, grabbing an apple and biting into it. With his mouth full, he began, "Melvin puts in bluebird boxes with cameras. He still has to manually open the box and remove the SD card from the camera and swap it out or download it to his laptop." He swallowed and laid the apple on a napkin. "That only takes a minute or so. He can probably slip in and out of someone's driveway in two or three minutes. He can watch the SD card or the download on his laptop or view it later on the office computer when no one's around." He looked up to see Jens in the doorway. "Isn't that right, Jens?" He picked up his apple and took another bite.

Jens nodded and pulled out a chair. "Excellent. You have a better grasp of electronics than I ever will. From what we've figured, Melvin does a lot of night explorations so he could pull in, download the SD card and be gone in minutes while people slept. He also could pretend to be checking the boxes and just switch a full SD card with a blank one. Say, Junior, can you tell them how the police transponders will work?"

Junior chewed fast and swallowed. "I think so. The signal from the transponder can be read from the policeman's reader. It's not a powerful signal, so the deputies will have to do more patrolling through farm country. I don't think the batteries last too long, so they may only have a week or two to find where the boxes are placed." He crunched off another bite.

"Okay, I get the electronic aspects, but why? What is Melvin hoping to accomplish?" Gayle looked confused.

Junior pointed at Jens. "I think you know more about this end of things, what with acting all friendly with the sheriff."

Jens faked a scowl at him. Emma winked at Jens as the other girls looked confused over Junior's last comment. "This can't leave the room, but this is what we think is going on. We think Farm Holding preys on elderly land owners. Gets the owners to sign land purchase agreements where Farm Holding will pay them a monthly amount, enough to live on, the property taxes and a percentage of crop income. In exchange, the owner signs over title so that Farm Holding owns the property."

"That doesn't explain the cameras." Connie looked frustrated.

"Cochran thinks Melvin targets the cameras for folks who haven't or won't agree to sign. He apparently monitors them to see who visits, see if they have any heirs. More importantly, he becomes their medical delivery person and delivers their medicine. We think there's tampering with the prescriptions going on, that the medications might make the old folks incoherent or ill enough to sign the papers. The thing is, it appears all contact with Farm Holding is over the phone and through the mail. There's a lot more Cochran is trying to figure out, but he can't tell me what it is yet." He turned and said, "I'm going to go take a shower, clean off this blue bird detective sweat."

~ * ~

Jens met Cochran at the tire dealer at five. The staff loaded the tires into Jens pickup.

Cochran was subdued as he climbed in carrying a bottle wrapped in a brown bag. "Umm, just run through McDonalds. I got two deputies out sick and another one has a family emergency. I got time to eat a quarter-pounder and take a swig of this, then go unload the tires. That's it." He pulled the bottle part way out of the bag. It was Mountain Dew. "I'll need the caffeine tonight. I'm going to be patrolling or on call all night. Sorry to screw up our first date."

Cochran looked so forlorn, Jens wanted to pull him over and kiss him. Instead, he said, "We'll live." They ate their burgers in the truck, driving down the road, sharing swigs from the Mountain Dew like they'd been friends forever. Jens hit a pothole while Cochran was taking a slug of soda causing him to inhale some. "Hey," Jens shouted, "do I need to pull over? Call 911? Sheriff Cochran is choking to death on Mountain Dew."

Cochran managed to flip him the bird between gasps.

At Cochran's garage, they unloaded the tires and lifted them onto the racks. After closing the doors, Cochran glanced at his watch. "I gotta get back to my jeep and the department to see what's going on..."

"You got time for this." His heart pounding, Jens pulled the man into a tight embrace. He waited till he felt Cochran relax before he nuzzled his cheek, then began a soft peck on the lips. That led to a long, deep kiss.

Groaning, Cochran broke away. "My first kiss with a man and we gotta stop. Maybe I'm too freaking dedicated to my job."

Jens sighed. Neither spoke on the drive to town. Pulling next to the Jeep, he laughed when Cochran said, "Sorry to screw this up. Can we go on a real date soon?"

"This was a real date. We did an activity together, we ate, we drank and we kissed. Best of all, our parents didn't have to drive us."

Cochran leaned over and gave Jens a kiss on the cheek, then quickly got out as if embarrassed someone might have seen them.

Jens swallowed and tried to sound light. "See ya around. I'll try to stop by next time I'm in town." He drove his slow rate of speed to Connie's, his mind whirring with thoughts about Cochran.

Chapter Twenty-Nine

Junior

Friday, noon, April 1

Junior stepped onto the back patio and watched Jens park between the garage and the office. "You find some transponders along the way? Lunch is ready, come and get it. Looks like you got a haircut."

Jens laughed. "Yup, I did. Cochran just called. He did a lot of patrolling last night. Apparently, the bluebird boxes are still in Melvin's truck which means he hasn't installed them elsewhere…"

Junior wondered why he stopped talking. He watched Jens start toward the house, but he kept looking back at the office.

"Just a minute, I got to measure something."

"What's that got to do with lunch?"

"Just give me a minute and I'll be right there."

Junior watched Jens dig a tape measure out of the truck and trot over to the where the office connected to Shed One.

"Sixteen feet," Jens yelled. "Remember that number." He tossed the tape back into the truck and rushed into the mud room. "C'mon, let me wash up and dig some hairs out of my ears. I'm starving."

Lunch was a hubbub. Sometimes, the conversation lagged. Junior thought everyone was wondering the same thing he was. What else were they going to learn? He turned toward Jens, ready to ask him why he was measuring the office wall when the sound of an explosion caused everyone to jump. "What was that?"

"It's at the Milliken mailbox." Gayle pointed at the monitor which showed wisps of smoke barely visible at the road.

Junior tore out of the house, followed by Jens and several sisters. He heard someone scream she was calling nine-eleven. Just beyond the garage, he heard Ellen yell that the car and truck tires in the garage were all flat. He raced on, Jens panting close behind him. He heard screams and shouts. Closer to the road, he saw pieces of the mailbox strewn around the splintered wooden post. He slowed to a fast walk. Screws, bolts, nuts and washers were scattered around, mixed in with pieces of the mailbox.

An old, skinny, gray-haired woman dressed in a long gingham dress, muddy apron and even muddier Nike Air Jordans, stood across the road on the edge of the ditch. Tears streaked the heavy make-up of her cheeks. Granny glasses rode low on her nose. She jumped up and down, screaming, "I knew he was up to something. I just knew it."

Junior didn't have time to think about where the heck she came from because she raced across the road and launched herself toward him. He had no choice but to open his arms and grasp onto her as the force almost knocked him over.

"Oh, my God," she squealed in his ear, almost deafening him. "That could have been you or the mail carrier." She hugged him around the neck so tightly, he thought he might suffocate. He managed to get the woman's feet to the ground and gently pushed her to a stand in front of him. It was Beany.

Beany yanked the wig off and choked out, "It was Melvin. I watched him put the box in. It looked like a shoebox wrapped in brown paper." Tears ran down his cheeks, further streaking the powder caked on them.

The wrapped boxes in Melvin's truck flashed through Junior's mind.

Emma yelled, "The mail carrier is coming." She ran down the road and waved her to a stop.

A deputy sheriff screeched to a stop, siren screaming and lights flashing. Cochran arrived seconds later. Beany's mom, Judy Sue, appeared, panting. She enveloped Beany and Junior. His sisters were talking through their tears.

"Quiet," Cochran's voice roared. "First, does anyone need medical attention? Beany, you okay?"

Beany sniffled. "I—I'm all right. I'll calm down."

"Okay," Cochran yelled, this time not quite as loudly. "What the hell happened?"

Again, everyone started talking at once. Cochran shook his head, raised his hand and pointed it at Beany. "You see something? That why you're so upset?"

Beany stepped away from Junior and his mother. "I saw it. I'm the one who made it go off, so no one else would get hurt. I hate that man." He started to tear up again as everyone stared at him.

"Okay, son, talk slowly and start at the beginning." Cochran motioned toward the deputy. "Get the boy some water." The deputy returned with a bottle of water, a snicker on his face.

Beany glugged it half down. Wiping his lips, he said, "Thank you." Taking a big breath, he began. "I was helping Mom in the attic look for some old pictures and I found my grandmother's dress, apron and her old wig." He patted his dress. "I planned to bring dinner over here for the family. It's April Fool's day, so I thought I would pretend to be an old maid or cook and surprise them. You know how I'm in school plays and like to act. I made a ham and scalloped potato casserole and was carrying it in a basket." He took a deep breath. "Anyway, by that big bush," he pointed toward an immense, leafless, lilac bush that spread almost into the road about thirty feet down Milliken Road toward his home. "I heard a vehicle and I thought, I can't be seen like this. I mean, if I was going on stage, I'd at least have better make-up on and nylons over my hairy legs." Beany frowned as the deputy snickered again and rolled his eyes. "So, I hid myself up against the fence and scrunched all down in the bush. Melvin drove up in his truck and stopped at the mailbox."

Cochran barked. "You sure it was Melvin?"

"Of course, I've been seeing him my whole life, I know his truck and it was him that got out, came around to the back-passenger side door, pulled out the box and put it in the mailbox. I even saw Rusty, his dog, and was afraid he'd see me and bark. I heard Melvin say something like, 'This is for messing with my boxes.' He was in a hurry. I could tell by the way he drove off." Beany took another slug of water. He pointed to the dirt in front of the mailbox, then at the deputy. "You all probably ruined good evidence. Maybe you can still get plaster prints of the tires or something cool like that."

"Got it." Cochran waved people back into the driveway. "But why the hell did you take it upon yourself to detonate the damn thing? For God's sake, what made you even consider it might be an explosive device?"

Beany placed two fingers to his temple as he thought. "I've never trusted him. I wondered why he would deliver a box wrapped in brown paper. I mean, if there was nothing wrong with it, why wouldn't he have driven it up to the house? Then, I remembered he wasn't supposed to be around the farm. I knew the mail carrier was coming soon. I knew someone, usually Junior, might come check the box." He squirmed around on his feet, waved his hand to stop Cochran's next question. "I didn't bring my phone, I forgot it. I'm always misplacing it anyway. See, it just felt suspicious. I wondered if there was a way I could set it off before anyone got hurt. If it didn't go off, I would carry it up to the house with my basket."

Junior blurted out, "That's crazy. What did you do?"

"Well, at home, when I put the apron on, I found a ball of ugly green yarn in the pocket. You can see some it over by the ditch. From watching reality cop shows on TV, I figured the box would only explode when it was opened or shaken hard. I opened the mailbox and very gently touched the package. I saw the way Melvin handled it. He was careful, but not jumpy, you know? Anyway, I got a long stick and jiggled the mailbox several times." He mimed poking the mailbox with a stick. "Nothing happened, so I slid the package out a ways and wrapped and tied my yarn around the box. Both ways, several times. This way, I had something to pull against. I strung a double strand across the road and got as low in the ditch as I could. It's a deep ditch on that side. I took the dish out of the basket, set it down where it wouldn't spill, and held the basket over my head. Guess I thought it could be like a helmet or something. Anyway, I yanked the yarn hard. It worked because the package flew out of the mailbox, hit the ground and exploded." Beany shivered and pulled Junior's arm around him.

Junior gazed at him in awe. "That was brave, but…"

"Stupid. I know. I'm more scared talking about it now than I was actually doing it. It just made sense. Melvin is evil." Beany stepped away and pointed to a disturbed area in front of the mailbox. He called to Cochran and the deputy. "You can see where it detonated and you can see the pattern of how far the shrapnel went. You should measure it and take pictures. I think it was designed to blow up close to someone when they opened the lid. Maybe there was a fine wire that triggered the bomb." He looked around the area. "I don't think any of the shrapnel got as far as me in the ditch."

Junior heard the deputy mutter something to Cochran about some gay kid in a dress telling them how to do their business. Junior turned, saw Cochran frown and heard him growl, "That kid in a dress has a better grasp on this than you. You're the one that didn't establish a perimeter with tape and those are your footprints through the detonation spot. Now get the state out here and tell them to bring the A.T.F. This is a federal crime scene now."

Cochran walked up to Beany and stuck his hand out. "Thank you, son. I think you just helped get someone on their way to jail. I'm not sure I approve of messing with suspicious boxes instead of calling the police, but I understand your reasons. I'm just thankful your judgment was solid and everything worked out well." He grasped the lacy edge of Beany's grandmother's dress sleeve and grinned. "You look mighty fine in this, but I missed seeing you with the wig on."

Beany grabbed the wig from his mother and pulled it on. "This is real hair. It's just a bit musty. I'll shampoo it before I wear it again." He marched across the road and down into the ditch, returning with his basket. He opened it in front of Cochran and lifted the lid of the dish. "See, I can cook more than just fried egg sandwiches."

"Oh, my god; and I haven't had lunch yet." Cochran turned to the rest of the family and the mail carrier. "Y'all can go back now. The state and feds will probably be talking to you later. We're putting the word out to pick up Melvin." He headed toward his car.

Junior watched his mother approach Cochran. "Fred, I'm sure Beany fixed enough to feed an army. Can you join us around six-thirty for dinner? Besides, we've got some questions to ask."

Cochran told Connie he would try to answer them. He glanced around and gave Jens a little wave. Junior noticed his face flush as he climbed into his Jeep.

Junior held Beany back a moment so they could walk beside their mothers up the drive. No one spoke. Even the girls and Jens walking ahead were silent. When they got near the garage, Ellen waited for them. "Both your vehicles and our rented one have flat tires. You need to let Cochran know. Maybe Junior can check the monitor to see if it picked up anyone coming around during the night."

Connie shook her head and wiped her eyes. Her shoulders sagged. "This is too damn much." She took a big breath, straightened up, and pointed to Junior. "You go check the hard drive." She pointed to Ellen. "You and Jens check the tires. He's experienced with flat tires. Tell him to call the same tire company he dealt with the other day with what we need." She pulled Judy Sue's arm around her waist and the two walked slowly toward the house as Junior and Beany sped ahead.

Chapter Thirty

Connie

Connie and Judy Sue paused on the patio as the crew rushed into the house. The clan appeared to be partly in shock, all chattering away and seeming anxious to find something to do. Anything to keep their minds off what just happened.

Connie looked up at the dull afternoon sun. "Is your jacket warm enough for a while? I can't deal with going inside to all that commotion. Can we sit at the patio table a few minutes?"

"Of course, I'm plenty warm enough. It's going to take me a long time to cool down anyway. I can't believe that son of mine."

The two sat down next to each other at the faded green table parked at the edge of the patio. Connie thought it seemed like they were next to each other most of their adult lives, long before the boys were born. She started to giggle. "Oh, Judy, I can't believe your son either. What did he have on his cheeks?"

"He didn't tell everyone, but he also found his grandmother's make-up case and liberally applied her powdered rouge." She started laughing as she put her arms around Connie. "Years and years ago, I gave up dreaming about having a child. Before that, when I did dream about one, someone like Beany never entered my mind. Oh, God. I took a picture of him in his grandmother's dress and emailed it to his father just before Beany left the house. His dad wanted to know the address of the nightclub featuring ancient drag queens." She nudged Connie. "Did you see and hear what that deputy said?"

"Yes. Did you hear Cochran's response? I bet that deputy never says anything about someone being gay again." Connie winked at her.

"What does that wink mean? Why is Cochran coming for dinner? When did this friendship start?"

"Actually, it started when he met Jens. I sense they might be interested in each other." Connie burst into laughter again as she watched Judy's face.

Their laughter slowed and they became quiet. Connie felt the weight of her future hovering again. Judy took her hand and squeezed it. "Do you have any idea what's going to happen with you and the farm yet?"

Connie patted Judy's hand. "About what's going to happen with the farm, I'm not sure. Jack Walker, our lawyer, is meeting with us Saturday or Sunday. He wants all the family here. I don't know whether to be worried or not. There's some holding company Shaw and Melvin were involved in. We know little about it. At the least, I think I'll have this half of the section with the buildings." She didn't tell Judy that the lawyer told her Melvin had to be present also. How was that going to happen if the guy was in jail? She heard Judy's sigh and realized she had issues regarding their future too. "How are you and Albert doing with your long-term plans?"

"We're still up in the air. Al is getting tired of traveling all over the area to sell his beef. He loves raising the organic, grass-fed angus, he loves mechanics. He hates all the marketing and personal travel it takes to get the meat into the good restaurants and quality butcher shops." She stretched. "If he hired someone to handle the sales, we would barely break even. We make enough to live on, but our only savings is equity in the farm. Anyway, I think you have more issues to deal with. At least no one is blowing up our mailboxes and slashing our tires."

Connie's heart broke. She sagged, crying, into Judy's arms. She was thankful Judy knew to just let her cry things out. She didn't need advice. She didn't need questions. She just needed to be hugged and held. Judy managed to pull some tissues out of her pocket. Connie wiped her eyes, blew her nose and carefully pulled herself out of Judy's embrace.

She waited. Getting her head on straight, as she liked to say. After several minutes, she stood. "I'm good to go. Thank you, I needed that. Can you stay for dinner?"

"The good thing about you and me is that we are rarely down at the same time. I'm glad I could be here for you. It's a no for dinner. Beany made extra for us, and Al should be rolling in about seven. I'll text you. You call me when you can. I love you." Judy scrambled out of her chair and marched her short body down the driveway.

The long and short of it, Connie thought as she watched Judy leave. *I'm tall and skinny, she's short and stocky. She picks me up. I pick her up. Thirty-five years, half of that her helping me raise the girls, now, seventeen years, both raising gay sons. I'm now a widow.* Connie shook her head, hard, like it might rattle things into place, so they made sense. *I may be a widow, but I'm still a mother, still a neighbor and even though I can't rattle things into place yet, they will fall in place.*

She bustled into the kitchen to find Junior dressed in a long apron, wearing a string mop-head as a wig. The girls were laughing and egging on the boys to dance. Thank god those two broke the tension, she thought. Our nerves need a break.

Jens waved her over for a hug. He spoke into her ear so she could hear above the hubbub. "Cochran called, they picked up Melvin. He's in jail. The boys figured that's a reason to celebrate. Junior found video of someone sneaking around the garage that resembles Melvin. He was only in there a few minutes. Apparently, he crawled through one of those old windows. None of your tires were slashed, just the valve stems pulled. The tire company will be here within the hour to fix them. Junior emailed a copy of the video to Cochran who should be here soon."

Connie turned and held her hand up without saying a word.

"Oops, Mom's got her hand up, so our mouths go shut. Why did we ever tell her that's how the counselors called everyone to attention at summer camp?" Gayle raised her hand, too. The talking ceased as all looked to Connie.

"I hate to change the subject, but we do have several things to discuss. One, the rental company arrives at ten tomorrow morning with the tables and chairs. With all the commotion going on, Shed One is not prepared. Should we cancel them and move the event inside our house?"

"Mom, that's too much commotion for in here. Could we pull it off? Yes, but why go through the extra aggravation?" Gayle looked around the table. "If we all pitch in, can't we get that place cleared out and swept by ten? We have the rest of the day to decorate and set up."

Junior looked across the table at Jens. "Jens and I can move the big equipment out and park it behind the bins."

"What's the floor like?" Connie looked concerned. "If there's a lot of grease and we have to spend hours scrubbing, I'm not sure it's worth it. Damn that Melvin. He could have been doing that, instead of spying on us and bombing us."

"Mom, who gives a rats' ass?" Jane waved her hand. "Oil on the floor or not. Dad was oily, hiding all this crap, hiding his other life. You're too nice, Mom. No one's going to care about a few stains on the floor of a farm shed." Jane shook her fist, before getting a drink of water. "Maybe this will cool me down." She waved away her mother's hug and gulped the water. "I'm okay now. You all can go on."

Jens looked around the room before speaking. "Connie, only the shop area is a bit dirty and we weren't going to use that area anyway. I thought we'd string some rope to cordon it off. The main floor is fine. It won't take much more than a good sweeping. I think Junior and I can have that place shipshape by this evening. If it rains or snows, that's still the best place for it. We'll crank the heat up, too."

Connie smiled. "Thank you, Jens. That does make the most sense. Now, second, Jack, our lawyer, finally got back to me. He wants to meet with the family tomorrow, Saturday, or Sunday. He said he has to read a letter Shaw wrote over the years, and updated before he went into a coma. He also wants to go over the will." She looked at Jane. "I'm glad you expressed your anger. I do feel angry at times as well, but I feel like we have to keep moving along with everything. Once this is all over, I might go punch some seed bags again."

Jane raised her fist again. Everyone followed. Fists raised, silent, each looking around the room and nodding in solidarity.

Junior broke the silence. Reaching into a bag of chips, he said, "It seems odd, talking about the will when Dad, Shaw, just died. Mom, do you think he changed the will about me in it? I mean, if anyone was going to be cut out, it would be me."

"Son, look at me." Connie waited till Junior looked her in the eyes. "Jack said to bring my copy of the will which I took to mean there hasn't been a change." She waited until he slowly smiled at her. "However, there's one more complication. Jack said Dad was insistent that Melvin be present when he reads this letter. Somehow, this letter he wrote will clear things up."

"Mom, what did Jack say was in the letter? This is crazy. Besides, Melvin is in jail." Emma sat down at the table.

Connie looked at the confused faces around the room. "It is crazy. Jack said Dad made him swear not to read it by himself and that Melvin must be present." She looked at Jens. "Can you contact Cochran to get Melvin out here? I'm not sure how I feel about hearing a letter read with a guy that wanted to kill or maim us sitting at the same table."

"Give me a few minutes," Jens said. He texted Cochran while everyone helped themselves to snacks.

Anything to keep busy, Connie thought.

Jens' phone rang. He listened a few moments, then hung up. "Cochran says they can bring him bound and gagged if needed. He'll have him here and he won't be able to hurt anyone. He promises. Says his last official days as Sheriff are not going to be ruined by that turd." Jens reached over and patted Connie's hand. "He swears."

Connie gave a tense smile. "That's good. Jack did say he will be able to answer some of our questions about Farm Holding. He didn't set it up, but said he has done a few title transfers for them. He understands how we might be confused and surprised."

Mary snorted. "Is that the best he can say? He understands how we might be, might be, confused? Try shocked and dismayed. Scared. Angry. Might be?" She pushed her chair back and started to stand, then sat back down. "I'm sorry, Mom. Were you through, or is there more crazy stuff to share?"

"No, Mary, I'm through." She held her hand up till Mary looked at her. She smiled till she knew her eyes twinkled. "I think I might be confused, too. Might be."

Mary started laughing and shook her fist in mock anger at her mother.

How many times do we have to keep breaking this tension? Connie reached into Junior's bag to grab some chips. *Thank god, we're still able to do it. I just hope hearing Shaw's letter answers some of these questions, for better or for worse.* "Kids, what happens if we learn more things? Bad ones?"

"Well, we have to take the bad with the good, Mom. That's what you taught us growing up. We'll survive. It would be a lot nicer to have nothing but good memories of Dad. However, that's not the case. It's painful, but that's our lives." Gayle spoke softly. "Don't forget the grief process."

No one answered for several minutes.

Connie cleared her throat. "We do need to grieve, but something has been at the back of my mind the longer your father held on. Each of you girls have a full life to live back home. I know some of you are losing income being away. While I want you to stay, I will totally understand if some of you need to leave before the memorial service. You've already been away from home five to six days. Adding three more makes it a long time. I feel like you got to say goodbye to your father." Her shoulders sagged. "Even if it wasn't a satisfactory goodbye."

"Thanks, Mom," Gayle said. "It would be nice if I can return to Seattle this Sunday, to begin a shift that night. Are you sure you wouldn't mind?"

"No, it makes perfect sense. Let me call Jack to come out tomorrow afternoon. By then the tables and chairs should be set up. We could meet in Shed One. I sure as heck don't want Melvin in my house." She looked around for Beany and pointed at him. "Could you have some cookie bars and lemonade ready tomorrow? That would be helpful."

"Cookie bars? Like sheet cookies? Sure, Mom Connie." Beany looked pleased to help.

Over a late dinner that evening, Connie felt a weight lifted off her and the family. Not the entire weight, but part of it. The girls agreed that Ellen, Mary and Gayle would leave early Sunday morning for the airport. The other three would leave Tuesday morning. She bit into Beany's scalloped potatoes with ham. "Oh, Beany. How did you do this? This is excellent and I'm sure it's low calorie."

Beany beamed with pride, his wig and his grandmother's makeup were off. She was thankful for Beany. Somehow, his exuberant behaviors seemed to level out the extremes for everyone else, the highs and lows, the hills and valleys. She was glad things were settling down. She was a widow now. Though sad, at least she could begin focusing on life as single woman. A single woman with lots of questions about things. At least she knew who she was.

The back doorbell rang. Before anyone could stand to go answer it, Cochran marched in. "You got a minute?" His voice sounded stressed. He looked around the kitchen. "Everybody here?" She nodded. He pulled out his kerchief and swiped his forehead and neck. "Melvin got out on bail." He waited till the chorus of expletives and voices stopped. "I agree, it's pure cow shit. Now, keep quiet while I tell you what I know."

Jens got up and brought him a glass of water.

"Thanks, buddy." Cochran took a long drink. He looked down at Connie, then around the table. "Okay. Melvin offered no resistance when the deputies picked him up at his house about two-thirty this afternoon. Didn't say a word other than he wanted to call a lawyer. He said he exploded two other packages behind his house. He told them where, and my guys checked it out. We believe him. They went through his house, found explosive-making things, but nothing close to another bomb." He took another drink. "They let him make several calls when they were booking him. This young hotshot lawyer from Worthington showed up and got the judge to hold an emergency bail hearing. Hotshot laid out the fifty-grand bail money in cash, plus another ten guaranteeing the lawyer would personally escort him around town, and to his arraignment coming up. I ran into Jack right after you set up that meeting, so Melvin will still be here tomorrow. Just now, he'll be with his babysitter lawyer." Cochran stepped back. "Now you can whoop and holler. I would." He drained his bottle of water and sat down on Connie's desk chair.

Connie placed her head in her hands. She was thankful no one whooped or hollered. That wasn't their style. Moan, groan, then ask questions. She raised her head to find her children watching her, waiting for her to speak first. "Are we safe? That's my first question."

Her kids all nodded.

Cochran stood. "Part of the bail release is that he can't have weapons or explosives. We removed everything from his home, he even pointed some out. The problem is, we have no idea what he may have hidden in all the farms they control." He pointed at Junior who raised his hand.

"What about his truck, does he still have that? Isn't that part of the evidence?"

"Yes, Junior. We confiscated it for the evidence team to go through. Luckily, his computer was in it, so we have that, too. The state and feds don't think this situation is the highest priority, compared to some things happening in The Cities, but they will be out Wednesday to start their investigation. They have a lot of material, so it will be interviewing folk, which is mostly Beany."

Connie stood and began pacing. She liked to walk when she was trying to think, another reason she loved her big old house. "So, help me get this straight. Melvin supposedly has no guns, he's being babysat by a young lawyer, the two found enough cash to lay out sixty thousand dollars for bail. Melvin has no truck, which I assume means he has to ride with his lawyer, and he only lives a little over three miles down the road. Are we safe?" Connie watched Cochran make several notes before stepping closer to him. "Doesn't a judge have to set bail? How did one do so, so quickly? Given the facts you have about the explosion, why?"

Cochran lifted his hat and scratched his head. "My staff are quite certain you'll be safe. They will be making extra patrols and will be checking closely on Melvin's lawyer's vehicle." He paused and glanced at Junior who smiled back. "The judge thinks Melvin over-reacted with the explosives after learning he couldn't come on the property. Melvin claimed he was upset over his bluebird boxes being tampered with and was just acting out. He never intended to hurt anyone." Everyone groaned. "Get this, the judge likes Farm Holding. When he heard the holding company being mentioned as something we were also exploring, and might be seeking a subpoena for, he said, 'Farm Holding was excellent in dealing with my grandfather. They paid his taxes for years and enough for him to live comfortably till he died. Plus, Melvin delivered the old guy's medication, checked his blood pressure and called the doctor to adjust his medication.' Go figure. I can't wait till this comes to trial and the judge realizes his father might have lived even longer."

Stunned silence was followed by Connie's gasp. "That's what they were doing? That's how Farm Holding acquired so much property?" She looked at Jens. "That's what you were going to tell us the other night before we got interrupted?"

Jens stood. "Yes, that's what this is beginning to look like." He pointed at Cochran. "He's trying to dig up more info. So that's all I know. However, those words almost echo the words we heard from an old couple who haven't agreed to sign with Farm Holding."

Everyone looked at Cochran. "I don't have much more to add, other than we need a whole lot more information. After this family meeting tomorrow, I hope we have more to go on."

Junior pointed at Cochran. "Hey, did those transponders we put in the birdhouses do anything?"

"Yup," Cochran replied, a slight smile on his face. "They led us right to Melvin's truck where you placed them. All three were there and came back with the truck when we confiscated it." He shuffled on his feet and grinned at Junior. "Of course, we pulled them for other assignments."

Connie touched Cochran's arm. "Do you want to see the files of the properties Farm Holdings controls?"

He thought a moment. "It's the ones they don't control yet that worry me."

"We don't have access to those, I think they're on the computer," Jens said. "Worthington Security has access, but he wouldn't share them with us because, according to his records, Connie doesn't have ownership in the holding company."

"Right now, that would take a subpoena from the same judge that loves Farm Holding. I got about a dozen sworn sheriff deputies and I'm calling most of them in for the next few days to do more investigating and talking with other county sheriffs. I'm concerned for the old people that Farm Holding is providing medical services to."

~ * ~

That night, Connie's mind twisted and turned as she tried to sleep. What else could happen? When would things settle down? Would they? She switched sides and slid another pillow under her head. Too much, she pulled it out again and tucked just the edge under her main one. How could she have missed this other side to Shaw? A side of a man, her husband, who would have killed her. A man who had an entire business she knew nothing about. Plus, another name she didn't know of. Were Shaw and Melvin responsible for other people's deaths? Old people? Would she learn more about this? Still, how did she miss what she already knew? With never a glimpse of their other lives?

She sat up, tucked the extra pillow behind her and sipped at her half-cup of cold Sleepytime tea. When would I have had time to find this out? It's not like we dated or had Match.com available to run background checks on each other. She knew of Shaw, met Alice, his first wife, around the area, at community events and occasionally at the library with the girls. She attended Alice's funeral, still in her own grief over Mrs. Hanson's death. She remembered the day, about a month after Alice Skogman's funeral, when she was in the library. She was volunteering almost full time, trying to decide what to do with her life. Move to The Cities and attend college? Except that would place her closer to Hans. How would they handle that? She wasn't worried, though, and it would be a chance to go to school. She still lived with the Hansons, Jens and the old man. Each of them was adjusting to the idea that Connie soon would be moving on with her life.

The library doors opened, Ellen and Mary had rushed in and almost knocked her over, hugging her. They came three times in the past week, just to see her. That day, Shaw walked behind them, an odd expression on his face. The girls pulled back from her and looked at their father. He cleared his throat, shuffled his feet and looked at the floor. "Miss Johnson, we could use some help here—"

"You need some books? I'll be glad to help. Besides, I'm Connie, not Miss."

Ellen snickered while Mary looked like she might cry.

Shaw's face turned red. He coughed.

"I'm sorry. I interrupted," Connie said.

"These, these girls need some female things…" His voice faded off.

Connie pulled the girls to her. "Let me take them aside and talk with them. Would that be easier for everyone?"

The girls flew into her arms. Shaw looked relieved, but still perplexed. He looked at his watch.

Connie glanced at the time. It was four-forty. The library closed at five. She whispered to the girls, "Do we need to buy some things?" They nodded. "Tonight? Now?"

"We think soon. We just want to be prepared and Dad seemed weird about taking us shopping, so we told him to bring us to you." Ellen looked up into Connie's face with a mixture of sadness, humor and embarrassment.

"Give me a second with your dad." Connie released the girls and walked over to Shaw. "Mr. Skogman, I have nothing planned for this evening. Why don't I help the girls find some books on puberty, then take them to Marshall for a little shopping trip. We'll eat at McDonalds and I'll have them home by seven-thirty or so. How's that sound?"

Shaw exhaled a big breath. His eyes focused on hers. They were a beautiful bluish gray. "You'd do that? I would certainly appreciate it. I was going to ask our neighbor, but the girls insisted we come see you first." He pulled out his wallet and handed her a fifty and a twenty-dollar bill. "Here, this should cover it and their food." He gave her a wistful look, turned and left.

Connie felt a spark with this quiet, out of place man. It surprised her. He was much older than her. She knew she loved the girls, but thought it was nothing more than helping them as another member of the community trying to support them.

After purchasing bras, some new underwear, sanitary pads and belts, followed by a discussion about puberty and sexuality while sitting in McDonalds parking lot, the girls opened up. They laughed and giggled all the way home. "You should have seen Dad's face when we told him we wanted to go buy pads and bras," Mary said. "Mom told us several times we were getting old enough and she was going to buy us training bras in a few days, but then..." Both girls sniffled.

"Anyway," Ellen said. "I thought Dad was going to have a cow. It was like he never thought of this situation. He's so out of it. I'm so glad you were available. We like Judy Sue, our neighbor, but you're younger and cooler."

The following week, Shaw began coming into the library with the girls instead of dropping them off. Connie noticed he read farm periodicals while the girls chatted with her and searched for books. Both were prolific readers. About the third week of him coming with them, Shaw noticed her shelving books away from the girls and walked over to her. "Could we have dinner?" He stared at the shelf above her head.

"Right now? With the girls?" Connie forced herself not to laugh at the man. He looked so uncomfortable.

"Umm, not right now. Not with the girls. Well, I don't know about the girls. I need to do something with them."

His shoulders dropped. He looked so awkward, Connie wanted to pat him and tell him he'd be all right.

"Tell you what," she replied. "Let me pick up something and bring it to your house and we'll eat together. I think that seems much more comfortable for everyone, don't you?"

He looked like her words were a life raft thrown to a sinking man.

She went to the girls. "What have you been eating lately? What are you hungry for that we could fix together at your house?"

The twins' eyes got large. "You'd come help cook something? We're tired of casseroles and hot dishes the old ladies from the church keep bringing." Ellen looked around to make sure she hadn't spoken too loud.

"I'm hungry for some good old spaghetti with Italian sausage and a big salad," Mary said. "We tried to make it the other day, but the spaghetti turned out all gloppy and came out in one huge pile. Dad tried to make some, but his came out like chewing on toothpicks." She giggled and looked around to see where her father was, then whispered, "Dad can't cook much. I'm so tired of scrambled eggs and cold cereal in the morning. Hey, could we make garlic bread too?"

Connie lightly poked the girls. "And spaghetti's not like a casserole?"

The girls giggled.

"No, definitely not," Mary said. "Not when it comes out of the cooking pan all steamy and the Italian sausages are cooked in the sauce. In a casserole, it's all smushed together and baked and looks like it's got mold growing in it."

"That's the parmesan, silly." Ellen nudged her sister. "It's just different when it's cooked fresh. Better."

Now, Connie took another sip of her cold tea and readjusted the pillows behind her. She remembered back to that night. How she purposely thought about what kind of man Shaw might be. While she and the girls fixed dinner, he sat in the family room, reading and watching NBC national news and the local news out of Worthington. It felt very comfortable. The girls were relaxed, she was surprised how relaxed she felt. The conversation over dinner was between her and the girls. Shaw would answer a question directly, but didn't join in the chit chat or laughter, yet seemed at ease. Gradually, she realized that was his nature.

The most emotional moment came as she and the girls were doing dishes while Shaw sat, drinking his coffee.

"Connie, when we're done, can you hang around till we're ready for bed?" Mary asked cautiously.

"Of course. Do you take baths or showers?"

Mary teared up as Ellen looked at the floor and said, "We used to take baths in Mom's big tub…" A sob erupted from her, then both girls fell into her arms, weeping.

Connie hugged them tightly. "I understand why you want to take showers." She glanced at Shaw and caught a glimpse of a tear as he sat, watching them. She stayed till after she reviewed their homework and they were in bed.

Shaw walked with her to the back door and watched her slip her jacket on. "Thank you," he said. He shifted his feet. "Could we do this again?"

She looked at him and laughed. "Of course, as often as you or the girls want."

He gave a brief smile, awkwardly patted her shoulder, turned and went back to the kitchen.

Three days later, she showed up again. The following week, she came three times. The week after that, five times. She realized the girls had many issues regarding their mother's suicide. Issues they had no place to express. The more she got to know them, the more they opened up with her. What had they done to make her kill herself? Why then? They were planning a weekend trip to Sioux Falls two days after she died to shop for bras, clothes, see a new movie and swim in the Holiday Inn pool. Just their mother and them. No cousins or their mom's friends or anyone else. At times, the girls were emotional wrecks. Several nights, they became so distraught, she slept over in their room.

By the fourth week, Connie loved the girls and, more importantly, knew she could help them. She recognized Shaw was not the type of father to parent alone, yet she was very comfortable in his presence and was quite sure he was interested in her, though it was in a strange, awkward, non-romantic, romantic way. She also knew it was time to leave the Hansons. Jens was stable in spite of an uncomfortable relationship with his father. He told her he would be fine if she needed to go back to school or to help someone else. "Just as long as we can talk on the phone or write each week," he said.

Connie slept over one Sunday night. After seeing the girls off to the school bus the next morning, she walked out to the farm office. Melvin startled and left the room. Shaw stayed at his desk and didn't seem surprised to see her. He broke the silence. "I'm not good at talking or expressing emotion, but I like you."

Connie smiled at him. "I like you too, but what does that mean?"

He shook his head and gave a rare smile. "I know it's soon, but I'd like to be in a relationship with you. You are wonderful with the girls."

"Do you want to be in a relationship because of me? Or because of the girls?"

His face flushed, almost bright red as Connie continued to stare at him, not angrily, just wanting, needing, to know. Somehow, at that moment, she knew she could either be a live-in caretaker for the girls or be a wife. She hoped it would be as a wife, though. There was something about this man that attracted her. Whatever was going on with Hans would never change, and she was glad for that. She sensed this man would allow her to be who she was and she could allow him to be who he was. Was it tingly-all-over love at first sight? No. Was it steady, dependable love? She thought so. She hoped so.

Shaw stood and stepped closer to her. He opened and closed his mouth a few times. "Because of you."

"Does that mean you want to marry me?"

"Yes, in a couple of months."

"Good. I'll move my stuff into the guest room today. After a month or so, we'll tell the girls we're thinking of marriage. If they have any objections, we'll hold off till they're comfortable with the idea. That gives everyone, including you and me, time to adjust or readjust."

She and Shaw never spoke of marriage again. A month later, at dinner, Shaw looked at her and smiled. She smiled back. He said, "Girls, do you have any objections to Connie and me getting married?"

Each gasped.

"We love Connie," Ellen said, "but what will we call her?"

"You can still call me Connie. I can never replace your mother."

Mary sat, chin on her chest, not looking at anyone, tears rolling down her cheeks. After a few minutes, Ellen asked her, "Are you upset? Don't you want Connie and Dad to get married?"

"No, I'm not upset. I'm still sad over Mom, but I'm happy Connie will be here all the time. We need her."

Late that night, Shaw slipped into her room, gently took her hand and led her back to the master bedroom. She was surprised at his passion, tenderness and attentiveness to her needs. After making love, his arms wrapped around her, she whispered, "I love you."

"I know. Thank you," he said and hugged her tighter.

Somehow, she realized that was all he could say. And that was enough.

Six weeks later, they married at the courthouse while the girls were in school. That evening, Judy Sue and Albert had them over for dinner, pie and ice cream. The men talked farming, the wives and twins about everything but. Back then, it all seemed so normal. So logical.

She got up and went to the bathroom. Climbing back into bed, she thought, *No, never in my wildest imagination could I have guessed Shaw Skogman led several lives.* She rolled on her side and drifted off to sleep.

Chapter Thirty-One

Jens

Later that same Friday afternoon, Jens, Cochran and Junior spent several hours in the farm office, trying to get a handle on the properties Farm Holding owned or controlled, frustrated they couldn't find any additional information regarding properties Farm Holding didn't own, but were surveilling.

Junior looked antsy. Finally, he said, "This is boring. I'm calling Beany and going for a run." He looked at Jens with a slight smirk as he left.

"Did he leave so that we could kiss again? Is this a working date?" Cochran stepped toward Jens, only to stop when his shoulder radio went off. "Multi-vehicle accident with injuries on State 12 and County 10." Cochran groaned. "Gotta run." He raced out of the office.

Jens followed and watched him tear off, his siren sounding at the end of the driveway. *When are we going to have a real date? Is that even possible with a sheriff/detective so dedicated to his community? Will this always be happening?* He returned to the office to close and lock the files and turn the lights out.

Saturday, April 2

At seven, Saturday morning, Jens received a text from Cochran. *Meet me at Syds at 8 for breakfast.* Jens was waiting when Cochran came into Syds at eight-ten.

Cochran yawned and waited for his coffee to be filled. "Quite an accident last night. One drunk teen with a carload of kids tried to pass a pickup hauling some chickens all covered up in their coops. He drove the oncoming senior citizen off the road before getting clipped by the pickup."

"Sounds like a mess. Anyone killed?"

"No humans, thank God. The old couple were bounced around, but no injuries. Their car is likely totaled from the mailbox they took out. For some reason, the kids were sane enough to all buckle up and most were high enough on pot to stay relaxed. The driver almost puked on my shoes." He grinned at Jens. "And the farmer with the chickens? Well, his driver's side front fender needs to be replaced..."

"What about the chickens? Is that why we're meeting here? Syd's making chicken pot pie today?"

Cochran laughed. "Surprisingly, only two chickens died, but it sure was a hell of a time chasing some of them down the road and in the ditches. I think they sensed their freedom." He took a drink of coffee and attacked the Danish in front of him. Both chewed for several minutes before Cochran said, "Nothing happened last night with Melvin. My deputies said his lawyer stayed at his house and his car never left. Listen, we still got work to do. C'mon, finish up then we're headed out."

"What the hell. It's a Saturday. Do detectives have to work weekends?" Jens faked a groan. "What's the big hurry?"

Cochran bit into his Danish, chewed and said, "For some reason, I want to see Melvin's delivery van. He told us he stored it in a shed about a quarter mile across the road from his place. Let's run by and see it." He drained his coffee, threw a ten on the table, grabbed the remains of his Danish and rushed off. Outside, Jens noticed the jeep was muddy with what looked like remnants of chicken crap. "Don't say a word about the condition of my car, unless you're prepared to clean it." Cochran tore out of the gravel parking lot like there was a fire or another accident. Jens followed him to Connie's, parked his truck and jumped into the Jeep.

Cochran drove past Melvin's place. "Guess his lawyer didn't bring his Mercedes." He pointed at a rusty blue Hyundai Elantra in the drive. Cochran pulled onto the property that held a garage, no windows, with a wood shed attached. Evidence of a razed farm house and barn showed in the dirt, waiting to be planted. The garage door opened by a key pad. The side door of the garage was locked. "Damn," Cochran said as he studied the padlock.

Jens stepped into the wood shed and let his eyes adjust. He began feeling around the edges of the door frame. "Bingo," he called out. "Sometimes it takes an old farmer to know another one. Melvin's so meticulous, I'm surprised he didn't keep this key on him, but then, with all these properties, how many keys did he want to carry around? Besides, he had the code for the big door." He unlocked the padlock and they walked in.

Cochran flipped on the light, illuminating an older, but well maintained, white Dodge panel minivan. On each side, a magnetic sign said Prescription Delivery. He peered through the passenger window. "It's set up like a delivery truck. Shelves, clipboards, a small medical bag…Hey, there's even a nurse's jacket hanging with a name pin on it. Some people will recognize him, though I'm surprised I never heard anyone mention Melvin claimed to be a nurse. I'll take a picture, zoom in, maybe I can blow it up enough to read what it says." Cochran took several pictures, then reviewed them. "Yup, it says Melvin Smith, L.P.N. This confirms the records I've seen."

He went outside and shot photos of the garage and surrounding area. Sitting in his Jeep, sipping coffee out of his thermos the Syds waiter filled for him, he mused, "If they're messing with pills, do you think they're doing it at Worthington Pharmacy? I realize Shaw is still licensed…"

Jens felt his eyes widen. Cochran must have noticed. "Oops, guess I shared too much. Anyway, yes, Shaw Phillip is a licensed pharmacist, still in good standing. No complaints against him. Trust me, I checked. Close your mouth before a fly dives in."

Jens swallowed. "I think if he and Melvin were coming in and out of the pharmacy, even in the night, and making pills up, someone would notice and start asking questions. I think they have another place where they can produce pills from raw material."

"I agree. Got any ideas where?"

"Yup, on the farm. Let's go back and I'll show you where the place might be." Jens made a circle with his hand as if to turn around.

"I'll be... Listen, we need to rule everything out. Why don't we go visit Worthington Pharmacy, then come back to the farm? I'll buy you lunch. There's a great little Mexican place. We have time. I think the meeting with Jack isn't until four."

At Worthington Compounding Pharmacy, Cochran and Jens asked to speak with the pharmacist and waited till he was through filling several prescriptions. He led them back to a tiny office.

"As I said, I'm Sheriff Fred Cochran out of Summerville. I understand Shaw Phillip owns the pharmacy." The pharmacist nodded. "I'm sorry to tell you this, but Shaw died. He had an accidental gun injury last Saturday and wasn't able to recover."

"My God. I'm shocked. I wondered why he or Melvin hadn't checked in. They usually do early in the week. Wow. Do you have any idea what might happen to this place? I know Farm Holding owns it."

"I think that's being worked out with the lawyer later today."

Jens was surprised again at how smooth Cochran could be, how little emotion he showed.

"Can I ask several questions?" Cochran asked with a small smile.

The pharmacist waved his hand to continue.

"Are you aware that Shaw's birth name was Shaw Philip Skogman?"

"No, not really. I knew he owned Skogman Farms, too, but never realized he went by two names. Why did he do that?"

"That's what we're trying to get a handle on. Listen, did Shaw ever come in here and compound prescriptions or fill them?"

"No, never. He always said he hired me to manage the business, fill prescriptions and supervise the part-time pharmacists and staff. He pays me well and I get a decent cut of the profits." The pharmacist looked perplexed.

Jens leaned forward. "What about deliveries? Was Melvin involved in making deliveries? How far out did he deliver? Who determines what drugstore fills and delivers what scripts?"

The man thought a minute. "Some years ago, the pharmacies in the area got together and subcontracted with several local people to deliver prescriptions and medical supplies, primarily to the elderly and isolated."

He paused to pick up an intercom call. "Tell them I'll be able to fill it in about thirty minutes."

Turning to the men, he continued, "Melvin seemed to know who everyone was, so he was hired to deliver the prescriptions to folks who lived between here, Marshall and Summerville. It's a big area, but he seemed to love squeezing it in with his farm work. Melvin handled most of the regularly scheduled deliveries. In other words, he had a forty-eight-hour window in which to pick up and to deliver the prescriptions. He usually made deliveries on Tuesday, Thursday and Saturdays. If it was an emergency, we had another person handle it. Why do you ask?"

Cochran settled back in his seat like he was at a family picnic. "So, neither Melvin or Shaw ever filled scripts here. Correct?"

"That's right. Melvin seemed to like the attention of helping others. He even carried a white jacket with his L.P.N. pin on it. Claimed he was licensed years ago, but let it expire, though he said he kept his First Aid and CPR current. He was very conscientious, and always contacted us and/or the physicians if he observed anything wrong with the clients. We have a local woman who uses our vehicle for local delivery in Worthington." The pharmacist looked at his watch. "Do you have more questions? I need to get a script filled."

"Two." Cochran stood. "Has Melvin been in so far this week?"

The man replied, "No. We've had no scripts to be delivered. He did leave a message while I was busy this morning. I haven't had time to call him back. Why?"

Cochran handed him his business card. "Do me a favor. Don't return it. If he calls or shows up, call me immediately. He's under arrest, but out on bail." He patted the man on the back. "Don't worry, if everything you say is on the up and up, you'll be fine. There's a meeting this afternoon that might decide who will be in charge of Farm Holding."

"Jesus. What the hell is going on?" The pharmacist sat back further in his chair and shook his head. "What's the second question? Is this one going to shock me as well?"

"Hope not," Cochran said. "How much compounding do you do? Where do you get the raw supplies or ingredients? What kind of records do you have to keep for ordering those supplies? Did Shaw or Melvin ever acquire raw materials from here?"

"That's four more questions. We do very little compounding anymore, but enough to make it worthwhile. We order the ingredients as needed from the major drug manufacturers. We keep records for the government. Shaw and Melvin never acquired any such materials from here. Five, it's fairly simple for any registered pharmacist to order such supplies directly."

"Thank you. You've been very helpful." Cochran barged thorough the door and down the hall toward the parking area.

Jens held back. "Quite a shock. Right?" The man nodded. "How long you been here? How's it been working for Shaw?"

"I've been here twenty years. It's been great. I have no complaints with Shaw. Melvin is a bit strange, yet he's extremely knowledgeable about medications and health care." He wiped his forehead. "Tell me, do you think this place will close? If it's going to, I'd love a shot at buying it. We provide great service to the community and it's a solid business, even if it is in a small market."

"I'll mention that at the meeting. Thank you."

Jens hurried out to find Cochran on his phone.

Cochran hung up. "That was a deputy. Melvin and his monitor ran up to Syds and back. Deputy says other than that, they haven't left the house." He unlocked the doors. "Hurry. We're going to get our burritos to go. Now I'm even more interested in where you think Shaw and Melvin have their own pharmacy."

When Jens returned to Cochran's jeep, carrying the burritos and horchata, he found the man waiting with a large towel tucked around his neck, covering his torso and upper legs. "How do you think I keep my uniform looking neat when I'm on the road so much? Besides, burritos are messy."

Jens buckled in and handed a wrapped burrito to him. "These are huge. Guess you must be a boy scout—always prepared."

They were quiet as they ate. Cochran handed Jens his half-eaten meal. "Could you wrap this back up, please? I could eat the whole thing, but I don't need the whole thing." He waited till Jens was finished wrapping up the meals and putting them back in the bag. "Okay, now tell me where you think Shaw and Melvin have their own pharmacy. I can't believe it's on the farm. Someone should have noticed something."

"Let's back up a minute." Jens sipped his horchata and smacked his lips. "I love this stuff. Okay. One, I believed the pharmacist in Worthington. They're not involved with Farm Holding. Plus, he was clueless as to Shaw's other name. Two. Shaw and Melvin must be able to assemble pills someplace and would need a space and equipment to do so. Three. We now know it's easy for them to get the raw materials, the chemicals to compound and prescriptions can be switched from tablets to capsules which would be easier to adjust."

"I got it. I got it. I'm way ahead of you. Now where do you think there's room to manufacture drugs on the farm?"

"We're about five minutes out. Just wait and I'll show you." Jens grasped the edge of the towel and gently wiped Cochran's mouth. "You left a few drips. Can I take this off you now?" He untucked the towel, carefully wadded it up and dropped it on the back seat. Cochran squeezed Jens' hand and held it for several seconds. They were quiet for the rest of the ride.

"Park directly in front of the farm office window." Jens pointed to the spot. "I'll get a tape measure out of my truck."

"I got one. It's in my kit in the back." Cochran eased the Jeep to a stop and killed the engine. He reached in the back, pulled up a case and took a tape measure out of it. "Fifty feet, that long enough?"

Jens directed him to the corner where the office wall met the long wall of Shed One. "See, it's sixteen feet wide."

"Big deal, you can read a tape measure. Bet you want me to measure inside now. Right?"

"That's right. You should consider becoming a detective someday."

Cochran flipped him the bird. Inside the office, he measured the width. "I'll be damned. It's twelve feet. There's four feet missing."

"Remember when I told you about the hidden monitor and computer equipment?" Jens pointed to the white board. "Well, it kept eating at me. Where did that space come from? C'mon, let's go around and go inside Shed One and see if my hunch is correct."

Inside Shed One, Emma and Gayle were spreading plastic tablecloths on the tables the rental company set up. "Wow. This looks nice." Jens called out.

He and Cochran gazed at the long wall shared with the office. There was no bump out where the hidden electronic equipment might be. They walked along the wall and entered the bathroom. "Wow. This is a big bathroom. It looks like four feet have been taken from each side of the original wall line." Cochran slapped his thigh in excitement. "That means there's a secret room, almost eight feet wide. Look. Next to the shower stall is a closet. The door is locked…" He quit speaking as they heard more voices enter Shed One.

"It's almost time for the meeting with Jack. I wouldn't say anything to anyone else till we're sure what's going on." Jens turned to open the bathroom door, but Cochran pulled him into an embrace and kiss. "Does this count as a second date? We did an activity together. We ate, drank and kissed. Plus, our parents weren't with us."

Jens snickered. "Geez, I never thought of that. Listen, what are we going to tell folks who see us coming out of the john together?"

"Maybe we need a third date to figure that out."

Chapter Thirty-Two

Connie

Saturday Afternoon

Shed One looked cavernous without the huge tractors, combine and planter. Connie thought the family did an excellent job of setting up an area that looked comfortable, yet not like a wedding reception. Jane managed to get several photos enlarged to poster size. One was of Shaw, Alice and the twins when the girls were around five. One was of Connie, Shaw and the six girls when the twins were home from college. Another was taken of Shaw holding the hands of the twins when they were preschoolers, walking away from the camera toward the big tractor, almost in silhouette. Connie knew Alice snapped the picture and the twins always said their father complained when she showed it. He hated his photo taken. A fourth poster was made from a photo taken at the hospital with her, Shaw and newly born Junior. Neither of them wanted the photo taken, but Judy Sue was insistent. Connie realized now that Shaw's tight smile was probably him gritting his teeth over knowing the baby wasn't his. She agreed to the photo being made into a poster partly out of revenge, to show the community she thought Junior was Shaw's kid. Let the rumors fly.

Good grief, why wouldn't Shaw confront her when she told him she was pregnant? Look at all the pain his stubbornness caused in the long run. Even if they divorced over her affair, at least they could have avoided this mess. Yet, could they have? Would his opinion on betrayal be any different?

She watched as Jens and Cochran came out of the bathroom together, laughing, but looking secretive. She wondered what they had been up to all day. The seven kids were present. Jack Walker came in, looking uncomfortable. They gathered around two tables placed together to resemble a conference setting. A blue plastic tablecloth set off the variety of large cookies on two silver trays in the middle. Coffee, lemonade, tea, hot water, glasses, cups, bottles of water, and large napkins in various colors made the table look more like a celebration than the reading of a deceased man's letter and a will. *Leave it to Beany to try to keep them relaxed*, she thought.

They grew quiet as Melvin and his lawyer entered. Melvin reminded Connie of a banty rooster strutting. What did he have to strut about?

Jack asked everyone to take a seat and then introduce themselves, starting on his left with Connie. When his turn came, Melvin's lawyer puffed out his chest. "I am Harold Mains of Mains Law Offices in Worthington and Minneapolis, Minnesota, and I have several questions about this proceeding."

Jack slapped his hand on the table, startling everyone. "This is not a proceeding. This is a reading of a letter by Shaw Philip Skogman to his family. For reasons I don't understand, he required that your client, Melvin Smith, be present. Per my understanding, the only reason you are in this room is because of the bail requirement that Melvin Smith may not be out of your sight on this property. Your questions will not be addressed." Jack looked at Cochran who grinned. Jack glared at the young lawyer again. "Sherriff Cochran is here to ensure that those bail conditions are met."

Cochran looked at his watch. "Plus, two deputies are patrolling this area. One will be parked outside this building in about…three minutes."

Lawyer Harold Mains slid back in his seat, his face turning pink. Connie noticed a brief smirk cross Melvin's face. She wondered if he knew what was in the letter. His smirk said he knew at least some of it.

Jack opened his case and pulled out a large envelope

Connie sighed. Her stomach was telling her she needed something other than coffee. Milk or acid reducer. How many pages did that man write? Over how many years? She looked around the table. Every eye was focused on Jack and the papers. Every face looked nervous. Jens gave her a slight smile and an almost imperceptible wiggle of his nose. She smiled. That meant to relax. She touched Jack's hand to signify he could begin reading.

He cleared his throat, laid the papers down, picked up a bottle of water, untwisted the cap and took a small sip. "Umm, this is a most unusual situation. I've never quite encountered something like this."

Connie touched his hand again. "Jack, don't explain, just read."

Chapter Thirty-Three

Shaw's Papers

Jack took another sip of water and began, his voice low and shaky.

Letter to Family by Shaw Philip Skogman, also known as Shaw S Phillip.

Supplemental Page, added March, 27, 2011

I wrote most of this years ago. It's almost like creative non-fiction. Yes, I do know what that is. I did learn a lot from Connie talking about her love of books. Telling my story in such a format seemed important to me, and I hope for the family as well. I review it every year or so. Seeing as I will die soon, I added this supplemental page, but made no other changes.

I did intend to kill Connie. She betrayed me. Yes, I know it was years ago. Connie, your strength and quick thinking saved your life. It wouldn't have if I hadn't lost my temper. Betrayal by two wives deserves revenge.

For the record, I did not intend to kill Junior, just scare him away long enough to kill his mother. Despite my enraged state of mind, I clearly knew what I was doing. I am one-hundred per cent positive Junior is not my son. It's extremely rare for the vas deferens tubes to rejoin when a section of the tube has been removed, pins put into each of the remaining ends, and the ends folded back and stitched around the pin. That is the method they used on me when I had a vasectomy performed shortly after Emma was born. Dig up my records at University Hospital, if you must.

I was surprised, very surprised, when Connie told me she was pregnant. I didn't show it, just quietly decided to go along with her that the baby was mine. I've always taken a long approach to revenge. I simply filed the news away in a part of my brain, closed the door on that little room, but didn't lock it. I was certain I would find out who the true father of the baby was in time. I thought the affair most likely would continue and I could catch her in the act or it would become obvious who the man was. I did wonder how she could act so confident and open, as if she had nothing to hide. I didn't think it would take eighteen years to discover her lover, nor could I ever have guessed it would be Hans. I always thought she and Hans were more like sister and brother, the way she and Jens are.

Hans Hanson? I never had close male friends, nor were Hans and I close. However, he is probably the one man I most respected and admired for his intellect, his accomplishments, his winning personality—of which I have none—and his generous approach to life. Like many in this community, I was proud of him, though secretly.

Maybe jealousy helped trigger my temper. If I had more time, I would think about that. Preferably from the seat of the tractor as I planted or sprayed. That's not going to happen.

Two things. One, Farm Holding Company is being liquidated and the resources established as a family nonprofit which Connie can direct in any manner she desires. Jack Walker started the changes and will see that everything is in order. Plus, the pharmacy will be offered to the current manager who knows nothing of what I am writing.

Two: I need to tell you the combination to the safe. In spite of my anger Saturday morning, I was rational enough to change the combination so Melvin couldn't open it. The information in there will answer many questions and provide proof beyond a doubt about the other lives Melvin and I lived. I changed it because I suspect he will want to remove some of the material in it.

The combination is: from zero, spin right three complete turns back to zero; left to forty-three; right past zero twice to twenty-one; left past zero to thirteen. I ask that you wait till the end of my story to look in the safe. Please have Cochran or one of his deputies present.

I can't believe no one has complained about Farm Holding. Melvin said Hans Hanson was the only person to dig for information about us and start asking questions. After Hans' death, he told me Hans asked too many questions while they were drinking cocktails.

Melvin, remember, you know what to do, and what we agreed long ago.

~ * ~

Jack stopped reading as Connie gasped. "What, what does that mean? Melvin, remember…agreed to do?"

Everyone's eyes turned toward Melvin. He smirked and stared at his coffee, then shrugged, never changing his focus on the cup.

Lawyer Mains nudged Melvin and looked at the group. "He doesn't have to answer that question."

Connie motioned for Jack to not respond. She wanted to jump up and wipe the smirks off both the lawyers and Melvin's faces. The thought of Hans drinking cocktails flashed through her mind. Cocktails? Hans rarely drank cocktails, usually beer or wine. Why would he drink cocktails that night? Was it because it was New Year's Eve and there were only three people present? She heard herself moan. Did Melvin make the cocktails? Hans barely knew how to make a seven and seven. At the time Hans died, his wife and everyone else thought he was in perfect health. No records of any health problems. That was part of the shock of his death.

Another thought struck. *Farm Holding Company was going to be a nonprofit? With her in charge? Was that a way to dodge liability for all the harm it seemed like Shaw and Melvin were responsible for? How would that work? Could she do something good with the proceeds, if there were going to be any?* She realized everyone was staring at her.

Jens mouthed at her, "Stay focused."

She forced herself back to the present and touched Jack's hand to continue.

Melvin still stared at his cup; the smirk gone.

~ * ~

Page 1

Betrayal is wicked.

Revenge is necessary.

Patience is a virtue.

I hate being betrayed. Always have. I have this deep-seated trait, or some might say, a psychological problem. The pain of betrayal is so endemic to my being that I never forget it and I always seek revenge. I know that about myself. I know a lot more, too. I have found a slow, steady, thoughtful approach to revenge is best.

My conscience demands I tell you a bit about my early life, along with further information about the holding company, Melvin, and some of our endeavors together. By the time I finish, some may wonder about my use of the word conscience. I do have one, it's simply not like most of yours.

I'll start with my father and mother. My father, Philip Shaw Skogman, was born in 1897, near New Ulm. His parents immigrated from Sweden and took over a failed homestead farm of one hundred and sixty acres. Father's older brother, Fordham Skogman, was born in 1895. Both brothers served in World War I. Fordham managed to wrangle a role in some headquarters and came home without a scratch. Father was gassed in the trenches and his lungs were permanently scarred. He spent six months in an Army hospital after the war and came home in terrible health.

Their mother died while Father was in the hospital. Their father died in 1920, which precipitated a battle for the land. Both were to share it equally. Fordham met a woman whose parents owned the Midville farm you live on right now. Then it was one hundred and sixty acres. Fordham wanted to move away with his share of their inheritance. He sold his half of the farm, took the money, moved to Midville, married Helen and went into farming with her father. After several babies dying in infancy, they had a son, Lawrence, born around 1930.

Part of what burns so deeply in my heart was that Fordham, my uncle, claimed the best half of the farm to sell. The eighty acres he claimed and sold were high, dry, tilled easily and produced wonderful crops. The eighty acres he left Father were low, mostly wet, and a creek ran through part of it which flooded in the spring. Save for ten acres, it was basically a flood plain.

Father, who couldn't draw a deep breath, limped along on the remaining farm. He kept a few cows for milk, raised chickens and a hog or two, put in a big garden and raised what he could on the good ten acres, at first with a mule. When the depression hit, Fordham and Helen were in great shape. They inherited her dad's land, plus bought the farm next to them, using the money Fordham brought from the sale of his half of the farm. During the depression, they managed to buy the next two farms so they had the entire section, minus the church and cemetery.

Somehow, in the 1920's, Father managed to talk the widow across the road into selling him forty acres of good land on land contract. Farming that piece was the most he could handle physically, and the widow was very accommodating when it came to late payments.

From what I could gather, off and on, Father would feel a bit better. I suspect it was when he wasn't breathing as much dust from tilling and harvesting. He was also very lonely. One winter, he placed an ad in the lonely-hearts section of some Minneapolis paper. He was thirty-six. Dorothy (Dot) Gustafson replied with a picture showing a young tall blonde blue-eyed beauty who expressed her strong desire to be a farm wife, especially of one who owned his own land during the depression. She was seventeen. They corresponded several weeks, met in person once in The Cities, and married the day after she turned eighteen. Their honeymoon was spent at the farm.

Before Dot's arrival, Father managed to paint several rooms, purchase new sheets for the bed, clean the floors and get several weeks of wood cut for the kitchen wood stove. The old house had the kitchen, living room and one bedroom on the first floor and two unheated bedrooms upstairs. The kitchen stove was the main source of heat as the living room chimney was plugged.

Dot quickly realized this was not the farm of her dreams nor the man of her desires. She became pregnant their first week of marriage, and as she used to tell it, she became a typical depression-era farm wife. She had to do any and everything to help them survive. Survive with a chronically ill husband. She never spoke of those times endearingly. Usually with a sneer.

I was born January 14, 1937. The widow across the road helped deliver me. As soon as she was able, Dot began taking me to The Cities. I think to show off, also to avoid the farm. I refuse to call her mother or mom, only Dot, for reasons that will become clear. By the time I could walk and was weaned, Dot began leaving me home with Father. As I understand it, her visits away were only for several days, maybe once or twice a month. Gradually, by the time I was three, she was gone three or four days a week. When she was home, she made weak attempts at keeping up the house and cooking. Mostly, she smoked, read dime store novels, and complained to my father about what a poor provider and excuse for a man he was. A month before my fifth birthday, Pearl Harbor happened. Dot got a job in a Twin Cities factory ramping up to produce munitions, planes, trucks and supplies for the war effort. She was a Rosie the Riveter, and proud of it.

Dot bought a used car and came home once or twice a month for several hours. She would bring some food, occasionally shoes or clothes and a sucker for me. She would put several bills in a jar used to save money for property taxes. I remember dreaming about Dot visiting. I was always excited to get the sucker. We never knew which day she might visit. One day, she came in and I started jumping up and down. "Did you bring me a sucker?"

She raised her hand and slapped me across the face so hard, she knocked me to the floor. I started howling. She picked me up, slapped me again and threw me onto the couch. "Don't you ever beg for anything," she screamed. "You'll turn out as worthless as your father."

She threw the bag of groceries down and left. It was a long time before she returned and I didn't beg for a sucker. From then on, I tried my best to ignore her.

Father never stood up to her. Physically, he was too weak, which probably exhausted his mental and emotional capabilities as well. Once, she was smoking in the house. He asked her to please step outside to smoke, it was hard enough for him to breathe as it was. I remember like it was yesterday, she blew smoke toward him. "I'll smoke where I damn well please. You can go outside when I smoke." He didn't say a word, just shuffled off to the cold bedroom and lay down. My heart hardened even more.

Maybe that's when I started to learn patient revenge. When she did visit, I began looking for opportunities to sneak cigarettes out of her purse. Not the whole pack, just several. I also began wandering out to her car while she was inside. If she had a carton of cigarettes, I would steal a pack or two. I was in country school and knew the big boys would pay or trade for cigarettes. I used their lunches to supplement my sparse diet or took their money home and gave it to Dad for food money or to buy feed for the animals. He knew what I was doing. That's when he started telling me how betrayal is wicked, revenge is necessary, and patience is a virtue.

Every night, he told me, "Your uncle Fordham betrayed me, our father, and this land. Your mother betrayed her vows to me and to God, and now whores around. Betrayal is wicked. Revenge is necessary. Patience is a virtue." Frequently, he made me repeat those words. When I asked how Uncle Fordham betrayed him, he would go on and on about how Fordham wouldn't visit him in the hospital after the war, didn't tell him his mother died until he came home, how he lied to their father that my father was near death in the hospital and couldn't bear the news about their mother, and, that instead of determining the value of the tractor and farm equipment to split evenly, Fordham simply hauled the good tractor and implements away. "Stealing is also betrayal," my father would say.

I asked him why stealing Dot's cigarettes wasn't betrayal.

"That's revenge, son. That's revenge for her betrayal. There is a difference." Shortly after that, he started telling me, "If you ever get a chance for revenge on Fordham and Dot, take it. Just don't be rash. Go slow, think it through, be patient. In due time, you'll have the opportunity. Never be afraid of revenge, son." That was drilled into me night and day.

~ * ~

Connie put her hand on Jack's arm to stop him from reading further. "This is intense. I need a stretch break. There are Beany's snacks. The shop bathroom is clean. I've been told Mary cleaned it so we know it's as good as it can be." She smiled and stood up.

"Mom," Jackie asked, "did you know any of this about Dad's childhood or his mother? Did you know he was such a good writer? This truly is creative non-fiction."

"No. He mentioned his mother ran out on him and his father. His father died when he was thirteen, which brought him to his uncle and this farm. I know he was bright and am not surprised he could write well. I read some of his correspondence and speeches he gave years ago. They were well done."

Ellen spoke up. "Jackie, I remember doing family tree stuff in eighth grade. Let's just say, Mary's and my tree looked pretty bare. No family Bibles that listed people all the way back to Noah. Our mother, Alice, had a few relatives, and Mom's an orphan who didn't know who her grandparents were. Dad said his parents never talked about their ancestors and they both died relatively young. It's a good thing we got graded for turning it in, not for the content."

Connie stretched, grabbed a monster cookie and walked around, catching snippets of conversations similar to what was running wildly through her mind. Could this be happening? Why had Shaw never shared any of his young life before now? What did Shaw mean that Melvin knew what to do? The girls looked as stunned as she felt. Junior sipped his coffee, going from photo to photo, stoically studying them as if there might be answers contained in the images. She glanced at the table.

Melvin was still seated, staring into his coffee, slowly shaking his head. I'd give a lot of money for his thoughts. Well, maybe not, at least I understand a little what may have driven the two of them. Lawyer Mains stood to the side of the room, gobbling cookies like he never saw them before, crumbs floating down his suit jacket. He looked as surprised as everyone else. She waved everyone back to the table and asked Jack to continue.

~ * ~

Father was not a warm man. He might have been if he wasn't always so ill, though I'm not totally convinced of that. With Dot gone for longer and longer periods of time, my only choice was to tag along with him. Wherever he went, I followed. I soon became his legs and hands for running to get tools, holding things for him and assisting in any way I could. He was very patient and serious in showing me how to do things. Things few kids that age would be doing. There was no play time. Work was work. I knew I was expected to work hard and steady. Praise was rare. Criticism sharp and more with a stern look than words. Often, Father would run out of air and have to sit down till he could suck enough into his lungs to continue. He would point at what needed to be done next and watch as I attempted. I learned I could do some of what needed to be done, even if it meant taking tiny shovel loads or with extra pounds of the hammer.

The closest he came to being warm was his commitment to reading and learning. He taught me my letters and numbers when I was three. I was writing them and reading at four. We always had library books. I think our neighbor lady, the widow, would bring books from the library. At other times, I remember our infrequent trips into town always included a stop there. He read to me until I was five. I loved it because it was the only time I could sit close to him, but I don't recall ever sitting on his lap or his arm around me when he read. He checked my homework till he knew I was old enough and disciplined enough to complete it without reminders. He was frequently short and impatient with me.

Childhood silliness was not permitted. There was no laughter or joking around, no going to visit with other children. At school recess, I occasionally watched the kids play. Usually I read or worked on my studies. It was clear they didn't want to have much contact with me.

I was barely tolerated at our one-room school. Partly because I got top grades and worked several grades ahead, but mostly because I was also the poorest and most unkempt. Sometimes, the teacher complained in front of the entire school that I smelled. I would go over to the widow's house and she would set up her tub in the kitchen and let me take a bath. She was never overly friendly, nor was she mean. She just was there when needed. She acted like it was part of her Christian duty. Still, it was humiliating.

When I was twelve, Father came home from town and showed me an envelope. "This is a deed to the forty acres across the road. It's in both our names, so when I die, it's yours. The deed to the main farm is in the buffet drawer, which is your mother's because she's paid some of the taxes and we're still legally married. When I die, make sure you take your deed before she gets hers." Next, he handed me a bank savings passbook. "This is in your name. The farmer leasing our land is to make payments directly to the bank into this account. The bank will take the taxes out and pay them. If you ever move, write the bank with your address. I want you to go to college and the income should help, plus you can use the land as collateral if you ever need to." Father went to bed, exhausted.

I put the bank book in the envelope with the deed and placed it in my bedroom dresser drawer, tucked behind my raggedy clothes, the few that I possessed. Father dying seemed a long way off to me. He'd always been in poor health. Why wouldn't he continue to be?

In 1950, the spring after I turned thirteen and was in eighth grade, Father grew sicker and spent more and more time in bed. I managed to keep the cow fed and milked, the chickens fed, eggs collected, and the hog fed. One day, it ran away. A neighbor brought it back and asked if he could buy it to butcher. I said yes and took the money to Father, who wheezed that was a good decision. "Sell the cow and chickens, too. I need to go into the hospital and probably won't come out."

I stared at him in shock, then took the old Dodge pickup and drove around to the neighboring farms until I found people to buy our livestock. I put the money in the same drawer as the main deed and paperwork. When I got back, Father said to put cleaner clothes on and to wear his boots because mine were too small. I was already going barefoot to school. I loaded him into the truck and drove him the fifteen miles or so to the hospital. I was told to wait in the lobby until they did the paperwork. In his room, I sat next to him and heard him fighting for breath. He slept for a while. The nurses checked him several times. One of them said, "It won't be long now."

About one in the morning, Father turned toward me. "Son, don't forget your property, don't forget betrayal and never forget revenge."

He quit talking and his breathing became more labored. I heard the nurses mention the word coma several times. About seven o'clock that morning, Dot marched into the room, dressed to the nines, and began crying. It was so fake, I wanted to slap her, but I didn't. She fell on the bed and put on a good show for the nurses. We both sat there, not talking for about an hour before Father breathed his last, loud, painful-sounding breath.

She turned to me. "He's gone. Here's ten dollars. On your way home, stop at Sears and get yourself a long-sleeved shirt, new jeans, and boots big enough you can grow into them. I'll send word to a neighbor to contact you when the funeral is. I'll see you then."

I walked out of the room, asked the clerk for directions to Sears and drove carefully there. Thirteen was too young for a driver's license, but most farm kids like me knew how to drive. I just didn't want to get caught and I wasn't familiar with town driving. It was only ten in the morning, so I drove to school. No one asked what happened and I didn't tell them. Three mornings later, early, a neighbor banged on the door. "Your mom called, said she's on the way, so be ready. The funeral's today at nine in the Lutheran Church. Whose funeral is it?"

"My dad's. I'll be ready."

"Your father's? I'll be damned. No one knew. I best get spreading the word. He was a good man with a tough life. Hey, why didn't you tell anyone?"

I shrugged. "Guess I wasn't sure what to do. Dot said she was handling everything." He looked confused. "Dot. My mother." He rolled his eyes and took off.

I washed up and changed into my new clothes, then went to use the outhouse. When I came in, Dot was going through the tax jar, counting the money. "You didn't take any of this, did you?"

"No, why would I." It hit me that she came even earlier than I expected and I hadn't time to pull my deed and passbook out of my drawer.

"Go pack your suitcase with everything you can wear. You're coming with me and I'm getting rid of this place. Hurry." She lit a cigarette and started tapping her foot.

The envelope with my deed and bank was missing. I was sick. I shoved what clothes I had into an old cardboard suitcase and rushed into the living room. She was gone. I heard the horn blow and rushed out to her car. I climbed into the back seat. She took off before I could even close the door. I was ready to yell at her about my deed when I realized there was another boy sitting in the corner, looking frightened. A paper bag of clothes was below his feet. His legs couldn't reach the floor. He was skinny, dirty, smelly, barefoot and stared at me like I was an apparition.

"That's Melvin, your brother," Dot screeched. "I got the deed to your forty acres. I'm keeping it safe till you turn eighteen."

"It's mine. Father set it up for me. I'm supposed to keep it," I shouted, trying to keep from crying. That was my whole future. I was ready to shout more, but realized all might not be lost. If I was going home with her, then I'd still be in the same house with it. I sat back and looked at Melvin. He moved a bit closer to me, maybe two inches.

"How old are you?" I kept my voice low. Dot had the radio blaring anyway.

He held up both hands to show nine fingers, then slid another inch closer, like a puppy not sure how to approach an adult dog. He looked like he was six years old.

I asked him what grade he was in. He shrugged his shoulders and inched closer. A mosquito bit my arm and I slapped at it. Melvin threw himself back into the corner of the car, his eyes wide with fear, his hands up in a defensive mode. I couldn't believe it. "That was a mosquito. Did you think I was going to hit you?"

He nodded and began edging closer again. I noticed sores on his arms and legs. Round ones, some old and scarred over, several still raw-looking. I pointed to them and raised my eyebrows in question. He mimed smoking and twisting a cigarette out into his arm. I gasped. He pointed to Dot just as she pulled into the church lot next to a cemetery.

"Melvin, you stay put or I'll beat your ass. Shaw, you come with me. Who's all these other people here? This was supposed to be private, family only. Godammit, some of them are neighbors. Now they got more to talk about behind my back."

I got out and followed her to the cemetery. I noticed a tall, gray-haired man who looked like a healthy version of Father. A heavy-set woman stood beside him. Both looked awkward about being there. About ten others, all neighbors, gathered around the casket. The pastor read some scriptures and said a few words about what a great guy Father was and how he served in World War I, ruining his health. That he suffered all his life and heroes like him go to heaven. By the way, those men waiting over there will lower the casket as soon as we finish. Amen.

Several neighbors stepped up to Dot and expressed their sympathies. One man asked why there wasn't an honor guard and flag for a veteran. Dot snapped she didn't have time to arrange it and this was supposed to be private anyway. No one else spoke to her. They walked away, shaking their heads. There was no meal in the church basement. The two men began lowering the casket in and shoveling the dirt over it. The couple waited by the church steps for us to get closer.

"Dot, is this Shaw Philip?" the man asked.

"Who else would it be? Shaw, this is your Uncle Fordham and Aunt Helen. Shake their hands. They're the ones been helping pay the taxes on that wretched place all these years."

I shook their hands, had no idea what to say to them. My father's words kept circulating at the back of my mind. How could I seek revenge, standing in front of a church? And they'd been helping Dot keep the taxes up? I wondered if Father knew that.

"Shaw, go over by the car and wait. I have something to discuss with your uncle and aunt. Wait, take your brother to that outhouse over there. I don't want him wetting the back seat."

Melvin followed me to the outhouse and I motioned for him to go in. He looked frightened. "Are you coming in with me?" Those were the first words I heard come from his mouth and I could barely hear them.

"Heck no, can't you go by yourself?"

He brightened up. "Yes, oh, thank you."

~ * ~

Connie took a quick glance around the table. Melvin looked like he was struggling to not cry. Everyone else looked like they were listening to a radio drama. Hanging on every word. She was. She didn't want to think about what this meant or how it affected her view of Shaw or Melvin. Right now, she just wanted to hear more. She wished Shaw had been a writer. Maybe he could have expressed his anxieties on paper instead of his dual personalities with one of them wanting revenge.

~ * ~

As we walked back toward the car, I saw Dot holding an envelope. I could tell it was the deed to the farm, not to my forty acres. "Fordham, the boys come with this deed," she said. "I'm going to prison. Either you take them or they'll go into the orphanage and I'll sell the farm. Your father always wanted this place kept in the family. It's yours, again."

My uncle's and aunt's mouths opened and shut a few times. Neither said a word. I don't think they could. Dot handed the deed to Fordham and stalked toward the car. "Boys, take your clothes to their car.

You're going to live with your uncle and aunt now. I'll check on you when I can. Behave. You're better off with kinfolk than in an orphanage."

We ran ahead of her to grab our clothes. Melvin managed to spill his and pick them up moments before Dot backed out and drove off. We stared at Uncle Fordham and Aunt Helen as they stared back at us. Aunt Helen broke the silence. "Well, boys, we weren't expecting this. Put your clothes in the trunk and get in the back seat." She tried to smile, but I could tell she was in shock.

Uncle Fordham opened the trunk and watched us put our luggage in. "Get in the car. Keep your feet off the seat and the back of our seats." It was a 1948 Plymouth Deluxe Sedan, four doors, dark blue and even had a radio. I was enthralled for a few minutes. I never rode in a car this luxurious or recent.

Aunt Helen tried to break the ice. She wanted to know our ages, grades, favorite classes. I responded with one- or two-word answers. Melvin squirmed or whispered his answers. After several miles, she said, "We knew Philip Shaw had one son with Dot. We had no idea there were two of you. What a surprise. Shaw, when was the last time you saw your mother?"

"Just after the war, 1945, she visited."

"Is that when you met your little brother? I know your parents lived separate lives since the war began." Aunt Helen's voice was syrupy sweet.

I was ready to say today was the first time I met this kid and I doubted if he was my brother, but Melvin poked me, his eyes large and teary. He mouthed to me, "Say yes. Please say yes."

"It was about then, I guess. Dot and Father didn't get on much, but yup, that was the first time I saw him. He was sleeping in the back of her car." I looked down at Melvin. His face beamed. He scooted next to me, pulled my arm around his shoulders and cuddled next to me. Within minutes, he fell asleep. I realized, for better or worse, I had a brother, even though I was positive he wasn't a full brother. Half, maybe, but not full. There was no way in heck Father could have impregnated Dot. By 1941, he rarely left the farm, and if he did, I was usually with him, plus he could barely walk from the house to the truck without leaning on me and gasping for breath. At thirteen, I knew there was no way the man could have had sex nine years ago with any woman, let alone the wife who betrayed him time and time again. He said she was a whore. The proof of her betrayal might be cuddled up against me, excited to have a big brother.

Melvin woke up when Uncle Fordham cleared his throat. "Boys, you're going to have to bear with us a bit. We didn't know you were coming home with us. We have an older son, Lawrence, who works the farm with us. He's twenty—"

"Do we have to sleep with him?" Melvin's voice sounded frightened.

"No, boys," Aunt Helen said. "We have a small bedroom upstairs near the back stairway we'll put you two in. It's small, but will be fine. We even added a bathroom upstairs."

Melvin relaxed and smiled up at me.

Uncle Fordham said, "Please don't interrupt me. I'm saying you both will be expected to help on the farm, the garden, in the house before school and after school, the weekends and summers. You need to realize that if you weren't our blood, we'd never do anything like this. What kind of grades do you get? I expect good ones. No one with a Skogman name is going to get bad grades."

"I get all A's. I love school, especially science, math and history," I said.

"That's to be proven." Uncle Fordham snorted.

Melvin looked up at me and shrugged his shoulders. I realized he hadn't been to school. "Can you read and figure?" I whispered to him. He smiled and mouthed, yes.

"Melvin likes reading and math. He's in fourth grade," I said. I needed to change the subject. "Uncle Fordham, what kind of cows you milking? I like Guernsey and Jerseys."

My uncle grunted. "Them are poor excuses, they give a lot of milk, but they don't stay healthy. We have Holsteins. Can't go wrong with them."

"Uncle Fordham, you milking them by hand, I'm pretty good at that." I felt like I needed to assure my uncle I was worthy of him taking us in.

"Call me Ford or Uncle Ford. We got surge milkers." He shifted in his seat. "Tell you the truth, young man, we're thinking of getting out of the dairy business and going to corn and soybeans. The state is talking of more regulations and it's going to make it harder for small dairy operations to hang on. Lawrence and I figure we can make more money for the same amount of time cash cropping. Now that we got us a section, I figure we'll be switching over in the next few years." He flipped on the radio and tuned it to the news. Like my father, he didn't talk for long, even with good lungs. He snapped the radio off when the announcer started talking about a military buildup in Korea. Aunt Helen wiped her eyes. In a few minutes, she began humming hymns.

Melvin's and my eyes grew huge as we pulled into the farm. The house looked like a mansion. The old barn and silo were behind it just west of where the sheds are now. There were cows in the field, looked about thirty or so. A fairly recent tractor was hooked to a manure spreader. The barn had a gutter cleaner that conveyed the manure from the barn and dropped it in the spreader. Even though I knew I was supposed to hate my uncle and be thinking of ways for revenge, I couldn't help but be impressed.

Aunt Helen led us to the bedroom, which today is part of the master bedroom. It was like a maid's room or for hired hands, she said. There was a double bed, a closet, small window and student desk and chair. She told us to empty our raggedy clothes onto the bed. She poked through them, sighing and moaning. "Most of these are going in the rag barrel, if they hold up through the wash. You won't be going to school tomorrow. We're going clothes and shoe shopping." She grabbed Melvin by the arm and pulled him down to the bathroom and began filling the tub. She must have realized he didn't know much about baths because she stayed in there with him and must have helped scrub him. He came out in the cleanest clothes he possessed. Aunt Helen muttered to herself as she led him like a preschooler to our room, "I never seen a kid abused like this one. Even his rectum looks tore up."

Melvin smiled at me. "I like Aunt Helen." He sounded more like a preschooler than nine.

I took my bath and scrubbed out the tub afterward. That night, we met my cousin Lawrence at supper. He was not impressed his parents brought two young cousins home. "Basically, she sold them to you. Who cares about that crappy piece of property over an hour away? If it was any good, you'd have taken it when you had the chance." Uncle Ford scowled at him.

I tucked that away in my mind as I dove into my food, only to be told to quit eating so fast, to use a napkin and ask for things to be passed rather than reaching. Aunt Helen screamed at Melvin when it was obvious he didn't know how to use a knife and fork. After several days, we found ourselves eating on the enclosed back porch, now the mudroom. Aunt Helen said she didn't have the patience to teach Melvin table manners. Over time, I taught him the little I knew and what I learned by watching others eat.

That first night, Melvin was skittish, getting into bed with me. He kept asking, "You going to hurt me? You going to poke into me?"

I kept saying no. In 1950 rural Minnesota, the topic of child sexual abuse was rarely mentioned. I asked him what he meant and he told me what big boys and men did to him. I was shocked. I promised him I would never do such a thing to him.

"That's because you're my brother, ain't it."

I told him most big boys and men didn't do that to little boys.

"A lot of 'em do. The ones I know do." All at once, he flew out of bed, flipped on the light, dug his paper bag out from the closet, and handed me something. "I snuck this out of Dot's purse while you all was in the funeral field. I knowed it was important to you. Aren't you glad you got a little brother to look out for you?" It was my deed and passbook. After the lights were off, he whispered, "Dot ain't going to prison. She just don't want us."

I asked him if he thought she might change her mind, come back for us, or for the deed.

"Nah. She flat out don't want us. She'll probably get another job in the factory or a nursing home."

We chatted late into the night. I told him of Father's repeated warnings about betrayal and revenge. Melvin cried a little. I wanted to, but didn't. I think the deep bond between two rejected boys formed that night and never left either of us. Betrayal is wicked. Revenge is necessary. Patience is a virtue.

The next morning, I told Aunt Helen I needed a piece of paper, envelope and stamp. I needed to send the bank my new address.

"Any money you got should go to your uncle. You're not old enough. Just give me the bank book."

I almost shouted at her, but Melvin piped up, "Why does someone big like you need two dollars?" That was the first time the kid amazed me. It wouldn't be the last. Aunt Helen shook her head in disgust and gave me an envelope and stamp. I sent the bank my change of address. Later, I asked him if he looked in the bankbook.

He grew nervous. "You gonna hit me?"

I shook my head.

"Yup." He rattled off the exact amount. "I'm good with figures and remembering what I see and hear."

I thought for a moment, then spoke out loud. "What happens if Dot comes back and wants the deed and bankbook?"

"What happens if Aunt Helen tries to find it, too?" Melvin smiled at me. "I'm good at hiding things. When we finish a loaf of bread, I'll get the plastic wrapper. I'm thinking high up in the outhouse. Ain't no way she's gonna check up there and Dot ain't smart enough to check there, if she did come back for it."

I could only shake my head and laugh at this squirrely little guy.

Aunt Helen soon tired of trying to be a nice Christian aunt who took in her husband's two destitute nephews. I guess she never read Melvin's birth certificate or she'd have known he wasn't even related to them. She gave us leftovers for lunch and supper, usually cold. She found an old toaster and kept loaves of cheap white bread, huge jars of peanut butter and jelly on the back porch, along with boxes of cold cereal for our breakfast. We had to wash our cast-off dishes in the old porcelain sink, the same place we could wash up before school. She allowed us one bath a week, as long as the tub and bathroom were kept spotless. Only in the middle of the night could we use the bathroom. The rest of the time, we were told to use the old outhouse. The back porch was enclosed, but not insulated, so when eating, we roasted or froze, depending upon the weather. She kept the heating vent in our bedroom closed. However, compared to Father's home, this was still luxury. I didn't have to cut wood or go to the neighbors for a bath.

Uncle Ford barely tolerated my presence. He barked orders and tried to find things to complain about my work, but usually couldn't, which made him grumpier. Lawrence outright despised us. Still, even he could rarely find fault with my drive and abilities.

The first Sunday we were there, Uncle Ford and Aunt Helen took us to the little Lutheran church next door. We walked there in our brand-new clothes and shoes. After hearing the Sunday School Bible story taken from Revelations about the blood running as high as a horse's bridle, Melvin got so scared, he wet his pants on the walk home. That night, his nightmares were so violent, his sounds woke Aunt Helen. She spanked him. The two of us never went back to church. We were told to stay in the house on Sunday mornings and not come out till after we saw most of the cars drive down the road from the church parking lot. Sunday mornings became our favorite time.

My uncle and aunt soon gave up trying to have Melvin do anything to help around the house or farm. He was afraid to be alone with the men, frightened they might hit or molest him, and Aunt Helen's constant nagging made him so nervous he kept running to the outhouse so he didn't pee his pants every few minutes. When he did something that they thought was wrong, they blamed me. After a few weeks, I told him to stick by me. He was soon fine and worked well alongside me. In the mornings, he helped me bring the cows in, feed them, wash their udders, clean the stanchions and ready them for the next milking, sterilize the milking equipment, throw down hay and straw from the loft, feed the bull, and clean the barn floor. In warm weather, we also hoed the garden, picked vegetables, washed the house windows, painted the out buildings. He even went with me when we were baling hay. For his size, he was strong and quick. He could stack the top bales that Lawrence and I threw up to him.

Melvin loved to tinker, take things apart and put them back together. One day, Lawrence and Uncle Ford were trying to repair the evaporator motor that kept the milk cans cool. I hung about, ready to run for tools or anything they might need. Melvin kept peering around me to watch. The men were getting more and more frustrated. Suddenly, Melvin jumped in front of me, reached in and took the piece they were struggling with out of Uncle Ford's hand. Ford started to bellow. He stopped when Melvin twisted the piece to a different position and slid it into place. "It goes in this way." Neither man said a word. I grabbed Melvin and rushed him to the garden. "I just see how stuff goes," he said.

Melvin was sneaky, but careful. Just as today, he only needed several hours of sleep a night. After going to bed with me, he'd wait till I was asleep, usually around nine. If the house was quiet, he'd slip out of our room and wander around the house or the farm buildings. He knew where everything was, inside and outside the house, canned food, tools, little things. I learned, though I probably couldn't describe it that way as a teen, Melvin has almost a photographic memory. Whatever he sees, reads or hears, he remembers. He also displayed a keen sense of caution as to when to share where something was that Uncle Ford, Lawrence or Aunt Helen were looking for. He didn't want to arouse any suspicions about his midnight prowling.

~ * ~

Connie kept glancing at Melvin. She watched his expression range from what looked like pride to fear to anger. When Jack read Aunt Helen's comment about his abuse, he rolled up his sleeves past his elbows. She realized, in all the years she knew him, she never saw his bare arms. Some scars still showed. Was he seeking sympathy? He stared at the table. She couldn't read his face.

At one point, when Jack read about Melvin being sneaky, he looked right at Connie and gave a tiny shrug of his shoulders and smirked. She wanted to jump up and choke him. Instead, she looked away and focused on listening to Jack read. *It's a soap opera*, she thought. Only one with frightening consequences. The things Shaw wrote pointed to Melvin being a seriously troubled boy who became a troubled man. *So was her husband, but was he as troubled? I'm bargaining,* she thought. *Focus.*

Chapter Thirty-Four

Shaw's Papers

Jack continued reading, his voice occasionally scratchy.

In August, things changed again for Melvin and me when Lawrence was drafted into the Army to fight in Korea. His application for a farm deferment was denied because his father, Uncle Ford, was deemed by the draft board to be able enough to carry the farm alone at his age of fifty-five. Lawrence was angry, his mother devastated and his father troubled. Lawrence left for boot camp two days before school started.

After Lawrence left, I thought my aunt and uncle might be a little warmer and more appreciative of our efforts to help. Not much changed in their attitudes, but, with Melvin's assistance, I was soon doing way more around the farm, plus going to high school in Midville. Aunt Helen tried to enroll Melvin in the one room, kindergarten to eighth grade school a mile away, but he put up such a fuss about not being with me, the teacher told her to enroll him in the elementary school in Midville, which was on the lower level of the high school. He was satisfied with those arrangements and rode the school bus with me.

Melvin's teachers weren't sure what to do with him. Within weeks, he read every one of his textbooks. Not only did he want to answer every question asked, but he would tell the answers to upcoming questions weeks or months in advance. Just to keep him occupied, they gave him other textbooks. By the end of his fourth grade, he read every text book through sixth grade and spent most of his time quietly wandering the halls. His teacher gave him a note for Aunt Helen about meeting with her to see what else they could do to challenge him. He showed it to me, and tore it up. Later, his teacher spoke to me about the possibility of him skipping several grades and asked me to speak with Uncle Ford about it. I told her, "It doesn't make a difference what classroom you put him into. He won't change. I don't think he can. Let him be, he will never hurt anyone, steal or misbehave. Besides, Uncle Ford doesn't want anything to do with him, or me." She must have spoken to the principal who spread the word, because they let him be. It wasn't like he didn't learn anything. The teachers let me be, too. I did my work, turned it in, participated when called on, almost always knew the correct answer, and rarely interacted with the other students or teachers.

We struggled through that first year of school without Lawrence. It felt like we were continuously walking on pins and needles to not upset Aunt Helen or get barked at by Uncle Ford. Never a compliment or thanks, only criticism or surly attitudes toward the two of us. That next summer was hell, too. Uncle Ford, Melvin and I were doing what we did the previous summer with Lawrence. Melvin was helpful, but he wasn't Lawrence, though he began fixing more and more mechanical breakdowns.

My sophomore year, Melvin was in sixth grade, though he spent most of his school days wandering in and out of my classes, sometimes answering questions or turning in the assignments the rest of my fellow classmates were doing. Around the third week of October, we got off the bus on 127th Street and noticed a plain, dark sedan driving slowly up the driveway. It pulled up to the front, and two men in uniform get out. Aunt Helen and Uncle Ford stepped onto the porch. We heard Helen scream and watched her collapse to the floor as Ford crumpled against the wall. Melvin and I overheard the words of Lawrence being killed in some battle called Heartbreak Ridge. I remember thinking, that was a hell of a name for a place to be killed.

We walked around to the back door, went upstairs, changed into our farm clothes and left to start the chores. We did them almost entirely by ourselves for the next ten days till the funeral was over. On the day of the funeral, cleaned up and in our best clothes, we prepared to walk to the church for the services. Aunt Helen saw us and hissed, "You will not disgrace my son's dignity. Get out of my sight." We stayed on the front porch and listened from across the field to the bugles play at the gravesite.

By the end of November, Uncle Ford sold the dairy herd. Suddenly, we had only the chickens to care for before school, almost nothing after. Three weeks later, before leaving for the school bus, Uncle Ford told me he and Aunt Helen were going south for a vacation. He had no idea when they would return, but would be gone at least one or two months.

"Do Melvin and I have to move out today?" My mind was racing with fear about our future.

"No. Someone needs to keep an eye on this place. Bring in the mail, take care of the chickens, make sure the pipes don't freeze, feed the dog and barn cats, eat whatever food you want, use the pickup for local errands and don't make a mess." He handed me forty dollars. "This is for food or supplies you actually need. Keep the receipts. If you need additional money for repairs or anything else, call Mr. Sloane at the bank and he'll get you some. He'll know how to reach me if there's an emergency."

They were gone when we came home from school. Instead of being joyful and excited at our newfound freedom, we were frightened. Could we use the kitchen? What about the food in the big freezer in the basement, and the canned goods? Did we still have to use the outhouse during the day? Mostly, I think we were afraid of what to do with our time. Since the dairy herd was sold, we were bored, trying to find things to do. Uncle Ford and Aunt Helen were so morose and in grief that we hadn't dared ask them anything.

Melvin said it was getting too cold to eat on the back porch, we would eat in the kitchen and do our dishes after every meal. He checked the fridge to find it filled with hot dishes left from the neighbors in the weeks following Lawrence's funeral. We cleaned everything out and poked through the cupboards and freezers to find tons of food. Tons, if you knew how to cook. Melvin pulled out a Betty Crocker Cookbook and looked up spaghetti. We ate that for our first meal. Of course, he remembered there was canned sauce in the pantry. As I recall, we ate a lot of eggs and bacon, plus learned to make pancakes from scratch. We didn't touch the oatmeal or peanut butter. I still hate both.

Several days later, an announcement was made at school that the pharmacy in Midville needed a person after school and Saturdays to make deliveries, clean the store, stock shelves and help the pharmacist. I left class and ran over there. Melvin followed. I was hired to start the next day. Mr. Gunther, the pharmacist, liked the fact I was quiet, attentive and asked intelligent questions. He hated chit-chatting with employees, he said, because he had to talk with the customers so much. For some reason, he never questioned Melvin tagging along and he started giving him small tasks. I was similar to Mr. Gunther, I didn't enjoy the customer interaction, but was prompt and polite.

~ * ~

"Let's take another break," Connie said.

She remained seated as others got up and moved about. Melvin remained seated. She kept looking at him during the reading. Though he was quite stoic, she could sense changes in his emotions, like pin pricks, not eruptions. Who was this man? What did he do? Why did he spy on people? How did that relate to Farm Holding?

She stood and went to the bathroom. She rarely used this bathroom. What were Jens and Cochran doing in it with a tape measure before the meeting? She dried her hands, closed the door and gathered everyone back together. Everyone looked drained and it looked like there were still many pages to listen to, plus the will to read. She sat down and touched Jack's arm. "How much more? This is taking so long and is very intense."

Jack riffled through the pages. "I'm guessing fifteen pages more. I'm ready for a stiff drink and am sure you are as well."

Connie grimaced. "That drink is going to have to wait."

~ * ~

I soon found the pharmacy business fascinating. Not the retail operations, those were basic and functional. It was the drugs, the chemistry, the elements, mixing things together, how different drugs had different effects on the body that intrigued me and indirectly fed my desire for revenge. Back then, most pharmacies did some compounding. Mixing different ingredients together and putting them through a press to make a hard tablet or pressing the ingredients into a capsule whose shell dissolved was also fascinating.

We settled into a routine. After school, Melvin did what little homework he had at the drug store. Next, he dusted, stocked the small gift section, cleaned the bathroom, and enjoyed plenty of time to read the reference books on drugs. Occasionally, he wandered over to the grocery store and picked up receipt's customers left behind. He never stole anything. I waited on customers, rang up their prescriptions and purchases, kept the empty bottles, labels and supplies stocked for Mr. Gunther, and gradually began assisting him in filling the prescriptions. I was right next to him and he double-checked each order. He quietly explained each drug, its uses and dangers. After I turned sixteen, I began making deliveries. On Sundays, Melvin and I drove in to wash the glass counters, mirrors and windows, scrub the floors, straighten up the supply room and basement, and carefully stock the drugs on the dispensary shelves. I knew Mr. Gunther always double-checked my work because he always complimented me on Mondays.

We rarely spent money. The farm gas tank was full. We traded eggs for milk with a neighbor. I kept my income from the pharmacy and Melvin kept every receipt he could find till we had forty dollars' worth. We wrapped a string around each day's mail and stacked it on the dining table. Melvin seemed to know what was in some of the financial envelopes, but never said much to me.

Melvin began complaining about the elderly people needing prescriptions. Sometimes, I brought him with me on deliveries.

Frequently, their homes smelled of age, medicine and poor cleanliness. "Why are they afraid to die? There's nothing after death, why don't people realize that?"

I tried to explain most people believed in the hereafter, either heaven or hell.

Once, riding back to the pharmacy, he became upset. "Them people who hurt me should go to hell, but there ain't one, so they should just die. All these old people pissing and pooping themselves, can't think straight, can't even get out of bed. They can barely get around. What's the use? Why are we keeping them alive?"

Several weeks later, I noticed the rat and mice population increasing around the grain bins. The cat population seemed to be decreasing. I mentioned it to Melvin. He wouldn't look at me. Eventually, under pressure, he told me he gave some of the cat's arsenic, a common poison on most farms at the time. "They was really old and decrepit."

I grabbed him and pinned him to the ground in the snow. "If you want to be my brother, then I have to know everything you're doing." He quit trying to get me off of him and nodded. "No nodding," I yelled. "Speak to me."

"I'll never hide anything from you again. I'll always talk with you about things I want to do before I do them." We got up. He pointed to the old collie painfully limping toward the back porch where he slept in the winter. "How long does Shep need to stay in pain? Isn't it cruel leaving him to live?"

That night, we mixed arsenic into the dog's food and watched him die within minutes. We put some out for the rats and mice and soon had them under control. First, though, we gathered up several of the youngest cats and moved them to the back porch for several days till all the rats died, along with the old cats.

About that time, I opened a bank account at the second bank in Midville, the one not used by Ford. I wanted as little of my money around the house as possible. We included the forty dollars from Uncle Ford.

Aunt Helen and Uncle Ford arrived home while were in school, must have been late February. They were tan and healthy-looking. We drove in about seven-thirty after working at the pharmacy.

"This place is a mess," Helen shrieked.

"Why did you have the pickup out so late?" Uncle Ford yelled.

No greetings. No hellos or, how are you? Just bitching and yelling. I gritted my teeth. "The house is cleaner than when you left, check the refrigerator, see any moldy hot dishes? Check the mail. It's all in order. You said I could use the truck. I have a job after school at the pharmacy." I poked Melvin who ran to our room and came back. "Here's the receipts for your forty dollars. Anything that broke, we fixed without spending more money. Did the banker contact you?" I glared at Uncle Ford until he shook his head. "Did you contact him while you were gone?" He lowered his eyes to look at the floor. "Did he have any bad reports on us?" He shook his head. "How about any good ones? The banker always said hello to me when he came in the pharmacy." Uncle Ford briefly nodded, still not looking at me.

Aunt Helen stepped to the fridge and looked in. It was spotless. She opened the pantry. "Where's all my food?"

"Down the toilet, we crapped it out. Ford told us we could eat what was here. I think there's still enough left to last till the second coming." I glared at her, which seemed to make her even angrier.

Her voice shrilled, "If you got a job, you better start paying us room and board. For the both of you."

I stared back at her and slowly enunciated, "We have done enough and do enough around here to earn the cold cereal, oatmeal and peanut butter you provide us. I will consider paying for gas until I find myself a car."

Aunt Helen slowly deflated and Uncle Ford looked worn out. I grabbed a loaf of bread from the bread box. Melvin and I went to the back porch and pulled out the peanut butter and jelly. We kept our coats on to ward off the chill while we ate. Back to the dungeon.

"I could kill them," Melvin muttered with his mouth full. "How long before they get old?"

I didn't answer.

In the morning, Uncle Ford came onto the back porch as we were eating. "You can take the truck today." He choked up a little. "Lawrence's car ain't much, but if you want it, you can have it. Needs a battery and a change of oil and grease. Starting tomorrow, I'm going to need my truck."

"I don't want your charity. I'll give you twenty dollars for it. I'll pick up a battery today at lunch." I looked at him. "What's Helen going to say about me driving that car around?"

He shrugged his shoulders. "Does it matter?"

I think that was the only moment he was ever a human to me.

I left school during lunch, withdrew enough money to pick up a battery and some oil and pay Uncle Ford. The next day, I started driving a 1939 Plymouth Coupe. It was not classy, not as Lawrence once dreamed he could make it. The car was dented, rusty, dull, had cracked windshield and side windows, along with dry rotting tires. But it ran good and it was mine.

This is getting long, so I wrote the following to answer questions I'm sure family members will have.

Why do I have two names?

In early spring of my senior year, Ford and I had a huge blow-up. Get this, he wanted me to stay on the farm. He was ramping up to produce corn and soybeans, big time. Especially for 1954. He ordered a big tractor, combine and planter, then realized he still needed a full-time helper. I already planned to move to Worthington, go to the community college for two years, and transfer to pharmacy school at U.M. Mr. Gunther already made arrangements for me to work at a compounding pharmacy in Worthington, starting after high school graduation. I had yet to register for the college.

"I need you here. How the hell am I going to manage without a full-time man? The new equipment comes next week, so we can get started. You gotta quit that damn pharmacy."

I remained calm. "Did you tell me your plans? Did you ask me about mine? I plan to enroll at Worthington Community College for two years and then transfer."

He was livid. "Worthington Community College? You can't go there. I forbid it. Lawrence went there, got straight A's. I will not have another Skogman going there to ruin his reputation. I'm not sure how you've made it this far in high school." He fumed and fussed.

I stood, thinking. Obviously, he took me for granted. I realized I might not want the Skogman name. I knew I wanted to own land, lots of land. I never wanted to be destitute again. Part of me hated the name. Everyone with the same last name had been terrible to me, except my father. He was so cold and ill; he was almost like having a rock for a parent. I would soon be leaving the farm, why not start with a different last name? Besides, I knew how long older teachers remembered good students. My freshman year, my high school teachers reminded me frequently of Lawrence and his abilities. He was big in sports and also the valedictorian. The teachers quit reminding me of him once they saw my grades, after I reminded them several times that I wasn't Lawrence and never would be. I didn't want any junior college teachers asking if I was related to Lawrence Skogman.

As for barely making it through high school? Clearly, Ford didn't read the report card section of the local newspaper when grades came out or refused to believe what he read. I was consistently in the honor roll section. I knew I was going to be either salutatorian or valedictorian. I didn't play sports, do any extra-curricular activities and had no close friends. The other students quickly learned to leave me alone and I left them alone. Melvin and I were like ghosts floating around the schools. The teachers learned I wanted no praise in front of others. I think most folk in the area never focused on me or Melvin. As I said, we were ghosts.

The next week, I registered at Worthington Community College as Shaw S Phillip. W.C.C. was held in the high school back then. I got another driver's license. I learned I could use AKA, Also Known As, for my new name. I filled in my new name on forms, then wrote in tiny letters, AKA Shaw Philip Skogman. Melvin managed to adjust copies of my school records. It was pretty simple in those days of carbons and forms. I didn't bother changing my social security number. It wasn't necessary.

I gave the valedictorian address as a Skogman. Ford and Helen were present. They hadn't planned to attend and were stunned when a neighbor congratulated them on my accomplishment. They would have been embarrassed not to be there, or admit to their friends they never read the student news in the local paper nor how they considered us to be imbeciles. They left the ceremony almost as fast as I did. That same day, I drove to Worthington as Shaw S Phillip and moved into an apartment above the Worthington Compounding Pharmacy.

Melvin, sadly, agreed to remain on the farm to help, with the agreement that Saturday afternoons, he could hitchhike to Worthington and I would bring him back Sunday nights. For him, it was not a peaceful situation. Helen's treatment toward him got worse. Ford realized Melvin was a mistake and tried to find another person to help out. Tough to do in the middle of the summer. One day, Dot drove into the farm. She informed Ford and Helen she was taking her son back and they could do nothing about it. They were so frustrated with Melvin, they readily agreed.

Melvin managed to call me and tell me what was going on. For some reason, he was calm. His calmness overrode the questions flooding my mind. Why is he so relaxed? Why isn't he telling me he'll slip away? He's not happy on the farm, but he sure as hell won't be happy with Dot. He didn't even ask about coming to stay with me.

He must have read my mind. "Don't worry about me. I'll come see you in a week or two. Dot's getting old, anyway."

That comment rang through me like bells clanging. "Be careful. Betrayal..." He joined me, "Betrayal is wicked. Revenge is necessary. Patience is a virtue."

Still, I was surprised when he showed up one week later at the pharmacy. He waved at me, set his bag down and put a nickel in the pay phone and dialed the operator. I heard him say, "There's an abandoned car behind Woolworths in the last row. Tell the police." He gave the make and plates number. "No, I won't give you my name. I had nothing to do with its disappearance. I just know it don't belong there." He hung up, turned toward me and said, "Where am I living now?" He seemed different, almost calmer.

Neither of us acted excited to see each other, though inside, I was and I think he was. It just seemed natural that we be together. I showed him my room and told Mr. Coughlin, the pharmacist, my brother would be living with me and helping out when he wasn't in school. Mr. Coughlin, the owner and pharmacist, was too busy at that moment to object. Two days later, he asked me how long Melvin was staying. I told him until I left, but he would be impressed what the little guy could do. He must have been because he never complained or asked again.

That night, I asked Melvin where Dot was. He shrugged. "Not sure now. She drowned in some motel bathtub after overdosing on valium with booze. I think she lost her mind. Kept driving us all over the state, saying she was starting a new business. I copped the valium from some lady who laid down her prescription of it as she checked out other things at the front counter of some drug store. Getting Dot to take it was easy with booze." He didn't smile, cry, show any emotion. He added, "I'd 'a done it sooner, but we kept sleeping in the car." He repeated Father's words. I knew right then that we were connected in everything each of us would ever do. We were a team. We both understood each other's pain and our deep-seated desire for revenge against those who betrayed us. And, as I discovered, for greed. We had to own land.

Melvin was fourteen. I signed him up for high school in the same building the community college was located. Not much changed. He wandered into my classes as frequently as he attended his own. Just another ghost. We lived and worked at the pharmacy. Both of us expanded our knowledge of prescription drugs.

Mr. Coughlin, a widower, was older, early seventies, considered old back then. His son was a career Army officer who died in World War II. His daughter died of cancer the year before I began working. He was also a diabetic. The spring of my second year living and working there, he started meandering on about dying and having no one to leave the place to. I carefully said, "What about me? If I haven't earned my degree by the time you die, I could manage the place and hire a licensed pharmacist."

His face lit up. "By golly. That's a great idea." Two days later, he met with a lawyer and, several weeks later, Mr. Coughlin told me the arrangements were finalized.

He began having more trouble regulating his insulin. He hired two pharmacists to work part-time. I made sure to be present with him if they weren't. I couldn't leave him alone, filling scripts. I began filling the syringes for him to make sure he was getting the prescribed amount. He didn't want to go into the hospital. More and more, he became unfocused. Muttering about why he was still living, wanting to be with his dead wife. I recommended he place an order for a vial of rarely used, high potency insulin that was becoming necessary for some diabetics. It had five times the strength of normal insulin and needed to be used with a separate syringe made to reflect the higher dosage. One day, a half-hour before the part-time pharmacist was to arrive, I handed Mr. Coughlin his regular syringe, along with the new potent vial of insulin. "Here, Mr. Coughlin, it's time for you to go." I showed him the vial of the extra potent stuff.

His eyes widened as he grasped what I meant. "It's time." He didn't pick up the syringe for the potent insulin, instead he managed to fill the regular syringe to its normal level, which was five times the normal potency, and shoot it into himself. Minutes later, he died in his office chair. I left the regular vial on his desk, pocketed the potent one, and called the police and emergency squad. They had no questions, shook their heads, pronounced him dead, and took him to the funeral home. I called his lawyer, I expected there to be a legal proceeding over my owning the pharmacy. Instead, the lawyer told me Coughlin simply added my name to everything to make me a co-owner and to carry on. I now owned a compounding pharmacy with no mortgage and a bank account with thirty-five thousand dollars. That night, I emptied the vial of strong insulin down the drain sewer and threw the container in with the pharmacy's other empty containers.

That happened in April. During May, I debated with myself whether I truly wanted to transfer to pharmacy school at the university. I was already accepted. I kept thinking about farming. I loved the land, the cycles of preparing, seeding, weeding and harvesting. I enjoyed studying the grain markets, learning about good farm management practices. I strongly considered using the pharmacy and money in the bank to put a down payment on some land not far from Worthington. Something told me to go to college and get the degree. I spent that summer in Worthington, hired a managing pharmacist and a part-time one. Late that summer, in The Cities, Melvin and I found a cheap apartment near the university. I started classes, Melvin got two part-time jobs, one at a pharmacy, the other working midnights in the hospital morgue. He said he loved studying anatomy first hand. We didn't bother enrolling him in school. Besides me, hardly anyone knew he existed. Somehow, he finagled himself into an LPN, Licensed Practical Nurse, course and passed it. He maintained his license for many years. After two months of classes, I realized I could handle their intensity and still spend most weekends in Worthington, which was a good three to four-hour drive. I bought a better used vehicle. Most weekends, school breaks and the following summer, we were in Worthington. I graduated in the spring of 1959, finished my internship that summer, wrote the state boards, and have kept my license current till this day. You can check the records of the pharmacy. I still own it. Actually, Farm Holding Company does.

One Saturday in May of 1959, at the pharmacy, Melvin answered the phone. His eyes got big and he whispered, "Take this one in the office."

It was Uncle Ford. "Son, I really need to talk with you. I'm in trouble."

"I am not your son. Don't ever call me that again." I hung up on him.

The phone rang again. I let the clerk answer it. She came into the office. "Shaw, this man says he desperately has to speak to you. He sounds very upset, not angry, though."

I waited till she left. "This is Shaw S Phillip. How may I help you?"

"Shaw, it's Ford. I'm so sorry about calling you son. We should have treated you like one."

"It's too late for that. Tell me what you want."

"Well, I can't keep help. Trying to farm a section is too much for one man, at least it is for me. I got a couple of tenants in with the idea that we would share my equipment and kinda work things out. Now, it's a mess. We only got half the seed in this spring. I'm about ready to throw in the towel and sell the equipment and lease out the land. Except I just can't stand the thought of a Skogman not farming the land."

"So, now you want me to be a Skogman?" I couldn't keep the sarcasm out of my voice.

"That was a big mistake. Word got out that we didn't even know our nephew was going to be the valedictorian and we took some heat in the community. It sounds like you changed your last name."

"I did. No way I was going to show up your infamous son, Lawrence. Listen, I'm busy right now. I'll be up tomorrow at ten to talk about this. Just know I will have some demands if I decide to help you."

"Can we make it one o'clock on Sunday? Ten is church."

"I said ten. As far as I can tell, church has never helped you a damn bit. Tell Helen to attend church. I don't want her involved in anything we talk about." I hung up.

Melvin sat across from my desk and smiled. "We moving back to the farm after you graduate? You could commute to finish your internship."

Uncle Ford and I met in the house. My requirements were that Ford write his will, leaving everything to me. When that was completed, Melvin and I would move into one of the tenant homes. Ford was responsible to move the guy out. I had final say on every decision regarding the farm. I would listen to his reasoning, but I made the final decision. "You've drained your equity in this place trying to go big and you don't know what you're doing." He also had to inform the banks that we were in this together, that I could renegotiate anything possible, and I had fifty-thousand in equity if we needed it. I thought that man's eyes would fall out of his head. I didn't tell him what my degree was going to be in, but I informed him he could tell others I was coming back from studying agriculture. I did squeeze in several ag management classes.

Farmers can never get the dirt from under their fingernails.

We went through more issues until I heard Aunt Helen coming in from church. She started to act all syrupy, but I cut her off. "If either of you say one thing critical or cross to me or Melvin, know that it will shorten your life." She flapped and flustered until Ford pointed toward the front stairs and she huffed up them. I waited till Ford was looking at me. "The last thing is, you will tell everyone you wanted to keep a Skogman on the farm, that's why you asked me to go into business with you."

"I can do that, I'm right proud of what you've done."

"Good, the only problem is, you have no idea of what I've done or can do. Sit back and watch me."

I walked out to find Melvin coming out of the new equipment shed, it's the old number four today. "What did you find?"

"The equipment hasn't been maintained, tools all over the place, nothing in its place. One of the tenant farmers was in here, telling how disorganized everything is. He's ready to leave. I asked him which house was the best one of the tenant houses. He said his was. I told him Ford's nephew was coming back and to be prepared for changes coming fast. He looked at me like I was a crazy teenager. I just laughed."

We started full time on the farm in August, following the completion of my pharmacy internship. For the most part, Ford was supportive. He even began to brag about his nephew around the community. It would take us three years to get the place turned around. Melvin had been the delivery person for the pharmacy. Once we moved, he continued delivering to the rural areas between the farm and Worthington, but not in the town itself.

In June of 1960, Melvin was in the grocery store, buying us some food supplies. We did learn to cook a little, though mostly eggs, pancakes, canned soup and sandwiches. Melvin mastered spaghetti. I never did. He overheard Helen talking in the next aisle with a neighbor woman. The neighbor told her she recently ran into Melvin and chatted with him. She told Helen she complained to him about her medicine not working. She said Melvin asked about her symptoms. He then suggested she talk to her doctor about a specific medicine. Melvin overheard Helen say, 'Pshaw. That boy don't know anything about medicine. He's a pretty good mechanic, but he is so messed up, he can't find his head with both hands.' She laughed until the lady said she told her doctor what Melvin said. The doctor agreed and changed her script. Melvin told me he waited in the back of the store till Helen checked out and left. He was shaking when he told me about it. I told him to calm down, to be patient.

Two days later, Aunt Helen died tending her garden. She loved working in her garden and would bring a big mug of strong coffee out. It's amazing she wasn't a diabetic, because she always brought the sugar bowl with her. After breakfast, Melvin watched from the garage as she kept sipping, then adding more sugar. Finally, she collapsed. He told me he walked over and asked her, "Can you find your head with both hands now?" Tears ran down her cheeks, then he figured she went into a coma and died several hours later. He emptied the bowl with the mix of sugar and arsenic in the outhouse, washed it out in the kitchen, refilled it with sugar and went back to the shed to work on equipment. Uncle Ford found Helen when he came home midafternoon.

Ford rarely saw a doctor, but he died that fall of a sudden heart attack. I expected Helen's death would be devastating for him. Because of that, we didn't expect much from him that summer or during harvest. I hired extra help as needed. Several neighbors pitched in. We did the same for them when needed. No one has ever said I was a bad neighbor who didn't like helping others out. No one. In November, Ford was trying to get back in the swing of things, helping with repairs, storing the last of the grain, and upkeep on the equipment. One day, he kept ragging on Melvin. Unnecessarily so. I finally told him to go home. "Remember, I told you that your life will be shortened if you criticize either of us? Remember? Now go to the house and cool down. Come back tomorrow in a better mood."

The next day, he started out fine, but soon turned on both of us, complaining about how we did so little for all he gave us, that we never thanked him for taking us in from a lousy mother and worthless father. We came prepared. We were standing near the edge of a pile of corn we had yet to auger into a bin. Melvin pulled a syringe out and removed the guard.

"What's that for?" Ford's eyes got big.

"It means we warned you," I said. It was warm, his jacket was open. I stepped behind him, grabbed his hands and twisted them up behind him. Melvin quickly felt over his chest, counting the ribs and gaps, determining where Ford's heart was, then thrust the needle through his shirt into his heart and plunged a lethal dose of potassium chloride into it.

He staggered a few steps and fell face down into the pile of corn. I quickly rolled him over, opened his shirt and used a razor blade to make a small nick over the site of the injection, plus two more below. I restored his shirt and rolled him back over. We left him there and went back into the shop and began working.

"Guess all those nights in the morgue studying anatomy helped," Melvin said as we walked back to the shed.

A parts supplier drove up and came running in, yelling how Ford was in the corn pile. As next of kin, I told the doctor who met us at the hospital that I didn't want an autopsy. "Ford's been acting a little strange lately, complaining about his chest and arms feeling heavy. Yesterday, he seemed a little nauseous. I told him I'd bring him in to the doctor, but he refused. He told me earlier today, he somehow dropped his razor and scraped his chest. Like his arm was weak or something. I reminded him again about going to the doctor, but he waved it off. He could be stubborn sometimes." The doctor shrugged. He listed the cause of death as a heart attack.

Farm Holding started shortly after Ford's death. I realized I held the farm in my Skogman name and the pharmacy in my Phillip name. We wanted to acquire more land, but weren't sure we wanted to be public about it. We each did some research and decided a holding company was the best way to go. I paid for and filled out a DBA form with the state that said Shaw Philip Skogman was Doing Business as Shaw S Phillip in the formation of Farm Holding Company along with a partner, Melvin Smith. For ten dollars, Farm Holding bought the Worthington pharmacy.

We made the upstairs apartment the legal address for Farm Holding and contracted an answering service to take messages we would check daily. I discarded my Phillip's driver's license and resumed use of the one in my Skogman name. We also sealed the Farm Holding registration records so it would take a court subpoena to access them.

We noticed older farmers dying off and their heirs selling their farms, or it going up for auction. We also realized many of the heirs had left the farm and held no interest in returning to farm it. We researched county land records in the area to get an idea of the older people still owning farms. Melvin began snooping around. Making prescription deliveries and running errands, he would pop in on people, trying to be neighborly and to ascertain their situation. Did they have children who regularly visited? What was their health like? How were their finances? Did they have much income? He expanded his information after he began making rural deliveries for Worthington, Midville, Summerville and Marshall.

If we thought someone might be open to a quiet purchase situation, a letter was sent from Farm Holding, offering to pay their taxes, give them a comfortable monthly income, a small share of the profits, and sometimes a payment to the heirs, all in exchange for title to their land. The letter was signed by Phillip Smith. It was a land purchase agreement. Melvin would follow up as Phillip Smith with phone calls and more mailings. The closings were handled by different lawyers. Neither of us ever spoke directly, face to face, with anyone involved about the holding company. Melvin's voice is not distinctive, plus he can mimic other voices. The minute I say hello, anyone who has met me knows it's my voice. Melvin now has a separate cell phone for the holding business. Face to face with his prescription deliveries, he was always Melvin Smith. On the phone as Farm Holding, he was Phillip Smith.

After an agreement was signed, Farm Holding would contract with Skogman Farms to farm the land or, if not close enough to be efficient, Farm Holding would lease the land out to other farmers. We gradually acquired holdings within a hundred-mile radius. Eventually, we slowed down, it took too much time for personal research. From the mid-seventies to the mid-eighties, we made few acquisitions. About then, technology changed dramatically and Melvin realized he could also make observations through remote means instead of him personally spending so much time chatting with people. That's when the idea of nesting boxes came. Alice loved bluebirds, Connie got into it for a while, but Melvin was intrigued by the birds. Even more so, the boxes allowed him to collect more information on persons who had not responded or who told us they weren't interested. Who doesn't want bluebird boxes on their property?

When Melvin delivered prescriptions, he also served as an occasional nurse. The local physicians were thrilled when he sent in an update on their blood pressure or symptoms. Of course, he didn't report all of the symptoms. Also, when fentanyl came out twenty years or so ago, we realized we could mix it with skin cream. Very low amounts would make a person ill, higher amounts could kill them. Several times, Melvin made up a Brompton Cocktail, morphine, cocaine, ethyl alcohol, chloroform water and cherry syrup. Add maraschino cherries plus a slice of orange and it could fool anyone. It was an old, but effective manner of easing someone onto their next life or killing them suddenly.

~ * ~

Connie shuddered, buried her head in her arms for several moments. Was a Brompton Cocktail what killed Hans? Jack stopped reading. She raised her head to see everyone but Melvin watching her. His eyes were focused on the ceiling fan. "Sorry," she whispered, "Keep reading."

~ * ~

When you open the safe, you will find the records of who we were observing. Our intent was to not kill them off, just make them sicker until they gave in and signed with Farm Holding. Of course, several existing

Farm Holding clients may have died sooner than anticipated. How long should people in poor health live? Believe me, no one we helped along their journey was in good health. We're not even talking years of slightly decent life left. More like months or weeks of poor life, if you call barely breathing with little or no cognition, life.

Alice.

I met Alice during junior college. She was a dairy farmer's daughter near Worthington. We dated sporadically for four years. If you consider two shy people barely talking with each other dating. She was somewhat insecure, seeking someone strong and stable. In 1960, I realized another man was interested in her and she seemed to be tired of waiting for me to pop the question. I bought her an engagement ring. She accepted my offer and I stalled for two more years till we married in 1962. At first, she seemed to love the farm, especially not having animals to care for. When the twins were born, we added the family room and remodeled the house much as it is today. A week after our marriage, I took out life insurance on both of us, but I kept increasing hers till it was five-hundred-thousand.

It took her a long time to make friends with our neighbors. Alice loved to run back to Worthington, not only to visit her family, but to shop and see old friends. I grew suspicious after the twins were born, and more so as they grew. Finally, I hired a private eye. Pictures of her with her friend, the same man interested in her before, are in the safe. I suppose the twins could be his, too, but I doubt it. Alice tried to get pregnant for almost a year. She seemed to be as interested and having as much fun as I was. It didn't make sense that she'd be trying with another guy at the same time. Besides, he was half Mexican and Italian. Alice was another Scandinavian like me. When I had no trouble getting Connie pregnant, I put thoughts of me not fathering the twins out of my mind. I hated for the twins to lose their mother, she was a good mother, though not as good as Connie became.

My advice is for you to open the safe with Connie (if she's alive, I'm still waiting to find out who fathered Junior), the twins, Jack Walker, Melvin and the Sheriff. Obviously, I will be dead so you can't prosecute me. Melvin knows what to do. He knows our agreement. You can try to prosecute Melvin, but the records stored in the safe of his diagnoses, psychotropic medications, and tortured background should convince a jury he's legally insane.

Also, I want to be cremated and my ashes spread across the fields.

I guess that's it. I'm sure the family will have many more questions. Some of them, they will have to discover themselves. Most likely in the safe.

Goodbye.

Chapter Thirty-Five

Connie

Jack took a huge breath and looked over the stunned faces. "I think we should take a twenty-minute break, then read the will. I need a bathroom break and to get some fresh air."

For several minutes, no one spoke. Mary lifted her hand, then put it down. Gayle shifted in her chair and looked as if she were going to speak, but didn't. Melvin looked like he was trying not to let his face fall into the table. Lawyer Mains scratched his head. Cochran sat, shaking his head.

Connie stood. "I don't know what to say either. I'm sure we'll have plenty to say later. Let's stretch, then finish this marathon."

Junior asked, "What about opening the safe? Melvin needs to be here for that. Why not do that before reading the will?"

Jack scratched his chin. "That does make sense. After we come back from our break, let's do that. I'm surmising most of the contents may be needed for evidence." He looked at Cochran who stood up.

"I agree. Melvin needs to be there for the opening of the safe. He sure as hell doesn't need to be here for the will. Just realize that no one is going to touch anything in that safe until the evidence team checks it out." Cochran stretched and poured himself some lemonade.

Connie watched Melvin, slumped over, head now on the table, slowly sit and open his eyes. "I desperately need to use the bathroom. Can I use it first?" His voice was almost childlike.

"Be my guest," Jack said.

Connie watched Cochran walk over to Melvin and lightly punch his shoulder. "Stay out of the closet." Cochran motioned to Lawyer Mains, who stood up as if to keep an eye on Melvin.

She had no idea what Cochran meant by the closet, but Melvin looked surprised as he rose and headed for the bathroom.

Jack turned to Connie. "How are you holding up?"

"I'm numb. Part of me wants to tear my hair out over how I lived with this man for thirty-five years, never realizing there was another Shaw, a Shaw Phillip, inhabiting the same body. It's chilling. I feel so stupid, so incompetent. Part of me feels terrible for the old people, and their families, he destroyed."

Jack put his arm lightly around her shoulder. "Connie, psychopaths fool lots of people, sometimes for years, sometimes forever. You can be thankful he lost his temper. You can be thankful everything is over now."

"Is it? Is it really over? There's years of murders and land grabs to account for. Are you certain I won't lose everything? That Farm Holding, even as a nonprofit, might take the farm down with it?" Connie stepped out of his embrace.

"Connie, I have a legal team working with me. I've gotten in touch with the firm that originally helped establish the holding company. They were astounded at what was done with it. I still think you will be fine. The formation of the holding company was perfectly legal. Land purchase contracts are legal. Proving how old people died might be difficult." Jack shook his head, stretched, walked to the snack table and began eating a cookie.

"Thanks, Jack. I may need a lot more reassurance. Right now, I'm going to the house." Connie grabbed a cookie and headed for the door.

Cochran stopped her. "Take a few minutes, but just know if the safe contains what we think it does, I plan to arrest Melvin on the spot. Deputy Ken is in his car near the garage, I'll have him at the door. Two other deputies are within a few minutes."

Connie nodded and walked to the house with Junior. Some of the girls were walking down the drive, apparently to clear their minds in the early April air. In the kitchen, Connie was greeted by Beany and his parents baking macaroni and cheese and fixing a huge salad for supper. "Oh, good. Comfort food. We need that desperately." She hugged Judy Sue and ran up the back stairs to her master bedroom.

Chapter Thirty-Six

Junior

Junior followed his mother to the house. He hugged Beany and used the bathroom off the mud room. He met Connie at the back door. They were halfway across the yard when Cochran shouted, "Melvin." Junior saw Melvin's lawyer race out of Shed One and Deputy Ken run from his car.

"He's gone. He went to the bathroom and now he's gone." Melvin's lawyer looked devastated. "I used it right after him, but Jack was waiting by the door when I came out. Sheriff Cochran was behind Jack. Melvin was poking around in the shop area. I got some lemonade and cookies, looked at the photos, next thing I heard, someone shouting Melvin's name."

"I saw him poking around in the shop area, too. He went out the side door, you damn fool," Cochran snorted. He checked his watch. "He had plenty of time, probably five to ten minutes. I went to the bathroom right after Jack and Melvin was gone when I came out. Damn you, Mains. You had one effing job."

"Where the hell could he go?" Deputy Ken threw his arms up.

Junior heard a metal door banging and Rusty bark twice. He turned to see the opened door of a grain bin slapping against the railing. Rusty sat on the top step of the curved metal stairway, like he'd been trained to do. "He's in Bin Five." Bin Five was the largest of their eight bins, thirty-six feet in diameter, rising almost thirty-seven feet to the eaves and forty-eight feet to the peak. It held over thirty thousand bushels of corn.

Junior followed Cochran and Jens up the metal stairs that circled the outside of the bin. No one thought to throw the breaker switch at the bottom to turn the lights on inside the bin. "Don't step inside," Junior screamed.

The steps he swiftly climbed during harvest time, now seemed like walking up a skyscraper in slow motion. He skidded to a stop behind Cochran and Jens. Both leaned into the doorway, their feet on the outside metal landing. Junior peered over their shoulders. Rusty came up one step and sat behind him. His nose lightly touched the back of Junior's knee.

The late afternoon sun shone in through the door to form a triangle of light that covered the middle of the bin, widening as it reached the curved far wall. To his left, in the shade, but almost on the edge of the light, Melvin sat on top of a grain crust, something that frequently forms across the top of corn due to moisture, cold temperature, or improper drying. Junior knew it could collapse at any moment.

Melvin sat about fifteen feet into the bin, his legs crossed, body angled so his back faced the door. In the dim light, Junior could see the straps of a safety harness over his shoulders and across his back, the lower straps around his upper thighs. A security rope ran from the safety harness to a pulley in the peak of the bin that then came down at an angle and was tied off to a brace next to the door. The rope was to prevent a person from sinking into the corn very far. No one was ever to step foot into a grain bin without wearing a safety harness attached to a rope while one person watched from the landing and a third person remained on the ground within eyesight to call for help.

Junior knew there could be several inches to several feet of air space below the crust and that it was weakest in the middle. He also knew if one went through the crust, it was extremely difficult to get out, and frequently fatal. Gravity pulled a person down into the loose corn as the kernels filled in around and above them, not only suffocating them, but almost crushing them to death. Your only hope was to be wearing a safety harness with someone holding the rope to pull you out.

"Don't touch the rope." Melvin's voice was low. "I need to be heard. It's my turn."

"Go ahead, Melvin. You have our undivided attention." Cochran spoke calmly.

He also turned slightly and motioned Deputy Ken back down the steps, making motions to call emergency services and mouthing 'no sirens.'

Though low, Melvin's voice was still almost childlike. "I always knew Shaw and me were related. Dot tried to tell me she got religion and took me out of some orphanage as a baby, but I never believed her. I saw my birth certificate when I could read. She must have lost her religion real soon, because I was passed around from friend to friend. When she got on drugs, the abuse started. Even when she got off them, she kept me around as a punching bag. Every time she lost a job, she would turn tricks. With me along, she could earn more. I saw my birth certificate again when we moved to Helen's. I was scared they'd throw me out cause technically, I wasn't a blood relative to them, but don't think Helen ever looked at it. I was afraid I'd lose Shaw then, 'cause we weren't full brothers. My certificate said my last name was Smith, but the father was of unknown whereabouts. That didn't matter to Shaw. He was the best thing that ever happened to me."

Through the dim light around Melvin, Junior could glimpse the man's hands moving, low, between his crossed legs, like he was scratching at the corn, maybe because he was nervous.

Melvin continued. "Dot frequently worked in nursing homes and would take me along. The old people loved having a kid around and she played it up. They were the cheap nursing homes for poor folk, often in people's raggedy homes, not the large clean-looking places. Everyone was waiting to die, except several had old men who weren't that ill, but had no place else to live. She earned nice tips when she left me with them for the night. I thought the others lived forever, just wanting to die. Shortly before I met Shaw, I asked her why she didn't help some of them die. 'I'd love to,' she said, 'but another one would just replace them. I wouldn't gain anything by it.' That kinda stuck with me, I mean, what's the sense of old folk who ain't ever going to get better still living? It just seemed like a waste to me. Besides, I hated what some of them did to me. The old bastards."

"How did your mother die?" Cochran asked.

"Quit interrupting me. It's my turn to talk. You just heard what Shaw wrote. It's the truth."

Cochran nudged Jens and Junior and pointed to the triangle of light which was shifting with the lowering sun and beginning to touch Melvin's elbow.

"The blue bird boxes were my idea. I kept seeing them around the whole area. Alice and the twins were big into birding and put in a few boxes. When the small cameras, surveillance equipment, and internet came out, it struck me it would be a lot easier to monitor a home. Only took a few minutes to download or swap out the SD card late at night. That way, I could review it on my laptop whenever I wanted, from wherever I was."

Cochran cleared his throat. "Sorry to interrupt, but Melvin, I still don't get it. What the hell were you looking for?"

"Jesus, you're dense. Old people who had few visitors, like family. People who got medicine in the mail, had it delivered or even picked up from a pharmacy. Some old people weren't interested in signing with Farm Holding. Some wanted to make sure their farm was inherited by someone else. If we knew they were on medicine. If we knew they didn't want to sign with Farm Holding. If we knew their kids weren't around or rarely showed interest in them. If they liked the friendly delivery man and nurse, that was me, *then* we could collect their signature on delivery papers and I could transfer it to our purchase agreement. Got it?" Melvin began wiggling around.

"Calm down, Melvin. Just calm down. You've got our attention." Cochran's words were soft and soothing. Melvin seemed to settle down, though Junior noticed his hands never stayed still. Small repetitive movements accompanied by a scratching sound.

Junior watched Cochran pull a digital recorder out of his pocket and check to make sure it was recording.

"Some of the people didn't know they signed away their farm to

Farm Holding. Just a few, though. Most people signed after they got sicker from the meds I altered for them. Most of the time, they got better after they signed and I switched their medicine back. Sometimes I did alter the medication for people who already signed so they would die sooner."

Cochran held the recorder out to his left in the shadows to better pick up Melvin's low voice.

"I mean, why waste time on old people who were going to die anyway? They were just waiting around, crapping themselves, hoping they'd die soon, if they could even think."

Melvin quit speaking. The only sounds were the soft scratches he was making in the corn, magnified by the surrounding metal. Rusty whined, nudged Junior's knee and he leaned down to pat him.

Cochran broke the silence. "How many old people do you think you helped die by altering their medications?" Junior was surprised how Cochran could ask such questions with a voice that held no condemnation.

Melvin stretched his shoulders while he seemed to think. "Over the years? All told, maybe ten or twelve. Like I said, they was gonna die anyway. I checked out several of their funerals, you know, trying to assess how accurate our research was. Hardly any family were present. They were old, sick, lonely folk. The records are in the safe."

The angle of light now covered part of Melvin's back and right knee. His hands were still in the dark.

"I did most of the compounding. Shaw got the degree and keeps licensed, but I know more than he does. He just orders the raw ingredients when we need them. We didn't make them at Worthington Pharmacy. They're legit. They know nothing of this. We had our own pharmacy. Sounds like you might have figured out where."

Cochran handed the recorder to Jens and grasped the rope with both hands. "Melvin, thanks for telling us all this. I have another question, if you don't mind. What did Shaw mean when he wrote that you knew what to do and, also, what you agreed to?"

"Take my medicine..." Melvin seemed to be thinking about what else to say.

"Thanks, Melvin," Cochran said. "Now, I think it's time you come in, so you can take your medicine and we can go open that safe. C'mon. I'll hold the rope."

Rusty began whining. Junior noticed the sunlight on Melvin was partially blocked by himself and Jens. More light could be available if they lowered themselves. "Squat down," he whispered to Jens. Jens dropped to his knees. Junior squatted. He pulled Rusty close to him and peered around Jens. That allowed the light to fully cover Marvin. All three gulped as they saw that Melvin held a screwdriver and was scratching with it into the corn between his legs.

"Nope, I'm done taking my meds," Melvin said. "Stayin on my meds, that's the first part of him saying I knew what to do. He was always reminding me to do that. We also agreed we would go out together if we ever got caught. We been together since I was nine. We thought alike. We both hate bein' betrayed and we both wanted lots of land, even though we knew we couldn't take it with us." He scratched deeper into the corn. "I don't consider anything we've done as wrong. Sometimes revenge can be humanitarian, too. Besides, you all are coming out of this just fine. I want my ashes to go with Shaw's."

With that, he began frantically stabbing the screwdriver deeper and faster. The crust beneath him cracked and began to tear open. "Junior. You take care of Rusty. He loves you, too."

Junior clung to the frantic dog as they watched Melvin's feet sink into the corn. It was as if watching in slow motion. Cochran pulled on the rope to stop him from sinking further. Each groaned as they realized Melvin's leg straps were unbuckled. His legs were never in them to begin with, nor had he fastened the front buckles across his chest and waist. He simply laid the leg straps over his thighs, tucked them under and sat on them to look like he was fully wearing the harness. He sank to his chest, still silent, then threw his hands up in the air which drove him down faster. Cochran yanked on the rope, but the harness slipped off Melvin's shoulders, past his arms, and dangled in the air as Melvin slipped into the slowly blending corn. His fingertips were the last the men saw of him.

Junior turned and vomited over the railing. Jens patted him on the back as Rusty whined and wriggled in his arms. Cochran trotted down the stairs and told the first responders it was a planned suicide, to get started on cutting several holes in the sides of the bin to let the corn flow out. Everyone knowledgeable about grain bin accidents knew not to turn on the auger to remove the grain. They also knew that it would take several hours before enough corn flowed out of the holes to safely find the body. Any faster, and the entire bin could collapse, endangering those nearby and further slowing the recovery efforts. The chances of Melvin surviving were none to slim.

Junior was conscious of his mother, sisters and Beany watching him as he slowly walked past the other bins and sheds. Rusty followed at his left knee. He picked up the dog, climbed the ladder, stepped across the steel landing and into the cab of the giant corn combine. He sat high above the twenty-row picker, cuddling Rusty in his lap. The combine faced away from the bins and commotion, toward the muddy fields, and was quiet inside. Besides running, it was the only place he could think of to be by himself. He leaned his head back. What else was left? Shaw said there was more. Was there an end to this nightmare? His father was not his father. The man he called Dad all his life shot at him and tried to kill his mother because she had a secret affair with a man who was his father. The man he thought was his father chose to die rather than accept an amputation that would have saved his life. The same man murdered a druggist, his own uncle and aunt, his first wife and was complicit in more deaths, including Dot's—his own mother's.

Rusty licked Junior's cheek. Junior loved the dog. It was the only thing Melvin ever shared with him. Junior was seven when Melvin brought the eight-week old puppy to the farm. Junior quietly asked if he could hold him.

Melvin flashed one of his rare smiles and placed the excited yipping pup into Junior's arms. "He's a Jack Russell Terrier."

Junior couldn't hear Melvin over the noises of the puppy and the softness of Melvin's words. "His name is Rustle?"

Melvin paused. "No, I said he was a Jack Russell Terrier, but

Rustle's not a bad name."

"Rusty is better, look at his spots," Junior replied.

"Well, you just named him."

He picked Rusty up and explained how Junior must ask permission to pet him, how he would teach Junior to walk the dog, when they could run wild and when they couldn't.

Junior thought about how Melvin was true to his word and taught him and Beany how to handle the dog, the commands, even the hand signals. Rusty grew to a solid fifteen pounds. Now that he was ten, he needed little direction. When he and Beany started high school, they saw less of Rusty, but were still welcomed by him whenever they were around the farm at the same time.

Melvin's last words to take care of Rusty coupled with the image of the man resolutely sliding under the corn without a word or a struggle, his fingertips slowly being covered by the corn, made him gag. He managed not to vomit again. How many people had Melvin and Shaw really killed? He hugged Rusty again as he felt the cab jiggle and watched the door open and his mother appear. He didn't mind. They needed to be together. He slid over as she squeezed onto the seat with him and wrapped her arms around his shoulders. Rusty dropped to the floor by his feet. The cab wiggled again, the door opened, and one by one, his six sisters squeezed into the cab or stood on the steel platform, crowded around the open doorway. No one spoke. They hugged, lightly patted each other and sniffled.

After what seemed hours, but was probably ten minutes, Junior felt the cab shaking again. Cochran climbed the ladder and stood behind the girls in the doorway. "Just wanted you to know, Jens, Jack and I think the safe should wait till tomorrow to be opened."

"Thank you. That makes sense." Connie took a deep breath. "How long before they find…"

"Maybe another hour or two." Cochran sounded worn out.

Connie lowered her head into Junior's shoulder and half-whispered, "Wish we could all go someplace. Like instantly."

Emma broke the tension by snickering. "I think we already have.

Can't Jack join us to read the will? He could climb up the other side of the cab and lean in through the window."

How can a person go from despair, pain and sorrow to hilarity so quickly? Junior thought, as he felt himself burst into laughter. It wasn't happiness, it wasn't enjoyment, but it did break the tension and showed the innate resilience built into the human spirit. He also knew that somehow, everyone squished inside this cab were meant to be together and they would figure out how to continue their lives, no matter what else happened.

When they calmed down, Junior said, "I don't want to be in the shed when they find Melvin. Can't we move to the house? I'll shut the cameras off so we can't watch the monitor. Jack can read the will. If it's good, so be it. If it's bad? Well, we'll survive. Anyone who can survive this past week can handle anything else. Right?"

His mom and sisters softly cheered.

Junior was the last to climb down. Ellen led the family toward the house. Rusty stayed tucked under Junior's arm as he walked past the hushed busyness near the bin; the first responders and neighbors shoveling the corn flowing out of the holes into piles away from the bin. An ambulance waited nearby. He saw a TV truck ease up the driveway and realized several photographers and reporters were already milling around. Emma stepped back to speak to Cochran. Together, they walked over and briefly spoke to the group. Junior heard Emma say they would have more information to provide later.

Oh, God, he thought. *Now we'll be a media frenzy. A suicide of a serial killer, following the self-inflicted gunshot wound of another killer, a dead first wife, and a second wife living with seven kids who never guessed the evil around them. Mom was right. They needed to leave.*

He went inside, found a towel for Rusty to lay on in the mud room, got him some water, then went into the kitchen and turned the cameras and monitor off. He sat down at the kitchen table. From the looks of nearly everyone else, all had the same thoughts he did—when was this going to end? Emma, Cochran, Jens and Jack came in together. It seemed no one knew what to say.

~ * ~

Water, lemonade and more fresh baked cookies waited on the table. Beany was subdued. Jack sat at the head and took a long drink of water. He looked around, took a deep breath and leaned back in his chair. "Relax, people. This tragic day is nearly over."

Connie snapped open the large envelope with her copy of the will. "Just get this over. Out with it. Will we have anything left or not?"

Jack tilted his head toward her. "First, the will you have in front of you has not been changed."

"That's good, but I need to hear from you about Farm Holding. Was Shaw just blowing smoke out his butt when he wrote it was now a nonprofit and I was the head of it? I'm thinking after the news hits about Farm Holding killing people to get their property, they'll still come after our assets, nonprofit or not. We're going to be screwed. I don't want to lose the home and part of the farm we live on. If we do, we'll survive, because as you can tell, we are survivors. We just won't be survivors with any land or a home."

Junior watched his mother slide dejectedly back in her seat.

She roused and sat up again. "Is this blood money? Will the nonprofit be utilizing blood money to help others? What sense does that make?" She shook her head and slumped back into her chair. "I can't even deal with that right now. It's too much."

Jack looked firmly at her. "Connie, I understand your thinking. I have several lawyers working on this situation. In the first place, Farm Holding did not own or control the two sections you already own. That is clearly spelled out in the will and I double-checked the land records. That file you saw in the back office was incorrect. Also, from our review of the records of the land that's been acquired, I don't think many, if anyone, will sue. If they do, we can work out something with them. I believe you have a good opportunity to use the nonprofit to help rural people with mental health issues. Let me repeat. You are not going to lose the farm. Your children will still inherit the resources separately set aside for them in the will and you will be able to determine what happens to the farm when you die or decide to liquidate it." He held up one hand toward her as he took a long drink of water. "Shaw was an odd man. Complex. The reason the kids have an inheritance is because he established investments and trusts with the insurance money he received from Alice. Over the years, he kept adding to it. It would be impossible right now to determine which part came from the original insurance payment and which is a result from growth and addition. I think he purposely mixed it up that way." He looked at the shocked faces around the table. "Plus, each of you seven children are receiving an equal amount. He double-checked with me in the hospital to make sure that was still the case."

"Oh, my God," Gail said. "I think more should go to Ellen and Mary—"

"No." Ellen stood up as Mary motioned for her to continue speaking. "We are seven brother and sisters. As much as I hate our father for what he did and who he was, he got this part right. I will not listen to any disagreements. Case closed. We share equally. Now move on with this conversation."

"Ditto for me," Mary said. "Move on."

"Wow," Emma said. "I guess sometimes we gotta trust the process. Mom, let Jack and the lawyers do their work. You can decide what to do with the nonprofit later. Some good needs to come out of this mess. Now, we need to focus on these next few days."

Connie slid her chair back. "Thanks, Emma. Jack, listen, if the will hasn't been changed, why do we need to read it right now? It isn't going to change. In fact, I can make copies for each of us."

Jack said, "Connie, that's an excellent idea. We do have to read it formally, but not everyone needs to be present. Let's put it off for a week or so. Besides, we have to open the safe and from the look on Cochran's face, I suspect he has more to say."

"Dammit, just dammit. What else do we have to hear?" Connie leaned in, grabbed a cookie and snapped a bite.

Cochran stood. "I agree. I think we should open the safe

tomorrow after this commotion with Melvin is done." He looked around table till every eye was on him. "Plus, Jens and I believe we now know where Shaw and Melvin had their pharmacy…"

"You mean they didn't use the one in Worthington?" Connie sounded dubious.

"No, Mom," Junior answered. "Melvin told us in the corn bin that they had another place and it wasn't the pharmacy. He said Worthington Pharmacy is a legit business and they wanted to keep it that way."

"So where is it?" Connie shrugged; just how much more were they going to learn?

"We're now sure there's hidden space between the office and Shed One walls. We just have to figure a way to get into it." Jens stood. "I think we should wait till tomorrow to open the safe. There's too many other people around here right now with the recovery effort."

Jack grimaced. "I heard Shaw told the family there was more. Hopefully, that's the last of it. Can we meet about ten tomorrow to open the safe?"

Connie looked around the table. Her kids agreed.

Ellen said. "I think we all have the gist of what those two were up to and what you'll find. Mary, Gayle and I won't be here. It's sad, but I don't think there's much else that can shock us. If Dad was correct, and there are photos of Mother with some guy, it won't change anything. She still died. He admitted he killed her. Her committing suicide never felt right. The idea that Dad would have killed her never felt right either. What a tragic experience. Anyway, let's try to relax tonight and make it a family night."

"Still. It would be nice to see the pictures." Mary straightened. "But we don't want to interfere with the investigation."

An hour later, Rusty started whining and scratching at the door. Junior picked him up and stepped onto the back patio. He watched the EMT's close the back doors of the ambulance. The vehicle slowly pulled away; its sirens silent. Melvin's lawyer followed. The first responders and volunteers finished shoveling the corn into larger piles, then quietly walked to their vehicles and left. Junior knew the neighbors would return in several days to patch the bin and auger the grain back into it.

When all were gone, Junior set Rusty down. The dog trotted toward the bin and began sniffing around the piles of corn. "He's gone, little buddy," Junior said, tears forming. He knelt down as Rusty slowly walked back to him. "I think we both lost our dads, the good parts and the bad."

He sat down and pulled the dog into his lap and let his tears flow. Tears for his family, himself, the old people who died, even Uncle Ford and Aunt Helen, though he wasn't truly related to them. He felt Beany slide down beside them and wrap his arms around him and Rusty. He raised his head and looked into Beany's eyes. "I think there's another orphan now. Dad was. Melvin was. Now Rusty is too."

Rusty licked Junior's hand and snuggled tighter into his lap.

Chapter Thirty-Seven

Cochran

Saturday Evening

After dinner was cleared away and the dishes done, the family gathered in the family room. Cochran and Jens joined them. Beany said goodbye to the twins and Gayle, then walked back to his home. No one seemed to want to celebrate the last night of the family being together. Cochran kept glancing at Ellen and Mary. He cleared his throat. "I'm thinking you'd like to know what's in that safe that deals with your birth mother. Right?"

The girls looked at each other with expressions of agreement. "You were reading my mind," Ellen said. "I was feeling a loss. If there's pictures of my mother, even if she's with another man… Is there a chance we could view them?"

"With me supervising, I don't see why not. There's just one condition. We're not going to look through the other records pertaining to Farm Holding and the people Melvin was spying on. I think only you girls leaving early and Connie should view them tonight. Agreed?"

Everyone nodded.

In the back office, Cochran had everyone put on gloves. He spun the dial and pulled the heavy safe door open. It was a large safe, an ancient bank one, nearly seven-foot-high by four feet wide, with multiple shelves and several locked drawers.

Mary touched the door. "I remember Dad saying his uncle

somehow hauled this thing out here when they remodeled the bank, about the time his uncle put the first shed up. Dad put this office addition on Shed One right after Mom died. Ellen and I watched them move the thing over with a huge front-end loader and place it on the concrete floor before the walls went up."

Cochran stepped in front of the opened safe. "You look around me and don't crowd in while I figure this out." He took his time visually examining each shelf. "They sure as hell were organized." He pulled a small basket off the top shelf. "These are keys labeled for the drawers below. Here's another for the pharmacy. Damn, they even called it a pharmacy." He pulled a key out. "Drawer 3, Alice."

He heard Ellen and Mary suck in their breath as he inserted the key and slowly pulled it open. "There's more than a few pictures in here. Why don't you pull in some chairs and sit down? I've got one here." He sat down and delicately began pulling out envelopes and looking at the contents. He slipped a typewritten report out of one with photos attached. "This is from a private investigator out of Iowa City." He glanced through it. "Very professional and detailed report. These photos are clear. I can't see any reason not to believe his conclusions." He looked at the twins. "You sure you want to see these?"

They took the package from him. Ellen skimmed through the report while Mary looked at the photos. "That's her, all right, and those look like her friends from Worthington. There was a small group that she kept in close contact with. We stayed with our aunt and uncle and cousins sometimes while she went on outings with her friends, but I think the relationships faded away. Maybe because they knew she was having an affair. Her parents died shortly after we were born. Mom was the youngest." She scratched her ear. "Seeing these, I think most of her later outings must have been with Robby. I remember him. He worked for the post office and coached Little League in the summers." She handed the photos to Ellen. "They sure look happy together. I'm not referring to the pictures of them kissing in the motel door, the other ones, too." She wiped her eyes.

Ellen looked through them and handed the package back to

Cochran. "I agree. I'm just glad she had some happiness in a relationship. She obviously wasn't having any with Dad."

Cochran passed them another large envelope. "It appears she was very unhappy. These are divorce papers served on your father two days before she died."

"Oh, my God. She was going to leave him?" Ellen scrambled to find some crumpled tissues in her pocket and began dabbing her eyes.

"Looks like it was for mental cruelty," Mary said after reading through the file. "Our poor mother, killed before she could get away and have a life. This is so much to grasp at one time."

"In eight days," said Connie. "Look at all we've learned in eight days. It seems like eighty years."

"Here's a diary," Cochran said, glancing through it. "The last entries appear to be in the late sixties, which would have been after you two were born, but while you were still young." He pulled out a bulging envelope. "Oh, my Lord. These are pill bottles with capsules similar to the ones in the file photos taken when the department investigated her death. There's even a note of the compounds used in making them." He kept looking through the envelope. "They made up capsules that looked just like the Librium your mom was taking. She was on a low dose, as I recall from reading the police files. Shaw exchanged them with high potency capsules and later switched the originals back, probably throwing some away, to make it look like she took a large quantity. God damn that man. If he lived, I'd be going for life imprisonment." Cochran stood. "I'll step back and let you girls look through this. I can only imagine the emotions it must bring. I'll be in the outer office, drinking up some of that cold coffee. Call me if I can be of help."

The four women passed around the photos, the diary and the bag with the extra bottles of pills and information. Connie stepped into the outer office and returned with a box of tissues and a waste can. She lightly touched each of the twins. "This must be like reliving everything all over, but with the knowledge that your father was responsible for the pain. I am so sorry you're going through this again." She sat and blew her nose.

"Mom, it's been over thirty-five years," Mary said. "On the one hand, it feels like yesterday, on the other hand, I have some perspective. Maybe it's shock. Either way, we lost a beautiful, loving mother who was seeking love because she couldn't get it from her husband."

"And he," Ellen said, "was so damaged emotionally from all the betrayals and rejection in his life, yet couldn't share it or see a way for help, if he even understood he needed help." She wiped her eyes. "What a tragedy. I'm seeking help when I get home. I need to talk with a professional about all this. I can't handle this on my own before..."

Connie waited a moment to see if Ellen would finish her sentence. "I think that is so smart. I think I will look into some help also and see if Junior wants some."

"Mom, it's not only for me. We've been too busy and focused on Dad to update you, but I began a relationship with a wonderful man, a retired music professor. I don't want to get too far into the relationship without being stable myself." Ellen smiled as her sisters and Connie congratulated her.

"That makes so much sense, getting help," Mary said. "Thanks for being so open. I think I will do the same in Prague. I know of several English-speaking therapists who work with American and English expats." She looked through the photos and gently returned them to the envelope. "I've seen enough. I'm glad we did this. It's better knowing than not knowing and wondering what was in the safe. At least we have some answers. It's good to say my mother did not commit suicide. It takes some of that childhood guilt away that always nagged at the back of my mind, like what did I do wrong to cause her to want to leave us? As Sis said, this is all such a tragedy, but there's nothing I can do to change it, except to look forward."

The girls watched Cochran return the items to the safe and lock it. Each touched the safe for a moment, then left, walking back to the house with their arms linked. Cochran turned out the lights and quietly followed.

~ * ~

Jack, Cochran, Connie, Jens, Emma, Jane, Jackie and Junior, plus Susan, a member of the state crime lab, were present at ten Sunday morning when Cochran opened the safe again. He quickly reviewed what the drawer on Alice contained. He turned to Susan. "For me, the first priority is to locate a file or information on who Melvin had under surveillance and was altering their medication or supplying doctored skin cream."

Susan agreed and quickly located several files that confirmed there were three people whose prescriptions had been altered. Cochran called Ken with orders to visit those people ASAP, collect their medications, any creams, to contact their physicians and pharmacies for a renewal of the original prescription.

Susan took charge and methodically went through each item and record. The files were detailed with back-up video on DVDs and SD cards of people who were surveilled, people who died from apparent natural causes and people who possibly died from altered medications, of which there were fewer than the group expected. One file held obituaries for each person who died and Farm Holding acquired their land. Another held Melvin's medical notes regarding the condition of elderly people he delivered medication to, their blood pressure, pulse rate, and other information. They found a file on Melvin, thick with his medications, his appointments with various psychiatrists over the years, and filled with his many possible diagnoses involving schizophrenia, flat affect disorder, PTSD from childhood trauma, obsessive-compulsive personality, avoidant personality. Susan muttered to Cochran, "What an alphabet soup. This poor guy was a mess. It's amazing he functioned as well as he did in normal society."

Jack kept shaking his head and finally sat down. "I had no idea they acquired so many properties. I handled only a few of these land acquisitions in terms of property transfers and titles. Why didn't I know more?"

"Because," Susan said, holding a file folder. "They used other lawyers. It appears enough of them so that no one person could get suspicious." She glanced through the records. "I guess there are eight to ten lawyers who each handled only two or three transactions over many years." She handed Jack the file. "Take a look. I'm not a property lawyer, but everything looks proper to me."

Jack looked through the file. "The transactions were all handled legally. Obviously, how they got to some of those transactions wasn't. This is so sad."

Connie started pacing. "Jack, is there any way we can make things right for the families or heirs of these old people who might have died from altered medication or fraud in obtaining signatures? I want everything done to assure they are satisfied. I want you to be proactive on this."

"We're thinking the same way, Connie. My reputation is at stake in this mess, too. I'll be very preemptive in sorting this out." Jack walked into the outer office. "Damn you, Cochran. You drank up all the cold coffee. Guess I'll have to start a pot."

Cochran noticed Junior getting antsy. He looked at Jens who looked the same. "Susan, can we have the key to the pharmacy? We won't touch anything, but want to see it. Afterwards, these folks can go back to the house while you catalog and document everything in the safe and the pharmacy."

Susan handed him the basket of keys and he pulled one out.

"Lordy, look at this, would ya," Cochran opened what looked like the door to a janitor's closet in the bathroom of Shed One and stepped into a long narrow room lined with a counter on one side and shelves above it. He pointed out things to the group as they gaped. "An old manual typewriter with a roll of prescription labels, from... Let's see, now..." He studied the labels. "These are very old, decades. I'm thinking once Melvin started delivering medications, he brought some back here and they perverted them and typed in the same name of the pharmacy. Plus, capsules can be substituted for tablets. Isn't that convenient?" He continued along the counter and shelves. "Empty prescription bottles, a tray to count and sort pills, here's a pharmaceutical scale, and a tray to punch capsules. All this equipment looks old, but functional." He explained how, after thoroughly mixing the ingredients and spreading them out on the tray, a pharmacist would take the small end of the capsule and punch it into the mix, then weigh it till the correct amount was secured and then slide the large half of the capsule over the small.

Junior opened a cabinet. "Look. Here's some drugs or chemicals they could mix together." He pointed to the bags, boxes and bottles, the mortars and pestles.

Jens moved past the group and tapped on a wall that jutted into the room, like the back of a closet. "Here's where the monitor, computer and hard drives are located and a door into it." He paused and looked at Connie. "You know, that day Ben from the security company showed us the set-up, the thought niggled at me about where the space for it came from. I just couldn't focus on it till I realized how the outer walls of the office seemed wider than the inner. Bingo. This is why."

They gathered back in the office. Cochran poured a cup of fresh coffee and took a sip as he turned toward the group. "You all seen enough? I think Susan can handle what she has to do. Unless you have any questions for her, I think you can go back to the house and relax."

Connie plopped down into the office chair. "That sounds good. I can't speak for the rest of you, but I've seen enough. I'm already on overload with details, loss, grief and anger. Part of me keeps beating myself up for not knowing this was going on right in front of me. Soon, I realize the minds of these two men were so warped, and being so smart, they had the ability to manipulate a lot of other people including our family." She shook her head and slowly stood. "It will take some time to put all these pieces together. The good news is I don't think we'll have any more surprises. I feel somewhat comfortable that Jack and the lawyers can straighten out whatever needs to be, plus maybe we can do some good for this community." She headed for the door, then stopped. "Jens and Junior, after the service tomorrow, when you're ready to move the combine and equipment in, take me with you. I need to learn how to drive them. Plus, Jack, pull a meeting together with the accountants later this week. I need to get a handle on our finances."

Chapter Thirty-Eight

Jens

Jens noticed a smile on Cochran's face as they left the office around noon on Sunday. They were the last ones out, besides Susan, who needed several more hours to document items. "In spite of all the stress from yesterday with Melvin, you look happy. What's up?"

"Yesterday was horrible. Last night, it took a long time to finish the paperwork and get the reports started by the staff."

Jens looked at Cochran, his eyes warm.

"Today, I feel like this nightmare is almost over. We won't be learning anything new. Even better, Ken called me. He said he couldn't officially order me to do so, but he thinks I should take the rest of today off."

Jens stopped walking. "In that case, would you like to go on a date with me? Maybe lunch in Marshall, Italian, a bit of wine, followed by some activity we can do together, followed by a kiss." He could see the answer in Cochran's eyes.

"Yes, but I can't accept your offer until I run the Jeep through a car wash and myself through the shower, plus change into real people clothes. This uniform still smells of chickens. How about I come back and pick you up in an hour and a half?"

"It's a deal. I can shower and change into socks that don't bunch up with quarters in them."

Jens was in the kitchen, chatting with Connie, when Cochran rang the back door bell. She looked surprised. "Why is he here again? I hope it's not more bad news." She let him in and stood between him and Jens, looking at them suspiciously.

"We're going out for dinner." Jens tried not to laugh.

"It—It's kinda like a date," Cochran said, blushing, not looking at her.

Jens put his arm around Connie's shoulders. "Yeah, if I'm not back for a while, it may be more than a date."

Cochran's face flushed even more as Connie looked at him, then back at Jens, whose face felt just as red. "Well, I'll be damned," she said softly. "This is the best news I've had in a long time." She reached up to softly touch each of them on the cheek, then laughed. "We'll still know what time you come home." She pointed toward the monitor in the kitchen and, smiling, walked back toward the family still chatting around the table.

~ * ~

Monday morning, Jens woke in Cochran's bed, sensing someone was watching him. It wasn't Rufus, who snored on his pad next to the bed. It was Cochran, laying on his side, looking at him, his eyes moist. "That was the most beautiful night I've ever had. I never guessed sex could be so wonderful. It wasn't just sex. It was making love. Now I understand what those words mean."

~ * ~

Monday, thirty minutes before the memorial service was to begin, Jens stepped out the back door of the house and glanced down the Milliken driveway. A sheriff deputy's car sat with lights flashing. It appeared someone was checking each car arriving. He stepped to the side of the house and peered down the 127th Street drive. Same thing occurring. He also noticed a TV van and several cars parked to the side of the driveway. Damn, the news is out. How are we going to handle this? He noticed Emma near the sheriff car.

297

He watched her walk up the 127th Street drive toward him. "Everything is under control," she said. "At least for the most part. The service is private for family and friends, the media may not attend, film or tape. One of my friends is at each drive with the deputies, telling the people not to speak to the media. We'll do a press conference right after the service. All Mom knows is that we're going to do a press conference later."

"How's she doing?"

"She seemed a little nervous about the press conference. She told me she's got nothing to hide and maybe the publicity will do some good for the nonprofit. How she's thought that far ahead is beyond me." Emma slipped her arm through Jens' and guided him toward Shed One. On the way, she elbowed him. "That man ahead of us is Judge Franklin, the one who gave Melvin bail." Jens stopped walking, but she pulled him gently toward the door. "I think it will be all right. I heard Cochran had a long talk with him out by the road."

Inside, Jens looked around, pleased at the number of people coming in, yet surprised to see a camera on a tripod with Ben from the security company standing by it. He caught Ben's eye. Ben smiled, tilted his head toward the camera and said, 'Connie's idea.' Jens decided not to worry about the camera, the judge or the press conference. Tomorrow was tomorrow. Right now, they had to sit through what was probably the strangest memorial service he ever attended.

Beany's group played classical music, not too loud, not too quiet. They were dressed in black suits, white shirts and skinny black ties. The only color was the purple hair and chartreuse eyeglasses of the bass player. Jens recognized some of the locals, the old timers his father's age, shuffling in with their canes, hearing aids and heavy winter coats. Several recognized him and expressed surprise he was still around the area. One asked about Hans and seemed shocked when Jens reminded him that his brother died eighteen years ago. Several mumbled about not talking to the media and seemed confused, but accepting.

About sixty people were present for the service. The Methodist pastor stepped up and motioned for the quartet to quit playing. He introduced himself and said he would not provide a eulogy, that Connie planned to introduce the kids and speak for a few minutes.

Connie stepped to the small podium with an air of strength and calmness. Jens realized, other than family and Judy Sue, few people ever saw Connie not in her self-confident mode. She welcomed the group, then introduced the children who were present and spoke of the ones who left the day before. She mentioned what each of them did and where they lived. Her pride beamed across the room. After introducing Junior, she asked Judy Sue, Beany, Albert, and Jens to stand. "These people share no DNA with me, but they are also part of our family." She paused a moment as everyone seemed to wait in anticipation.

Sitting back down, Jens wondered what she would say in this complicated situation. What could she say? How much do you tell? How much don't you? Jens watched her, knew she gathered herself by the way she straightened her back and shoulders.

"Many of you were surprised when I married Shaw shortly after Alice's tragic death. He was fifteen years older than me. He didn't express emotion. He wasn't warm and cuddly, or outgoing and social. No, he wasn't my type, as I heard several people say back then. I'll admit I first loved his daughters, the twins. They needed a mother, they needed love, they needed help and I immediately recognized that Shaw was not the type of man who could raise kids by himself. Some men are. I'm sure you all will agree Shaw wasn't."

Jens noticed several people nod and smile.

Connie continued, "However, I didn't marry Shaw out of sympathy for Mary and Ellen. After being an orphan myself, after living with and seeing how Mr. Hanson was somewhat of an emotional man who I could never tell which way his wind was blowing, I knew I needed someone steady. I needed someone who would allow me the freedom to raise kids and run a household, to share my love, to be a wife who could help her partner achieve his goals and flourish. I wanted and needed stability, roots, a home, everything I didn't have when young." She paused and looked at the group, her eyes bright and focused. "I needed and deeply loved Shaw."

She stepped to the side of the podium and smiled. "Most of you have heard this old story, but I'm going to tell it again. A journalist for the local paper was at an open house for a couple married sixty-five years. He asked the old man, 'Sixty-five years is a long time to stay in love with the same person.'

'Yup,' the old guy replied. 'Sure is.'

'So, what's your secret? Giving her lots of flowers, helping with the dishes, giving her breaks from the kids?'

'Didn't do too much of that, I guess.'

'Well, did you tell her you loved her every night?'

'Nope. I told her once.'

'Once? Only once in sixty-five years? That's terrible.'

'Twas not terrible. I told her on our wedding day I loved her and if I ever changed my mind, I'd let her know.'"

Jens looked around and heard the chuckles.

Connie raised her hand. "I'm not finished. The young reporter goes into the kitchen where the wife is sitting with her friends. 'Is it true your husband only told you he loved you once in all your life together?'

'Sure is,' the old gal said. 'An' guess what? I believed him.'"

Connie pointed around the room as the laughter subsided. "You all know that was Shaw. The first night in bed together, after making love, I looked into his eyes and said I love you.

"Can anyone guess what he said?" She paused as everyone began to smile. He said, 'I know. Thank you.' Now you know why I told you the story of the old couple. That was us. That was Shaw and me. That was our relationship. Committed, firm and steady." She took a sip of water. "Now, tell me, did he ever refuse to help anyone who asked or needed? Did he hold back on paying anyone what he owed them? Did he ever say he was going to do something and not do it?"

No one answered, but Jens noted heads shaking.

"That was the man I married and loved. I thought he would live long enough so that I could say I was old, too. However, that was only half of the man I loved and married and bore more children for. The other half, I knew nothing about. Nothing. Zilch. Zero. I never heard the words

Farm Holding Company uttered until after he shot himself while attempting to shoot me. I never had an inkling he had a vasectomy after Emma was born. I never would have guessed he would wing Junior with birdshot to keep him away long enough to kill me."

Connie took a long drink of water and began pacing again. Dropping the volume of her voice, she went on, "Farm Holding has been dissolved. A nonprofit charitable organization is being established to help elderly farmers hang onto their property and dispose of it the way they desire. Also, to help farm families with mental health issues. There's too much going on below the surface in our isolated communities. We need to quit the ineffective gossip, openly discuss our problems, and establish professional networks that can truly help people. I realize some of you may have issues with Farm Holding. Bring them to me. I will make sure everything possible will be done to make things right. You each know me as honest and straightforward. That's not going to change." She pointed to a white board with her name and phone number. "Make a note of that. If you have any questions or problems related to Farm Holding call me. Anytime. By the way, that is my cell." She pointed toward Ben and the camera. "I asked that I be videotaped. Ben is only focused on me. Any of you whose face accidently ends up on the tape will be blurred out. I am doing this so there will be no questions as to what I said today. Like Shaw, I don't go back on my word."

Connie stopped pacing and looked around the room. She moved closer to the front row. "You know there is more to my story and the reason we're here today. I'm sure it's been in the back of people's minds, if not on their lips. When I was still in high school, Hans Hanson and I fell in love. That love for each other lasted until his untimely death eighteen years ago. It lasted when we each married others. Love is not something of limited supply. Our love for each other did not mean we did not love our respective spouses. It did not mean we suffered in our daily lives until we could see each other. It did not mean we made false promises to each other about leaving our spouses and uniting full time. It was a special, unique love that I have no regrets for." She returned to the lectern. "I had an exciting, deep bond, soul mate kind of love with Hans, as occasional as it was, but it wasn't steady. As I've described, I needed steady. I loved Shaw and part of him loved me. I just didn't realize it wasn't all of him, nor ever could have been."

She resumed pacing and glanced at Junior who sat straighter and smiled back. "Can any of you imagine naming your son Junior if you thought he wasn't your son? I'm sure the gossip lines have been buzzing. There's reason for it. I get it. I did consider Hans might be Junior's father when I discovered I was pregnant. But as you recall, Hans died suddenly four months before Junior was born. We have reason to believe Melvin Smith was responsible because Hans was asking too many questions about Farm Holding. That is still being investigated." She paused by the lectern and took a sip of water. "However, at that point in time, I had no idea Shaw had a vasectomy and couldn't have fathered Junior. Though grieving Hans' death, I was thrilled to be pregnant. Shaw never indicated any dissatisfaction or concern. He agreed to name him Junior. For me, it was natural to bury those thoughts of the possibility that Hans might be the father. So, say what you will, but quite frankly, don't say it to me. Life moves on, and so will we."

Jens watched Connie seem to deflate for a minute or so, but she took a deep breath and continued. "So that everyone is on the same page, we have sent in DNA samples. We will not hide the results. Nothing will change the relationship between Junior, myself, his sisters and our good friends." She held up her hand, five fingers, signaling the musicians. "This was supposed to be a memorial for Shaw. It still is. I hope each of you can remember him as you knew him, stoic, solid and dependable. I also want you to remember him as secretive, compartmentalized and revengeful. There were two sides to Shaw Philip Skogman. I don't think we can choose which side to remember. I know I can't. Thank you for coming, for your support, love and friendship. Please mingle and enjoy the food and drink. If you're like us, you never can tire of Syds food. Eat up. There's containers to take home the leftovers. We love you."

Jens glanced at Junior. How was he taking all this in? His mother publicly confirming not only her affair, but the results of it. Junior looked back at him and smiled with a quick nod. *He's all right*, Jens thought.

He's doing fine.

The pastor stepped to the podium. "This has been a memorial service for Shaw Skogman. As everyone knows, Melvin Smith died yesterday, seemingly at his own volition. Melvin, it turns out, was Shaw's half-brother and the two have been together since Melvin was nine. The family asked that I ask everyone to remember Melvin at this time, also. He had no other family. He and Shaw suffered great abuse as children which resulted in double lives for both of them. It's sad. At this time, I'm going to ask if anyone wants to share any memories or thoughts about Shaw, and/or Melvin."

Several did, hesitant at first, expressing their shock at the double life both men led, but then focusing on the good things the men did for them and the community. Jens was surprised at the number who said positive things about Melvin caring for their relatives, or helping them out on their farms. All mentioned their love and respect for Connie. Jens was pleased with the comments and sense of community that held these friends and neighbors so tightly together.

The pastor paused as Judge Franklin walked slowly to the front of the room. He pointed at Ben and the camera. "Keep that on me. Like Connie, I want a record of what I'm about to say." Jens watched the looks of anticipation and confusion flash across the faces, especially Connie's.

"Most of you know me. Most of you would say I'm a fair judge who goes by the book. I've been part of this county, either as a lawyer or judge, for forty years. If I don't know each of you, I dare say I know someone close to you." Judge Franklin looked at the floor. He straightened up. "I want you all to know I made a mistake. Last Friday, I allowed Melvin Smith to go free on bail. I didn't know he was a part of Farm Holding until then. I let my emotions for this man helping my father in his last days skew my judgement. I wouldn't accept the idea there might be a connection between Farm Holding, whose payments kept my father in his home until his death, and Melvin's efforts. Maybe if I listened better, Melvin would be in jail and still alive." He turned away, pulled a starched handkerchief out of his pocket, carefully wiped his eyes, then blew his nose. "Now, what I'm about to say will sound strange, but hear me out. In many cases, it sounds like some of Shaw's and Melvin's efforts to acquire property through Farm Holding were underhanded, but not illegal. In what I've discerned, several cases were by nefarious means. I would be for throwing the book at them if they were alive. The two are not. I trust Connie and Jack Walker to make things right with whomever believes they've been wronged. Sit down and talk with them. Do it quietly. This community and county have been through enough with this situation. We don't need to blow it up and ruin relationships. If someone doesn't get satisfaction, then take it to a lawyer. Contact the media as a last resort." He pulled his handkerchief back out and wiped his brow. "I also want to say this. You know I still teach the adult Bible class at First Methodist Church. Not sure why we still call it First. After one hundred years, it should be obvious there's not going to be a second." He smiled as several chuckled. "Here's what I want to tell you. It seems the Bible teaches that everyone has a time to die. That time is predetermined and is not affected by what we do. I'm not saying we should do nothing to help someone in poor health. I'm just saying, life is a lot easier if we don't play the what if game. Shaw and Melvin think they might have helped some old folks die a little sooner to fulfill their greedy desires, but only God knows for sure. Again, I'm not excusing those two's actions. I am saying, if you have concerns, speak with Connie and Jack. As for me, I'm at peace with my dad dying at his appointed time, regardless of the circumstances."

Whoa, Jens thought. *What happens if one doesn't believe in God?* He looked around the room. Nearly every elderly head was bobbing, seeming in acknowledgement of the judge's words.

The pastor closed the service with a brief nondenominational prayer. Beany and the quartet broke into an upbeat version of Mozart. Ben took the camera off the tripod.

Jens' thoughts returned to Connie. Holy cow, how did she do that? So blunt, on target, so descriptive of the reality of her life and loves. He watched as people went up to hug and talk with her. The girls milled around, greeting people they hadn't seen in years and telling their stories over and over.

Chapter Thirty-Nine

Connie

As the last guest walked out the door into the damp, misty, almost snowy early April day, Connie sat down at a table with the girls. "I'd love a glass of wine. Can someone get me one?"

"Mom, you were wonderful. I don't know how you stood up there and bared your soul without losing any of it." Emma set a glass in front of Connie. "Take a few sips, then let's go meet the vultures."

Jack walked over to the table. "That was impressive and meaningful. So transparent. So honest. You ever thought about going into law? We need someone like you."

"Nope. I have enough to learn about farming now, without taking on another career. Thank you, Jack, for all your help." Connie waved Beany over. "Can you boys pack up in the next few minutes?"

"Sure, Mom Connie. You were fabulous. So were we, weren't we?"

The folks around the table clapped as Beany bowed and pointed to his accompanists.

Jane called across the room, "We're bringing the rest of the wine and some snacks to the house. When you're done talking to the press, you're going to sit in the recliner with your feet up and do nothing. Judy Sue and the neighbors took care of sending nearly all the leftovers home with other folks and stripped the tables. Cochran and Jens said they'll do any dishes. We're in good shape. Go on, before you get too relaxed."

Cochran, Connie, Jack, Emma and Junior walked down the drive.

As they approached the small group of media members, Emma put her hand up to stop their chatter and questions. "I'm Emma Skogman. I'm the family spokesperson. Any future communication is to be made only through me." She handed out business cards Connie knew she printed off that morning. "I will make a statement. My mother, Connie Skogman, will make a statement. Our attorney, Jack Walker, and County Sheriff Cochran will try to answer any questions you may have. Please be aware this is an ongoing investigation and they may not be able to address everything you want to know."

Emma summarized the situation, stressing that Farm Holding was being dissolved with plans that any proceeds would be used to form a nonprofit to address farm and small community issues.

Connie stepped to the microphones. "Thank you for coming. Emma will hand you a press release when we're finished. Trust me when I say that I knew nothing of Farm Holding or some of the activities my husband, Shaw Skogman, and his half-brother, Melvin Smith, were involved in. To that end, I plead with anyone who has been financially or emotionally injured through their actions to contact me directly through information noted in the release. I will make it right to the best of my abilities. I will never make excuses for my husband's or Melvin's actions. No matter how psychologically injured they were as children, they were still wrong. Our foundation will try to make things better for adults injured emotionally as children, lonely and aging farmers, families residing in rural areas and small towns."

She turned, took Junior's arm and they walked toward the house as Emma, Jack and Cochran addressed some of the questions being called out.

"Your sister deals with the media like a pro." Connie squeezed Junior's arm.

"I know, Mom. I can't believe how good she is."

They stopped in front of the house and turned to watch the media crews put their equipment away. Several minutes later, Emma, Jack and Cochran joined them as the crews departed. "How much worse will things get with publicity before they settle down?" Connie asked. "Will things never settle down?"

Jack replied, "Connie, Emma has handled the press wonderfully. The press release she issued is professional, gives them enough to have a story, yet lets people know there's a human side to all this and we will do our best to set things right."

Emma patted Connie's hand. "Mom, I'm going to be the point person till this settles down. I'm going to be getting more advice from several friends who do freelance PR. I think there's a real story here about making things right when you inherit a freaking mess."

"In the army, we called that FUBAR." Cochran nudged Jack.

"Yup. That stands for Fucked Up Beyond All Recognition. Connie, this is a mess, but I think it's a manageable one. Judge Franklin said some wise words. I think he set the tone for those present today whose relatives were involved with Farm Holding. Personally, I think the more we can tell this story, the better it will be in the long run. So many corporations and business want to hide their wrongdoing or blame others. You don't. That's admirable." He smiled at Connie. "Emma and I will handle this and involve you only when necessary. I'd tell you not to worry your pretty little head, but I don't want to go home with a black eye."

"You would, too." Connie mockingly shook her fist at him. "I trust you and Emma to deal with this aspect. Now, I need some wine."

She turned toward Emma. "Daughter, I think you should consider expanding your career search."

"I know, Mom. I am."

Chapter Forty

Jens

Tuesday morning

The sound of reveille blasted Jens awake. He tried to figure out where the obnoxious sound was coming from and why. It took him a second to realize he was in Cochran's bed who was laughing at him. "Dammit. Who the hell plays reveille on their alarm clock?"

"Sorry, I set it extra loud. We have to listen to the local news at seven. It's six-fifty-five. You've got time to go pee."

Jens shuffled to the bathroom and returned in time to hear the local radio station announcer greet them with the farm forecast, then say, "In local news, yesterday was the memorial service for Shaw Skogman and Melvin Smith, both of Skogman Farms. Smith died Saturday in a corn bin, apparently of suicide. Skogman succumbed to an accidental gunshot injury on Thursday. Emma Skogman, spokesperson for the family, said the following…"

Emma's voice came through the speaker. "Melvin was my father's half-brother and a long-time employee. He apparently was distraught over the death of my father, Shaw Skogman, who recently died from an accidental gunshot wound. This is a double tragedy for our family and community. We discovered they were involved in another business, Farm Holding. If anyone has any information or questions about Farm Holding, I ask you to contact us. In the meantime, we ask for privacy as we grieve their deaths and the knowledge of the pain they may have caused others. Connie Skogman, my mother, has stated the farm will continue to be operated and a nonprofit is being formed to assist the psychological needs of rural and small-town residents."

The newscaster added, "We will be doing an in-depth look at the issues with Farm Holding in an interview with local attorney Jack Walker at nine this morning."

Cochran motioned for Jens to sit next to him on the bed. "There's more."

The newscaster continued, "Also in local news, Sheriff Fred Cochran surprised the county board and county management last night when his longtime assistant, Irene Fawley, submitted a letter to the board for him as he was on detail elsewhere in the county. The letter was of his immediate resignation from the department. Plans were underway for him to step down as Sheriff and take the open county detective position. In his letter of resignation submitted and accepted by the board, he stated, 'After further thought, I have decided it is time for me to develop a personal life and cease my employment with the Sheriff department. This county, the employees, the residents, the department have been my family for over three decades and I have loved each and every day. I leave with no ill will or because of any controversies. It's just time to take another step in my life.'" The newscaster went on to play several quotes from the county supervisor and administrator, and Deputy Ken, each lauding Cochran.

"Does that mean you're not going in to work this morning?" Jens struggled to get his head around the news.

"I'm going in to clean out my desk, say goodbye to people and sign forms that will wrap up my employment and begin the process to continue my insurance, as well as apply for my retirement income. That's about it. What are you going to do?" Cochran looked as awkward as Jens felt.

"I have to be back at the farm by eight. The other girls are leaving. They each have flights later today. I want to say goodbye. After that, I thought Connie and I would start moving the equipment back in the shed. Junior's driving into school late, all excited over taking the Camry. It's going to feel crazy for them to go back to any sense of normalcy. I figured Connie would want a day to crash, but she says not yet. She plans to work half days and rest a couple of hours a day for a week or so."

He felt Cochran take his hand and pull him closer. "That's for today. I want to know what you are doing in the near future? Maybe forever?"

Jens swallowed. "I have been seriously thinking about staying on at the farm to help Connie for the season, maybe longer. I've always enjoyed farming, just not with my father who didn't think farmers could be gay. I haven't thought much beyond that. Except..." He snuggled closer. "Except, I know one thing for sure. I want my future to at least begin with you."

"Ditto. Think you can use a helper on the farm? We can live here and commute the ten miles. In time, we'll know if we can stand to be around each other twenty-four seven. Though I hope we can."

Jens kissed his answer. "I agree. My heart says I never want to be away from you, but my brain tells me to take my time. Us coming together happened so fast. Now, we need to take our time. You may tire of a gay undertaker turned farmer."

Cochran kissed Jens back. "Makes sense. You may tire of an old retired sheriff turned gay farmer. I was worried that you would reject me or be angry about some of the information I held back from you about Shaw and Melvin. I realized over the past few days how, even as a detective, I couldn't share my entire life with you. I would always know things about someone around the area I couldn't divulge. I decided I didn't want to live that way with someone I loved. Especially in this small of a community. I was hoping, gambling, actually, on you hanging around here, at least for a while. Figured gambling on love was worth the risk for me."

"I was frustrated you and Jack didn't share things earlier, but when it all came together, I understood. Inside, I do think we belong together, but need time for things to work out. We're off to a good start." Jens stretched. "Hey, do you know how to shovel corn?"

"Can I interrogate it first?"

Chapter Forty-One

Connie

Mid-October 2011

It was nearly time for sleep. Connie was in her pajamas. She sat in her bedroom reading chair, sipping Sleepytime Tea. Her feet rested on the ottoman as she read, *Sapiens: A Brief History of Humankind* by Yuval Noah Harari. Rusty, curled up and snuggled against her feet, became her dog, too. He refused to be far from either she or Junior and settled for Jens or Cochran as second best. Tonight, Junior was out with Beany in her truck, and Rusty seemed to sense he was hers for the night.

She was tired. They were in the middle of harvesting fifteen hundred acres of corn. She, Jens, Cochran and Albert, Judy Sue's husband, with help from Junior, pulled it off. So far. It was amazing. She ached from driving the combine and trucks. It was a good ache. Better than the headaches and emotional turmoil of last April as they adjusted to the deaths of Shaw and Melvin, to several months of media scrutiny. Emma and Jack managed the investigations with professionalism and transparency.

With help from Jack and other lawyers, the proceeds from Farm Holding were being used to establish a foundation to address mental health issues in farmers, their families, plus assistance to older farmers and their spouses who needed companionship and health services. Thus far, negative feedback from the immediate community about Farm

Holding had been minimal. *A sad commentary on the elderly in the area,* she thought.

The two most recent elderly couples to sign with Farm Holding approached them. She and Jack quickly arrived at a market-based appraisal for their land. Three heirs also met with her and Jack. Two accepted settlements, the third asked them to establish an annual scholarship program named after the deceased. Even with all the curiosity raised by the media's investigations, there were few strong complaints, and those came from people not related to the deceased. While it would take some time to finalize the nonprofit, some of the funds were already being used to expand an existing visiting nurse and home aide program throughout the area.

Junior's DNA results came back in late May, just before school ended. There was little surprise that Junior was not Shaw's child. Hans was his father. Somehow, Cochran got a DNA sample from Melvin in the jail which confirmed he was a half-brother to Shaw.

Junior was thrilled that Jens was his uncle. Connie was pleased to see Jens and Cochran interact with him in ways Shaw never would, or could. The four of them occasionally discussed Junior's thoughts on changing his name. He was taking his time in coming to any conclusion, which she thought was wise. He kept asking her and Jens questions about Hans. She could see more and more of Hans in him as his personality opened up with the close interest and support of Jens and Cochran. For Junior's birthday, she had a composite made of the few photographs she and Jens possessed of Hans. Junior was delighted when he realized how much he looked like Hans. She laughed when he held the composite next to the photo of Shaw and joked that all Scandinavians must look similar.

She placed her book on the night table and removed the cameo hanging around her neck. The one Jens gave his mother forty years ago. The one he discovered in his old house just before it was demolished. She remembered buying it with him, telling him he had to pay her back before he could present it to his mother, recalled how thrilled his mother was to receive it. How she noted the chain was eighteen-carat gold and the cameo high quality.

Jens showed her the necklace and an envelope a week after the memorial service. "I was supposed to be at that New Year's Eve Party the night Hans died, but didn't drive out for it. Being around my father was not easy and I chickened out about the weather and driving all the way from The Cities with such a big snowstorm predicted." Jens cleared his throat and wiped his eyes as Connie did the same. "I think in all the commotion of Hans' death, Dad put the letter aside and forgot about it. I barely noticed the necklace, what with all the dust. I found the letter in his drawer just before they demolished the house. Yesterday, I took the liberty to read it. I meant to earlier, but things kept getting more and more wild with Melvin and Shaw and all the decisions being made the following week. Now, it's time." He placed both gently into her hand. "It might add to your sorrow, but the cameo will definitely add to your joy. I want you to have it."

"Jens, I'm thrilled to have it. Did you realize your mother wanted to be buried with it on?" Jens looked surprised and shook his head. "Your father saw it with the clothes I set out for the undertaker and said he wanted to keep it. He also told me, 'Give it back to Jens when I die.'" She touched Jens' arm. "Don't faint on me. I'm so glad you saw this. I totally forgot about it in all these years."

Connie laid the necklace on top of the book. She would wear it again tomorrow, and the days after. Wear it tucked carefully beneath her T-shirt to remind her she had a mother for part of her life. She wiped her eyes again and picked up the yellowed envelope. The front was printed in Hans' legible, but sloppy hand, *Dad, Give this to Jens to give to Connie next week when he sees her. Thank you. Hans.*

December 31, 1992

Connie, I write this at Dad's and will leave it for Jens to give to you as I'm leaving for Fargo from here. I understand he intends to come here after this storm clears and plans to stop by your place on his way home. I'd mail it, but I might blow away or freeze to death getting to the mailbox and back. Besides, Dad has no stamps. Imagine that.

I'm not writing this to alarm you, simply to make you aware of something I've discovered Shaw and Melvin are involved with. In the conversations you and I have held over our many wonderful years, I never heard you or anyone else mention Farm Holding Company. Last summer, when I dropped by Dad's on my way home from a dig in North Dakota, he showed me a letter from this company offering to, in effect, give him a reverse mortgage in exchange for deeding the farm to them. He would receive a monthly stipend, more than the amount of a lease, ten percent of the profits from grain sold, and they would pay the property taxes and insurance. Unlike a reverse mortgage, no equity was factored into determining the amount. I think it's doubtful, very doubtful, Farm Holding could lose a nickel on this kind of deal. This was their third letter. He also received several phone calls from a Phillip Smith. Polite, but persistent, he said.

I never heard of them, neither had Dad. This fall, I did some digging. Being an archeologist helps sometimes in searching for information. Through some effort, I discovered Shaw used the name Shaw S Phillip years ago. I'm quite certain he and Melvin are part of Farm Holding. I mean, the name Phillip Smith seems a bit obvious. I checked further and could find no complaints registered against Farm Holding. I found FH on the plat maps owning a number of farms, all of elderly folk or deceased. My concern is, if this is them, why are they so secretive? The phone is answered by a very polite person at an answering service who can only take messages and knows nothing about the business. Their office is in Worthington. Dad is very interested in signing with them. He's tired, he's getting old, looks older than he is, though heaven knows, these old Scandinavians can last for years looking like they're at death's door. I suppose that might be true for me someday, too. Ha ha. He's tired of receiving low lease payments for his land and the inconsistency in his income from a percentage of the grain sales. Plus, he's got monthly payments on that new pickup truck he bought and can barely climb into. Of course, he didn't get the plow for it, or I could now be plowing the drive.

I suggested he sell the place outright, take the money and move to town or someplace warm. He refused to consider it. "Not yet, not yet," he kept saying. We had a rather heated argument when I tried to point out to him that even if he lived to be a hundred, he'd never receive what he'd get if he outright sold now. Didn't matter. He told me if I kept arguing with him, I could leave right now. I explained he invited me to celebrate the new year and was the one who suggested I have several friends over. Well, the way this snowstorm is developing, I'm wondering how many people, even those close by, will make it. Anyway, I need to move onto more exciting things. YOU.

I am so excited you are pregnant. I know it's a surprise, how you thought you were in menopause, but I love to hear how excited you are anyway. You are one of the most incredible mothers I have ever known. Not only did you mother Jens at a young age, but taking on the twins to mother at the age of twenty-four was astounding. I have so much admiration and respect for you, not only as a mother, but as an intelligent, resourceful, creative, thoughtful, caring person. I remember after I married Judith, how you and I were still sorting through how to keep our oh-so-special relationship going. I suggested you go to college and stay till you earned your Ph.D. You said my mom and Jens needed you for several more years, then you would think about it. Of course, Mom died, Alice died, and you willingly stepped into instant step-motherhood before beginning your own brood. I never cease to be amazed by you, nor with our love for each other, as unique as it is.

As an archeologist, I do have some abilities with calendars. You wrote that your OBGYN determined the size of the baby indicates your due date is in early May. If that time frame holds, have you considered the baby might be mine? Ours, I mean. Two-hundred-eighty days, forty weeks. We were together the night of July 30 when you attended a seminar for library volunteers. Forty weeks would bring a baby May 6 to 8. I did not wear a condom. I recollect I thought you were still on the pill. I realize that, if after you went home, you enjoyed sex in the next few days with Shaw (I'm so glad you have always enjoyed sex with him) that the baby might be his. Either way, I am delighted you are pregnant again, feeling well and juggling all those balls you somehow manage to keep in the air.

I would be delighted if the baby is mine, even if kept a secret. For some reason, if Shaw were to find out and react in some negative way, please know that I will stand beside you in any manner you desire. Judith, my wife, cannot conceive. As you know, she is also aware of our bond. She would be supportive of me being involved with a child fathered by me and borne by you. She has nothing but respect for you and has never been jealous of our long-time special relationship and infrequent meetups.

Sitting here, I get excited, thinking about a child with you. Would it be a girl or boy?

Will you find out before it's born? Whether mine or not, I don't want to know the sex until it's born. That's just the way I am. What traits from each of us will it display? What traits from our parents and ancestors? I know that would be harder for you to ascertain, being an only child orphan. What color eyes and hair? Tall. Surely the child will be tall. We are both tall, it can't be short. Can it?

The thought of a child somehow in my life, either secretive, openly or even if Shaw's, inspires me. I never forget how Ellen went into archeology because of the stories I told her one time. One time. I can't wait to tell this child stories. I need to calm down and go figure out how to bake frozen pizzas. How many hours do they take? Ha ha.

I'm so sorry you, Shaw, and the girls (the ones still left at home) will not be joining us tonight. The weather is horrible. Dad just informed me that the other area friends have cancelled as well. I see Melvin managed to drive in. He would make it through the apocalypse. That means three people to eat 8 frozen pizzas, corn curls, un-branded soda, cheap beer and Walmart brownies. Do Dad and I know how to party or what?

I briefly thought about giving Melvin this letter to give to you, but I intend to confront him about this Farm Holding thing. He doesn't handle conflict well, especially without Shaw around, so I doubt he would get the letter to you, simply out of spite. He is such an odd little man. I have never understood his and Shaw's relationship. Whatever it is, they certainly are good farmers and businessmen, though I don't like their suspected involvement in this holding company venture.

Goodbye, I love you and always will.

Hans

Like she did every time she read Hans' letter, Connie pulled a tissue, wiped her eyes and blew her nose. She always thought of the same questions after reading this. All the what ifs. What if she hadn't stuffed her early suspicion that the baby was Hans? The first thing she thought when the doctor told her she was pregnant was how this was likely Hans' baby. Several weeks later, Hans was dead. She quickly locked those thoughts deep inside of her and threw away the key. The transition to the baby being Shaw's was not only expedient, but easy to convince herself of, especially during her hidden grief over Hans.

What if she told Shaw back then about the affair, that the baby might not be his? What if they divorced and she raised Junior with Hans' and Judith's support?

How would that have affected the girls?

What if Shaw killed her back then? He killed Alice for having an affair.

She shuddered. Her fists clenched.

The son of a bitch tried to kill her. He spied on her for eighteen damn years.

Her mind shifted to that snowy March day out on the front porch, after Shaw fired at Junior. Shaw was turning to shoot a slug through her when she launched herself toward him. Self-preservation, instant reflexes, shock, anger that anyone would try to kill her, let alone her husband. Whatever it was, took over. His hands lost their grip when his feet went out from under him on the snowy porch. As he fell, she grabbed the gun entirely away from him. He lay on his back. She saw the fear in his eyes as she aimed at him. She moved her finger from the guard to the trigger. Shaw twisted and kicked at her. The momentum of stepping back to avoid his kick caused her bare feet to slip. She intended to shoot him in the chest. As she was losing her balance and his leg was coming toward her, she squeezed the trigger. The slug tore through his lower left leg.

She still wished she'd hit him in his chest.

What if she had killed him? There were no witnesses. It would have been deemed accidental. Or would it? If someone wanted to pursue the case, could her fingerprints on the gun tell the true story?

A month after Shaw's service, Connie was guiding the big tractor and planter across the large field, planting corn, using the GPS to maintain straight rows. She was also fulfilling Shaw's and Melvin's final wishes. Wearing gloves and noting which way the breeze was blowing, she reached into their cardboard urns and released a small scoop of dust out the tractor's windows to mix with the dust rising from the wheels. Dust to dust. She was ready to perform this final task. It was a closing ceremony for her, though she realized it would never stop all of her emotions. After several trips of the long field, she shook each urn's bag out the window to empty the last of their remains, took a big breath and felt a release, a sense of emotional and mental lightness. Not giddy, not full closure, simply a sign that she was on the right track and would survive and succeed.

A few minutes later, a sheriff's car drove slowly down the road and parked at the end of the field, waiting where she would turn. It was Acting Sheriff Ken. She dropped down from the tractor's cab and walked up to him. He held out the shotgun wrapped in plastic.

"You're pretty good with that tractor. I got off the farm quick because I couldn't drive a straight line with those things." He gave a small smile. "Here, I'm returning Shaw's gun." He handed it to her.

She almost forgot the gun would be returned. Looking at it brought the whole experience back, but she controlled her feelings, smiled and took the gun from him. "Thanks, Ken. I can't say as I'm glad to remember all this, but I appreciate your help."

His eyes tightened as he pointed toward an envelope taped to the plastic covering. "That is the fingerprint report. You can read it later, but in a nutshell, your right thumb print was very clear on the stock, your right index print was clear on the left trigger, and your left-hand thumb was on the forearm, like..." His words trailed off.

Connie mentally heard his unspoken words, 'Like you would hold and aim a gun.'

She thought a moment. "I'm not surprised my prints were on the gun. I was trying to save my life."

"Yeah, I know. We found yours in other places, too, not as clear. They were mixed in with Shaw's." Ken's eyes squinted as if waiting for an explanation.

They both stood silent, staring at each other for several moments. He sucked in a big breath of air, let it out slowly, and said, "Well, guess that's it."

"It was a terrible experience. I'm glad it's over."

Connie watched Ken turn and stride back to his car. She didn't read the report. She knew her prints were exactly where she grabbed the gun to tear it away from Shaw, and right where they would be if she raised it to her shoulder to fire. She didn't tear off the envelope, but placed the gun on the cab's floor. When she got home, she leaned the gun in the corner of the mud room. Unwrapping it, loading it, and hanging it back on its rack felt too soon.

Connie uncrossed her feet on the ottoman and sighed. What if Shaw did die on the porch and no one besides Jens ever knew of her affair with Hans? Her wonderful, beautiful, life-giving affair. Would she have unlocked the cage with her early suspicion that Junior was Hans'?

Would she have learned everything about Farm Holding? About Shaw's and Melvin's double lives? About other people they killed?

Connie shook her head. What ifs. I refuse to live in what ifs.

She went to the bathroom, brushed her teeth and climbed into bed. Rusty was already waiting for her. She felt small on the edge of a king size bed. She also felt strong.

Shaw's words floated around her as she drifted off.

Betrayal is wicked.

Revenge is necessary.

Patience is a virtue.

Sometimes that's true, she thought. *Sometimes.*

Chapter Forty-Two

Junior

Late October

Junior stepped off the school bus and strolled up their 127th Street driveway; the first time he walked the drive since he began driving to school last spring. Rusty met him and trotted along beside him. It felt odd to ride a bus again. The Camry died yesterday and was now in parts heaven, being prepared to provide other needy Camrys life-giving transplants, at least for a few miles. Two weeks before, he noticed strange sounds in the engine, and the transmission seemed to slip.

He stopped to see a mechanic who ran several diagnostics. "You need to rebuild the engine and transmission. I'm not sure I'd invest any money in this old girl. I mean, she's got two-hundred and forty thou on her."

"Really? What about buying a used engine and transmission from the salvage yard?"

Junior hated to give up the Camry. His mother told him her water broke in it on the way to the hospital to give birth to him and he was brought home in the same car.

"What's your name?"

"Shaw Skogman, but I go by Junior."

He wondered if he would get a strange look from the guy over who Shaw Senior was. For a few weeks last spring, there were lots of news and investigative articles about Shaw and Melvin.

"I know who you are. You're the runner. The kid that placed in the top twenty-five in the big marathon over in The Cities last weekend. You were in the paper." He stuck his hand out to shake Junior's. "Congratulations, that's a real accomplishment." He patted the roof of the Camry. "Another used engine may not be any better than this one. Here's my advice, but first, let me ask you something. You carry a cell phone with you?"

"Yeah, why?"

"Well, my advice is to make sure you always have it with you anytime you take this old girl out. Make sure your phone's got enough battery for two calls. Go save your money for a down payment on another car and drive this baby till she dies on you. Got it?"

"Makes sense. How long you think it's got? Why the two calls?"

"No idea how long. Could be a few days, weeks, maybe months, but unlikely. Also, I was wrong. You only need to make one call. See, ordinarily the first call is for someone to come pick you up and the second is for me to come haul the old car to the salvage yard to part it out. Except, seeing as you're a runner, you can probably get yourself home under your own power, so you only gotta call me." He grinned and patted Junior on the back.

Junior went home, put the title in the glove box and kept driving the car. He and Beany talked to it, patted it and sang to it. Yesterday, driving home from school alone, the car coughed, wheezed, rattled and clanged to a stop. Junior signed the title, put it back in the box, called the mechanic and jogged the seven miles home. He wasn't too worried about new wheels. His mother was so busy, she rarely drove her pickup and told him he could use hers occasionally until he decided what to do.

New wheels were only one of the decisions he needed to make, though. The mechanic recognizing him as his own person, a runner, and not the illegitimate kid of Shaw Senior, impacted his thinking about who he was and whether he should change his last name or not. A week ago, over dinner with his mom, Jens, Cochran and Beany, he said, "I've made a decision about my last name. No offense, Mom and Jens, but I'm keeping Skogman."

Jens smiled. "Kid, that's fine with me. I hope you didn't feel any pressure from me about changing it."

"I didn't. It was mostly pressure I put on myself to at least think about. The bottom line is, I don't want a last name different from my sisters and mother. I know I'm not related to Shaw, but look at what the Skogmans have done for farming and this area for all these years. There's parts of Dad Shaw I abhor, and I won't ignore those, but for me, I'm at peace keeping the name." He looked at Jens again. "However, I still want to know as much about Hans and my Hanson family as possible and I don't think I will have any trouble stating I belong to two families."

Junior startled, surprised to find himself now sitting on the front porch, his fingers touching the embedded slug in the porch floor, Rusty's head resting on his foot. Almost seven months since he flew off these steps and ran down the same driveway he just leisurely walked.

Today, he was in no hurry. He was scheduled to cook dinner and didn't have to go to the fields to haul corn to the bins or fuel the combine. He planned to make hamburgers stuffed with cheese on the grill, like Beany taught him. He would grill potato wedges too, along with peppers and cipollini onions, plus throw together a slaw, his favorite, red-cabbage-and-apple. The hamburger came from Beany's farm. Albert, Beany's dad, now worked for Connie, mostly as the mechanic. Albert hired a meat salesman which allowed him, Albert, to do what he enjoyed most, raise his organic beef cattle and fix things. Beany worked after school three to four days a week and Saturdays at Syds. He cooked some of the food, but primarily baked rolls and pastries. He loved it and bragged how customers were coming from further and further away to eat his baked goods and experience Syds food. Beany was growing up and Junior knew he was too. He was not the same kid who, last spring, raced to save his life.

His mother, Jens, Cochran, himself and Albert were amazed at how Shaw and Melvin managed the farm and leases. What Junior and the family took for granted, primarily because Shaw never shared with them what he did to make things appear so smooth, was the result of his in-depth planning, strong management and scheduling. Shaw scheduled monthly management meetings with Melvin and the accountants. Costs and income were carefully tracked and analyzed. Commodity futures, long term weather, and farm management procedures were studied. Notes and records were kept and updated. It was impressive, but then, Junior wondered why shouldn't it have been? Yet, he couldn't help thinking that the hidden side of those two was also impressive, just immoral.

His mother ate up all the findings and procedures like a starving waif at an all-you-can-eat buffet. Junior saw her joy from being challenged, how her skills at researching information and ability to make astute decisions came to bear on their situation. He doubted she would ever sell the farm. She was in her element now, a new one, but hers. He thought she was thriving.

The question was, did he want to continue on the farm? There were areas of it he enjoyed, but did his aptitude run toward continuing a family farm dynasty? He didn't think so. Sitting on the shaded porch stairs, the fall sun casting long shadows, the rattles from stray stalks of dried corn in the field, and the light chill settling in—the goals of the family foundation being developed kept entering his mind. Not that he wanted to direct a foundation, but the social work aspects of working with needy children and hurting families kept popping up like spring corn unfurling. He stood and spoke out loud. "Rusty, that's something I need to pay more attention to. Social work." Rusty jumped and nuzzled his hand.

He and Beany already planned to take a year at Minnesota West Community to get some of the basics completed. Beany was thinking of going on to culinary school, but it had to be one near a theater, even if it was only a community theater. The boy had to perform.

In the kitchen, Junior tested the hamburger in the fridge to make sure it was thawed, and checked that the charcoal and lighter were in the mud room. He noticed the shotgun, wrapped, still standing in the corner. He figured when his mom brought it home last spring, things were too fresh for her to unwrap, load and hang it again. Besides, did they need to keep a loaded gun in the house? He didn't think so. He slid the gun out and hung it on the rack. He started to wad the plastic and noticed the sheriff's department envelope taped to it. He slipped the letter out. It was the fingerprint report with diagrams. He moved outside to the patio table and sat down. Rusty curled up at his feet. It took Junior several minutes to realize the implications of the report. His mother didn't simply grab onto the gun. The print on the left trigger and the placement of her prints on the stock and forearm meant she also gained total control of it and aimed it. Did it fire accidentally when her feet slipped? Did she purposely pull the trigger? Either way, her finger was on the trigger that sent the slug into Dad Shaw.

Junior didn't notice his mother step onto the patio until he heard the scraping of a chair being pulled out. She didn't say anything, just watched him read it again. Junior thought, *This means Mom fired the second shot that injured Dad Shaw. It didn't go off when she was trying to get it away from him and his finger was still on the trigger. His print is fairly clear on the right trigger.*

Junior quit reading and looked toward the fields. Turning to look at his mom, he asked, "Did you know this? Have you seen this?"

Connie looked him straight in the eyes. "I have not read it, but I can guess what's in it." She reached across the table and patted his hand.

"I—I remember Dad Shaw telling us in the hospital that he would have killed you if he could have and saying you would have killed him if you could have. At the time, that last part of his comment went over my head. Would you have? Killed him, I mean."

Connie took a deep breath. "There are times I wished I would have." She looked across the fields toward the Lutheran cemetery. "Those prints tell a lot more, too. You do realize that, don't you?"

"Yeah, Dad Shaw's were right where they would be if he shot at me and aimed at you. I guess not everything is black and white. Maybe I've learned that people aren't always who you think they are, but more importantly, I have no idea how I would have reacted in that situation." He paused. "Well, maybe I do. I didn't try to grab the gun when Dad Shaw aimed it at me in bed. I ran. You fought." He hesitated as he looked into her eyes before saying, "Of course, I didn't have any secrets to hide."

His mother looked back at him. From her eyes, he knew neither of them needed to say anything else.

Junior stepped into the mud room and brought out the bag of charcoal and lighter fluid. Wadding up the pages of the report, he placed them on the rack, poured in briquets, then soaked the pile and papers with fluid. Connie stood next to him. Her hand on his, they aimed the long-necked lighter toward the papers and squeezed the trigger.

Acknowledgements

This is a much different novel than my first three. It involves medical, legal, pharmaceutical, security and farming research. Any misrepresentation of facts is totally on me. Thank you Dr. Bob Stanley, M.D.; Marty Densch, retired pharmacist; Jerry Sveum, retired pharmacist; Adam Simon from Alibi Security; Hon. Kenneth W. Forbeck, retired judge, lawyer; Denny Morris, agricultural consultant; Bill Henderson, lawyer.

Many thanks to the beta readers who read, listened to and provided helpful—sometimes lifesaving—comments on the manuscript: Steve Purdy; Ann Sitrick; Marty Densch; and the members of the Stateline Night Writers group chaired by Jerry Peterson at the Beloit Public Library.

Special thanks to Rick Dexter and Kathie Giorgio. Rick, my partner, reads my early drafts, patiently listens and interprets my nighttime mumbling as I wrestle with the characters, and, somehow, he still supports me in every way possible. Kathie is my writing coach, a dispenser of blunt but kind advice, cheerleader, author and an inspiration to many others through her own writing and coaching; http://www.allwritersworkshop.com.

Finally, a debt of gratitude and respect for Christine Young and Arlo Young of Rogue Phoenix Press; their staff; Gene of Web and Graphic Designs by Ms. G for the cover art; and Sherry Derr-Wille, manuscript editor.

About the Author

Revenge is Necessary is Bill's fourth novel. Bill grew up in a village in a Midwest farming community where nearly everyone had large families. Hence his proclivity for writing about families, warts and all (though he's not sure how many families he grew up with actually included psychopaths). He began writing after retiring from careers in YMCA camping and foster care, and, he admits working with children for forty years may have affected him. Bill resides in Beloit, Wisconsin, and looks forward to again traveling. He enjoys reading, writing, photography, art and volunteering. He likes connecting with his readers. Feel free to contact him at billmathiswriter@gmail.com. Check out his website: http://www.billmathiswriteretc.com. Keep track of and follow him and his future books on Facebook:

https://www.facebook.com/BillMathisWritersEtc/. For a variety of short stories read the author's blog:

http://billmathiswriteretc.com/blog/.

More books are in progress. Watch for *Memory Tree* and *Journie Morgan's Legacy.*

Help Spread The Word!

If you enjoyed this book, please leave a review on Goodreads, Amazon or other similar websites; ask your local library to order a copy; invite Bill to a book club meeting either in person or via Skype, Zoom or Facebook Live; tell your friends to order a copy; post your comments on your Facebook page and Bill's page:

https://www.facebook.com/BillMathisWritersEtc/.

The Rooming House Gallery
Connecting the Dots

Josh and Andres unexpectedly inherit an old rooming house in Chicago.
Each discovers they have a long and deep history with the place.
Thrilled to have a home of their own, plus a place for Andres to make
and sell his art, the two are challenged to turn the place into a
community art center. The challenge becomes more personal as each
deals with their own backgrounds, family issues and differing personal
interests. Tough decisions are made about their new/old home,
relationship with their fathers, and their conflict over starting a family.
The neighboring family and new friends play a key role as they bring
the art center to fruition, move into a new personal home, and begin a
non-DNA family.

Chapter One

Josh Sawicki, Age 29
Andres Rodriguez, Age 28

4822 South Justine, Chicago, IL – Back of the Yards Neighborhood

Monday, June 8, 2009

The old house smelled. To Josh, it was a musty mix of dust and age, but the closer he and Andres moved toward the kitchen, the stronger the odor became of urine and Pine Sol overlain with coarse cigarette smoke.

Manny Rodriguez, Andres' old uncle, rested on top of a grungy, threadbare sheet in an ancient recliner, his feet up, his back almost straight. An oxygen tube ran across the floor from the large container of liquid oxygen and over the top of the recliner, its nosepiece rested close to Manny's left ear. Josh wondered why he wasn't wearing the oxygen mask. Was it turned on? Why was a recliner in the kitchen? He glanced around and noticed the chair's proximity to a bedroom and the bathroom. Guess it made sense.

Manny wore a stained tank-style undershirt with burn-holes and clean blue pajama bottoms. A dented plastic juice bottle, half-full, sat on a stool, tucked against the right side of the chair. A cordless phone rested in his lap, next to the twisted fingers of his left hand, his left shoulder bent at an odd and awkward angle, as if out of joint. The tobacco-stained fingers of his right hand held a hand-rolled cigarette upright, carefully balancing a tall pile of ash. Josh stared at the cigarette, then the oxygen nose piece. He took a half step closer.

Noticing Josh's concerned looks at the oxygen piece, Manny rasped in a Spanish accent, "Only use it at night. It's turned off when I smoke." He grimaced and looked from one to the other as he growled, "About time you two got here. Andres, I'm still pissed your dad waited two months to send you over." He broke into a hoarse, deep cough and hacked up a honker, leaned over and without spilling the ash, lifted the bottle with his right hand and spat into it.

"Hi, Uncle Manny," said Andres. "You don't look good."

"I'm dying. Soon, too. If I wasn't, I'd be looking better. I told your dad in April, I needed to see you two before I croaked." He started coughing again.

Josh looked around and filled a glass with water from the sink faucet and held it for him to sip.

He wheezed a thank you. "So, you two are still lovers, huh? Been together about ten years. Right?" He tried to smile.

"*Si, Tio.* You can't go wrong with a gay Polack."

"*Bueno, bueno.* You know I'm gay too." Both nodded as the old man wrinkled his forehead into a deep furrowed frown. "Did Art-the-fart tell you I have AIDS? He's such a *dupek*." He spat the words out, then coughed again. Josh snickered at the Polish word for asshole. Manny managed a weak wink at him. "I swear good in Polish, too."

Andres replied, "Dad tried to tell me that years ago, but I didn't believe him. You'd be dead by now if you had AIDS. I think it's these cigarettes killing you." He bent over and gave the old man a hug.

Uncle Manny put his head back. Just before his eyes closed, he lowered his right arm and dropped his cigarette into the juice bottle. It sizzled as the acrid smell of stale urine and ashes wafted up. Without opening his eyes, he muttered, "You two go look this place over, it's going to be yours, both of you. Don't take long. I want you to see the papers while I'm still around."

Josh froze, staring at Andres, both in shock. He started to speak. Andres put his fingers to his lip and motioned toward the door, which, they discovered, led to a back apartment, along with stairs to the outside door and the basement.

In the back apartment; a kitchen-living room with a cramped bathroom and small bedroom, the double bed still covered in an old flowered quilt, Josh let out his breath. "What does he mean, this place is going to be ours?"

Andres shook his head, looking perplexed.

"Andres, Andres. What does he mean? Do you know something else?"

"No, Josh. I don't know anything else. Dad left me several voicemails yesterday morning. We connected last night. He said he didn't realize it was so urgent, just to get out here today, pronto." He paused.

"What else did he say?"

"Give me a minute, Josh. Just slow down and let me finish. He said *Tio* Manny had been wanting to see me and you together and for us to get our butts our here ASAP. He said Uncle Manny was dying. He didn't know when. He sure didn't say he should have told us two months ago." He paused. "He should be here, too. They're half-brothers. That's the way things are between them. And between him and me. You know how Dad is." His voice trailed off.

Josh shook his head again, touched the mole on his left cheek, a habit when he was concerned or trying to concentrate. "I understand how he might want you to have this place, but why me too?"

They spent less than thirty minutes exploring the outside and the upper floors. It was a weathered gray, three-story rooming house with nearly thirty rooms between the second and third floors, plus the two apartments on the first.

Somehow, a faint recollection of a rooming house drifted through Josh's mind. *Where did that come from? Why wouldn't Andres inherit it in just his name? It would be a great place for Andres to make art in. What would we do with the bedrooms? We don't even have kids. Besides, Uncle Manny probably was senile and the place wasn't truly theirs.*

After poking around, they ran down the two flights of stairs and into the living room. They slowed as they passed through the hallway between the living and dining room and heard Uncle Manny groaning and cursing from the kitchen, cursing in English, Spanish and Polish. He was attempting to stand up, but he was so weak he kept falling back into the recliner. "Help me, you two, I gotta piss." Andres slid his hands under his armpits and carefully pulled the frail man to his feet and waited for him to move toward the bathroom. "In the bottle," he rasped through the cigarette dangling from his mouth.

Josh grabbed the bottle, pulled the shrunken man's pajamas down and aimed the bottle roiling with urine, ash and cigarette butts at Manny's penis. "Ahh, *amigos*, you are just in time." Manny stumbled as a coughing fit engulfed him. Josh followed the flopping penis, trying to keep the trickle of dark yellow urine from hitting the floor, or either of them.

"*Bueno. Bueno.* Put me back now. I have much to tell you."

Josh ran the bottle to the bathroom, emptied it and rinsed it out. When he returned, he straightened out the sheet under the old man as much as possible, saw an afghan and covered him.

Exhausted, Uncle Manny leaned his head back and closed his eyes, his cigarette still fuming, ash floating down onto the afghan. Andres looked at Josh and shrugged.

"See that dresser? In the dining room. There's the papers I want to show you." Manny's voice was weak, barely audible. "There's lots to talk about, especially with Josh, there's secrets in those ledgers." His raised his right hand from the wrist and pointed his index finger toward the dining room.

Josh looked at him in surprise, but the old man's eyes were closed. He seemed too worn out to open them.

Or breathe.

Josh and Andres stared at him. Josh noticed Manny's breath become lighter, raspy and slow down. He glanced at Andres, ready to ask if he noticed the same thing. Before he could speak, the kitchen door opened. Two men entered. One was older, gray-haired, the other of slight build with jet black hair; both wore black short-sleeve shirts with clerical collars. They stepped close to Manny and all four men watched him suck in a large ragged breath, before slowly letting it out in irregular gasps. Each man leaned in closer, waiting for the next breath. There wasn't one. The cigarette dropped from Manny's lips onto the afghan. Josh pulled it away and tossed it into the sink where it sizzled out.

Andres pulled out his phone. "I'll call 911. Josh, start CPR."

The smaller of the two men placed his hand on Andres' arm. "Manny's gone. He didn't want any resuscitation efforts made." He pulled the afghan up and covered the dead man's face, tucking the faded yarn gently around his body. "Father Frank will call the funeral home. All the arrangements are made." He stuck his hand out. "Hi, I'm Padre An, that's spelled with just an A and a N." He next shook Josh's hand, then placed his hand on Andres' shoulder, patting him. "We're surprised he made it this long. We think he's been hanging on, waiting for you two."

Andres put his arms around Manny's covered shoulders. "*Tio* Manny, *Tio* Manny. *Por que? Por que?* Why?"

Father An said, "That's a good question. I think we can help with some answers. At least the basic ones." He paused, then pointed to the other priest. "This is Father Frank, we're both from St. Bobola's Church, just west of here. We've known Manny for a few years, but got better acquainted the past few months as his health deteriorated. We've been checking on him several times a day. Two days ago, we managed to give him a shower. This morning, he only allowed us to give him a sponge bath and put on clean pajama bottoms. When we went to remove his t-shirt to put on his clean pajama top, he told us he had to save his energy for you two coming. Said he didn't want to die before. Looks like he timed it as close as possible. Surprisingly though, he allowed us to give him last rites this morning."

Father Frank shook Josh's and Andres' hands. "Manny managed to phone us while you were looking around, said to get over here, that he hoped he could hold on. He was either going to piss himself or die. He hoped to see you guys before either happened."

Andres wiped his eyes and grasped the priest's hand. "I'm Andres Rodriguez and this is my partner, Josh Sawicki. We don't know what to do, we had so many questions. This is such a surprise. Now he's gone." He scratched his head. "It took both of us to help him pee. Then he told us to go check the dining room buffet. Something about paperwork. Then…"

"Was…was he of sound mind? We haven't seen him in over five years and he just said this place belonged to both of us. I'm confused…" Josh quit talking. Did he just sound rude? Asking about the place being theirs before the guy was cold or in the grave? "I-I didn't mean to sound selfish. This is such a shock and I don't know what to think."

"He was of sound mind," Father Frank replied. "A physician examined him, along with a lawyer. He knew exactly what he was saying to you. Let's have Padre An take you two into the living room while I call the funeral home." Noticing their reluctance to leave, he added, "It's okay. There's nothing else that can be done for him. He's at peace. We will feel the pain of his passing for many years. Though, knowing him, I'm sure he would want you to get on with your lives, which is the reason we're all here."

Josh and Andres followed Padre An through the dining room, down the short hallway lined with aged photos of family members, and into the living room. He motioned for them to sit down on the old, overstuffed couch, the dust rising as they lowered themselves. "I am the one who helped get all the financial papers in order…"

"Is this for real?" Josh interrupted. "He told us this place was ours. Both of us. He said to look at the papers, something about secrets…Well, then you came in and he…"

Padre An smiled. "Yes, that's true. I'll try to quickly bring you up to date. I know you haven't seen Manny in years and this is a shock." He motioned for the two men to slide back on the couch. "About two years ago, Manny learned he suffered from advanced lung cancer, stage four. He refused invasive medical treatment. This spring, he asked me, I'm also a notary public with extensive experience in financial matters, to prepare his will, get a lawyer and finalize his desire to transfer the property to you two." Padre An paused when Josh started to interrupt. "Josh, let me finish, then I can answer your questions."

Josh nodded, still confused and surprised.

"At first, the house was going to just Andres, but when he realized how you two seem to have a solid, long-term relationship, he became so excited. He kept saying, 'I can keep it in both families. Both families.' He was as happy as I've ever seen him."

Josh couldn't contain his anxiety. He shifted forward on the couch, dust motes flying in the early evening light. "I don't understand. It's wonderful. I just don't get it! And what's he mean, both families? Is that what he wanted to tell me? Is that the secret?"

Padre An motioned toward Josh and Andres to remain seated. He stood, walked into the dining room and returned with a ledger. He slid between the two of them on the couch and opened it to the middle pages, where everything was written in Polish. "Josh, do you recognize that name?"

"Um, it looks like it could be Sa-wic-ki. A Josef Sawicki?" His eyebrows started to rise.

Padre An turned more pages. He pointed to a name written in English. "And that name?"

"Hank Sawicki. Oh my God! Hank Sawicki was my great-grandfather's name, his wife's name was Mae. They owned a rooming house my Grandpa Joey was raised in. You mean this is the same place?" He looked at Padre An in amazement at the significance that his blood ran deep in this old place.

Padre An smiled. He waited for Josh to calm down and Andres to wipe his eyes. "Men, this is happening in real time. Now, when you're ready, follow me to the dining room. I want you to see the materials Manny was referring to."

At the oak arts and crafts style bureau in the dining room, near the hallway to the living room, they waited as Padre An slipped the ledger he carried onto a stack of three others and rearranged some papers across the top. He motioned for Andres to pick up the top paper. It was a Cook County receipt for property taxes paid, followed by receipts for the gas, electricity and water bills. He gently moved Josh's hand to pick up a bank savings book showing a balance of twelve thousand dollars.

The two men carefully surveyed each piece spread across the top of the buffet. Still not sure why the old man did this, still wondering if this was for real. Josh glanced at the stack of ledger books again, each numbered. He wondered why there would be secrets in them.

Padre An picked up two papers and showed them to the men. One was a title with their names alongside Manny's. It was clipped to a quit claim deed removing his name and signing over the rooming house to the two of them. In wonderment, Josh glanced at Andres who looked equally as shocked. He picked up the other paper, another bank statement with two cards clipped to it, awaiting their signatures. A drawer was partially open. Josh noticed scads of photographs and albums stuffed inside.

Andres pulled Josh into a hug. "Is this a freaking dream?"

Father Frank walked up to them. "The funeral home is on their way. Here's a copy of his funeral plans, already paid for. He's to be cremated. We will inter him Wednesday morning, unless you have major conflicts with the date." He looked at Andres who shook his head as if the suddenness of a funeral was too much. "Manny never liked waiting around or wasting time. He said the quicker we get this over, the quicker you two can move on with your lives." He shook their hands. "I need to leave for the hospital to visit an elderly parishioner. Padre will stay with you and help with any details needed today." He smiled. "My sincere condolences. Manny was the type of guy I wished I knew all my life. Oh, by the way, Manny insisted we leave you some refreshments. It's homebrew beer. The bottles look old, but the last brew was made several months ago, still safe, and good. I hope eight are enough. Doesn't matter, that's the last of them. Just be careful, they can knock you on your butt if you're not used to them." He stepped toward the front door, then turned back. "Men, why don't you ride with us to Oakwood on Wednesday? It's simpler than you trying to find us there. We'll pick you up here at the house, around nine-twenty." He walked briskly away.

"Good idea," Padre An said. Looking at the two men, he asked, "Would you like to spend a few moments alone with Manny? The funeral folks will be here momentarily."

Andres looked at Josh. "Briefly for me. I haven't seen many dead people. I think I'd like to remember him from when he was healthy, not the way he looked today."

They followed Padre An into the kitchen where he started to remove the afghan.

"Wait." Andres said, "I don't need to see him uncovered. Leave him covered." He pulled a kitchen chair closer to the covered body and sat. He pulled a pencil and small pad from his bib overalls pocket and began sketching.

~ * ~

Andres forced his mind to focus on sketching; something that normally came easy for him. He'd developed the discipline to tune out the world around him when he sketched. This was harder, though. He had few relatives and had never seen one dead. While his visits with Uncle Manny were scarce, they did have a bond. Both gay, both not accepted by Art Junior, Andres' father; Manny's half-brother. Both barely knew Art Senior who treated Manny horribly and was a vague, demanding presence to Andres as he was growing up.

He sensed Josh's hand on his shoulder and felt the warmth, the support. His sketched lines quickly suggested the shape of an old man: head slouched to one side, sitting in a recliner. He added some texture to show the afghan. He left the face blank. *I'll fill that in later,* he thought. *Right now, I just want to capture the essence and sadness of death. Later, I'll decide where to take this.* His hand flew as the lines expanded to include a sense of the kitchen, the cabinets, old refrigerator… old, old, old. Death, death, death. His eye caught tulips. Wooden, once bright, hand-made, red, blue green and white: tulips marching over the cabinets.

He glanced up at Josh. "Look, Josh, look. The tulips; I noticed some plants by the front porch." He put the sketch book and pencil back into his pocket.

What a loss, he thought, glancing at the covered form of Uncle

Manny. *I barely knew him. I could kill Dad. Two damn months, we could have been getting to know each other, now we're burying him Wednesday and all I know is he left us an old rooming house. As excited as I am, I think I'd rather have had time with Manny while he was alive than inherit his house.* Andres stood up as the people from the funeral home entered the room, trundling a gurney with a white sheet.

~ * ~

Josh stood with his hand on Andres' shoulder and watched the fingers fly. As usual, he was amazed at the emotion and sense of reality Andres produced in the few lines, curves and shaded areas. He squeezed Andres. His partner could tune out the world in almost any situation. Yet when one saw his art, you grasped all the thought, emotion and imagination that flowed through the man. Over time, he realized viewing Andres' art made the lack of connection with him when he was making it, bearable. Usually.

Josh and Andres stepped back. They watched as two men in coveralls and a tall, business-looking woman with short gray hair, dressed in dark slacks and a blue jacket bearing the name of the funeral home, gently handle Uncle Manny's body.

"Do you wish to view the cremation?" the woman asked. Josh and Andres shook their heads. "That's fine. He already provided us with a pottery urn with sunflowers on it made by a Mexican artist friend of his. It's beautiful. I will be present at Oakwood Cemetery for the interment of the urn in one of the Sawicki plots. I understand those arrangements were made nearly fifty years ago." She looked puzzled. "Our funeral home goes back to the late 1800's and I discovered we have buried many Sawicki's." She looked like she wanted to ask why they were burying the ashes of an old Mexican alongside them, but she didn't.

Josh shivered at the thought his relatives helped make arrangements for Manny's place of rest all those many years ago. Just how deep did their connections go in this place? Unconsciously, he slipped his hand into Andres' and squeezed. Andres squeezed back, then put his arm around Josh, hugged him and gave him a quick kiss on the cheek. Josh tried not to snicker at the fleeting expression of shock on the woman's face or the surprised looks of the assistants. He purposely snuggled closer into Andres' embrace. *Deal with it,* he thought. *It's 2009 and you act surprised at a Mexican being buried in old Polacks graves and young men in love with each other.* He winked at the woman and watched her face turn pink. It was his turn to look surprised when she winked back and gave him a thumbs up from behind her back as she turned to follow the gurney.

Also by the Author
at
Rogue Phoenix Press

The Rooming House Diaries
Life, Love & Secrets

Six fascinating and touching diaries are discovered in an old rooming house that detail the lives of the owners and tenants spanning over a century of change in Chicago's Back-of-the-Yards neighborhood. An unwed pregnant teen shows up; a teen from Paris, France appears, the result of a relationship during World War I; the first Mexican in the neighborhood is given a room and eventually inherits the place, his diary describes his young life running the streets in Tijuana, Mexico and how the rooming house served undocumented AIDS clients. The matriarch leaves a long-hidden diary that details her undisclosed life of brothels. Filled with love, life and family secrets, The Rooming House Diaries prove DNA does not always make a complete family.

Face Your Fears

Face Your Fears is filled with vitality as it challenges the traditional concepts of normalcy, family, disability and love. Nate is a quadriplegic with cerebral palsy raised in a family of achievers. He must be fed, dressed and toileted, yet has unique skills and abilities he gradually becomes aware of. Jude is able-bodied, one of 10 children raised on a hardscrabble Iowa farm. He can change diapers, cook, fix equipment, milk cows, and discovers his vocation as a physical therapist. Both experience tragic teen-age losses, navigate family tragedies, and come to peace with who they are individually as gay men, and eventually together.

This book shows how normal comes wrapped in different packages, yet inside each package, people are the same, whether able-bodied, disabled, black, white, brown, green or LGBTQ+.